Katie Mettner wears the ti... her leg after falling dow... decorating her prosthetic le... northern Wisconsin with her own happily-ever-after and wishes for a dog now that her children are grown. Katie has an addiction to coffee and X (formerly Twitter) and a lessening aversion to Pinterest—now that she's quit trying to make the things she pins.

New York Times and *USA Today* bestselling, award-winning author **Lisa Childs** has written more than eighty-five novels. Published in twenty countries, she's also appeared on the *Publishers Weekly*, Barnes & Noble and Nielsen Top 100 bestseller lists. Lisa writes contemporary romance, romantic suspense, paranormal and women's fiction. She's a wife, mum, bonus mum, avid reader and less avid runner. Readers can reach her through Facebook or her website, lisachilds.com

THE PERFECT WITNESS

KATIE METTNER

COLTON'S DANGEROUS COVER

LISA CHILDS

MILLS & BOON

First Published in Great Britain 2024
by Mills & Boon, an imprint of HarperCollins*Publishers* Ltd
1 London Bridge Street, London, SE1 9GF

www.harpercollins.co.uk

HarperCollins*Publishers*
Macken House, 39/40 Mayor Street Upper,
Dublin 1, D01 C9W8, Ireland

The Perfect Witness © 2024 Katie Mettner
Colton's Dangerous Cover © 2024 Harlequin Enterprises ULC

Special thanks and acknowledgement are given to Lisa Childs for her contribution to *The Coltons of Owl Creek* series.

ISBN: 978-0-263-32218-7

0224

This book contains FSC™ certified paper and other controlled sources to ensure responsible forest management.

For more information visit: www.harpercollins.co.uk/green

Printed and Bound in the UK using 100% Renewable Electricity at CPI Group (UK) Ltd, Croydon, CR0 4YY

THE PERFECT WITNESS

KATIE METTNER

For Linda

Thank you for believing in me when I didn't believe in myself. The memories of your loving encouragement in every aspect of my life are the reason I had the courage to make *our* dream a reality. Wherever you are over the rainbow, I still love ya more.

Chapter One

"Meanwhile, in Minneapolis, the trial for Cynthia Moore, aka The Madame, the famed head of a sex trafficking empire, is underway after a lengthy eighteen-month delay. The extensive evidence for the case was nearly insurmountable for both the prosecution and the defense. The trial is expected to last several weeks while the jury remains sequestered. Later today, the defense will put a woman on the stand who was in charge of the household at the Red Rye escort house before it burned. That witness, whom courts are only identifying as Marlise, is expected to testify against her former boss, Cynthia Moore, while revealing what she knew about other illegal activities under The Madame's eye. Former FBI agent Mina Jacobs, the undercover agent sent in to find evidence of prostitution, is expected to testify after Marlise. Jacobs's testimony is expected to take several days, considering her connection to her then boss, and Cynthia Moore's husband, David Moore."

Marlise's gaze flicked to the screen as her heart rate crept up to near heart attack level. She was waiting for Cal to pick her up for the drive to the courthouse. Secure One was three hours away from the city, so they'd all driven in last night and stayed at a hotel. Cal didn't like it, but realistically, they had no choice. With The Miss still on the run, everyone was worried she'd pick today to tag them. Marlise knew it was a real possibility, but if she made it to the courthouse today and gave her testimony, The Miss would have no reason to hunt her. Unless she wanted revenge. If that were the case, Marlise would never be safe or free.

"We've asked our law expert to break down the case for us," the newscaster continued. "He is in no way affiliated with the case but can offer insight into both the defense and the prosecution's plan of attack. Thanks for being here, Barry."

"It's my pleasure," a man in a tweed suit said. He was sitting in an office on a blue couch, and the windows behind him gave the audience a view of the Minneapolis skyline lit with a thousand sparkling lights. It was early, and the sun wasn't up, but that didn't mean the city was quiet. That was one thing Marlise hated about the city. The dark. It hid the worst side of humanity, and she'd experienced the worst side of humanity enough times in her short life to fear it. She preferred the quiet solitude of Secure One, where she worked keeping Cal's men fed every day. Whenever she was scared or nervous, she could walk out to the lake and watch the water ripple while taking deep breaths. Cal's property lent itself to isolation and made you forget the outside world existed. Marlise had lived on the streets for years, and no one knew what a jungle they were more than her, so she appreciated being wrapped in a womb of safety and protection at Secure One.

"There is no perfect witness," the lawyer said when she tuned back in to the news program. "Both sides will find something to use against any witness. A small misstep, a social media post or even an image taken out of context can throw doubt into the minds of the jurors. You have to remember that the prosecution has to prove beyond a reasonable doubt that crimes were committed, but all the defense has to do is prove reasonable doubt that the defendant is innocent. Each side will look for any chink in the witness's armor before putting them on the stand."

A shiver ran down Marlise's spine. *There is no such thing as a perfect witness.* Was that true? She still had to try. She had to do her part to put The Madame and her husband behind bars. She refused to acknowledge the woman's real name. She would always be The Madame, a badge of shame for the damage she'd done to girls like her. Yes, The Miss was still out there, but Marlise had to start where she had a little bit of power and control. Her entire life had been about lack of control, and she was tired of it.

Living and working at Secure One had changed her. She was stronger, both physically and emotionally. When Mina was kidnapped by The Madame, she had hurt her foot beyond repair and, because of that, was now an amputee. Marlise watched her come back from that stronger and more determined to make a difference in the world. Mina's fighting spirit inspired Marlise's.

Absently, she rubbed the leathery skin on her arm. She had healed from the extensive burns she'd endured at the house in Red Rye, but the nerve damage and disfigurement were still hard to live with some days. Cal had insisted that his nurse, Selina, treat her skin with a gel to care for the disorder better, which was something she could never afford on her own. The skin felt better with each passing day, and she had hope that it might lessen the burning pain even more. When she'd first woken up in the hospital after the fire, she'd wished she'd died there rather than be alive inside her burning body. Her heart paused in her chest when memories of that day came rushing back to her.

"I heard them talking. They know you're an FBI agent. You're not getting out of here alive, Agent August."

The woman Marlise had come to see as her only friend in the house hesitated before a shaky smile lifted her lips. Marlise turned back to the mixer, the cookie dough swirling around inside the bowl while terror swirled through her gut. She worried about what would happen next if her friend actually was an undercover FBI agent. Would she be arrested? Marlise wanted to throw up at the thought. She was just the cook! She wasn't involved with the escort service. At least she wasn't anymore. They could still say she was or at least say she knew about it and should have reported it. She knew better, though. Red Rye was like fight club. That was the only rule.

At least she had Agent August. Maybe she'd tell the authorities that Marlise didn't go out on dates the way the other girls did. She swallowed over the nervous lump in her throat. Her life was about to change again, and she wasn't ready. She wasn't ready to go back to the streets.

"Thanks for this, Marlise," Agent August said as she snagged a cookie from the tray with a wave.

Marlise didn't react. She didn't look at her or do anything until she was gone. Then she calmly turned and pulled out another pan of cookies from the oven.

"What does your gut say about the agent who was undercover there?" the newscaster asked, bringing Marlise back to the present. "Wouldn't she be considered the perfect witness?"

"No," the lawyer insisted as Marlise's attention snapped back to the television. "Again, there is no perfect witness. The defense will try to discredit the agent. They'll say her boss at the FBI, former special agent David Moore, who is also The Madame's husband as you'll recall, put her there unknowingly, but she was there long enough to find a smoking gun. She was injured while undercover and again while arresting David Moore. The defense will try to convince the jury that she's got a vendetta against the Moores now."

"Could you blame her? I don't know anyone who wouldn't feel intense hatred toward the people responsible for their torture and attempted murder."

"On the human nature side of the case, that will play well for her, but it could harm her on the legal side of the case."

"The same can be said for Marlise?"

"Absolutely. Of course, Marlise is a victim of The Madame, and on the human nature side of the case, she will be a stellar witness, but they will find something to discredit her. It will be harder with her since her past was wiped away, but if they have to, they'll twist something perfectly reasonable into something ugly."

Marlise flicked the television off, disgusted with how the media had turned The Madame's trial into a sideshow. She knew firsthand that it wasn't a sideshow for the girls in those houses. The human nature side of those houses was a terrifying way to live while constantly worrying about dying. It tossed her right back to that day, and the swirling in her mind dropped her to the bed.

A thud. A muffled scream. Another thud. A moan of

agony. Why didn't the FBI come and help her friend? Where were they? Marlise had noticed Agent August tap out a message on her phone before she left the kitchen.

Do you want to be here when they show up? that little voice asked. It's time to make like a tree and leave.

The voice was right, and she had to do it now. She scurried to her room, another thud from overhead bringing her shoulders up to her ears. Marlise waited for the scream from her friend to follow, but this time, the house stayed silent. She ran down the hallway now, her feet swift. It was only then that she realized the other girls weren't in the house. She swallowed around the truth that clogged her throat. They didn't care what happened to her. The other girls were cash cows for the organization, but she was disposable. She always had been.

Her gaze swept her tiny room for someone waiting for her, but it was empty. She reached for her backpack and hesitated. She should only take her money. No bag to slow her down or make it evident that she was running. She pulled out a wad of one-hundred-dollar bills from under her mattress with a grim smile. It wouldn't get her far, but it would get her out of Red Rye. She grabbed a jacket and threw it on, stashing the money in a secret pocket.

The Miss's words ran through her mind. "I'm taking the girls and getting out before the FBI breaks down our door. Only the moneymakers. Yes. No. She's dead weight to me now. I don't need her. I think she knew all along the FBI were involved."

Marlise didn't know her friend was an FBI agent, but she wasn't sticking around to get the same kind of treatment

Agent August was suffering. Another thud, another scream, and then something tickled her nose. She sniffed.

Smoke.

The cookies were burning! Too bad. Marlise wasn't going back to the kitchen. They could be waiting for her there. She hoped the smoke would distract them and give Agent August a reprieve. Marlise had to get out before she couldn't. If they stopped her, they'd kill her. She had to get out of Red Rye, but she had one more thing to do. She hated to waste precious time on it, but if she didn't stop for her treasure, the proof would be gone for good.

Run, her brain told her feet, but she forced herself to enter the hallway at a normal pace. Smoke filled the space, and she realized nothing was normal. It wasn't her cookies burning. The house was on fire, and she had to get out! Choking on the acrid smoke, she got as low as possible and kept her hand on the wall. She was desperate for fresh air as the cloying thickness choked her, tempting her to open her lungs to it. It wanted to work its tentacles through her until she followed it down into the bowels of hell.

She wouldn't. She couldn't. She needed to get out of this house alive, or everything Agent August had worked for would be lost. If they ever caught The Madame, she'd have the evidence to help put her away for good.

There was a knock on the hotel room door, and she jumped. Her heart rate, already up from being trapped in the memories of Red Rye, kicked up another notch until she heard his voice.

"Mary."

Cal.

He'd started calling her Mary last summer when she'd

moved back to Secure One to work for him. She hadn't used the name in a decade, but he insisted on using it when they were alone together. She wasn't sure why. She'd ask, but she was too afraid of the answer. Cal held power over her life, whether it was intended or not. He kept her employed, housed and fed while they awaited the trial, but there was more to it. He sheltered her—both physically and emotionally.

She checked to make sure it was him before she opened the door. He was inside the room with the door closed before she saw him move. He was that way. Even at six foot four inches tall, two hundred and fifty pounds of muscle and with tats covering both arms, he moved like a ghost. Cal was always intense, but this morning, he was laser focused on the details as he prepared her for the trip to the courthouse.

He slung a bag onto the bed and started pulling out items. "Mina and Roman are preparing the cars. It's time to get dressed for court."

Marlise glanced down at her pants and long-sleeve blouse. "I am dressed for court."

"Correction," he said, handing her a black jacket. "For the drive to court."

She took the jacket, but her eyes widened when he pulled out a bulletproof vest. "Don't you think that's going a bit far, Cal?"

"If anything, it's not going far enough, but it's all we have, so put it on."

Marlise had learned when Cal issued an order, he expected you to follow it. He lowered it over her head and then tightened the side straps down.

"I should have gotten a child's size. You swim in this thing."

"If they make child-sized bulletproof vests, I don't want to be part of humanity," she muttered.

He cocked a brow at her, and she sighed. Of course, they made them. Cal held up a small walkie-talkie and attached it to her vest before he helped her cover the vest with her jacket. "The walkie-talkie will only contact the other people on our network." Marlise nodded, but she swallowed over the fear in her throat when he turned away. She could see in his dark brown eyes that he was scared too. If Cal was scared, there was a good chance she could die today.

When he turned back to her, he handed her a small hand-gun and showed her the full magazine before popping it back into the gun. "You can't take this into the courthouse, obviously, but until then, it stays within reach."

She grabbed his hand before he could tuck the gun into the front of her vest. "That doesn't look familiar."

"It's just like our training guns, but it shoots live ammu-nition. Remember, the safety is on the trigger. Don't aim. Just point and shoot. And while you're shooting, run."

"Cal, this feels a bit overboard for a fifteen-minute drive to the courthouse."

"Maybe, maybe not," he said with a clenched jaw. "If The Miss is out there, and she's worried about what you'll say on the stand, she knows exactly where you will be and when."

"We don't even know if she's still in the country. It's been radio silence for years, Cal."

He grabbed her packed backpack off the bed and slung it over his shoulder. "That doesn't mean she's not in play. I've worked too hard to keep you alive the last year to take any chances on the one-yard line. Mina is dressed to look like you and will be riding with Roman. I'll be driving the other SUV with you in the back."

"It's not smart to put Mina at risk, Cal. She has to tes-tify too."

"We're making it look like we're bringing you in one at a time. If my car is empty, they'll think on a passing glance that Mina is you. They're trained agents with more years under their belts combined than you've been alive, so don't worry about Mina and Roman. We'll get you to the courthouse safely, and once we do, you're one step closer to living your life free of The Madame."

Cal walked to the door and checked the peephole before radioing down to Roman and Mina in the underground garage. He was right. The media had broadcast loud and clear when she was testifying at the trial. It had been on the evening news a week ago, and she wouldn't forget that scene anytime soon. Cal had been so angry he'd thrown his coffee cup against the wall before he walked out of the control room and disappeared for an hour. Roman had assured her that his brother was just frustrated with the media turning the trial into a circus and putting people's lives at risk, but she still carried guilt about it. If Roman hadn't gone to Cal for help when he found Mina, Cal would never have met Marlise, and his life wouldn't be so complicated.

Mina told her she couldn't think that way because Cal didn't, but it was days like today that she wasn't so sure. As much as it pained her to think about leaving Secure One, and this man, she wouldn't have a choice if she made it through today. They both deserved to be free.

CAL BRAKED AT the exit to the parking garage. Roman had just pulled out with Mina in the passenger side dressed as Marlise. With a wig down over her face and a pair of sunglasses, Mina could pull it off. He didn't like putting his brother in the position of risking his wife, but she was a former FBI agent and could hold her own. Two years ago, his brother showed up on his doorstep with his compromised partner in tow. Mina had been on the run from a woman they called The Madame for a year, but she was desperate for protection and a chance to heal.

He was convinced Secure One could take care of her. He'd naively believed he had all the safeguards on his property to protect them, but he soon learned nothing was further from the truth. The Madame's men infiltrated his borders and took Mina right out from under their noses. They got her back, but he'd learned some hard lessons that day, and he wasn't giving anyone another chance to attack his home or his people.

One of those people was in his back seat dressed in bullet-proof armor, and he hoped this ruse would work long enough to get her to the courthouse. Marlise used to live in the Red Rye house, an escort service and modern-day brothel, run by The Madame. She was also Mina's only friend on the inside. When that house burned to the ground, with Marlise still inside it, The Miss and The Madame thought they'd mitigated a threat. They were wrong. Marlise knew things no one else did, and that was why The Miss could be waiting to ambush them on their route. She was a dangerous, invisible woman, but the chances she'd become visible today were almost 100 percent.

Truthfully, he didn't know if she was even in business anymore, but the part of him that had done bad things in the name of helping good people told him she would soon turn up. The Miss was hunting for the last two people who could identify her. In the eyes of The Miss, Marlise was a nobody, but she also knew more about the operation than even Mina did. The Miss didn't want either woman spilling the beans about what went on in Red Rye, but she would see Marlise as an easy snatch and grab. Worst-case scenario, she was willing to shut her up any way she could, including with a bullet from a distance. He wouldn't let that happen.

"Are you okay back there?" he asked, waiting for his turn to leave the parking garage.

"Snug as a bug," she replied sarcastically, and he snorted.

"I know it's uncomfortable, but it's better this way."

"If you say so."

Cal slid his sunglasses across his face and followed his brother down the street. Following his brother defined his life. The moment Roman joined the army, Cal never considered doing anything else. He signed up at seventeen. At eighteen, Cal followed his brother into special training for the military police. By nineteen, he was the youngest member of the Special Reaction Team at Fort McCoy. They'd called him "kid," but Cal didn't mind. He knew why he was there. To do the job. Protect his country. To stand next to his brother again. His team may have teased him about being a kid, but they knew he wasn't one. They had each other's back every time and all the time until that one time.

People always said blood was thicker than water, but not when it came to Cal Newfellow and Roman Jacobs. They may not share a last name, but they shared a bond that went deeper. They grew up together as best friends and foster brothers, but Roman never treated him like a kid. Over the last decade, Roman looked to his little brother for help more often than not. When Mina had gone missing, driven into hiding by The Madame after their undercover operation went south, Cal helped Roman find her. They complemented each other's strengths and weaknesses, and that made them an effective team.

That was the reason Roman and Mina left the FBI last year to be part of Secure One. Roman's extensive combat training had made his men sharper, stronger and more advanced in self-defense and combat fighting than half the guys in the military. Mina's skills at a computer kept his security business running smoothly. Over the last year, she had stopped two cyberattacks aimed at several of his VIP clients.

On days like today, he was glad to be working with his brother again. Cal had done enough bad things in his life. Now his goal was to do good things to better the world. He blew out a breath as he checked all the mirrors of the SUV. He had to stay sharp. He had a witness to protect.

Is she just a witness though?

That is all she can be, he reminded himself.

Marlise had arrived at Secure One broken, in pain and terrified. He'd made sure she healed better than anyone could have predicted. Once she had her strength back, he trained her in self-defense and gun safety. While she could bake a mean chocolate chip cookie, she also had deadly aim with a firearm. He got off on giving her back power over her life. He hoped that she could find newfound freedom once this trial was over. He wanted her to stay at Secure One, but he understood she'd been bought and paid for over the last decade. Hell, her name wasn't even Marlise. It was Mary.

Cal shook his head and readjusted his focus on the road. Fifteen miles separated them and the courthouse, and he had to get her there in one piece. He reminded himself to send a thank-you to the media and their useless mouths. Now was the time to attack if The Miss wanted to throw the entire trial into chaos and get away a free woman. If she tried hard enough, she could get a twofer with Mina without even knowing it. He could feel the evil coming. The hair on the back of his neck was electric and fear crackled in his chest.

"Do you think there's such a thing as a perfect witness?" Marlise asked from the back seat.

"Absolutely not. Humans are imperfect, so it's relatively easy to discredit a witness. Why do you ask?" Cal asked, waiting at a red light.

Roman was third in line, and he hoped his brother remembered they both had to clear the green light, so they didn't get separated. Cal hated driving through the concrete jungle with a witness as hot as Marlise, but he had no choice. If they hadn't stayed over last night, the drive would have been three hours long, and by the time they reached the city, they wouldn't be sharp or reactive. Unfortunately, the city made escape routes challenging to plan, and he always felt like a caged animal trapped by the street grids with no easy way out.

"I heard a lawyer on the news say no witness is perfect. The newscaster asked about Mina, and the lawyer said the defense would claim she stayed in Red Rye too long and should have had the evidence sooner."

Cal pressed down the accelerator to clear the yellow light. "I'm sure they'll throw anything at the wall and hope it sticks, but we know none of it is true. Mina never had the evidence because her boss was pulling the strings to keep her there."

"It made me think that I might be the perfect witness."

"I don't follow."

"Think about it, Cal," Marlise said. "Thanks to David Moore, my past before I moved into the Red Rye house is gone. There's nothing for the defense to dig up."

"That's true, but everyone is vulnerable," he reminded her. "They can twist simple things to make you look bad."

"It would be hard to discredit someone held against their will."

"They'll simply say you were free to leave at any time."

"I wasn't though!" Marlise hissed. "I wasn't. You know I couldn't leave. If I left, they'd have killed me." He heard the terror of those years in her whispered words. Cal wanted to pull the car over and gather her in his arms to protect her. That was a reaction he'd had a lot since she'd first stepped foot on his plane, injured and scared. A reaction he didn't like. He reminded himself his only job was to get her to the courthouse to testify. Once that was over, they could part ways and go on with their lives independently of each other.

That little voice inside his head laughed.

"Deep breaths, Mary," he encouraged, his focus still on the back of Roman's SUV. They were ten minutes out now. "We know you couldn't leave, but the defense will try to throw doubt into the jurors' minds any way they can. That's their job. It's widely accepted that women who are sex trafficked into those houses aren't there by choice. It's the prosecutor's job to explain that to the jury. You just have to relax, okay? You're not going to be charged with a crime. I won't allow it."

"I don't know if even your steely determination can outpower The Miss," she whispered. "But, just in case something happens, thank you for taking care of me the last few years and getting me this far. You didn't have to do it, but I would be dead already if you hadn't let me stay at Secure One."

"I'm going to get you there safely, Mary. Don't give up on me now," he begged.

"I'm not," she assured him. The sound of Velcro being unstrapped reached his ears. "I've got my gun, and I know how to use it, thanks to you."

His lips broke into a grin that made him glad that neither she nor his team could see it. "Mary, it has been my greatest honor to be part of your life. You don't need to thank me for anything. Just get up on that stand and put these people away. I'm proud of you and your tenacity, so let's cross the finish line. We're in go time."

Marlise knew what that meant. He heard her take a deep breath before she went silent. He punched a button on the dash that connected him to Roman's car. "Five and in. What do you see?"

"Road construction up ahead. Slow traffic."

Cal hissed out a cuss word before he responded. "There was no planned construction anywhere on the route."

He heard Roman's laughter before he answered. "As if the city of Minneapolis cares?"

He was silent, and Cal waited for an update as they crawled forward. Since Roman was the lead car, he would have to be the one to assess the scene.

"Utility work. Looks like a city truck. We're fine. Just go slow around them."

"Six and in now," Cal said, updating them on the GPS arrival time.

He wasn't happy about the added minute. Extra seconds could mean lives, and the one he was carrying was a life he'd worked hard to save for reasons he refused to address. He might bury his head in the sand about how he felt for the tiny woman in the back seat, but he would never give up on keeping her safe.

Roman's SUV skirted the truck with ease, but Cal's bigger vehicle would be a tight squeeze, so he slowed to pass the truck. "Almost there," he said to keep Marlise calm.

There was laughter from the back seat. "No, we aren't, but nice try, Newfellow."

As he approached the truck, his lips turned up in a grin, but his amusement quickly disappeared when the scene before him registered. The truck wasn't from the City of Minneapolis. The last time he checked, they didn't arm their city employees with automatic rifles.

"Stay down!" he yelled as the first bullet collided with the side of the SUV.

Marlise's scream filled his ears as he yanked the car to the right and slammed into the parked truck in an attempt to unbalance the shooters. He didn't wait to see if it worked before throwing the SUV into Reverse and slamming his foot down on the accelerator. He should have listened to that hair on the back of his neck. It had never let him down.

Chapter Two

"Cal!" Marlise yelled from the back seat, where she hid under a heavy black blanket. She no sooner got the word out than the SUV lurched and nearly threw her to the floor. She had a seat belt around her waist, and she threw her hand out to brace against Cal's seat. "I'll return fire!"

Before she could, his words chilled her to the bone. "Stay under that blanket, Mary! We're outnumbered, and they have way more firepower!"

Another bullet slammed against the SUV's window, and the bulletproof glass cracked. Marlise tossed the blanket off her head and noticed the front passenger-side window was also hit.

"Cal!" Roman's voice on the radio filled the car as the utility truck rammed them from behind. "Evade! Evade! There are more waiting ahead. We're going left! Do not go to the courthouse! They know you have Marlise!"

A barrage of bullets hit the car, and this time, Cal must have slammed the accelerator because the car jerked, the tires spun, and then they were flying across the city streets, barely avoiding oncoming traffic. All she could do was pray no innocent people got hurt because of her. Marlise wrapped one arm in the seat belt and held her gun in the other. She was ready to defend their lives if it came down to it. That was the least she could do for this man after everything he'd done for her.

"Scatter plan!" Cal yelled.

"Ten-four," Roman answered, and then the radio went silent.

Cal muttered a string of cuss words that would make any girl blush, but she noticed that he didn't slow down. A terrified pit had opened in her belly, and she wanted to cry, but she refused. She would not let The Miss win this time! A bullet slammed into the back window, and then another one tagged the rear door.

"Hold on! We don't stand a chance if I can't lose them!"

"I'm returning fire!" she yelled, but the window refused to budge when she hit the button.

"No!" He yelled the word in anger as he twisted the wheel hard to the left. "If you stick your head out, you're dead. Stay down!"

The words weren't out of his mouth when another bullet smacked the back of the SUV. They'd managed to damage the glass to the point if they got a clear shot, a few more rounds would shatter it. Marlise's arm burned from being twisted in the seat belt, but she didn't have time to worry about it. Sirens had filled the air, and she was worried more people would get hurt because of her.

"Hang on!" Cal yelled to her. "We're using the cops as cover and going off-road!"

"Cal, we're in the city!"

"No choice. Hang on!"

The SUV jumped and metal grated on the undercarriage before they fishtailed, landed hard and straightened out.

"What's your plan, Cal?"

"Once we're clear, we have to find a new vehicle and work our way back to the gathering point so Secure One can extract us."

He fell silent as the SUV hurtled down a bumpy surface while she was rocked back and forth like a boat. A boat!

"What about the river?" she asked, throwing the blanket off her face, securing her gun back in her vest and preparing to unbuckle her seat belt when he stopped. She had memorized the same plans Cal and Roman had and knew exactly what steps to follow.

The bullets had stopped coming for now, but that didn't mean more weren't waiting for them up ahead. "If we could find a boat, we could use the river to get out of the city and closer to Secure One."

"We'd still need a car," he muttered. "We can't take the river any further than St. Cloud."

"At least we wouldn't be here!" she exclaimed, her voice holding all the fear bubbling up in her belly despite trying to remain calm.

"If the opportunity presents itself, I'm not against it," he said as they bounced over something that made a grinding sound under the car. "Get ready. I'm about to dump this in a grove of trees, and we're going to bail. Grab the go bags!"

She leaned over the back of the seat and grabbed the two black backpacks. Her arm burned, but she ignored it to focus on the plan. After hauling them onto the seat, she unbuckled her seat belt and braced her feet on the front seat until Cal slowed the car and threw it into Park. It had barely lurched to a stop before they were out and running for the trees along the river.

Engulfed by green branches, Cal weaved through them, and she knew he expected her to follow without question. She was grateful for the strength and stamina workouts Cal insisted she do, but the longer they ran, the heavier she breathed. Cal was pulling her along behind him now, and she went down to one knee, his arm pulling hers taut for a moment until he turned back.

"I need a break," she said, her chest aching from carrying the pack and the heavy vest.

He leaned toward her, scooped her up and started running again. "We need more distance between them and us," he huffed as she held on around his neck.

Marlise jumped in his arms. "I have to testify! You have to take me back!"

"That ship sailed, Mary," he said, his breath coming harder now that he was carrying her. "There's no way you're getting near that place. If we're lucky, the cops pick up some of The Miss's women, and they lead them to her."

"And if they don't?"

"Then this doesn't end until someone roots her out of her hole and kills her."

"Stop and put me down!" she ordered. She held her demand in her gaze when Cal glanced down at her. Eventually, his pace slowed, and then he stopped next to a large tree trunk and lowered her back to the ground. "Thank you." Marlise straightened her vest, stiffened her spine and lifted her chin high.

"We can't stop for long. We have no idea if anyone followed us, and the SUV isn't exactly hidden. I don't even trust the cops at this point."

"Understood, but you have to think smart, Cal. You told Roman to follow the scatter plan, which means we do too."

His hand went into his hair as his chest heaved. "I was prepared for an assault, but my heart is still pounding. I can't believe they tried to take us out that close to the courthouse."

"It was their only choice," Marlise said, her trained eye searching the shoreline past the trees. "They didn't know what direction we'd be coming from, but they knew once we funneled down into the hot zone, there would be only so many choices we could make."

Another cuss word fell from his lips, and she bit back a smile. Men were so transparent, even when they thought they were big bad security agents. "We need to distance ourselves from that mess."

"They're going to be looking for us, Cal. I'm one of their star witnesses."

"You're not going near the courthouse right now. The FBI should have done their job and found The Miss before the trial!"

Marlise rested her hand on his giant forearm. "Cal, take a deep breath. I understand that I can't go there now. We have to get out of here since the prosecution will be on the hunt for their star witness. Besides, we were the ones who decided not to use the FBI for protection."

"Not true," he said with a shake of his head. "They were supposed to be part of the transport team for you. That was why we were in the hotel this morning."

"You never told me that," she said, planting her hand on her hip.

Cal took his hat off and wiped his brow before putting it back on. "It was need-to-know information, and I didn't want you to worry. Ultimately, it was still Secure One that was protecting you. The FBI just wanted a hand in getting their witness to the courthouse. They were in the air as well as waiting on the surrounding streets."

"Then where the hell were they when we needed them?" she demanded. It made her angry that even surrounded by the FBI she wasn't safe.

"I don't know," he admitted with a puff of air. "That's what scares me about this. We need to get back to Secure One and get Roman and Mina on the official wire with them."

"How did the FBI miss this?"

"Maybe they didn't," he said, cocking a brow.

"No. There's no way the agency still has someone in play, Cal. It's been years since David Moore was arrested, and Mina said everyone in the field office went under a microscope before they were allowed to continue working."

"Sure, in Minneapolis. That doesn't mean every office worker and agent in the FBI was looked at under a lens. Remember, money talks."

"What are we going to do, Cal?" she asked, anxiety filling her.

He tipped her chin up to force eye contact. "We're going to stay alive. Are you ready to run again?"

"We could run, but we need to conserve our energy, Cal. The scatter plan says we find a way back any way we can. We can't use one vehicle longer than an hour before finding another. Gloves must be worn at all times, and the last five miles to the extraction zone has to be approached on foot." Marlise took pleasure in the way his mouth dropped open when she finished the instructions.

"You memorized the scatter plan."

She stepped up to him, chest to chest, and poked herself in the vest. "Of course, I did. It's my life on the line. I've been in life-or-death situations more times than I want to count, Cal. I know how to live and hide on the streets. You'd do well to remember that."

A smile tugged at his lips, and he wrapped his arms around her, giving her a brief hug. Marlise languished in it, glad to be in his arms again in a way that wasn't scary. She would never admit to his face that she was terrified, but she had been for days. There was never any doubt that if The Miss were still out there somewhere, she would look for her at the trial. At this moment, she just needed to feel safe, and his arms always did that for her.

When he released her, he straightened her vest and ensured her gun was secure. "I would never discount your experience, Mary. But this is an urban jungle, and we have few choices but to run."

Marlise motioned him closer to the edge of the tree line along the riverbank and then squatted down. Cal knelt next to her, and she made an arc with her arm as it swung out to the left. It stopped on a bobbing speck on the bank of the river. "That's our run target."

"How did you even see that?" he asked, pulling her up to standing again.

"The Jolly Green Giant was carrying me, and the light glinted off it and into my eye."

Marlise took great pleasure in his snicker as he shook his head. "I'll let you get away with that once." His brow furrowed, but she saw the smile tugging at his lips. "It looks like we're about three miles out from the boat. Let's move."

Cal grabbed her hand and headed deeper into the trees again. She knew he would wind his way there rather than attempt the path of least resistance. He was always looking for a secondary path if their first one was blocked. She matched her steps to his, hard as it was, so she didn't let him down. Marlise would follow him anywhere, but she'd also be ready to defend herself if she had to. He'd said it himself; they were in the concrete jungle now, but she knew that life like the back of her scarred hand.

CAL KNELT, and Marlise slid down his back as she did the same. They'd reached the end of the trees near the back of a property on the Mississippi. There were multiple boats and kayaks tied up to a dock, but he had his eye on just one. A brown Jon boat. It was built for the waters of the Mississippi. He'd had enough experience with them in the service to know their capabilities.

"I need to do some recon before we make any decisions."

"We don't have time to use military strategy, Cal," she hissed from behind him.

He spun and took a knee, grabbing her shoulders so she didn't tip over. "We don't have time not to, Mary. For all we know, that house is full of people! There could be cameras anywhere on that property. We can't waltz in and take a boat if we don't know what we're waltzing into."

He felt her defiance wane as he held her. "Fine, but I'm going with you."

"You don't know the first thing about recon, Mary. While I'm gone, you have a job. Listen and look. You've got the bird call?" She nodded and dug it out of one of her pockets. "Good. You're my eyes from up here. If you see or hear anything, blow that call, then get hidden and stay hidden. Remember the sound of the drones at Secure One?" he asked, and she nodded again. "Listen for that sound. It's unlikely they'd send them this far down the river, but the police will be searching for us eventually. Understood?"

"Got it. I'm not helpless, Cal. Go."

A cuss word slipped out when he ran his sentence back through his head. "We can't go for the boat."

"Why?" she asked. Her question sounded frustrated, but Cal heard the fear and fatigue hiding under it.

"Drones. I can hide you from anyone on land in the center of that boat, but not from the air." Her face fell, and he swore a blue streak internally. "I'm still going to go check the place out. We may not have a choice." He double-checked his gun and turned to her. "Stay alert. Keep your head on a swivel. When I'm ready for you to join me, I'll blow the bird call."

He winked before he headed to the left of her and down a steep embankment. A quick flick of his wristwatch told him it had been two hours since the first bullets flew. He wouldn't hear from Roman again unless he could send out a text. No voice communication could be risked, so he had switched his walkie-talkie off when they'd stopped the first time. When he got back to Mary, he'd check the phone in her pack for a message. It was silent and untraceable, but, with any luck, Mack would have an extraction plan in place.

Cal knew Roman and Mina were fine. The Miss's gang saw right through their plan to keep Marlise hidden and went for his SUV. He kicked himself for not realizing that was a dead giveaway. He and Roman had hoped that the flak jacket and double car entourage to the courthouse would fool them, but they were only fooling themselves.

How could he have been so stupid? Mary could have died today! Cal's steps faltered, and he nearly fell down the slope headfirst. His breathing was ragged, so he took a second to slow his heart rate and calm his breathing. He prided himself on being a ghost, but he felt like a bumbling oaf right now. His focus was split between getting them to safety and how close they came to death today.

Focus. Slow. Steady. Look for signs of life. Are there dogs? Where are the cameras?

The questions forced him to concentrate, and he picked his way down the embankment, avoiding sticks and leaves that could alert a homeowner or a dog. Autumn had arrived in Minnesota, and the dry, fallen leaves weren't doing him any favors. He paused at the bottom of the hill, knelt and let his gaze travel the eaves of the house. They would have to avoid the area if the house had cameras. He saw none at the back of the building, which didn't make sense. They had nearly a quarter of a million dollars' worth of boats at the dock, and they weren't monitoring them?

Sliding along the side of the garage, Cal peeked inside a window. It was empty of cars, but that didn't mean no one was inside the house. Another few feet, and he could stick his head around the side of the garage. His trained eye took in the uncut lawn, the wilting summer flowers, and the front porch swing wrapped to protect it from the winter weather. He ducked back and let out a breath. It looked to be a weekend and summer cabin, but with no cameras on the property, that meant one thing—the boats themselves were protected from theft.

Even if he could break through one of the security devices with his limited tools, he had to face the truth. It wasn't safe on the water. It left them far too exposed, especially in the daylight. A boat battle was nasty business, and Marlise didn't have the experience to live through a gunfight on the water. Especially the Mississippi. They needed a new plan, and quick. Marlise wasn't going to like his decision, but it was his job to keep her safe. He'd already failed once, and the next time might be the last.

Think, Cal.

He scanned the property again, and then he saw it. Salvation. He put his bird call to his lips and blew.

Chapter Three

They hit a boulder and caught a little air before settling back onto the trail. Marlise gripped the door handle on the old door as they tore across the tundra. The Jeep turned off-road vehicle had been a lifesaver when Cal found it hidden under a tarp at the back of the property. It might be the only thing that kept them out of sight long enough to find safety.

A shiver ran through her as she remembered the gunfight a few hours ago. There was no question in her mind that The Miss was doing business again. The bullets told her The Miss was worried that what Marlise knew would put her newborn business at risk. Marlise did have a secret, but she was afraid to tell Cal or Mina the truth. If they knew what she was hiding, they might kick her back to the streets, where she wouldn't last a day.

Did that make her a bad person? She was holding out on the people trying to help her, which was wrong, but she didn't think it made her a bad person. It made her a person with no good options. Telling them the truth wouldn't help matters if she couldn't cough up the proof.

"How much further?" she asked, noticing the sun was

starting to set. Her back was sore from riding in the bumpy Jeep for the last two hours, and she needed to stretch her legs.

"Not much since we're almost out of gas," he said, his jaw pulsing as he avoided another rock in the nick of time. "We don't dare stop for a fill either. We're too memorable in these vests, and we can't risk taking them off. Check for a message from Mack again, please."

Marlise fished the secure phone out of her pocket and flipped it open. The last message had come through about two hours ago from Roman that they were safe and awaiting further instructions.

"He sent a message fifty minutes ago. It says 'Trigger Lake. Mack. Seven. End.' What does that mean?"

"It means Mack will extract us if we get to Trigger Lake by seven tonight. Otherwise, we're on our own."

Marlise glanced at the clock on the phone. It was a little after five. "How far is Trigger Lake?"

"An hour."

"Then we have time," she said, buoyed by the idea of getting out of this alive, even if it was only a reprieve while they regrouped.

"An hour by vehicle. We maybe have fifteen minutes before we run out of gas."

"Then we find another car. We need the servers at Secure One to find The Miss," she said, a tremor in her words. "She knows where I am, Cal."

"We don't know that," he said, glancing at her for a moment. "She knew where we were going to be. That doesn't mean she knows where we're going."

With a deep breath in and out, Marlise tried not to let

the panic take hold. "If that's the case, we need to find her before she finds us."

"Now there's something we both agree on, Mary," he said with a smile.

"Why do you call me Mary?" she asked, her words soft against the grumbling of the Jeep's motor.

He gave her a shrug. She figured he was going for nonchalant, but it didn't look that way to her. The shrug told her the answer wasn't simple. "I like the name Mary."

"But I go by Marlise now, Cal."

"Is that by choice though?" he asked, steering around another boulder on the path.

The Jeep was silent other than the growling of the engine. It was the first time she'd thought about it. Was she using Marlise by choice now or by habit? It was easy to give up Mary to become Marlise when The Madame recruited her. It was a second chance for her—a new beginning. A season of change to be someone other than Mary Liberman— a homeless nobody. Then along came The Madame who made her Marlise—a woman people depended on every day.

"Do you know what the name Mary means?" Cal asked.

"No, Cal. I grew up in foster care, trying to avoid the abuse at the hands of older kids and foster dads. There was little time to look up the meaning of my name."

When she turned to look at him, his jaw was pulsing as though he were working hard not to say something to upset her. She got it. Foster life was miserable for her, but it had been fantastic for his family. Roman was his foster brother, and they'd grown up together and fought together in the service. There were two sides to every coin. She was just one of the unlucky ones who got tails instead of heads.

"The name means rebellious. I have never known a Mary who wasn't rebellious. You included."

"I'm not rebellious. I'm lost, Cal. Lost in this big world without an identity that I can relate to."

"We're all a little bit lost, Mary. You might as well accept that now. You have several identities, but only you can decide which one you connect to the most."

"What identity do you connect to?" she asked, watching as the gas gauge hit the last line on the dial.

"I'm a ghost, Mary."

Her amused snort could be heard over the engine's sputtering as it tried to keep going despite its lack of energy. "You might be a ghost when you're on missions, but people know that Cal Newfellow runs Secure One. No one outside of Secure One knows Marlise or Mary even exists."

"That's not true. The Miss knows, and as evidenced by this day, you mean something to her. You mean something to me, Roman, Mina, Selina and Mack. We will give you your identity back and a real second chance."

The Jeep sputtered and died, coasting down the path until the last of its forward momentum was spent. "I guess that's that," Marlise muttered, grabbing her backpack off the Jeep's floor. "We better hoof it if we're going to make Trigger Lake in under two hours."

Cal turned and touched her forearm before she could get out of the car. Her yelp was immediate, and he lifted his hand from her arm as though it had burned him. When he saw the blood covering his palm, a look crossed his face that she couldn't define.

"Are you hurt?"

"It's nothing," she insisted, bringing her left arm to her side to hide it.

"You're bleeding, so it's most definitely something." He gently pulled her arm back over where he could see it. He turned his headlamp on and grabbed scissors from his bag, slicing her coat open. "Why didn't you tell me you'd been cut?"

"I don't know what happened to it," she muttered, keeping her eyes off the wound. It had been burning for hours, but she refused to let it slow her down. "It started burning in the SUV while we were under fire. It doesn't matter. We can worry about it later. We have to get to the extraction point."

With a grunt, he dug in his pack and came out with gauze and tape. Cal wrapped the arm tightly to stem the oozing blood. At first, it burned worse, but then it slowly became numb.

"I can't believe you knew you were hurt and didn't say anything." He snatched the phone from her vest and flipped it open, typing something out in silence.

"When you're a girl like me, you learn what injuries need immediate care and what injuries can be ignored. You learn to separate yourself from the pain and keep moving. You learn that you're always in pain, and there's no sense fighting against it. Stop the bleeding, accept the pain and soldier onward. Isn't that what they teach in the military too?"

Cal tucked the phone back into her pocket and held her gaze with his steely one. "The difference is, you're not a soldier in the middle of a war."

"That's where you're wrong, Cal," she said, opening the door and stepping out of the Jeep. "I've been a soldier in one war or another for the last twenty-eight years and survived them all. Don't forget that."

HE HOVERED IN the med bay while Selina worked on Mary's arm. When he discovered her injury, he'd sent a text to Roman telling him she was hurt and they should wait at all costs for them. By the time Mack got them out of there and back to Secure One, her wound had soaked two bandage wraps. She was getting paler by the minute, so he'd taken her directly to Selina. He was supposed to meet Roman and Mina in an hour, but first, he had to be sure Mary would be okay.

"It's oozing because a piece of the seat plastic is stuck in her arm," Selina explained from where she sat working. Rather than stand over her shoulder, he forced himself to take a step back, so he didn't crowd her.

"I think a bullet must have come through and hit the back of the seat, which sent the plastic shrapnel into my arm," Marlise said. "Look at it this way. At least it's not a bullet lodged in my arm."

"Can you get it out, or do I need to find a doctor?" Cal asked, his lack of faith making Selina roll her eyes. She had sass, that woman.

"It's fine," Marlise said from where she lay on the hospital bed with her arm stretched out. She was already getting IV fluids and antibiotics and was less pale, but he still worried about infection.

"It's not fine," he snapped, and she shrank back against the bed. Selina glanced over her shoulder at him with impatience and disgust. "I'm sorry," he said, running his hand through his hair. "She's injured and acting like it's no big deal because she's afraid to be a burden. It's not fine, and we will take care of you," he promised, walking to Mary and taking her other hand. "I didn't mean to snap."

"It's okay," she promised with a shy smile. "It was a long day, and we're all tired."

"Amen," Selina whispered as she kept working. "Can you feel this?" she asked Marlise as she poked her arm.

"No, it's numb."

"Excellent. Let's get that debris out of there, and then we'll stitch you up so you can rest."

Cal knelt in front of the bed to focus Mary's attention on him. "I need to meet with Roman and Mina. Once you're patched up, have Selina help you shower and then go to bed."

"But I have to cook—"

He put his finger to her lips to hush her. "You're not going near the kitchen until tomorrow. There are plenty of premade meals available. You need to rest, or I will have to find someone here with the same blood type to give you blood, considering how much you've lost."

Marlise glanced at Selina, who nodded and added a shrug at the end. He appreciated that she didn't undermine him even if the truth was something else. He didn't know if she needed a blood transfusion, but he knew she needed rest. They were in the calm before the storm. There was a tornado on the way, and the tingle at the back of his neck was intense. He wasn't listening this morning, but he was tonight.

"I do have a headache," she admitted with a sigh.

Cal stood and kissed her forehead, stroking the hair back off her face and running a thumb down her cheek. When her eyes widened, he yanked his hand back as though the heat of her skin had burned him.

What was he doing?

He stepped back and avoided their gazes as he backed up to the door. "I'll leave you to it. Radio if you need anything, Selina. Mary, rest. I'm serious."

She gave him a salute, and he turned on his heel sharply and strode to the control room while berating himself the whole way. He had to keep his hands and lips off that woman before things happened that he couldn't take back. Mary wouldn't be part of his life once they caught The Miss, and he planned to do that sooner rather than later. Relationships were a no-no for someone like him. They caused entanglements that dulled your senses and shifted your focus away from the job at hand.

He slammed his way into the control room like a bull in a china shop, and his trained gaze picked out the vital activity in the room. His security team was in place monitoring his clients' businesses and homes. The other two people in the room took him by surprise—his brother and Mina. "I thought I told you two to rest," he said as a greeting.

"Hello to you too, brother," Roman said, biting back a smile. "What crawled up your pants and bit you in the a—"

"How's Marlise?" Mina asked, interrupting her husband's tirade.

"She's in the med bay," Cal said, running his hand through his hair again. "She has a piece of plastic in her arm because I dropped the ball." His finger in his chest punctuated his words. "She's tired, scared and lost too much blood. That's my fault."

"No," Roman said, standing and walking over to him. "That's The Miss's fault. You got Marlise out of there alive. She has lived through much worse than plastic in her arm and a little bit of bleeding. She's tougher than both of us combined, Cal."

"But she shouldn't have to be," he said, his shoulders deflating. "We should have seen this coming."

"We did," said Mina from where she sat at the computer. "We all knew if The Miss was still in play, the trial was where she would try to pinch Marlise. I just wasn't expecting it to get so far out of hand. The FBI should have given us cover to escape, and that didn't happen."

"The FBI," Cal snorted. "That must stand for Ferociously Bad Intel."

Both Roman and Mina bit their lips to hide their grins, but he saw them and let one lift his lips. He was tired and angry, but he always enjoyed a good dig at the FBI.

"What do we know?"

"We know The Miss is in play and wants Marlise," Mina said, stating the obvious. "We don't know where she is or how to find her."

"What's the chatter from the trial?"

"It's on an indefinite hiatus while the judge determines their next steps," Mina answered. "The prosecution is arguing they can't go ahead with the case if they can't get their witnesses there safely. The defense is arguing to dismiss the witnesses and continue the trial."

Cal grunted with laughter. "Sure, just continue the trial without their biggest players. Of course, the defense would want that, but we can't allow it to happen. Do we need to remand you and Marlise into FBI custody?"

"Absolutely not," Roman said, standing to his full height and blocking his wife from view. "Mina will not step foot into that circus until we have The Miss under lock and key."

"We may not have a choice if the FBI demands it," Mina said, leaning around her husband. "But I'd like to avoid it because they're zero for two in my opinion."

Cal pointed at her. "Marlise and I both wondered if someone on the inside tipped off The Miss."

"I want to yell that's impossible, but I can't," Roman said, rubbing his hands down his face. "Anything is possible when it comes to these people. The government claims they found no evidence of anyone else involved with The Madame from the field office, but that doesn't mean there isn't someone."

"I agree," Mina said, standing and stretching her leg. "It could be someone who works as a janitor or support staff. Like if Marlise could move around the Red Rye house without being noticed, this person could do the same. We can assume she heard it on the news, but until we know what happened today with our air support, we have to assume someone on the inside is pulling strings."

"Which is why neither you nor Marlise is going into FBI custody. You won't make it a day," Roman said, his tone fierce as he reached for his wife of less than a year. "I lost you once and nearly lost my mind. I won't put you into a situation where I could lose you again."

She slipped her arm around his waist and hugged him while Cal looked on. He noted a bit of jealousy toward his brother but immediately shut it down. He couldn't risk his business or life by getting involved with someone because he was horny.

Was he horny, or was he lonely?

Cal refused to answer that question. His job was to protect everyone on the team at Secure One, not just the person in his bed. Mary's face materialized, and he forced it away. He might want her in his bed, but she never would be.

"I agree," Cal said, his voice a little rougher than he expected. "Our priority is to find this woman and expose her. Once we do that, we can uncover any moles left in the FBI."

"I wish we had a place to start," Mina said, kissing Roman before returning to her computer. She stared at the screen for a moment and then started typing.

"What are you doing?" Cal and Roman asked in unison.

"Making a list of the mayors and city managers in small towns around Red Rye and Santa Macko."

"Why?" Cal asked, walking over to stand by her.

"She's looking for someone with an unusually cushy campaign fund," Roman said, a grin on his lips. "That's my girl."

Mina pointed at him, barely missing a beat on the keyboard. "If The Miss learned her lesson from The Madame, she would need to clean the money coming in. She'll likely fall back on the same way they did it in Red Rye."

"Fair point," Cal agreed, "but that's like a needle in a haystack."

"Not untrue, but we have to start somewhere," she said, her fingers typing almost independently of her brain.

Mina's skills were why he'd hired her on at Secure One. She'd saved a client several times from being hacked by immediately shutting the hacker down and closing the door they got through. Before the trial, she was going through all of his clients' servers, looking for weaknesses. He wanted her to get back to that job, which meant they had to find The Miss sooner rather than later.

"Boss," Eric called from his booth that held the surveillance equipment for the property. "We've got company."

Cal, Roman and Mina were standing next to Eric within a second, and he pointed at the camera that ran along the fence line.

"Lock it down," Cal told the man, then turned to Mina. "Get Marlise in the bunker." He had barely finished the sentence, and she was out the door. He turned to his brother. "Shall we go meet our guests?"

Roman raised a brow and then nodded, a grim smile on his face as he reached for his gun.

Chapter Four

The bunker was silent other than Mina's grunt as she closed the door and locked it from below. When Cal first told Marlise about the bunker, she expected a doomsday scenario with cots lined up along the wall, dried food at the ready and a cache of weapons. Instead, it was filled with state-of-the-art computer and surveillance equipment, a kitchenette and bunks. Not everyone had access to the bunker either. There was a hatch in Cal's room on one end of the lodge and a hatch in the guest room at the other end of the lodge. There was also an exit from the back of the bunker that came out at the boathouse on the lake, but Cal told her if they ever took that exit, they'd better never plan on coming back.

She bit her lip, worry filling her at the thought of Cal being out there somewhere trying to keep her safe. He was one of those guys who kept his thoughts and emotions close to his vest. He was gruff and bossy, but he always had the well-being of everyone on the compound at the forefront of his mind. Especially so since she came to work here, at least according to Roman.

"Would you like something to drink?" Mina asked, breaking into her thoughts.

Marlise shook her head no rather than answer.

"It's going to be okay," Mina promised, walking over to hug her. Since she'd gotten a new high-end prosthesis, you could barely tell that she was an amputee, but Marlise still felt guilty. The Miss had been torturing Mina while she was running from the house without thought of saving her friend.

That wasn't entirely true. She'd wanted to help Mina, but she knew if she'd gone up those stairs, she'd never have come back down. It had been wiser to get to her secret stash, or so she'd thought. Karma must have been why she hadn't made it out of the fire unscathed either. When Roman had gotten to the house, he'd found her by the front door nearly dead. He'd saved her, but not before the flames destroyed the skin on the left side of her body. It had been almost two years, but she still dealt with pain and nerve damage from the fire.

Her face was no longer symmetrical, and she couldn't smile or blink her eye well on the left side. Self-conscious, she always kept her hair over the weblike skin and wore long-sleeved shirts to hide the burns on her arm and side. Tonight, her arm was sore and tight where Selina had stitched it. The numbing medication was starting to wear off, and it felt like she'd been shot, even if it had only been plastic that had pierced her skin. Her nerves were so damaged on that arm that she worried this injury would only worsen it, but there was nothing she could do about it now.

"What's going on, Mina?" Marlise asked as she perched

on the edge of a chair. "The lights went out, and Cal said that only happens if someone tries to infiltrate the perimeter."

"Someone did, but we were prepared for them this time. All of our alarms worked and alerted us to them early. Eric was sitting right at the computer when they showed up on our cameras. I don't know what's going on. Cal asked me to bring you down here, and I took off."

"Should we be worried?"

Mina shook her head with a smile. "Not even a little bit. We had so much warning that the team was on it right away. They just want to make sure we're safe until they send the all clear."

"Do you think it's The Miss?" Marlise asked, her voice wavering slightly.

Her friend's face didn't give away what she thought, but her shrug wasn't relaxed. The Miss was the reason Mina was an amputee, and the idea she had found them didn't sit well with either of them.

"No way to know. It could be anyone. Let's face it. Cal has made a few enemies himself over the years."

An eye roll slipped out, and Marlise huffed. "Sure, and it must be a coincidence that his enemies decided to break into Secure One the same night we were nearly killed going to The Madame's trial. I might look stupid, Mina, but I'm not."

"I never said you were stupid," she clarified. "I meant that we shouldn't speculate until we hear from Cal or Roman."

Mina started tapping away on a keyboard, and while Marlise had no idea what she was doing, she didn't bother asking. She wouldn't understand anyway. Mina's job was far too technical for Marlise to understand when her skills ended at how to do a basic internet search. She paced the length of the bunker, wishing she knew what was going on and if Cal and Roman were safe.

If The Miss showed up with enough people to overrun Secure One, there was no telling how long Marlise would be alive. Mina was confident Cal had found all the weak points at Secure One, but he'd said that when he was tasked with keeping her safe two years ago too.

"Stop worrying," Mina said firmly. "No one is going to get to you here. Cal won't allow it."

The scar on Marlise's arm burned to remind her what happened the last time The Madame got to her. "That's what they said before you were taken."

Mina held up a finger. "And Cal learned a hard and fast lesson about his vulnerabilities. Since Roman and I started working here, they've analyzed every angle of this property, retraced the steps The Madame's men took to get to me and turned Secure One into a fortress. Cal spared no expense in fortifying the perimeter, buying new equipment and train- ing his men. No one walks onto this property unannounced now. That's why we're down here. Someone tried and set off every alarm in the control room."

Mina turned her attention back to the computer while Marlise started pacing again. Something big was going on above their heads, and she had a feeling she was smack-dab in the middle of it.

THE DAY CAL feared had arrived, and he had to force his mind to be calm. He didn't want to do something to put Marlise at risk again. He was already exhausted from their day on the run, but this turn of events most certainly had to do with Marlise. The then meek woman had sent him into a protective tailspin the moment he met her, and that hadn't changed. He refocused his attention on the shores of the lake rather than the woman hiding in the bunker. Tonight might be his chance to end The Miss's reign of terror.

From where they crouched in the grass, he held up one finger and flicked it to the right side.

"Only one guy?" Roman whispered. "Where are the other three we saw on the fence camera?"

"Maybe they just sent one scout to save time," Cal whispered. He scanned the area again and froze, dragging his head back to the left. "Wait. It might be a girl scout."

"A woman?"

"She just turned sideways, and it looks like it, but I can't be sure. She's one of the targets we saw on the fence camera. Wait." He paused and felt Roman tense next to him. "She just leaned her rifle down on a log and walked away."

"Walked away? It could be a trick," Roman said between clenched teeth. "We need to stop her before she gets much further. No one will get near my wife again."

"There has to be more than one scout, right? This has to be a distraction. Mack and Eric," Cal whispered into his wire, "there's only one scout. It could be a woman."

"Woman?" Mack asked in confusion.

"I can't be sure, but I don't trust this. Work your way back to the front of the lodge and cover it, then await further instructions. Roman and I will handle this girl scout."

"This doesn't feel right," Mack said.

"Agreed," Cal whispered.

"You know if we capture her, we have to turn her over to the FBI," Roman whispered.

Cal bit back the snort that tried to come out. "That depends on who she is and what she wants."

"She's got a gun that could put down a horse, and she's dressed in tactical gear with a vest. I think I know what she wants."

"What do you say we find out?" Cal asked his brother with a cock of his brow. "If she crosses the electric fence, she will need to recover from the voltage before she can speak."

The electric fences were designed to stop someone long enough for his team to secure them without scrambling too many brain cells. That didn't mean it didn't hurt, and Cal took a little joy in someone getting what they deserved when trespassing. He'd even started suggesting the fences to his security clients since they offered a level of protection even guards couldn't. A fence never had to sleep.

Cal and Roman worked their way to the right under the cover of darkness and trees. If The Miss found them, she wouldn't send one woman to Secure One. She'd send a dozen. Something was off. They paused in the woods, and they took in the tiny woman standing on the sand, spinning in a slow circle. She wore all black and had a flak jacket and combat vest, but she'd left the gun fifty yards away as though she'd forgotten it.

Cal glanced at Roman, who was crouched next to him. "It's like she's dazed or confused, not to mention her size. She's smaller than Marlise and Mina."

Roman nodded. "It's like she's a lost kid looking for her parents. The rifle is no longer a threat, but she could have a smaller pistol."

"Agreed, so watch yourself, brother. When she turns

around again, we go. All we need to do is secure her arms. Let's try to avoid injuring her. I want to get some answers."

Cal moved the night vision glasses to the top of his head, and they waited inside the tree line for the woman to turn away. When she did, they seized the opportunity.

"Lights, lights, lights!" Cal yelled into his wire as they ran out of the trees.

Awash in light, they watched the woman fall to her knees with her hands up. "I surrender! I surrender!" she yelled.

Roman and Cal glanced at each other, but slowed their approach, watching for any tricks. They both had dead aim on the trembling woman still on her knees. Hell, she looked like a kid from what Cal could see. Her blond hair spilled out from under her black stocking cap, and her petite frame was nearly swallowed up by the tactical vest.

Looks can be deceiving, a voice whispered.

Didn't Cal know that better than anyone? He didn't need a reminder. "What do you want?" he asked, only a few feet away from her now.

"I want to surrender," she whimpered. "I surrender."

"Lay down on your stomach and put your hands behind your back," Roman ordered as he glanced at Cal.

She did as he instructed, even crossing her ankles and lifting them to be secured. Roman nodded at him, so Cal holstered his gun and motioned for Roman to cover him while he zip-tied the woman's hands together. He left her feet unsecured so she could walk.

"I'm going to ask you again. What do you want?" Cal said, walking around in front of the girl. She was young, and her face told of the horrors she'd lived. He'd seen that haunted look in another woman's eyes before. She was currently hiding out in his bunker.

"I don't want to do this anymore. I need help. Please, help me."

The girl started crying softly, and Cal glanced up at Roman, who gave him the what-the-heck hands. Cal shrugged and grabbed hold of the woman's arm, helping her up. "Consider yourself surrendered. Where are your friends? There were four of you."

"They left," she said through her tears, and Cal lowered a brow at her. "I swear. I'm alone."

"Come on," Roman said, grabbing her other arm. "The fences will get them if she's lying. We need answers from her before the other three arrive with backup."

Cal sighed, but agreed with his brother. "This isn't a trick?" he asked the woman, who shook her head as tears streamed down her face.

"I'm tired, hungry and scared," she whispered. "I just want this to be over."

Cal released her arm, jogged over and grabbed her rifle. He covered their backs on their way to the lodge just in case others were lurking. Why did this woman think she had to surrender? Was she being forced to do something against her will? She was part of the group that had arrived near the fence, but where did her companions go? Even if the other three still wandered the property, they didn't have the firepower or the skills to outgun or outrun his men—none of this made sense.

Her head hung lower and lower until her chin touched her chest, and her feet shuffled along as though they weighed one thousand pounds. It wasn't from dread or a ploy to hold them up. It was pure exhaustion. He had two secret weapons he could deploy to get to the bottom of this.

Mina and Marlise.

Cal's mind went straight to Marlise, the woman he'd rescued with his plane two years ago, who'd worn the same look of fear and exhaustion. Maybe she could be the one to get answers from this woman. If they got lucky, Mina might be able to tag her as one of The Madame's, and they'd be one step closer to bringing The Miss down. Cal had promised Marlise last summer he wouldn't stop until she was behind bars, but that was easier said than done. Regardless of how often Cal put his ear to the ground, it was radio silence.

The woman he'd been protecting for over a year now deserved to be free. She had seen things in life that no one should, but she still got up every day and tried to make a difference at Secure One. Cal wanted Marlise to be free to find happiness. She hadn't known a lot of happy times in her life. Raised in foster care and then put out on the streets at eighteen, she had seen things no one should have to see. By twenty-four, she was running the household of a madwoman hell-bent on destroying other women's lives. By twenty-seven, she was recovering from burns over a quarter of her body and wondering why she was fighting to live.

Cal wanted—no, he needed—to be the one to give her that answer. He was confident the woman before them was the key to unlocking The Miss's secrets. He was less confident that doing that wouldn't result in carnage they wouldn't see coming.

Chapter Five

"Who is she?" Mina asked when she joined them in the control room.

"We're hoping you can tell us," Cal answered.

"You're sure she was alone?"

"From what we can tell," Roman said from where he leaned on a table. "We know she wasn't alone when they tripped the alarms in the woods. When we hauled her in off the lakeshore she told us the other women had left."

"That doesn't make any sense," Mina said, biting her lip for a moment. "Do you think she's a decoy?"

"All I know is, this entire compound is lit up like it's daytime, and guards are at battle stations. If someone approaches, we'll see them coming. We need to talk to this woman and find out who she is and what she wants. She kept saying 'I surrender' until she broke down into tears." Cal lifted his palms up to relay his confusion.

"She also said she was tired, hungry, scared and wanted help," Roman added.

"She didn't put up a fight?" Mina asked with surprise.

Roman walked over to his wife. "No. It was like she

wanted to get caught. She even walked away from her gun, which is suspicious, if you ask me."

"Let's see her."

Cal hit a button on the computer, and the two-way mirror activated. A woman sat alone at a table, huddled in a chair with her arms wrapped around her knees. She'd been checked for explosives and bugs and wore nothing but gray sweats, with her blond hair pulled back in a ponytail. She reminded Cal so much of Marlise in the early days—scared and alone.

"That's Charlotte."

"You recognize her?" Roman asked with surprise.

"Yes! She's from the house in Red Rye. She was one of The Miss's drug mules, but was just being introduced to it when everything went down."

"She's higher up in The Miss's organization?" Cal asked.

"I can't say," Mina said with a shake of her head. "I don't know what's gone on over the last two years. Something has because that's not the same woman I knew."

"What do you mean?" Cal asked as Mina stepped up to the mirror.

"She's lost weight. Easily fifty pounds. She looks sickly and terrified."

"Maybe she's hooked on the drugs The Miss was making her traffic?" Roman asked. "Could be that's how she was being convinced to stay."

"That's possible, but she doesn't appear to be tweaking. She just looks…"

"Tired, sad and scared," Cal finished. "She looks like Marlise did when we first picked her up."

Mina pointed at him. "Exactly."

"We need information from her," Roman said, putting

his arm around his wife. "Are you willing to ask the questions? She's not restrained, but I don't think she's a threat."

"She never was," Mina agreed. "She was always just scared and confused in Red Rye. In her current condition, I could take her even without my prosthesis. Something isn't right here," she said on a hum. "Charlotte was only one step above Marlise in how she interacted with the men on dates. She could talk to them with more confidence, but she was scared. The Miss sent her on dates with older men because they demanded less of her."

"She didn't want to be part of the house either?" Cal asked.

"Absolutely not. She was tricked into it just like Marlise. A few days before the fire, she secretly told me she was scared and showed me several hand-shaped bruises on her thighs."

A word dropped from Roman's lips that summed up exactly how everyone felt about what went on in Red Rye, Kansas. "Do you think this is a defection then?"

"Honestly, from what I see right now, yes, but I don't trust The Miss."

"Do you think Charlotte will talk to you?" Cal asked, nervously tapping the floor with his boot. "We need to know why she's here, and we need to know fast."

"I could go in and talk to her, but if I were you, I'd send in Marlise."

"Absolutely not," Cal said immediately. "Marlise is not getting near this woman."

Roman lifted a brow at Cal, but he didn't care. Marlise had gone through enough because of The Miss and was finally putting things right in her head. He wouldn't throw her back into that life when other people could ask the questions.

"I'll go in with her," Mina quickly said, "but Charlotte will see me for what I am. An FBI agent. She'll connect with Marlise as someone who lived through the same things she did."

"She's right," Roman said, his brow still in the air.

"Marlise is just getting back on an even keel almost two years later, and you want to stick her in there and bring it all back? No. I won't allow it."

Mina gently touched his arm until he made eye contact with her. "Don't you think we should let Marlise decide? She's a grown woman and a lot stronger than you give her credit for now. If I go in there alone, I could do more harm than good. Marlise has earned the right to make her own choice about this."

Cal ground his teeth together to keep the scathing rebuttal from escaping. The last thing he wanted to do was expose Marlise to anything that had to do with The Miss, but he also knew Mina might be right. Marlise had a gentle touch with even the toughest of his men. She'd hand them a cookie, and they'd be putty in her hands.

"Fine, but she's never alone with her."

Mina and Roman both nodded in agreement.

"I'll go talk to Marlise. Mina, would you grab some food from the kitchen? If she's going in, I want her armed."

Mina grinned. "Meet back here in ten."

MARLISE HATED BEING cut off from whatever was going on, but she had followed Mina's orders to stay in her room. She trusted that Cal would fill her in soon, but that didn't keep her from pacing the small space while she waited.

Her room was right next door to Cal's. In fact, when she moved to Secure One last summer, he'd installed adjoining room doors, so she had access to the bunker at all times. A smile tipped her lips up when she remembered the argument they'd had about where she'd be living. She had insisted a cabin by the lake would be fine, but Cal had flat-out refused to hear of it. He was adamant that it wasn't safe for her to be anywhere she didn't have instant access to the bunker. If tonight were any indication, maybe he'd been right.

A knock on the door made Marlise jump. "Mary? It's Cal. We need to talk."

Her shoulders relaxed as she walked to the door and checked the peephole to make sure Cal was alone before she opened it. The door was no sooner open than he was in the room and it was closed again.

Cal was…formidable. You wouldn't want to meet him in a dark alley if you operated on the wrong side of the law. He wore full sleeves of beautiful tattoos featuring the Greek gods that she'd spent hours gazing at without him even knowing. She'd memorized their placement, colorings and little nuances of shadows and light. Marlise suspected he had more, but she was far too drawn to him to ask where and if she could see them. She needed to stay ten feet away from Cal at all times.

"What's going on?" she asked, taking a step back to remind herself not to touch him. "And don't lie to me."

"I wouldn't do that, Mary, but there has been a development."

"The Miss."

He tipped his head in agreement. "It appears so. We took a woman into custody, and Mina made an identification."

"You captured The Miss?" Marlise stumbled backward and would have fallen if Cal hadn't grabbed her.

"Are you okay?" he asked, and she nodded robotically, even though the heat of his hand seared her arm.

"I'm f-fine. I wasn't expecting you to say you had The Miss."

"We don't," he said patiently. "Mina identified the woman we took into custody as Charlotte. Do you remember her?"

Marlise nodded again, but couldn't make words leave her mouth. *Why is Charlotte here?*

"There were originally three other women with her, but she was alone by the time we took her into custody."

"Where are the other three?" Marlise asked, her voice low and shaky.

"That's what we need to find out. Mina thinks you're the best person to talk to Charlotte. Were you friends with her in Red Rye?"

The nod she gave him was exact. "If you can call what went on in that house friendly. Charlotte was a lot like me. She didn't like the men, but she couldn't find a way to ingratiate herself to The Miss the way I did. She was just starting as a drug mule when the fire happened."

"How did she feel about that? Did she talk to you about it?"

Marlise wrapped her arms around her waist and swallowed over her dry throat. "She had only been doing it about a month, but she didn't like it. She begged The Miss to book her with the older men. She said they didn't expect her to do as much."

Cal's nod was sharp, but his smile was comforting. "That's exactly what Mina said."

"Was that a test?" Marlise asked with confusion. "I wouldn't lie to you, Cal." She turned her back and walked over to her bed, putting distance between them so she could think. If Charlotte was here alone, it was either a trap or something terrible had happened, which meant she was sick or hurt.

"I wasn't testing you, Mary. I was gathering information. Mina may have been told one thing while you were privy to something else."

Her shoulders rolled inward, and she dropped her chin to her chest. "Is Charlotte hurt?"

"Not that we're aware of. Why?"

"It doesn't make sense that she's here, Cal." She stood to pace the room again. "Why would she think she could just walk in and surrender? It has to be a trap."

"It could be. That's why we need to talk to Charlotte."

Marlise squared her shoulders and nodded. "Take me to her."

Cal stepped up into her space, and she fought against taking a step back. His gaze was intense as he drank her in, but she wouldn't back down. His brown eyes darkened to deep chocolate before he spoke. "You don't have to do this. You're just starting to find level ground, and I don't like reminding you of your time in Red Rye under The Miss's rule."

"I'm reminded every time I look in the mirror, Cal," she said, stiffening her spine to appear taller. "I'm not the fragile flower you think I am. I've gone through a lot in this life. Things I haven't told anyone. Talking to Charlotte will be the least difficult thing I've done in my life."

He took another step before he grasped her shoulders, connecting them in a way she couldn't deny. "I don't think you're a fragile flower. You're stronger than I'll ever be, and I'm twice your size. The last thing I want to do is cause you pain though."

"You need answers, right?" she asked, and he nodded, his jaw pulsing as though he hated to admit it. "Then let's go get them."

MINA HANDED MARLISE a plate with a sandwich, cookies and a glass of milk. "Your job at the house in Red Rye was to take care of the girls. Let's go at it from that angle."

She opened the door, and Marlise walked through, the moment captured in Cal's eye as he stood in the recording booth looking through the two-way mirror. He had a wire on both women, so they could hear loud and clear what was said in the room. Roman stood beside him while Mack stood outside the room the women were in, just in case muscle was needed. Cal didn't think it would be. It was easy to see Charlotte wasn't a threat to anyone except possibly The Miss.

"Charlotte," Marlise said to the woman sitting at the table. "I can't believe it's you!" She set the plate and glass down on the table and pulled her into a hug.

His girl could act. He had to give her that.

No. She's not your girl, Cal. You don't deserve a girl. Your lifestyle doesn't lend itself to having any vulnerability in your life.

"Marlise!" Charlotte exclaimed. "You're safe!"

"Yes," Marlise answered, pushing the food toward the woman before she sat down. "I'm the head chef here now.

Mina got me the job." She hooked a thumb at Mina, who had sat down at the table.

"Agent August, you mean?" Charlotte asked quite suspiciously.

"Not anymore," Mina clarified. "I left the FBI after what happened in Red Rye. I want to help people, Charlotte, not hurt them. After The Madame was caught, I spent a year helping the FBI take care of the girls from other houses."

Charlotte looked to Marlise, who nodded. "It's true. She helped many girls just like us get therapy and find jobs."

"She didn't help me."

"We couldn't find you, or she would have," Marlise clarified. "Where have you been for two years?"

Charlotte refused to answer. She picked up the sandwich, took a bite and washed it down with a swallow of milk. It was like she hadn't eaten in days, and she attacked the food without another word while Mina and Marlise stared at each other.

"She's starving," Roman said while the woman moaned as she ate.

"I haven't eaten real food in days," Charlotte whispered when she finished the milk. "I don't even care if that was drugged. It was so good."

Mina leaned forward across the table. "The food wasn't drugged, Charlotte. We would never do that to you. We don't know why you're here, but you must be desperate, so why don't you talk to us?"

"How did you get here tonight, Charlotte?" Marlise gently asked.

"We had a car with a preprogrammed GPS to this location."

"We?"

Charlotte nodded and leaned back in her chair, wrapping her arms around her waist. "There were four of us."

"We noticed that on our cameras," Mina said. "But you were the only one who came in via the lake."

"We were just supposed to scout the property and find a way to attack. As soon as we saw the electric fences, we knew that her plan wouldn't work."

"Her?" Marlise asked.

"The Miss," Charlotte whispered after she swallowed nervously. "She wants you. She said you know too much and can't be allowed to testify at the trial. The Madame's men were supposed to have killed you both two years ago, but they failed."

"Why did she wait so long to come after Marlise?" Mina asked with heavy suspicion.

"I don't know," Charlotte answered, and Cal believed her.

"This girl followed orders, but she wasn't privy to important information," Cal said, and Roman nodded his agreement. "She's also terrified. You can see it in her demeanor."

"She reminds me of Marlise when we first talked to her after the fire—skittish and on guard."

Cal didn't say that Marlise was still skittish and on guard, but she'd earned the right to be. Her life had been hell, and trusting people would never be easy. She trusted him though. She'd told him as much several times over the last year. At least she trusted him with her safety. She shouldn't trust him with her heart or her body.

He shook his head and focused on the women in the room again. He had no right to her heart or her body. He was a loner. A ghost. Someone with no roots. He had to remember that before he did something to jeopardize both his life and Marlise's.

Chapter Six

It was easy to see that the woman sitting across from her wasn't the same woman Marlise had lived with two years ago. What wasn't easy to see was why. She knew Cal must be getting frustrated in the control booth with their lack of answers, but she couldn't push Charlotte to open up to them until she believed they'd help her. That was life experience speaking. Marlise remembered those first days and weeks after the fire at Red Rye when she was scared and in pain. She hated that Charlotte was feeling the same way now.

"You've been with The Miss this whole time?" Mina asked.

Marlise forced herself not to grimace. She would have approached the question with a gentler tone, but Mina was the one trained in interrogation.

Charlotte was silent for several seconds before she nodded. "I don't want to live that way anymore." Tears fell down her cheeks, and Marlise handed her a tissue. She dabbed at her face and then twisted the tissue in her hand.

"Where are the other girls you were with tonight?"

"Gone. They said trying to access the property by the lake was a waste of time, and it wouldn't work."

"It is, and it wouldn't," Mina said with conviction. "You had already tripped the alarms on every part of the property."

Charlotte lifted her chin, even if it was still trembling. "I wanted to get caught. When no one came out after we tromped around in the woods, I convinced them to let me check out the lake alone. They said it was my funeral and they were leaving. I told them I'd meet up with them at the car."

"Do you know where the car is?" Mina asked, glancing toward the mirror.

"Long gone," Charlotte answered. "I gave them a head start back to the car before leaving the woods along the lake. I wanted to miss our agreed-upon time so they'd know I wasn't coming and take off. They don't care. I'm expendable."

"Weren't you afraid of getting shot?" Marlise asked. "You had to know someone would be waiting for you once you showed yourself."

Charlotte nodded, and a tear ran down her cheek. Marlise's heart squeezed tightly in her chest. She remembered what it was like to live that life and how terrifying it was.

"I knew it was a possibility, but I hoped I'd be okay if I surrendered right away. It was a chance I was willing to take. We're never far from death when used as pawns in other people's games. At least I had the control this time."

Mina and Marlise both nodded, but they glanced at each other. Marlise saw the nervousness in Mina's eyes and was sure it reflected in her own. They didn't know if Charlotte was telling the truth or if she was trying to give the other group time to penetrate the perimeter with more firepower. Marlise had to believe that wasn't the case.

"Why did you think it was safe to come here?" Marlise asked the question burning in everyone's mind.

"You're free of The Madame, right?"

Marlise made a so-so gesture with her hand. "I get paid to work here, and I'm not being forced to stay, but I also can't leave as long as The Miss is out there."

Charlotte's shoulder shrugged in a motion of weighted fatigue. "That's true, but you know you're protected here, and no one makes you do…" She paused and closed her eyes on an inhaled breath. "Things you don't want to do with men, right?"

Mina took the girl's trembling hand, nodding at Marlise to answer. "That's right. I don't have to do anything I don't want to do."

Her eyes came open, and she stared into Marlise's with round, blue, hopeful ones. "Then, the way I saw it, this was a safe place. I know I'll go to jail eventually, but I had to get away from The Miss," she whispered, tears streaming down her face. "She's making us do bad things. Worse things than we already do. She wants us to kill people!"

Charlotte broke down into uncontrollable sobbing, and Mina stood, making the cut motion at her neck before trying to comfort Charlotte. Marlise sat back against the chair and tried to process what the woman had told them, but she didn't know where to start.

"Marlise," Mina said sharply, dragging her attention back to the room. "We need to get her to the med bay."

Mina hadn't finished her sentence before Mack opened the door, rushed in and caught Charlotte just as she passed out. He was running with her down the hallway to the med bay before either of the women could speak.

"Life just got interesting," Mina said, staring at the empty chair at the table.

"Again," Marlise finished.

"THE PLOT THICKENS," Cal said once they gathered together again. Charlotte was in the med bay with Selina, being hydrated with an IV and something to calm her. "I'm not sure what happened in there to have her react that way."

"I am," Marlise said from the corner where she leaned against the wall. She walked over to them and leaned on the table. "I remember the plunge of adrenaline when I realized I was safe here. That's what happened. Charlotte realized she was safe."

"You believed her then?" Cal asked, walking over and standing next to her.

"Does it make me naive if I say yes?" she asked, glancing at him and then Mina.

"No," Mina said. "I feel the same way. I just wish we had gotten more out of her before she collapsed. I have so many questions."

"We all do," Mack said. He'd been standing at attention at the door as though he were a sentry for the people inside. In a way, Mack was, but he was so much more than that. He was a brother in arms, and when he needed a place to recover from the trauma he'd suffered in the military, Cal was able to offer him a place to heal and, eventually, a place to work and find a community again.

"Let's make a list of questions, so when she's able, we can ask them," Roman said, pulling out a chair and sitting at the sprawling table in the conference room. Everyone sat except for Cal, who wrote the questions on a whiteboard as they were asked.

Cal stood at the board and pointed at each question. "Here's what I know. We have two major questions we need answered. The first—is The Miss working alone or at the direction of The Madame? The second—where is The Miss hiding out, and how do we get to her?"

"Followed by, is it only The Miss from Red Rye behind this, or did the few who scattered during the raids link up?" Roman finished.

"How many of the misses were unaccounted for after the raids?" Cal asked Mina.

"There were twelve houses, and four didn't have a miss. At least no one fessed up to it."

"Wouldn't the other women have singled her out?" Cal asked, but Mina shook her head.

"Absolutely not. They were traumatized and scared of their shadows. There's no way they would risk their life by ratting out their miss."

"I agree," Marlise said with a nod. "I wouldn't have if you'd caught her that day."

"But then she could start another house and do this to more women. Wouldn't you do anything within your power to stop that?" Cal asked, his head tipped to the side in confusion.

Marlise crossed her arms over her chest and held his gaze. She wasn't backing down on her statement. "You're a man who doesn't know the first thing about being tricked, used and abused, Cal Newfellow. You can stand up there and be judgy and righteous because you've never been sold like a piece of property and treated like garbage. Until you have been, never suggest anything I do is wrong."

Mina stood and put her arm around Marlise, squeezing her. "It's okay. I don't think he meant to be judgy or righteous."

Cal walked around the table and approached her. "I'm sorry. You're right. I can't make a blanket statement like that if I haven't been in the situation. I apologize for being disrespectful. That was never my intention. I was simply trying to suss out the major players here."

Marlise swallowed around the dryness in her throat that being near him always caused. If only he knew how he affected her, but she was glad he didn't. She was glad he didn't know how attracted she was to him. Besides, it was probably nothing more than reverse Stockholm syndrome now that she was here and he was the one protecting her.

A little voice inside her head laughed. *Sure. Keep telling yourself that.*

"I shouldn't have said that. I'm sorry." She broke eye contact and looked away, ashamed that everyone in the room saw her lose her cool.

"No," Roman said from where he sat, and she glanced up at him. "Everyone in this room has a right to their opinion and respect when it comes to anything that directly affects them. You don't have to apologize for standing up for yourself and Charlotte."

"That's what I'm worried about, see," Marlise said, glancing between everyone in the room except Cal. She could feel his gaze on her with an intensity she was afraid to confront. "Charlotte is a new defect from the house, so if someone says the wrong thing or asks the wrong question, she might get scared and clam up because she thinks we're judging her."

Marlise's shoulders slumped, and she lowered herself to a chair, completely ignoring the man standing next to her until he walked around the table again and gave her breathing room. That was the most forceful she'd been about her opinions since she'd arrived here, and now she was worried she would lose her job for crossing the one person who had hired her.

"She's right," Cal said from where he stood by the board, and Marlise snapped her head up in surprise.

"I am?"

Cal, Roman and Mack all chuckled together while Mina reached over and squeezed her hand.

"You are. I forget that I have a privilege here that you, Charlotte and Mina don't have, and that privilege is being male. I have power, strength and the ability to make my own choices. The women with The Miss don't, and I need to remember my place. This is what I think we should do, but I want you and Mina in agreement before we move forward."

"We're listening," Mina assured him, and he leaned over on the table, his size an unscalable wall against the outside world in Marlise's mind.

"I want one or the other of you with Charlotte tonight. Mack will pull guard duty when you're there, alternating with Eric." Marlise saw Mack nod out of the corner of his eye. "Once Charlotte is strong enough to answer these two big questions, I want Mary—" Cal paused and cleared his throat. "Sorry, Marlise to ask them conversationally. No Mina, Selina or Mack in the room. We will record the conversation and listen to it when you're done. Do you think she will be at ease enough then to discuss the finer points of the organization? At least so we have a starting point?"

Marlise glanced at Mina, who nodded and shrugged one shoulder. "All I can do is try, Cal. I'll try my hardest because there are more girls like Charlotte with The Miss. If what she said is true, and The Miss is teaching them how to kill, we need to find her and stop this train before it goes off the rails."

"Everyone in this room agrees on that," Roman said. "The sooner, the better too. Mina, let's head to the control room to look at the video footage from the fence cam. Maybe you'll recognize one of the other three women in the shot. Marlise can take the first shift with Charlotte."

"Sounds good. Then I will dig into the files of the women we rescued from the four houses with the missing misses. If I find any who have disappeared again after we helped them, that's another lead we can follow if necessary."

With the plan agreed upon, everyone stood and filed out to assume their positions. Before Marlise could leave, Cal gently grasped her arm and held her in place. "I'm truly sorry, Mary. It was never my intention to insult or upset you."

"I know, Cal," she whispered with her gaze pinned to the floor. "It's fine. Consider it forgotten."

He tipped her chin up and forced her to meet his gaze. "It's not fine, and it's not forgotten. It was a lesson I learned and won't forget. You might think I believe that brute force and barked orders get things done around here, but that's not true. I listen to what my team has to say and consider everyone's opinion on the situation before going forward. That's what keeps everyone alive."

"And I'm a member of the team by default, right? I'm here because I need protection from the bad guys still after me, but as soon as you catch them, you'll cut me loose?"

"Wrong. You're a member of this team because you earned your place here. We might be closer than ever to the bad guys who are out to get you, but catching them doesn't mean you're off the team. Catching them gives you the chance to make your own decisions about your future. You're part of this team for as long as you want to be. I think we work well together, and you give the group insight into issues around jobs that we wouldn't have had without you here. Don't underestimate your contributions to this team, Mary. Understood?"

Marlise nodded rather than spoke. She was afraid her voice would hold all the emotions welling inside her chest. She felt pride that she was an integral part of a team that needed her insight as much as she needed theirs. She knew what she had to do as she walked down to the med bay to check on Charlotte. Once she had more answers, she would put her fear aside and talk to Cal. It wasn't fair to put the fight for her independence squarely on his shoulders. She would have to dig deep, trust the man who was keeping her safe and prove that she was a team player once and for all.

Chapter Seven

"How is she?" Marlise asked Mina when she walked into the med bay the following day. She'd gone to bed about 2:00 a.m. and then got up at 6:00 a.m. to make breakfast for everyone before her next shift with Charlotte. Cal was insistent she stay out of the kitchen, but he didn't understand that cooking helped her relax when things were stressful. Besides, she'd suffered worse injuries while working in Red Rye and never broke stride, so a small cut on her arm wouldn't slow her down.

"She's been sleeping most of the night. She just woke up and had some juice. She was much calmer, so we let her rest until you arrived," Mina explained, standing outside the door to the med bay.

"I brought her breakfast," Marlise said, holding up the tray. "I will let her eat and then ask the big questions. Time is short."

"Agreed," Mina said with a head nod. "Selina needed a break, so I told her you and Mack had the space covered. She's going to grab a shower and some food. That will give you the opening you need to ask your questions."

"I can do this," Marlise said, taking a deep breath. "We

have to stop The Miss before she gets girls to kill for her. I don't think they'd be doing it willingly."

"Me either," Mina answered with her lips pursed. "The idea that The Miss is teaching young, innocent women to be assassins for her gain is terrifying and enraging. If the FBI doesn't stop her, we will."

Marlise glanced over her shoulder at Mack before leaning into Mina's ear. "Will we get in trouble if we don't hand Charlotte over to the authorities?"

"Turning Charlotte over to the authorities would only put her at risk, and other than trespassing, they'd have nothing to charge her with right now. She defected and essentially claimed asylum from The Miss. Besides, sex trafficked women aren't held accountable for anything they do against their will that breaks the law."

"Okay," Marlise said with a nod. "If she asked, I wanted to reassure her, and I know she'll ask."

"Good luck, and let Mack know if you need anything."

Mina waved and walked down the hallway while Marlise entered the med bay and smiled at Charlotte. "Good morning. I brought you some breakfast. I thought you might be hungry."

"Good morning, Marlise. I'm glad to see you. I was worried when I woke up and Mina was here."

"She's a friend, Charlotte," Marlise promised, sliding the tray across the table so she could eat. "Mina doesn't work for the FBI anymore."

"That's what she said. She told me that her boss was The Madame's husband. I would never have expected an FBI agent to be married to a woman like The Madame."

"Money will corrupt people fast and ugly, Charlotte,"

Marlise said, pulling the chair up to sit by her friend. "We saw it over and over at the house in Red Rye. I bet you've seen it more since."

"Like The Miss," Charlotte said between bites of toast and eggs.

"She was angling to be the closest confidante of The Madame's. We saw that in Red Rye."

"Now she's decided to be the woman."

"You mean she's not working for The Madame still?" Marlise asked, hoping Cal was recording the way he promised. She hadn't expected Charlotte to start spilling the tea within seconds of sitting down, but she didn't want to stop her. At the very least, she noticed Mack move closer to the door, so he must be listening.

"How could she? The Madame is in prison."

Marlise shrugged, hoping she looked relaxed. "There are plenty of people running outside operations from behind bars. I wondered if there were plans for The Miss to continue if The Madame was caught."

"From what The Miss said, The Madame never expected to get caught. She was too confident that no one would ever tag her, so she never put any backup plans in place. Anyway, that's what I gathered from The Miss over the last two years."

"And she's not working with any of the other misses right now?"

Charlotte waved her hands in front of her chest. "Not that I'm aware of, but I didn't know the ones from the other houses. We got a lot of new girls joining the ranks though, so I can't say for sure. They didn't catch all the misses?"

"No," Marlise admitted on a breath. "There were four houses where they couldn't prove who was running them."

"And no girl would snitch her out if she valued her life."

Marlise pointed at her and hoped Cal was recording. He needed to hear that she wasn't the only one who believed that. "Exactly. It's entirely possible the misses were taken in with the other girls and then processed back out as survivors. There's no way to know for sure."

"I can tell you that no one else is as high up as our Miss. She's on the top rung and keeping everyone else at the bottom. You only get the information needed for each specific job. I usually overhear things because part of my job is cleaning and laundry duties, so I'm around her trailer more than anyone else. If we aren't doing chores, or out working a job, we're expected to be training."

"Training?"

Charlotte nodded, but dropped the toast back to the tray and pushed it away. "Working out, running, working on our combat training or practicing at the range."

"You were serious when you said she's teaching you to kill?"

"Dead serious," Charlotte said, "no pun intended. If you refuse, that's how you end up."

"Did all the other girls from Red Rye run with The Miss that night?" Marlise asked. She had the answer to one question for Cal, and now she needed to get the second one.

Her nod was enough of an answer.

Trying to gauge the size of the current operation, Marlise asked, "So, ten of you left Red Rye, including The Miss and the two guards?"

"Yes." Charlotte nodded. "But more have been added since then."

"Were you warned about the fire?"

"From what I could understand by eavesdropping on The Miss in the van, she was the one to tell The Madame that Mina was an agent. The Madame wanted Mina tortured to find out what she knew, and then killed to ensure she couldn't spill any secrets."

"But they already knew Mina was an agent. Mina's boss put her there."

Charlotte held up her hands again. "True, but The Miss didn't know that. She was livid that she'd been lied to."

"I don't have any solid memories of the timeline from that night because of the fire. What happened?"

"The Miss sent us to the airport to wait for her and the guards. By the time she joined us, everything had changed. She had changed. Suddenly, her need to please The Madame was gone, and she just barked orders and expected you to comply. She told us we were going by car so The Madame couldn't find us."

"But why? It was another year before The Madame was caught."

"She didn't know any of that though. She also didn't know The Madame put Mina in the house. She knew that an FBI agent had been living with us for a year, and that put everything she'd worked for at risk. If you want my opinion, I think she saw it as a chance to break away from The Madame and do what she'd always wanted to do."

"Run the show?" Marlise asked, and Charlotte nodded once.

"What happened after you left the airport in Red Rye? Where did you go?"

"A van showed up and we rode in it, blindfolded, for days. Breaks were always in the woods, and there were never any signs to tell us where we were. When we got to where we were going, it was hot. That's all I know."

"Hot?"

"Hot, dusty, doesn't rain much, and there are lots of cactus around the mobile homes. The new home base is in the middle of nowhere."

"You live in mobile homes?"

Charlotte's shrug was jerky. "They might be old camping trailers? I'm not sure. They're silver on the outside."

"How many trailers are there, and does The Miss have her own?" Marlise asked, leaning in as she waited for the answer. She was getting the information Cal needed, and she didn't want to give up now. She had to get as much from Charlotte as possible before the girl got too tired.

"The Miss has a big trailer in the middle," she explained and then motioned to show how the other trailers surrounded it like sunrays.

"What happens if a girl doesn't want to stay?"

Charlotte's head shook, and her lip trembled. "Not a good idea. Not a good idea."

Before Marlise could say anything more, she broke down into racking sobs again, and Marlise took her hand to comfort her, knowing Selina would swoop in and give her something to calm her.

Mack walked in and took Charlotte's other hand with both of his, his thumbs rubbing over the back of her hand in a pattern that seemed to calm her friend. He motioned for her to go, which meant Cal wanted her.

She stood, gave the now hiccupping woman one last look and steeled herself for what was to come.

"WHAT STATES HAVE cactus besides Arizona and California?" Cal asked the team gathered around the control room and computers.

"New Mexico, California, Arizona, Texas, Nevada and Utah," Mina reeled off.

"That's a lot of acreage," Roman said.

"But we narrowed it down to six states," Cal added, his mind spinning as he tried to sort through the information Charlotte had shared. "Mina, you said that the women who went on the drug dates flew to large events. Do you remember what cities? Was there one they went to the most?"

"I don't know."

"I thought you scheduled the dates," Cal said, frustration forcing his hand into his hair, still cut in the military high and tight style.

"I did the regular dates, but the travel dates were different. I scheduled the girl out of the house on the calendar, but The Miss dealt with the rest. I called the pilot and let him know to check for a flight plan for what date, but I wasn't privy to any other information."

Marlise walked in the door, and Cal motioned her over. "Great job, Mary," he whispered, putting his arm around her and squeezing her. "That was flawless questioning."

"I wasn't questioning her," Marlise said, shrugging under his hand. "I just let her talk. Maybe once she rests, she can tell us more. I don't think she knows where they're based though. The vibe I got from her is The Miss doesn't want them to know."

"Charlotte said they were blindfolded the entire drive to the new camp. The Miss must be paranoid," Mina said with a head shake. "Paranoid people are dangerous when they feel trapped."

"Our next question when she's rested again is, are they always blindfolded when they leave the camp?" Cal said. "Mina, did you recognize any of the other women with Charlotte at the fence?"

"No," Mina answered. "The other three were not from Red Rye, at least the best I could tell from the grainy images."

Cal turned and took Marlise's shoulders. "Do you have a gut feeling about where they might be based now?"

He noticed Marlise glance around the room before she shook her head. "Could be anywhere. I'm from Arizona, and there are a lot of cacti there." She shrugged, but Cal could see she was filled with fear.

Cal released her and turned to the rest of the room. "I want to know how The Miss is funding this."

Mina let out a loud *ha* from her chair by the computer. "The Miss controlled the money in Red Rye. I know she was skimming. She got on the boss's good side and then ate up every detail of the operation. I was more afraid of The Miss than I was The Madame," she said with a shoulder shrug. "We never saw The Madame, but The Miss was ruthless."

"And since The Madame was never there, it would have been easy to skim money without anyone suspecting?" Cal asked.

"She's right," Marlise agreed. "The few dates I went on,

I was supposed to get a certain amount of money, but sometimes I got a lot more. I gave it to The Miss and then got my cut, which wasn't much. She easily could have kept anything extra before she logged it for The Madame."

"Is it a stretch to say that she could have been running her own enterprise by piggybacking on The Madame's business?" Cal asked.

"When it comes to sex trafficking and drugs, anything is possible," Mina said with a sigh. "There was so much money coming into Red Rye, not to mention drugs, it wouldn't be hard for her to build up a parachute fairly quickly without The Madame ever knowing."

"I need to ask Charlotte how The Miss pays them," Marlise said, adding it to her list on a notepad.

"Or doesn't pay them," Roman said. "Charlotte indicated it wasn't a good idea for a girl to say no. Maybe she's just holding them hostage and forcing them to work."

"That or she's promising them great returns on the back end once their operation is up and running," Mina added. "After living with her for a year, I could see her pulling that off with those women. Maybe she's dangling part ownership in the adventure."

"Possible," Marlise agreed. "She was always spouting girl power when she wanted us to get on board with an idea."

Mina started to giggle until they were full-on laughing to the point they couldn't stop. Cal helped Marlise to a chair, waiting while she wiped her cheeks with her shoulders.

"I'm sorry," she said with contriteness. "It probably doesn't seem like a laughing matter to you, but you'd understand if you'd lived there. The Miss was evil, and we all knew it, but she pretended to like us, hoping we'd do anything for her. It worked on some of the girls, and they were the ones who got the bigger jobs out of state, but it didn't work on Mina or me."

Mina cleared her throat and shot Cal a look of understanding. "She's right. The Miss was wicked, but for the women who bought into her girl squad nonsense, they were rewarded. Charlotte was one of them."

"Apparently not any longer," Cal said with a shake of his head.

"I think Charlotte acted like she was, but only as a way to protect herself," Marlise said. "If she only wanted older men, she had to move up the ladder by helping The Miss."

"I wonder how many other women have tried to defect and what happened to them," Roman said.

"I'll ask her."

Cal heard the tremble in her words and noticed how her pen shook on her pad. "You don't have to ask her, Marlise," he said, resting his hand on her shoulder for comfort. "Mina can ask her."

"I said I would ask her." Her tone was fierce and defiant in a way he'd never heard before. His little mouse was becoming a lion.

Cal lifted his hand and held it up. "Whatever you're comfortable doing. In the meantime, everyone should get some rest. Until Marlise can get Charlotte to answer a few more questions, we're looking for a needle in a haystack. Hopefully, she'll feel up to a longer questioning session in a few hours."

Cal waited while everyone filed out of the room, but he held Marlise back. Once everyone was gone, he turned to her. "I don't want this to upset you, Mary. If it becomes too much, say the word, and I'll have Mina take over."

He noticed her stiffen, and she took a step closer to him before speaking. "Once again, I'd like to remind you that I'm not a wilting flower, Cal Newfellow. If I ever want my life to be my own again, I have to step up and do the hard stuff too. I know you want to shelter me from having to relive my life when I was held captive, but it might be the only way to be free of it."

He gently grasped her wrist. "But you've come so far since that day you ran onto my plane, and I never want to see you in that kind of shape again. You have to promise me that you'll ask for help if you need it."

She nodded, but Cal couldn't help feeling that she was hiding something. When she picked up her pad and left the room, he stared after her, but his mind was stuck on that scene on the plane the first time he saw her. Their eyes had met, and hers were filled with bottomless terror that he'd felt in the pit of his stomach. He knew that kind of terror, and seeing someone like her experiencing it raised a shield of protectiveness inside him. He wanted to give her room to grow and breathe now that she was out of that situation, but her time with The Madame came back to haunt them every time he tried. She could work for Secure One with no expiration date, but Marlise deserved the chance to experience freedom.

Real freedom. Not protection disguised as freedom. Sure, Marlise knew she could leave Secure One at any time, but she wouldn't survive a week unless The Madame was behind bars and The Miss was caught.

Chapter Eight

Marlise paced her room, but stopped by the adjoining door each time, only to turn away before she knocked. She didn't know what to do. Maybe she should wait to talk to Cal in hopes Charlotte could answer their questions. If Charlotte could tell them where The Miss was, she wouldn't have to upset Cal. If she told him what she'd been hiding and he got upset, he might cut her loose from the lodge, and she wouldn't live through the night.

Another trip around the room had her convinced he wouldn't do that, but she wasn't convinced he would ever talk to her again once he found out the truth. Maybe that was okay. Then she wouldn't have to fight this constant attraction she felt for him. She couldn't explain it, but every time he took her shoulders and stared into her eyes, it was like he was trying to fight the same battle.

Exhausted, she plopped down on her bed and sighed. She had to tell Cal. Maybe it wouldn't matter, but she'd never know if she didn't come clean with him. Marlise pushed herself up, walked to the door and raised her fist. After a short pep talk, she knocked on the adjoining door. He said they should get some rest, so she hoped he had taken his own advice and was in his room. Since she'd come to stay here, everyone said he was different. He was happier and didn't work everyone past exhaustion. She chalked it up to his brother moving here when she did, which meant Cal was happier having family close again, but Mina just rolled her eyes at that response.

When Cal didn't answer the door right away, she lowered her arm, ready to give up for the day, but the swish of the door opening ran a shiver up her spine. His whispered "Mary" in a sleepy voice ratcheted her heart rate up a few notches.

"I'm sorry I woke yo—" She'd spun around to see Cal standing before her wearing nothing but a pair of basketball shorts. Marlise begged her mind to work, but it wouldn't form a sentence. Her brain was too busy snapping images of his tatted chest. She could never have imagined what he was hiding under his tight T-shirts. His chest sported an image of Zeus and Leto, side by side. Zeus was gazing at Leto with admiration, while all around them, storm clouds gathered and lightning bolts rained down.

On an inhaled breath, she took a step closer. One of those lightning bolts followed a jagged scar down his chest. Her finger traced the bumpy skin, and his muscles rippled under her touch. "Your hand wasn't your only injury from the war."

Cal's hand had been injured in a car bomb, and that had ended his military career. They'd saved his hand, but he'd lost two fingers at the middle joint. He had a special prosthesis he wore on his hand that filled in for the missing digits. She didn't even notice it anymore, but this injury was new, and the jagged scar that ended in a round one told her it had involved a bullet.

"A long time ago, Mary," he whispered, capturing her hand and lowering it, but he didn't let go. "Did you need something?"

"What happened, Cal?"

"Why do you care?" he asked, his head tipped in confusion.

"We're all scarred," she said with a shrug. "I wish I could turn my scars into something beautiful like yours."

"You are beautiful, Mary," he whispered, his gaze sweeping the length of her without hesitating for even a moment on her scarred skin. "You don't need ink to make it so."

"How can this be beautiful?" she asked, flicking her hand at her scarred face and arm.

"It's beautiful because you are, and the scars are a beautiful reminder that you survived and thrived despite what someone else inflicted on you. Don't ever, ever tell yourself you're anything but beautiful."

If only that were possible, Marlise thought. He might say she was beautiful, but he didn't have to look at her every day. At least not in a romantic way, but then a man like Cal Newfellow would never consider her a romantic companion. She doubted any man would. Her scars went far deeper than her skin, and sometimes those scars were harder to hide. Working for Cal had taught her to trust him, but once out in the real world, she'd have to protect herself from men who wanted to use and abuse her. She'd had enough of that growing up.

"Where did you just go, Mary?" Cal asked, and she snapped her gaze back to his.

"I—I was just thinking about dangerous men."

"I'm not dangerous, Mary."

"Oh, but you are, Cal. Physically, emotionally and vocationally, you are the most dangerous man in my life. You have the power to put me back into The Miss's line of fire."

Marlise wrung her hands and turned her back to him, walking to the other side of the room. There was no way she could tell him the truth about Red Rye. He would get angry and send her away, but the image of Charlotte sobbing and alone drifted through her mind. It wasn't unlike the memory she had of herself in the same place a couple years ago. She had to do this for the other girls who were still suffering.

The door clicked closed, and a sigh escaped her lips. Had he left? She turned to see him lounging against the wall, his broad and beautiful chest making her forget why they were there. He needed to put more clothes on if she was ever going to tell him the truth. Cal didn't look to be going anywhere though. He had one bare foot crossed over the other as he met her gaze.

"Is that why you're afraid to tell me about whatever is bugging you? You know I don't threaten anyone's job as punishment."

"But you might when you find out the truth," she whispered. "I like you, Cal, and I like working here, but I have to help the other girls Charlotte left behind."

She squared her shoulders and inhaled a deep breath as he pushed off the door and strode over to her. Even barefoot, his size was formidable and overwhelming. She wanted to sink back into the bed, but she wouldn't. She had to stand up for herself and all the other girls who couldn't right now.

"I like you too, Mary. You wouldn't have the run of this place if I didn't. Tell me what you think is so bad that I'd kick you out."

She closed her eyes and let the memories of that night wash over her. The voices, screams and thuds filled her head. The smoke clogged her throat, and the wall of flames throbbed at her from all sides. "The night of the fire," she said, her voice choked as she inhaled again, the scent of acrid smoke filling her head. "I was trying to save the girls, Cal." A shiver ran through her, and he took her elbow to help her sit.

"How were you trying to save them? They found you by the front door. Were you running back in instead of out?"

"I had to get out. The smoke and the flames, Cal, they were everywhere."

"It must have been disorienting to be inside that kind of fire. Were you trying to get to Mina?"

"No," she whispered. "I was trying to get out!"

"Relax, Mary. I'm trying to figure out how you would save the women."

His warm touch jerked her mind back from the fire, and she focused on him. She was sure he could see the terror in her eyes, but she couldn't stop now. She had to convince him to help her.

"In Red Rye, I did what I wanted without anyone taking notice. I was expendable."

"No." His voice was firm, but there was a steel edge to it. "You are not and never were expendable, Mary."

"To them, I was, Cal. I knew it. Mina knew it. All the girls knew it. I think that's why they talked to me."

"Talked to you?" he asked as he dropped to one knee in front of her.

"More like confided in me," she explained, rubbing the scarred skin on her hand. "They told me things about their dates, and…" Her voice dropped to a whisper as she leaned into his ear. "I recorded it."

Cal's eyes widened at her admittance. "You recorded the conversations? On the computer?"

"No!" she exclaimed. "I'm not dumb, Cal!"

He rubbed her arms up and down to calm her, the metal of his prosthesis cold against her skin. There was something uniquely Cal about it though. "I didn't say you were. If not on a computer, then where?"

"When I first started doing all the grocery shopping and errands, The Miss always sent one of her guards with me to 'help.'"

"But it was to make sure you didn't run?" he asked, and she nodded.

"Eventually, they knew I wasn't going to run because I had no money to do it."

"You weren't getting paid to take care of the house?"

"No. I got to live there and eat. The Miss said that's all she would allow since I wasn't bringing in any money."

"If I ever find this woman…"

Marlise took his hand and offered him a sly grin. "I got her in the end though, Cal. It was easy to siphon money off the cash she'd give me for groceries. I bought a smartphone one day but never activated it. I just used it to hold pictures and recordings. Then I rented a post office box to keep it safe. That's where I was going the night of the fire."

"The post office?"

After a nod and rough swallow, she admitted something she never thought she'd tell another soul. "All the girls told me things about their trips, the men and The Miss. When one phone was full, I bought another."

"You don't have to whisper, Mary. No one here is out to hurt you."

"I don't want you to be upset," she said, jumping up and walking to the other side of the room. "I should have told you sooner, but I was scared and didn't think it mattered."

"What changed that makes you think it matters now?" he asked, rising to his full height of six feet three inches. He was taller than her by a foot. She should have been scared of him, but all she wanted was to be wrapped in his arms. She didn't trust most men after what happened in her life, but she trusted Cal.

She trusted Cal.

That thought stopped her in her tracks. She was twenty-eight years old, and for the first time in her life, she trusted a man.

"I trust you, Cal," she blurted out. He didn't say anything. He just rested his hands on her shoulders and squeezed them. It was like he knew how big of an admittance that was for her. "I trust you, and that's why I'm telling you about the phones. The lawyer on television said there's no such thing as a perfect witness." She flipped around to face him. "Maybe there isn't, but I could be as close to perfect as they come since my past is gone. If I can get the phones, I could testify against The Miss and The Madame!"

"The recordings would help the case, but the lawyers will say they were gathered illegally and therefore not admissible in court."

Marlise paced away from him and then back again, worry filling her that maybe he was right. "I wondered the same thing, but I searched the internet when I lived at the group home, and it said as long as one person in the conversation gives consent, then it's a legal recording that can be played in court."

Cal's lips pursed, and he dipped his head in question. "I can ask Mina or Roman. They'd know, but I'm not sure the recordings would add anything to the pending case against The Madame. The risk to reward is too high. I'm sorry, Mary."

"No, just listen, Cal!" she exclaimed, running to him and planting her hands on Zeus and Leto. "The recordings can answer some of the questions that no one else can."

His hands came around her wrists and held them, his brown eyes almost black in the dim light of her room. "Such as?"

"The cities they most often went to on dates, for starters. If you can just get me to Red Rye, I promise they're worth the time."

"Absolutely not," Cal said, his voice dark and heavy. He pushed her hands away from his chest before he set his jaw. "You'll never step foot back in that town. I'll discuss it with Mina and Roman, and if they think it's worth the risk, I'll send my men. End of story."

"That's impossible, Cal. I have to go."

"No!"

Initially, she stepped back, scared by his fierceness, until she remembered he wouldn't hurt her. He'd already shown that a million times over. She advanced on him instead, and they stood chest to chest.

"Yes. I don't have the key anymore since the house burned down. The only way to get into that box is with my face."

A curse word fell from Cal's lips, and she cocked a brow, waiting for him to say something else. When he didn't, she played her final trump card.

"Those phones also hold real recordings of The Miss as well as a photo of her."

He leaned forward to hear her better. "Did you just say you have her photo?" Marlise nodded as she swallowed around the lump of fear that was trying to keep her secrets inside. "Why didn't you mention this sooner, Mary?"

The tone of his voice told her he was angry, and she shrank back against the bed for a moment. Then she remembered she had the right to defend herself and her choices just like he did. She stood, ready for battle.

"What good would it have done, Cal? They caught The Madame, and we had no idea where The Miss was or if she was even in business anymore."

"If I had known you had a photo, I could have found her!"

"How?" Marlise exclaimed, her arms going up in the air. "We're more of a ghost than you are, Cal!"

"Why did you take her picture if you knew it was useless?" This time, he asked the question without anger, but rather in confusion.

"I had no idea that we didn't exist in any database when I took it. Once the FBI told me that, the picture of The Miss became useless, at least in my mind. Now, I'm not so sure."

"What do you mean?"

"Well, maybe, if we figure out where she is, the image will help us find her. I don't know, okay?" she asked, frustrated. "Something is telling me to get the phones. That's what I was trying to do the night of the fire, but I never made it out of the house!"

He turned away from her, his hand in his hair, and she noticed his shoulders rise and fall once. "I can't risk taking you back there, Mary. It's too dangerous!"

"Cal, I can handle myself. Besides, we know The Miss is nowhere near Red Rye."

"Haven't you learned anything?" He hissed the question more than he asked it. "Now that Charlotte is here, The Miss also knows you're here!"

"All the more reason to leave." Her raised brow did nothing to goad him, so she stepped into his space again and rested her hand on his arm. She wanted to put her hands all over his hard chest, but she knew there was only one way that could end, and it wouldn't be in her favor. "The Miss has been gone from Red Rye for two years. There's no way she has anyone local on the payroll."

"You can't be sure of that," he insisted. "I can promise you she's got someone on her payroll there. You going there can't happen."

"It has to happen, Cal. I only paid for three years on the post office box, and my time is almost up. There's no other way to get into the box either. You can't break into a post office and not get caught."

"I'm a ghost, Mary. I can be in and out of a place before anyone is the wiser."

"Not in Red Rye," she said, standing her ground with crossed arms. "It's a hub. Someone is always there sorting mail and loading trucks."

She tried not to take joy in his grimace, but a tiny part of her enjoyed playing that card.

"Stay put. I need to talk to my people." He strode to the door and yanked it open.

"Fine, but I'm not telling you the box number unless I'm along for the ride!"

The door slammed behind him, telling her exactly what he thought of the gauntlet she'd thrown down.

CAL'S THOUGHTS WERE as dark and dangerous as the lake that spread out before him. He was still reeling from the bombshell Marlise had dropped on him. She'd had ample opportunity to mention the hidden information, but she hadn't. He paced the dock, wishing the lights weren't on so he could hide in the darkness. Instead, his lakeshore was lit up with security lights to warn anyone they wouldn't be taken by surprise. No one took Secure One by surprise anymore.

"You better have a beer in your hand," he called out to his brother as he approached from the lodge.

"Do I look stupid?" Roman asked when he joined him on the dock and handed him a bottle.

Cal looked him up and down as he pulled the cap off the beer. "You want me to answer that?"

Roman shoved him in the shoulder with laughter before bringing the bottle to his lips. "Everything status quo out here?"

"As far as I can tell," Cal said. "All the alarms are silent, and there's been no movement. I'm inclined to believe Charlotte when she said the other three women left."

Roman nodded, but didn't speak as he stared out over the lake. "You know they're going to attack by air, right?"

"Yep," he agreed, acid swirling in his gut. "It's their only option, but I'm not convinced they have the ability to come in by air. She's sending scared women in to do recon. My confidence is low that she could get a plan together to attack."

"Facts. We still need to assume she can and be prepared though."

"I would like you and Mina to move into the guest room in the lodge. She's still hot, and you know The Miss would take her as fast as she'd take Marlise."

"Something we both agree on," Roman said. "We'll sleep there, but we're spending most of our time in the control room. If you want my opinion, you should go to Red Rye."

Cal grunted rather than answered, and Roman laughed, but his head shook. Whatever he was thinking, Cal didn't want to hear it.

"I think you have a screw loose. Red Rye is dead to us."

Roman's shrug said he didn't believe him, which annoyed Cal. "I know how hard it is to put someone you care about in danger to further a case, but from what Marlise told us while you were out here brooding, the information in the post office box might be worth the risk."

"How?" Cal asked, his arms going up in the air as beer flew across the dock. "Okay, so we know what The Miss looks like, so what? Marlise, Mina and Charlotte do too. That doesn't help us when she's untraceable."

"We could run her voice through our programs and see if we get a hit."

"I don't think she's doing television or radio interviews, Roman." Cal sat, and exhaustion hung like a cloak across his shoulders.

"Maybe not," Roman said, sitting next to him, "but that

doesn't mean she didn't in her past life. The recordings might give us information about where to find the woman."

"It's unlikely that any of the women knew her bug out plan."

Roman pointed at him as he finished his beer and set it on the dock by his feet. "That's true, but have you considered human nature in this situation?"

Cal stared at him in confusion. He wasn't processing things as fast as he should, and he knew it, but all he could see was a scared Marlise sneaking a phone into the house, likely at great risk to herself, to try and stop what was happening under its roof. Roman grasped his shoulder in a show of brotherly support, almost like he knew Cal needed it. He did, but he would never admit weakness to his brother or anyone else on this property. He was supposed to be steady as a rock and block the blows no matter how hard or fast they came. And he did, except for the blow he took an hour ago. That one hit him out of left field and nearly knocked him out.

"What are you talking about, Roman? I've had two hours of sleep in the last two days. I'm not going to solve riddles."

"It wasn't a riddle," his brother said with a laugh. "It was a genuine question. You say that the women wouldn't know her bug out plan, and that's true, but they knew her, and humans are nothing if not predictable. When we feel threatened, we fall back on the people and places we know best. It's possible that with the information Charlotte can give us, along with those recordings, we might narrow down where The Miss is hiding out."

Cal tipped his head in agreement but stared out over the

lake instead of answering. He was stuck between a rock and a hard place. "Risking Marlise's life for 'might' isn't reassuring."

"Might is more than we have right now, Cal. If we want our lives back, we have no choice but to take any chance we have to find The Miss, even if it's the slightest chance."

Cal stood again and set his hands on his hips. "Marlise is refusing to cooperate."

"No, Marlise is trying to take her life back. She's learning to stand up for herself for the first time ever."

"She had to pick me to be the one to stand up to?"

Roman stepped up to him and stuck his finger in his chest. "Yes, and it's time you stop acting like she's putting you out because of it. She picked you for a reason."

"I'm convenient."

"No," Roman said with a shake of his head. "You're safe. It's taken her two years to learn to trust a man, but your tirade is setting her right back where she was when we brought her here."

"What does that mean?" Cal asked with his jaw clenched. When Marlise arrived at Secure One, she was timid, scared and afraid to do anything that might upset him.

"She's inside the lodge asking Charlotte questions, trying to get more information. I overheard her tell Mina she would do anything to find The Miss so your life could go back to normal. She thinks you feel responsible for her because she's damaged." Cal opened his mouth, but Roman held up a finger. "Those were her exact words. She wants to be part of Secure One and not just as a support person who cooks and cleans for the team."

"Everyone is part of the team at Secure One," Cal said. "No one is any better than anyone else here, and you know it."

"You're missing the point, Cal. Marlise needs to be part of finding the woman who tried to kill her, not hide while other people do it."

"She needs to take her power back."

"Yes!" Roman exclaimed with laughter. "Finally. She has never had any power in this life, but now she finally does. Those recordings only exist because she took a huge risk to make them."

"And now she's the only one with the power to retrieve them."

Roman pointed at him. "I've known Marlise for years, and I'll tell you this, she's firm on her decision to be the only one who goes to Red Rye. Accept it, or don't, that's your choice, but you will damage her confidence by refusing to talk to her. Just think about it."

Roman turned and walked away, leaving Cal to stare after him while his words echoed in his ears. Marlise's power had been taken away at birth, first by her birth parents and then by her foster parents. That dictated the path for the rest of her life. Then she came to Secure One, and he gave her back the power to decide what she did, how she did it and when she did it. He gave her back the power to take care of herself by teaching her self-defense and how to use a gun. He gave her power by asking her to talk to Charlotte and ask the critical questions.

Cal swore as he jogged toward the lodge. Roman was right. He'd been the one to teach her how to harness her power, and he couldn't be the one to take it away. He had to get her to Red Rye, no matter what it cost him.

Chapter Nine

Marlise sat next to Charlotte and held her hand. She was still in the med bay so Selina could keep an eye on her, but she was determined to get more information about The Miss's operation for Cal. If she could, maybe he'd see she was a valuable member of the team and consider taking her to get the phones she'd hidden. The look on Cal's face when she told him about the post office box crossed her mind, and she grimaced. Chances were good he might never speak to her again, much less take her back to Red Rye.

"Are you feeling better?" Marlise asked the woman who reminded her so much of herself just a few years ago. Charlotte was depressed, angry and terrified, but Marlise could see the relief in her as well. She wasn't here as a pawn in a game. She'd found a way out and took it.

"I'm sorry that I lost it earlier. The memories, sometimes they swamp me, and I can't force the emotions down."

"You don't have to apologize," Marlise promised. "I remember living there. Working for The Madame has lifelong effects, but it does get better. I'm proof of that."

"I know," Charlotte agreed with a wan smile. "I always looked up to you, Marlise. You knew how to work the room, so to say, and keep yourself safe. I told myself if I ever got a chance to run, I would be as brave as you were."

"I wasn't brave," Marlise said with a shake of her head. "I was trapped in the house and almost died. I got lucky and only survived because Roman found me. A few more minutes in that house, and I wouldn't be sitting here right now."

Charlotte shrugged as she toyed with the mug in front of her. "Maybe, but you're working here now and trying to shut her down. I want to be part of that."

"Good," Marlise said, squeezing her hand. "I have a few more questions."

"I'll try, but I know so little." Charlotte shook her head and sucked in a deep breath.

"Sometimes we know more than we think we do," Marlise reminded her. "For instance, can you tell me what cities The Miss sent you to for dates when in Red Rye?"

Her mouth twisted to the side, and she glanced up at the ceiling as though she had to think about it. "I had only been on three of them before the fire, and two were in Kansas City. The third one was probably in Texas, though I wasn't told where. I was in a hotel the whole time. Maybe Dallas? I wasn't privy to any documents with an address."

"I wondered about that since you weren't doing it for long before the fire. What about the other girls? Emelia and Bethany, where were they sent?"

"I don't know. We weren't allowed to talk about it, and we didn't. We were too afraid The Miss would overhear and call us out."

Marlise nodded, but she was thinking about the phones again in Red Rye. She wondered why the girls talked to her without fear. Maybe it wasn't that they were afraid of The

Miss, but they were afraid one of the other girls would try to home in on their clients. Then again, maybe they were afraid someone would narc to The Miss about them to get a better standing with her. Marlise couldn't remember all of the cities and what girls went where. Not without listening to the recordings, at least. She struggled to remember a lot of things about her life in Red Rye before the fire. "One question the team had was, how is The Miss paying for all of this? Does she pay the girls?"

"She was confiscating bundles of money in Red Rye when we returned from our dates. She kept them in the safe at the house. I think she also trafficked drugs that The Madame didn't know about."

"She was siphoning off The Madame to set up her own business."

"Absolutely. The Miss believed she was a better leader than The Madame. It was only a matter of time before she tried to part ways and do her own thing. The fire at Red Rye accelerated her plan, but she had the money to get what she needed quickly. As for paying us, she doesn't. If she paid us, we'd have money and might try to run. Our payment is room and board. The Miss is incredibly paranoid. She doesn't let us off the property without a blindfold and a guard. She even has some male guards now. When girls return from dates—" she put the word in quotation marks "—they turn over the money to her immediately."

"If you have to be blindfolded, how did you get to Secure One? How did you even know I was here?"

"We get to take the blindfolds off once the plane is in the air. We can't see out the windows anyway. Once we landed, a car was waiting, and we followed the prepro-grammed GPS."

"You're saying that she doesn't want you to know where home base is, so if you're captured, you can't talk."

Charlotte pointed at her with a nod.

"Does she send a guard? How else can she assure that you don't defect?"

The other woman was quiet while she stared at her lap. Whatever the answer to that question was, it took a toll on her.

"There was a guard with us. If anyone tried to run, they'd be—" she glanced up at Mack before she dropped her gaze again to her lap "—shot." The whispered word ran a shiver up Marlise's spine.

"You said it was a bad idea for a girl to say no. Is that what happens if they do?" Her nod was immediate, but her hand came to her mouth to cover it. Marlise wasn't sure if she was going to be sick or was trying not to sob.

"Emelia and Bethany tried to say no, and we haven't seen them since."

Marlise lifted a brow in surprise. "Emelia and Bethany were her top girls in Red Rye."

"They were, and they didn't like how they were treated once we got to the new place. They decided they wanted more of the pie and challenged The Miss. If you ask me, she made them an example for the rest of us."

"If you challenge her, you're buried."

Marlise worried about what would happen when the other three girls returned to home base without Charlotte. Chances were good they'd be buried too.

"We didn't know why we were sent here until I heard on

the radio in the car that the trial for The Madame had been postponed because someone tried to kill the lead witness. I might not have a college degree, but I'm smart enough to know you were one of the lead witnesses. Once I heard that, I knew The Miss had failed to get rid of you and had to make a new plan."

"I wonder how she knew I was at Secure One."

"She talked nonstop about the plane you took off on a few years ago, and she finally figured out who it belonged to."

"What were you supposed to do when you got here?"

"The guard had to take pictures and draw maps of the property with entry points for the team that would follow us."

"There are no entry points," Marlise said with a shake of her head. "Secure One is a fortress now."

"Which we figured out quickly. That was why I had to convince the other girls to let me try to infiltrate via the lakeshore. The guard was new, and she was as overwhelmed as we were. She said I could, but they'd leave without me if I didn't return to the car by a set time. She reminded me that meant I could never find my way back to The Miss, but The Miss would find me and kill me if I defected."

With a cocked brow, Marlise asked, "How would she find you?"

Charlotte leaned forward and whispered into Marlise's ear. "My tracker."

Marlise's eyes widened, and she leaned forward so Mack couldn't hear her. "You have a tracker?"

She nodded, and Marlise could read the terror in her eyes. "I cut it out and buried it in the sand." Her whispered confession was tearful and told Marlise of the level of paranoia

The Miss had reached since leaving Red Rye. "Once the battery is dead, she'll think I am too."

She held up a finger to Charlotte and walked over to Mack. "Do they make trackers small enough to implant in humans?"

"No, not that I'm aware of," Mack said, his gaze flicking to Charlotte for a moment. "Why?"

"Charlotte said The Miss had a tracker in her. She cut it out and left it on the beach."

Mack's brows went up in tandem. "They make small ones for purses, but still over an inch thick. I suppose you could implant it, but it would be painful. The battery isn't going to last longer than a couple of days."

Marlise walked back to Charlotte. "When did she put in the tracker?"

"Right before we left. She put it under the skin and sewed it up. It was so painful, and we had to try to walk through the woods with it in our legs. She said they'd keep us honest because she could track our movements."

"Is that the wound they found in your thigh when they searched you?" Charlotte nodded, and Marlise sighed.

"I was glad I got rid of it before Cal captured me since they searched for a tracker."

"The Miss will either think you're dead or a hostage now."

"Or that I defected. Regardless of what The Miss thinks, I doubt she will bother with me. She wants to stop you from testifying. Nothing else matters."

"I need to talk to Mary." Cal's voice was loud from the door where Mack stood. Mack whispered something, and then Cal's voice boomed through the hallway. "I don't have time to wait on this, Mack!"

Marlise stood and squeezed Charlotte's hand. "I'll be back. Rest now, and let Selina know if you need anything for pain."

Charlotte nodded with a sad smile. "Thanks, Marlise. Be careful. She's hell-bent on stopping you from testifying any way she can. She just has to find you first."

"I've got one of the best teams looking out for me. I'll be fine."

Marlise turned and walked to the door to deal with her team leader. His attitude with Mack told her he was back in work mode. She had some things to tell him, and she hoped the information Charlotte gave her would tip the scales in her favor and get them back to Red Rye.

"ROMAN SAYS MISSION ACCOMPLISHED. Be careful and follow the plan." Marlise's voice filled the quiet car.

"Tell them ten-four and to keep us in their sights." She nodded and typed his response out to Roman.

At least that was one problem solved. Roman and Mina had found Charlotte's tracker on the beach, driven it out to a lake in the middle of nowhere several hours from Secure One and buried it on the lakeshore. Once The Miss triangulated on the location and figured out it was a lake, she would hopefully believe that Charlotte was dead and no longer a threat. Hopefully. There was no guarantee, but it was the best way to buy time if nothing else.

After a long and complicated planning meeting and a night of sleep, they waited for dark to descend and then headed south to Red Rye, hoping the phones Marlise had stashed could break the case wide-open. Cal wasn't convinced, but he trusted her instincts. He hadn't heard the recordings, so he couldn't say they wouldn't be helpful until he did.

He glanced over at the woman in the passenger seat. Their plan was tricky. They'd left Secure One in a dummy van and switched cars two hours later. They'd drive their current vehicle into Red Rye as soon as the post office opened, and Marlise would get the phones from the box. Once they had them, they'd transfer cars again and drive west several hours to a hotel. If they didn't pick up a tail from Red Rye, they'd switch cars and drive back to Secure One during the night.

"I wish we could have taken the helicopter." Marlise sighed. "This is tense."

Cal squeezed her shoulder for a moment before putting his hand back on the wheel. "I know, but taking any mode of transportation that could be traced back to Secure One was too risky. The Miss tagged my plane, which means she knows my chopper too."

Cal didn't say how angry he was that The Miss had found Marlise because of him. Once again, he'd failed to offer the protection his entire business was based around. Instead, he'd led bad people to good people not once but twice. Secure One. What a joke. He was the least secure one in the area, and The Madame and The Miss were the ones to teach him that both times.

"And you don't think a van with a fake technology repair logo will trick someone watching?"

"You'd be surprised how easy it is to overlook the obvious. I run a company that depends on technology. Besides,

I don't believe The Miss is monitoring Secure One. She doesn't have the manpower."

"More like woman power," Marlise corrected him.

She was right. If The Miss was running this operation with scared women and no one else, then going to Red Rye was worth the risk. Charlotte did say that there were male guards now, but she didn't know how many. If The Miss had enough, she might send them to Minnesota to attack Secure One. Better to find her before they showed up.

He didn't like that they had no backup, but Roman was right. The more cars in play, the greater risk of showing up on someone's radar. It was up to him to keep Marlise safe, and he'd die to make sure she didn't. He shook his head to clear his thoughts. Did he just think that? He'd never thought that about a woman before—not even when Mina had been kidnapped.

Mina was Roman's. Marlise is yours.

No. That was not an option. He had led The Miss to their door. He should have taken more time to develop a better plan, but they didn't have time on their side two years ago. The Madame had forced their hand. And this time, The Miss was forcing it. His jaw pulsed with the internal anger he had toward himself for even thinking he could be with someone again. Being with someone was dangerous, and an excellent way to get your heart broken or someone killed. He had learned that the hard way. While he was on this side of the grave, he would never take that risk again.

Marlise held up the small device in her hand. It was bigger than a cell phone but smaller than an iPad and allowed them to communicate with Secure One on a dedicated line. The information stayed on the screen for only three minutes before it disappeared. It was a solid way to get information back and forth when a team member was in the field without risking it falling into the wrong hands.

"Mina finished her deep dive into the Red Rye postmaster. From what she can see, he's squeaky clean. There were no large deposits made in his accounts, and she couldn't find any gambling debts or communication with anyone she couldn't validate. He has several car loans, credit card balances and a mortgage. She doesn't think he's on any payroll other than the US government's. At least not that she can find."

Cal pointed at her. "That's the important caveat. He could be on the payroll but paid in cash. We'll have to trust that Mina's information is correct, but we need to get in and out fast just in case. Since Red Rye is a hub, it means there will be a lot of employees, and we can't check them all."

"That's true," she agreed, "but the sorting will be mostly done by the time we arrive. We'll only have to deal with the postmaster. I know it's a risk, Cal, but Mina has done the legwork to minimize it as much as possible."

Cal set his jaw and kept the van hurtling down the highway. The sun was coming up, and they'd have to stop soon and use the facilities. He glanced at the clock. It was almost 6:00 a.m. They had an hour left to drive and then an hour to surveil the post office before it opened to the public. He refused to get his hopes up for an uncomplicated mission. Nothing ever went according to plan when The Miss or The Madame was involved. He had to stay two steps ahead of them.

"We have to find this woman and stop her."

Marlise's hand clamped around his giant forearm, and

he swallowed down the sensation of solidarity it gave him. He could not fall for this woman. Once they found The Miss, Marlise had to be free to live her life for herself. She couldn't be tied to him emotionally or financially. She deserved to make her own choices independent of him once this psychopath was found and stopped.

"I know you think this is a bad idea, but thank you for taking the chance on me. I won't let you down."

The air left his chest in a whoosh. "Mary, you could never let me down."

"I'd be more convinced if you hadn't stormed out of my room when I told you about the phones."

"I'm sorry about that," he said, running a hand down his face. "The information took me by surprise. It had been years since you left Red Rye, and you never mentioned it."

"I didn't think they mattered," she said, and he could hear the pleading in her voice. "I wasn't withholding them on purpose. They were just a dead end in my mind until Charlotte arrived and told us The Miss had built a new empire."

"Then suddenly those old phones became important."

"At least I hope so, because I know how big of a risk we're taking, Cal."

"Nothing ventured, nothing gained."

A head shake accompanied her snort of laughter. "That is not a motto Cal Newfellow lives by, but nice try."

"You think you know a lot about me."

"You aren't that hard to figure out, Cal. Something happened in the military that you don't talk about now. I respect that. There are things I don't talk about either. Whatever happened is the reason you started Secure One. You want to protect people from the bad guys and go to any lengths to ensure it. You consider everyone at Secure One family rather than employees."

"In the army, every member of your team is a brother. I built my business the same way."

"Why Secure One then? That's incredibly singular."

He didn't answer as he neared the rest area where they'd stop and prepare to make their only move on the board. He pulled into the empty parking lot, chosen because it was nothing more than a small building on the side of the road with plenty of trees to hide their vehicle. They would stay hidden until it was time to finish their drive back into hell.

Once he'd put the car into Park, he turned to her. "Secure one was the last thing I said to the only woman I've ever loved. It meant the area was secure, and it was safe to move. It wasn't secure, and she paid the price. I named my business Secure One so I'd never make that mistake again."

"Falling in love or not securing an area?" she asked, her gaze intent upon him.

"Both."

Without a backward glance, he climbed from the car to prepare for the next mission.

Chapter Ten

Secure one was the last thing I said to the only woman I've ever loved.

The words hadn't left Marlise's mind since Cal had uttered them an hour ago. Since then, he'd done nothing but bark orders at her like she was a soldier on his team. She tried not to take offense to it. He had opened up to her, and she knew how difficult that was for him. She understood it on a personal level most people wouldn't. Whatever happened the day his girlfriend died wasn't all on his shoulders though. When it came to the military, it was never up to one person to secure an area. That was why they had teams. Regardless, Cal was the kind of guy who would bear the burden of any failure so the rest of his team didn't have to. While she understood it, she hated it for him. No one should live that way.

"I killed a man once," she admitted. Did she say that aloud? She threw a hand over her mouth and hoped he didn't hear her.

His hands froze on the straps of his vest. He was standing in front of her and, in another breath, pushed her back against the car. "Excuse me?"

"I'm sorry. I shouldn't have said that." A tear ran down her cheek, brought about by the admittance and the guilt. "I didn't mean to say that out loud."

Her whispered confession softened him, and he pulled her into a hug. "Something tells me you didn't mean to kill him."

"He was assaulting me," she said in a choked whisper. "If I didn't get him off me, I would die. All I had within reach was a shiv. I accidentally hit his carotid, and he bled out."

"I'm sorry, Mary. I wouldn't wish that kind of experience on anyone."

"You're not alone, Cal. There are a lot of experiences I don't talk about either. You were in the military and probably saw many horrible things, but they don't define you. You're a good person who takes care of your family without hesitation. Whatever happened to your friend was a series of unfortunate events but not your fault. There's a chain of command in the military for a reason."

"You don't know any such thing, Mary. You've never been in war."

"That's not true," she said, pushing him away. "A war is a war, whether it's fought on the street or on foreign soil. You do things in war you would never do in peacetime. No one understands that better than me, Cal," she said, poking herself in the chest. "Don't tell me I've never fought for my life or for something I believed in because you don't know that!" This time, her finger went into his chest, and he closed his fist around it, the metal and rubber fingers clacking as they closed.

"I'm sorry. You know that wasn't what I meant. I simply

meant that if you haven't been in the military, you don't understand the intricacies of the missions. I dropped the ball."

"Did you though? Have you taken the time to consider that maybe someone else dropped the ball, and the game was over long before you got on the field? You'll never find peace until you consider that as a possibility, Cal. You're too damn young to sit around brooding for the rest of your life because of one mistake."

"That mistake cost a woman her life!" he ground out.

"But was it your mistake?" she quietly asked. "Really think about it. I've known you for two years, and you're meticulous when you run a mission. You're not like that because of what happened to her. That's your personality and who you are as a person. Have you ever considered that what happened that day wasn't your fault?"

"Absolutely not," he said, his gaze pinned on hers. "I was the team leader, so the mission failure was on me. My intel was bad, but I should have approached things differently. I should have held the team back until I knew for sure. I should have done something more than I did."

"You were given bad information, followed orders, and the mission failed. That's tragic, but that doesn't make it your fault."

Cal slid his hand up her cheek as they stood in the early air of a cool October morning. "Hannah's death will always be on my hands, Mary."

She grasped his wrist and stopped his hand from touching her scarred cheek. "Do you think Hannah would feel that way if she were here? I wasn't in the military, but there isn't a veteran who won't tell you they knew the risks when they signed up. What would Hannah think if she knew your life revolved around her death? Would that make her happy? Would she take comfort or joy in knowing you punish yourself every day for her death?"

Cal's gaze was so intense she was afraid she would combust under it, but what she saw in his eyes scared her the most. He truly believed he had killed the woman he loved, and she would never convince him otherwise. He needed to stop beating himself up for something that went beyond the scope of his job that day.

Slowly, his hand slipped from her face, and he took a step back without saying anything. Cal Newfellow was a crypt, and he couldn't make it clearer that she was not the keeper.

He pulled the car door open and motioned her in. "Are you ready for the resurgence at Red Rye?"

Was she ready? As she lowered herself to the car seat, the answer was easy. No, but she didn't have the luxury of time. If she wanted her life back, she would have to do the hard work, which started back where it all began.

Red Rye, Kansas. Population: four thousand.

WHEN SHE NOTICED her reflection in the post office door, she was glad her coat hid her bulletproof vest. At least she had that going for her. Her fingers played with her blond hair before she took a breath and pulled the door open. Being back in Red Rye hit her in a way she hadn't expected. She'd expected the anxiety to hit hard and brutal. Admittedly, she was anxious to get the phones and get out of town, but that was the only anxiety filling her belly. She was pleasantly numb to any other emotion as she walked into the lobby of the place she had once considered a fortress for her secrets. Once she left here, they wouldn't be secrets for long.

Cal had her back, but now that she was inside, she was on her own in retrieving the phones. They'd been watching the post office for an hour, and nothing seemed amiss, according to Cal, but then The Miss was never obvious. Subtle is your middle name when you're running an illegal prostitution ring smack-dab in the middle of a small town.

With a glance behind her, she made eye contact with Cal. He was loitering outside the door, pretending to smoke a cigarette. His head was on a swivel though, as he "took in the town's charm."

After a deep breath, she approached the counter, grateful Roland was still the postmaster. He was always so kind to her when she lived here.

"Marlise!" he exclaimed the moment he laid eyes on her. "Well, I never thought I'd see you again! But here you are."

"Hi, Roland," she answered, though her voice wavered. She cleared her throat before she spoke again. "I wanted to pick up my mail before my box expired. Unfortunately, I no longer have the key. You know, after the fire and everything."

"Oh, sure, sure," he said, nodding as though he didn't want to bring up the way the town had been tainted by The Madame either. "I'm happy to get it for you."

She held a bag out to him. "You can use this. Thank you."

The postmaster took the bag with a smile and walked back behind the bank of post office boxes. There would be no mail, only the cell phones. She prayed they'd still charge so they could access the information. Cal told her to act casual, as though it were any other day, and she was simply picking up her mail. She didn't know how hard that would be until she stood there exposed. She forced herself to remain calm as she waited, but he needed to hurry.

There was a bounty out on her head, and if she didn't find a way to stop The Miss, she wouldn't have one. The thought sent a shiver down her spine. The Miss would love nothing more than to have her head, but Marlise had worked too hard and suffered too much to fall back into that woman's grasp.

"Not much in there considering how long you were gone," the postmaster said, jarring Marlise from her thoughts. She jumped but covered it by reaching for the bag.

"I'm sure not. I changed my address immediately when I moved. Thanks again for getting this for me," she said, holding up the bag. "You can let the box go now. I won't be back."

"I'm sorry to see you go, Marlise, but I understand. What happened to you here in Red Rye was terrible. Don't be a stranger if you ever find yourself this way again."

Marlise thanked him and waved before she headed for the door. Not a chance she'd step foot in Red Rye again. This was her past. Her future was out there to find once The Miss was captured. Her gaze locked with Cal's, and she wished for a moment that he were her future. He was the kind of man you trusted without question because there was no doubt in your mind that he'd keep you safe.

Remembering their discussion, she didn't make eye contact on her way past him. She noticed him drop the cigarette and grind it out with his foot before catching up to her, his hands in the pockets of his coat that hid his bulletproof vest. He'd told her to pretend they were a couple on the outs, so she yanked the door open to the car and tossed the bag inside. On a huff, she slid into the passenger seat.

"Did you get them?"

"Yes. Let's get out of here." She donned a pair of sunglasses and crossed her arms over her chest, staring out the window as though she were mad at the man next to her.

The car rumbled as they headed away from the town that had broken her body, mind and spirit. The car was silent and tense until they reached the next county, but when they made it without a tail, she breathed a small sigh of relief. They were still in the race and, with the phones, a few steps closer to the finish line.

"I'm proud of you," he said, glancing at her for a moment.

"For what?" She bent over and tugged a brunette wig over her hair. It wouldn't fool anyone who knew her, but it would fool everyone else.

"You walked into that post office with your head held high and not a nerve in sight. You did what had to be done in a place you wanted to forget. Not everyone can do that."

"Oh, there were nerves," she said with a chuckle. "A whole lot of them."

"You wouldn't have known it, and that's why I'm so proud of you. You've come a long way since Red Rye, baby."

Baby? He didn't mean that as a term of endearment, right? She shook her head at the thought that he meant it exactly like that.

"We've come a long way," she corrected him, offering him a rare smile of genuine happiness. "But we have a few more miles before we can say we crossed the finish line."

His lips pursed, and he nodded. "I know. It doesn't look like we picked up a tail out of Red Rye, which is good. We're still switching out cars before we drive to the hotel. Don't give up. We've got this."

She glanced down at his hand on her shoulder and was suddenly afraid that he got her in a way that went deeper than she might like. She might escape The Miss without further damage to her body, but she'd absolutely leave Secure One with a broken heart.

Chapter Eleven

The walk through the dark streets of Salina, Kansas, had rejuvenated Cal after the long drive from Red Rye. He'd specifically asked for a late and contact-free check-in. They were almost safe for the night, and for that, he was grateful. Once he got them into their room, he'd let Marlise rest while he reached out to Roman at Secure One. He wanted an update on chatter about the trial or The Miss, so he could make a plan to return home. He'd rather not be in the wind with the hottest witness in the country, but he may not have a choice if Secure One was no longer secure.

His disobedient eyes glanced at the woman next to him. She was beautiful as a brunette, but he still preferred her blonde. It was as though she lost her innocence without the blond hair. He was so incredibly proud of her though. They'd been running nonstop for days, but she kept up with him and never complained. He'd been terrified for her when she walked into the post office this morning. Not just about The Miss either. He was worried that being back in Red Rye would trigger memories she couldn't fight through to finish the job. He should have known better. Marlise was tougher than both Roman and him combined.

Cal had been overwhelmed with a feeling that he'd kept tamped down for years, and he'd been breathless for a moment until he pushed it back. He would not fall for another woman, and he certainly wouldn't fall for a woman who was just as headstrong, stubborn and brave as Hannah had been. He forced them both from his mind to concentrate on their next steps. Hotel. Shower. Clean clothes. Food. Recordings. He was anxious to hear and see the woman at the heart of all this chaos.

"Are we almost there?" Marlise muttered next to him.

"Almost," he promised with a smile and tossed his chin at the lights ahead. "A shower and comfy bed are just up ahead. You deserve it." Rather than drive to the hotel, he'd left the rental an hour's walk away at a depot and they'd come in on foot. It was safer that way. If they had to run, they weren't tied to the city grid the way they had been in Minneapolis. On foot, they could go where cars couldn't, and Cal knew if they had to escape, that would be the only way.

"Do you think we're in the clear?" she nervously asked, her gaze flicking around the darkened street as they crossed to their hotel for the night.

"No. I think we're in a lull. The Miss hasn't found us yet, but she will, and when she does, she will hit us with everything she has. Before that happens, we need to access those recordings, find her and hit her when she's not expecting it."

Marlise was quiet the rest of the way to the hotel room. Because of his late check-in request, the hotel had texted him the room number and code for the side and room door. He wanted to bypass contact with the desk clerk. That mattered to Cal for both their safety and the safety of the innocent people they might come in contact with over the next several days. He punched in the code and pulled the door open with a quick glance around the area, but they were alone. He'd insisted on the room closest to an exit as an escape route as well as to avoid being seen by anyone. Marlise's brunette wig was long, and it hung down over her face to hide her burns. It was harder for him to be unmemorable. His size alone stood out, but there wasn't much he could do about it other than get inside the room as quickly as possible.

"Almost there." Cal pressed in the code for the room, and the light turned green.

He held the door for Marlise, and she slipped through, the heat of her skin brushing against his to remind him of a woman's touch. To remind him of the sensation of holding a woman he cared about in an intimate way. It had been too long since he'd experienced the touch of a woman, but Marlise would not be his next.

You don't mix business with pleasure, Cal.

That little voice gave a hearty guffaw as he secured the door. He ignored it. It could laugh all it wanted, but it would not get the last laugh.

Marlise had stopped in the middle of the room to stare at the king-size bed. "There's only one bed."

Cal was as surprised as she was, but he couldn't let it show. "I asked for a room closest to an exit. I didn't think to ask how many beds." He took her backpack from her shoulder and the hat and wig from her head and set them aside. After he'd straightened her hair, he motioned at the bed. "It's no big deal. One of us can sleep while the other listens to the recordings. Okay?"

"Sure, yeah," she agreed while she nodded. "It's no big deal."

As she gathered her things to shower, he had no doubt in his mind it was a big deal to her. It was a big deal to him too, but he'd never let on, not after their discussion about Hannah earlier. It was a firm reminder that he had better stay in his lane when it came to Marlise, and his lane was not the carpool lane.

WHEN MARLISE FINISHED in the shower, Cal had a pizza and a cold Coke waiting. After they'd eaten, she had to face the phones. She was terrified of them charging and equally terrified of them not charging. If they didn't charge, they were back to square one in the investigation. If they did charge, she'd have to face the woman who'd tried to kill her. She wasn't sure where she'd find the strength to do it.

She glanced at Cal, who was setting up the equipment they would need to listen to the recordings and consult with Secure One. He was her strength. He always stood by her, whether in silent solidarity or to hold her up. He helped her face the trauma from her past life, and she walked away stronger each time.

She yearned to do it by herself though. To rely on herself when the going got tough. Her mind traveled back to Secure One, where Mina sat at a computer while wearing a piece of carbon fiber and steel on what was left of her leg. The Miss had done that to her, and Mina still needed Roman's help when the going got tough. Maybe it was okay that she depended on Cal for moral support?

Don't get used to it, that voice reminded her.

There would be a day when Cal was gone, and she'd have to stand up for herself. She knew it was coming, but for now, for tonight, she'd let him help her through this new wrinkle from her past. After their discussion at the car this morning, she understood him better. He was just as scared as she was. Scared of losing someone again. He kept everyone at arm's length because if he didn't get close to anyone, they wouldn't end up like Hannah. Marlise doubted that he was to blame for her death. A link broke on the chain long before Cal took over the mission, but he was the kind of guy who wouldn't see it. The mission failed, and the woman he loved was dead. That was his fault. It broke her heart to think he lived with that every day.

Wars were ugly. They left carnage and death behind. There was no way to predict what the enemy would do. You just had to be prepared to react when they attacked. Unfortunately for Hannah, she was a casualty of a war she didn't start. The man Marlise had killed was a casualty of a war he chose to start. Someone was always going to lose. Mary had lost a lot in life and so had Marlise, but as Marlise, she saw hope for her future.

"I don't want to go by Mary," she blurted out before slapping her hand over her mouth.

Cal set the tablet he'd been messing with down and walked over to her on the bed. He knelt in front of her. "You've been thinking about it?"

She nodded and swallowed to quell her dry throat. "Mary was someone who suffered a lot in the war on the streets. She did a lot of things Marlise isn't proud of, and that's saying a lot considering who Marlise is."

"And you're speaking about yourself in the third person now." He gave her a wink to tell her he was teasing, but it lifted her lips into a smile. "You do what's right for you. Whether you go by Mary, Marlise or a new name entirely, your past experiences and the people you knew will always be part of you. A name change won't wipe your memories away, even if it wipes away their past from society. Does that make sense?"

"You're right," she admitted, staring down at her hands. "Every experience I've had as far back as I can remember has made me the person I am today. All I know is, I went from Mary to Marlise and, despite being trapped in the sex trade, took a step up in life. Once I figured out how to play The Miss to gain immunity, the stability of Red Rye helped me find even ground for the first time ever. I had plans to put The Miss away, and I worked toward that goal every day. In hindsight, I realize my mistake. I didn't predict how brutal and evil she truly was."

"You couldn't have predicted the fire," he said, taking her hand. "That was set by an agent of the FBI."

"I know, but do you understand what I'm trying to say, Cal?" Her tone was imploring, and he took her other hand with a nod. His thumb rubbed across the scarred tissue of her hand, and she wondered if he even realized that he did it.

"I do understand, and I know whether you go by Mary, Marlise or any other name, you're courageous enough to do anything. You'll put The Miss away for good, so she stops hurting others. If you're ready, we can start to unravel her web of lies so you can have your freedom back."

"What about you?" Marlise asked, her gaze pinned on his handsome face. He was sporting a heavy five o'clock shadow that he was using to his advantage as a disguise.

"What about me?"

"When will you get your freedom back?"

"Never." The word was a rasped whisper, and Marlise shook her head.

"You can't lecture me about being brave enough to take my freedom back if you're unwilling to do the same thing."

He didn't speak or even move. He just knelt there with his gaze so intent it made her insides tremble. This morning when he'd stared at her with the same look in his eyes, she swore he was going to kiss her. There was an internal battle going on behind those eyes. If she had to guess, his steely resolve would win, and he'd put distance between them again. It was his way of beating back the enemy. She wasn't the enemy, even if he saw her as one. The enemy was the voice that told him he didn't deserve to be with anyone again. It told him no one could heal his heart, so it was better not to try. She doubted he ever would. He was too busy taking care of everyone else to worry about his own—

Marlise's thoughts went off the rails when Cal reared up and planted his lips on hers. He grasped the back of her head and kissed her with the hunger and ferocity of a man who had been alone for too long. In her, Cal had found a connection that was undeniably frayed but still holding up to the demand asked of it. Now, he was trying to shore up the connection. Reweave the frayed fibers into a connection he could trust when the time came.

She tipped her head to get closer, to dig deeper. Marlise had dreamed of kissing this man since the first summer she'd lived at Secure One, but he'd hung a do-not-disturb sign long ago. The sign was gone tonight, and his lips were soft as he teased hers. There was the promise of more as his tongue traced the slit of her lips in an unspoken request for entrance. He wanted to be the first to claim the part of her that no man had yet entered. Marlise had been with many men, but she never let them kiss her. That was the only thing she could control back then. She'd wanted to save something for the man who might someday love her despite what all the other men had done to her. Was Cal that man? She doubted it, but her lips parted anyway, giving him the first right to taste her.

When his tongue slipped inside, his heat came with it, and she worried she'd burn up under his lips and hands. It wasn't a bad way to go. His right thumb ran across the scarred flesh of her face as though he were healing it with each caress. Maybe he was. It was easy for Marlise to think he could. When she'd seen the damage to her face and arm for the first time, she'd mourned the last hope that one day someone would love her.

"Cal," she whispered when he broke the kiss for air.

"I'm sorry," he rasped, running his hand down his face. "I shouldn't have done that."

He tried to turn away, but she grasped his chin and held tight. "Don't run away from me, Cal. I'm not the enemy."

"You're right. I'm my own worst enemy. I'm the reason The Miss found you, and I don't have the right to kiss you!"

"Cal," she said, grasping his shirt so he couldn't turn away. "What are you talking about?"

"My plane led her right to Secure One." Cal stuck a finger in his chest. "If she hadn't tagged my plane, you'd still be safe!"

Marlise shook her head while she tried to understand what he was saying. "No," she said without breaking eye contact. "You and your plane saved my life, Cal. I'd be dead if you hadn't come for me when you did. You had no choice but to use the plane."

"I could have gotten you out in an ambulance," he insisted, his gaze focused somewhere over her shoulder.

"Oh, you mean like the one Mack was driving when The Madame attacked? We could never outrun them in an ambulance." His grimace told her he knew it too. "The plane was the only option you had, even if it wasn't a good one."

"I made my business and home vulnerable to these people, and now we're paying the price. I will not lose you the way I lost Hannah."

"So what if she knows where you live? She doesn't have the manpower to attack it, or she wouldn't have tried to pinch me at the trial. Stop looking for any excuse to put distance between us, Cal. You played the hand you were dealt."

"And that hand put us right back in danger."

"Why are you so hung up on the idea that The Miss tagged your plane? It doesn't matter other than knowing we can't use it right now. We knew if The Miss came back into the mix, this would always be the result—us stopping her."

"I've let everyone down since you and Mina entered our lives two years ago. I didn't have enough time to plan efficiently, which led to too many missteps."

"In the end, you saved the day, Cal. We will again this time too."

He gently took her face in his hands and offered a tender caress of his thumb across her temple. "Maybe that's true, but I liked that kiss way too much for it to be good for either of us."

"I liked it too, Cal. It was my first kiss, and I'm glad I waited for you."

His head tipped slowly in confusion, and he blinked once. "You've never been kissed before?"

She pinned her gaze to the carpet and shook her head. "No, I never allowed it. I wanted to save something for a man who might someday love me despite everything else I've been through."

"Marlise," he whispered, pulling her head down to his until their foreheads touched. "Not despite everything but because of everything you've been through."

"What did you see in me that day on the plane, Cal? I was a shell of a woman who was battered, broken and burned. You risked your life and the lives of your team for someone with little hope for a future."

"I didn't see the shell of a woman who was battered, broken and burned. I saw the woman you would become with a little care, love and respect from people who wanted nothing from you. People who wanted to help you heal from your physical scars and help you live with the emotional ones. That day on the plane, when we locked eyes, I saw the woman who ran through the woods for hours without complaint, all while bleeding. I saw the woman who would help put away a woman hell-bent on mistreating women like herself. I saw the woman sitting before me right now."

"You're just saying that to be nice," she whispered, wishing she could take his lips again and make him forget about everything around them.

"I don't say things just to be nice, Marlise. You know that. If I didn't trust my instincts, you wouldn't be here right now. You'd still be at Secure One if I didn't believe that you had the courage and guts to walk back into Red Rye and revisit your past."

"I even surprised myself," she said with a smile. "But I'm terrified of what will happen when the phones come on, and I have to see the face of the woman who tried to kill me."

"Use that fear," he said, moving his jaw forward and kissing her lips once before speaking again. "Put her image front and center in your mind and keep her there. Remember all the things she did to you and is still doing to other women. Use that fear and anger to help me find her and put her away for good."

"You believe I can, don't you?"

"I always have. I just need you to believe it too."

Marlise stared into his eyes, noticing they were the deepest, darkest brown they'd ever been since she'd been part of Cal's world. Was she the woman he believed her to be?

"You're right," she whispered, her breath held tight in her chest. "I've already done so many things I thought were impossible two years ago. If I could do those things, I can do this. I can help you find her and save the other girls."

"That's my girl," he whispered, his lips dangerously close to hers. "Are you ready to do that now? The phones should be ready to start up."

"I'm ready," she promised, taking his warm face in her tiny hands. She wasn't ready. She didn't want to break the connection they'd found here tonight, but she knew what her reality was, and it wasn't having Cal Newfellow once this case was closed.

"Before we do, I have to ask you something."

"Anything," she promised.

"Would it be okay if I kissed you again? When my lips are on yours, I forget all the responsibilities I face and the heartbreak I've suffered."

"No," she whispered and noticed the light dim in his eyes. "This time, I would like to kiss you because you do the same for me."

There were no more words then, just the sensation of floating in a different plane of existence while Cal teased her lips and showed her, rather than told her, how beautiful she was to him. When the kiss ended, they were both breathing heavily, and they took a moment to catch their breath.

"I know we have a lot to unpack with those kisses," she said, tucking her hair behind her ears. "But they gave me the strength and the courage to face The Miss again, and I don't want that feeling to disappear yet."

He let his hand slip across her face on his way to the desk. "Whatever makes this the easiest for you," he said, unplugging a phone and holding down the power button. She heard the *whoosh* when it came on, and she sat up straighter, strapping on her armor to prepare for battle. "I'll show you this, and then we'll call Roman and Mina and track this woman down. Are you with me?"

She took the phone from his hand and opened the gallery, taking a deep breath before letting her gaze flick to his. "This one's for Emelia and Bethany," she said right before hitting the hidden folder and accessing it with the password. A face filled the screen that usually only filled her nightmares. Not anymore. The Miss was real again. "You're going down," she whispered, right before she turned the phone for Cal to see.

Chapter Twelve

While Marlise processed the image on the screen, Cal took a step back and ran his hand through his hair. He was still reeling from the kisses they'd shared. He tried to conjure up an image of Hannah to clear his head, but he couldn't. His mind wouldn't show him anything but the woman he'd just kissed breathless. It had been thirteen years since he'd been remotely interested in a woman beyond a one-night stand, and then along came this little slip of a thing who ripped the carpet out from under him.

You have a job to do.

He did, and letting Marlise cloud his mind and steal his focus wouldn't get the job done. Resolving not to kiss her again was impossible, but he could flip into his mercenary mode and stay on a singular path. Find The Miss.

That little voice in his head laughed.

That worried him. He had to put Mary out of his mind, or she might end up in his heart. That was an excellent way to get them both killed.

"That's her," she said, rotating the phone for him to see. Staring back at him was a woman who could be anyone's sister, cousin or girlfriend.

"She looks so…"

"Normal?" Marlise asked, and he nodded.

"Look at her eyes."

Cal brought the phone to his face and concentrated on the woman. "They're hollow."

"As is her soul," Marlise agreed. "She won't stop until someone makes her."

"Then let's make her," he said, handing her the phone back and turning on the tablet he had set up to connect them to Secure One. He dropped his boss mask down over his face to hide the man who'd had his lips on a beautiful woman just moments ago.

"Secure two, Romeo," a voice said over the tablet.

"Secure one, Charlie."

The screen came on and Mina and Roman were squashed together to get into the camera. "So good to see you both!" Mina exclaimed. "Are you safe?"

"For now," Cal answered, motioning Marlise over to sit by him at the desk. "We had dinner and then fired up the phones."

"Did you find the image?" Roman asked.

"Yes," Marlise whispered after she sat. "Mina, I want to spare you from seeing her again, but you should confirm her identity."

Cal noticed Mina's lips purse as Roman put his arm around her. "You don't need to spare me, Marlise. I'm in it to win it with you. Show me."

Marlise turned the phone, and Mina's eyes closed for a moment, and she swallowed before she spoke. "That's her. That's The Miss. She looks so innocent, as though she could be an accountant or a teacher. But she's diabolical."

Roman leaned in closer to get a good look at the picture. "I saw her once from a distance in Red Rye. I didn't know it was her until after the fact. On closer inspection of that image, I wonder if she's a different nationality?"

"I always thought she was Latina," Mina answered.

"She did speak a lot of Spanish on the phone," Marlise pointed out.

Cal lifted a brow. "What did she say?"

"I don't know. I don't speak Spanish."

"I do," Roman and Mina said in unison.

"I never heard her speak Spanish," Mina added, "but I couldn't snoop the way Marlise could."

"She has no soul," Cal told his brother. "We have to find this woman before more women die."

"How's Charlotte?" Marlise quietly asked.

"She's okay," Mina said. "I'm checking on her often, but Selina is with her at all times. Mack and Eric are trading off guarding the med bay. I think she'd be more comfortable in a room though. She doesn't need the med bay anymore."

"Put her in my room," Marlise said immediately, but Cal shook his head.

"No, that's not a good idea. Keep Charlotte in the med bay until we get back, but put a better bed in there if you need to. Have one of the guys do it. I want eyes on her at all times."

"Cal, she's not working for The Miss," Marlise insisted.

"Maybe not, but I'm not risking it. I want her with someone at all times."

"Understood," Mina said.

It was Roman who spoke next. "Have you listened to the recordings?"

"Not yet," Cal answered, glancing at Marlise. "We just got in, showered and had dinner."

"Get me a recording of her voice and that image as soon as possible," Roman said. "I'll start voice and face recognition with them, but I doubt that will reveal much."

"I'll do that," Cal said. "Then we'll listen to the recordings and make lists of names, cities and any women she might mention. We need to find her quickly, so we have to be efficient."

"Agreed," Roman said with a head nod. "As soon as you have something, send it. We'll run it down while you keep listening."

"I may have gotten her on the recordings speaking Spanish," Marlise said. Cal turned and noticed it was as though she were talking to herself.

Cal's glance at the camera showed Roman and Mina were just as surprised as he was. "But you don't know who she was talking to?"

"No, but I remember a couple of times the phone was running when I was cleaning because her door was cracked. It always frustrated me when she spoke Spanish because I didn't know what she said."

"If you come across any Spanish recordings," Mina said, "send it over immediately, and we'll translate it."

"It may not matter," Marlise said, her shoulders heavy from fatigue and frustration.

Cal put his arm around her to give her a comforting squeeze. "Maybe not, but all we need is a name that we can trace, and her web starts to fall apart."

"That's our plan of action then," Roman said. "And you need to stay put until we have more to go on. I don't want you driving back here until we know you don't need to chase down a lead closer to Kansas."

"Understood," Cal said. "We'll listen to the recordings and then get some rest while you're reviewing anything we find. My hands are tied here, so I'm counting on you, brother."

"We're a team—remote or in person. We'll get the job done."

Roman and Mina signed off, and Cal turned to Marlise. "Ready?"

"As I'll ever be," she said, but he could tell she was lying.

"Why don't you rest while I start listening? You're ready to collapse."

Her shoulders squared before she spoke, and he bit back a smile. She wasn't going to rest. "I passed exhaustion about six hours ago. I won't lose sight of why we're here. I can rest when we've sent the information to Roman."

"But…"

Her brow lowered, and it stopped him in his tracks. "No buts. Here's the thing, Cal. You can listen *to* the recordings, but you don't know what you're listening *for*. I do."

"Fair point," he had to agree.

"There are only a few hours of recordings, so let's just get at it. The sooner we finish, the faster we find The Miss, get her into custody and free all the girls she's torturing."

He tapped the desk with a grin and pulled the phones and two notepads over to them. He pushed one at her and handed her a pen. "Ready?" On her nod, he opened the first phone, and they settled in. They needed to find one needle in the haystack, and once they did, he'd make The Miss wish she'd forgotten Marlise existed.

MARLISE WOKE SLOWLY, her gaze sweeping an unfamiliar wall. Where was she? It took her a few minutes to remember she was in a hotel with Cal. Their late night filtered through her sleepiness and she remembered they'd stayed up until 3:00 a.m. listening to the recordings. Cal was still messaging Roman when she went to bed, but she couldn't keep her eyes open a moment longer. She was just going to close her eyes for a few minutes, but now the sun was up. She couldn't help but wonder what Roman and Cal had found after she went to bed.

She tugged the blanket up to her chin, but met resistance halfway there. When her brain sorted out the incoming messages, she glanced over her shoulder. A man, giant really, had his nose buried in her hair as he slept. He had his arms wrapped around her, and when she tried to squirm out of them, he pulled her in closer.

"Just a little bit longer," he whispered, his warm breath raising goose bumps on her neck. "If we get up, we have to face bad guys again."

"You mean bad gals?" Marlise asked with a chuckle.

"Them too. I need a few more minutes to hold you and remember the good in the world."

Marlise leaned back and gave him the time he needed. She understood how he felt. No one wanted The Miss found and neutralized more than she did. More than Charlotte did. More than all the girls still under her thumb did. It was up to them to do it. They were the only ones with the means and skills to find her and make her pay. In fairness, she had no skills. Cal had skills. Marlise had knowledge, but knowledge could be a powerful thing.

She rolled over to face the man behind her. They were

both dressed, and she noticed his gun on the nightstand next to him. "What happened to sleeping in shifts?"

"I couldn't wake you," he mumbled, but his eyes finally came open and blinked a few times. "I didn't think you'd mind as long as I stayed on top of the covers."

"I wouldn't have minded if you were under the covers. You're like a furnace, and I'm always cold."

"Is that your way of saying you trust me?" he asked, tracing his finger down the scarred flesh on her cheek. She didn't know why she allowed him to do it, but she'd probably make him stop if she ever figured it out.

"I guess it is," she agreed with a soft smile. "The last person I trusted nearly got killed though, Cal. Being around me isn't good for your health."

"No," he said, resting his finger against her lips. "Mina nearly got killed because of The Madame, not you."

"The common denominator then and now is still me, Cal."

"Again, no," he insisted. "The common denominator is evilness and greed. You talk about wars. Well, we're fighting one against evil and greed right now. We're in this together, and it will stay that way. Got it?"

Marlise had no choice but to agree. She knew he'd come up with rebuttals for any argument she made. Her battered heart had to admit that she liked being in this together with him. "Got it. Did you and Roman discover anything after I went to bed?"

"That's a negative. Roman's running her voice through voice recognition and putting her picture into the facial recognition program, but I doubt that will get us any hits since we know she was scrubbed. Mina and Roman are translating the Spanish conversations this morning and will get back to us."

"Listening to those recordings again was difficult," she admitted. She couldn't admit it last night, but the intimacy of this moment made it easier for her to be vulnerable. "I let myself forget some of the terrible things that went on there. When I heard Bethany and Emelia, my heart broke."

"Hey," he said, wiping away a tear from her cheek. "It's okay to feel that way. What you went through in Red Rye was traumatic, and facing it again is like digging it all up after you just buried it."

"Yes," she breathed out. "So much. I knew we had to, but I didn't want to battle it again."

"But you did. That's what makes you a warrior. You faced a demon from your past, and by doing that, she no longer holds any power over you. I could only hope to be that strong one day."

"You are that strong, Cal. One day should be now. Stop living your life like you're already dead. You're not. You're the backbone of a team that relies on you and looks up to you. You're their leader. Be that leader, Cal. Lead by example."

"I wish I had the belief in myself that you have in me, Mary. I mean, Marlise. I'm sorry."

She rested her finger on his lips. "I don't mind it when you call me Mary. I just don't want everyone to."

"But you said you didn't like that girl."

Her words from last night came back to her, and she realized she'd confused him. She had to explain it in a way that made sense to him. "If I ask everyone to call me Mary, I worry I might become that girl again."

"But you don't mind if I use it?"

"You use it softly. When you call me Mary, there's a layer of understanding there. It's solidarity between warriors. It's an understanding between two souls who have suffered through the same atrocities in battle. You say the name with reverence, and that makes me feel…" She paused and met his gaze, unsure what the right words were. "Cared about as a human being. When you call me Mary, I feel like I deserve to be cared about, and I'm not a lost cause."

"Oh, sweet Mary," he whispered, his eyes revealing his emotions better than his words. "You deserve so much more than caring. You deserve love, happiness and joy in this life. You are not and never were a lost cause, baby."

Before she could say another word, his lips were on hers. It wasn't a hurried kiss of passion, but a tender kiss of caring. Even his gentle kisses raised her blood pressure and made her heart tap faster in her chest. He'd called her baby again. Whether it was consciously or unconsciously, she didn't know, but she would store it away in her heart for when he was no longer part of her life. And there would be a day when he let her go. Especially if he couldn't find a way to let go of the past.

Chapter Thirteen

He ran his fingers through her hair, his lips still on hers in a kiss that went from tender to passionate with one flick of his tongue. Cal leaned over, pinning her head to the pillow as a moan left his throat to fill her mouth. She fought to control the kiss just as a device across the room started buzzing, and Cal groaned. "That will be Roman."

"You'd better get it."

Cal climbed from the bed, and the loss of his heat was palpable. Feeling so bereft quickly scared her more than facing down The Miss.

Cal finally hit the button to end the buzzing.

"Secure two, Whiskey." It was Mina's voice this time.

"Secure one, Charlie."

The team all had code names from the alphabet that matched the first letter of their name. Roman was Romeo, and Mina was Whiskey since her real name was Wilhelmina. They opened any communication with their code phrase, so if the person on the other end was compromised, they didn't put the entire team at risk.

"Did I wake you?" Mina asked when the camera flipped on.

"Just woke up," Cal said, and Marlise noticed him subconsciously straighten his T-shirt. Everyone looked to him when they needed guidance and reassurance, and the way he switched into work mode in the blink of an eye meant he knew it too. He just needed to own it.

"I may have found something," Mina said without further preamble.

Marlise was off the bed and standing behind Cal immediately. "Did we get a hit on her picture?"

"No. We got a hit on the conversation you recorded in Spanish."

"Which one?"

"The long one that you risked your life to record. It was just before the fire. Your subconscious must have told you it was important. I translated the whole thing, but I'll give you the highlights."

Cal grabbed a pen and paper and waited for Mina to speak.

"She kept referring to the other person on the phone as *papá*, which means *dad* in Spanish."

"That's weird," Marlise said, joining them at the desk. "She always told us she was just like us and didn't have any family. That was her whole shtick about girl power."

Mina pointed at the camera. "That's why it caught my attention so quickly. At first, I thought she was talking to a client. Sometimes they wanted to be called daddy."

Marlise and Mina simultaneously gagged and shuddered at the memory of those men.

"But that's not the case?" Cal asked, somehow knowing they both needed to be redirected.

"I don't think so." She picked up a piece of paper to read. "Everything is ready. I'm prepared to do what needs to be done to get out of this hellhole." Mina paused and then said, "That was loosely translated."

Cal and Marlise smirked at each other while Mina continued.

"My best girls are ready for the challenge. It's time to expose the agent. No, Dad, I'll take care of her myself. You don't need to come here. Stay far away from Red Rye, or this deal goes bad. You have taught me well, and I will not fail. This is our last contact until we reach the desert."

"The desert," Cal repeated, and Mina nodded.

"That was all she said about location, though Charlotte already confirmed they were living in a desert somewhere."

"A state that meets the border?" Cal asked.

"Honestly, it could be any of those, but we have a place to start. That narrows it down to Arizona, New Mexico and Texas. All about the same driving distance that Charlotte mentioned."

"Three states are a smaller hole to hunt than six, but we need more," Cal said, tapping his finger on the desk.

Marlise stood up and started to pace. "The other conversation she had in Spanish didn't reveal anything?"

"No, but she was talking to the same person. That one was quick, but she said they'd hit the jackpot, and she had to move if they wanted to collect."

Marlise paused on her way past the screen. "Jackpot is a street name for fentanyl."

Mina tipped her head for a moment. "You're right. The conversation was so innocuous and rushed that I didn't link that when I listened. She was excited and talking fast, which made it harder for me to translate. I sent you the transcripts of both conversations. Read them over, and I'll do the same again. Call me when you're done."

The screen went dark, and Cal opened his encrypted phone and handed it to her. "You read it and tell me if you can pick out anything. You lived with her. I didn't."

The short conversation wasn't as innocuous as Mina thought it was. "She also mentions Cactus, a street name for peyote, Red Rock meaning methadone, and Beans meaning ecstasy. If she's referring to drugs, they're moving the hard stuff around."

"More likely her women were moving it."

"And when you move those kinds of drugs around, women disappear."

"Anything else?" Cal asked. Marlise knew he was trying to keep her focus on The Miss and not the missing girls. Those girls didn't deserve what happened to them any more than she did, and Marlise would be the one to vindicate them.

"Well, we know her dad, whether he is her real father or someone else, was funding her time at Red Rye, and set her up in the new town, wherever that may be. They were using the women as drug mules in Red Rye, possibly with or without the knowledge of The Madame, and she piggybacked on The Madame's operation to build her own."

"But we still don't know where she is."

"Where's that list of cities we made last night?" she asked, handing him the phone and grabbing the pad he held out. She read off the cities to him. "Oklahoma City, Dallas, Fort Worth, Albuquerque and Phoenix were the cities where they did the most business. That matches up with the three states that sit on Mexico's border. If her 'dad' is south of the border, it would make sense she's in one of those states. I would pick someplace around Albuquerque."

"Tell me why," he said, ready to write on his notepad.

"It's the most centrally located to the other four cities. If The Miss is somewhere in New Mexico, her reach to the other cities is like a satellite," she explained, holding her arms out. "East or west, and she reaches one of the cities she used to send the Red Rye girls for dates. She probably kept those clients when The Madame went down because The Madame didn't know they were drug dealers. She was only seeing the escort side of the business."

"Possible," Cal agreed. "I'll call Mina back."

Once Mina and Roman were on the line, Marlise explained what she'd read and her thoughts on where The Miss could be.

"That's excellent linear thinking, Marlise," Roman said, bringing a smile to her face. "It's a place to start."

"Did Charlotte say anything more since we left?" Cal asked, clearly frustrated by their lack of progress.

"She's trying, Cal, but The Miss has them so isolated that she doesn't know much. Even when she flies them out, they're blindfolded until they're on the plane, and the plane has no windows. They fly into small airports, but it doesn't matter if the women know what city they're in by then because they're already away from home base."

"I'm going to be real with you, Mina. We may not be able to locate her. Secure One is good, but without a starting point, no one will find her. We may have no choice but to draw her out, capture her and then find the women."

Roman and Mina glanced at each other before they nodded. "That's what we were thinking too. Drawings of cacti don't help us find a madwoman."

"What?" Marlise asked, leaning on the desk to stare intently at the two people on the screen. "Drawings of cacti?"

"Yeah," Mina said, leaning out of the camera angle for a moment. "Charlotte is trying to help by drawing pictures of what she was able to see around home base." Mina held up a pad of paper with a pencil drawing. "It's like pods that stem off the main house."

Marlise studied the image Charlotte had drawn. It was surprisingly intricate and was easy to picture sitting in the middle of the desert somewhere. The middle house was a large camping trailer, and sitting at angles like sunrays were smaller ones.

"She told us that each of the smaller pods," Mina said, pointing at Charlotte's rounded campers she had colored silver, "house two women."

Marlise counted quickly. "There are fourteen pods."

"Which gives us a good idea of how many women are working for her," Roman said. "But that still doesn't matter if we can't figure out where this pod group sits."

"Wait, what's that?" Marlise asked, pointing at a drawing at the back of the image.

"One of the cacti she drew," Mina said. "I have a better image. Hang on." She shuffled through some papers and then held up another drawing. "Charlotte is an amazing artist," Mina said. "She helped us with several things we needed laid out here, Cal."

Marlise registered Cal's nod, but her focus was on the paper that held images of several different but intricate cacti. "That one!" she exclaimed, pointing at the paper on the screen.

Mina turned it around. "What one?"

"The big one. It's a saguaro cactus."

"A what now?" Cal asked, turning to her.

"A saguaro cactus. The kind you see in old movies that look like trees. They're tall and have arms that come up like branches," Marlise explained excitedly.

"We're on the same page," Cal said calmly and with great patience. "Why does that one stand out in your mind?"

"They only grow in one place in the country! The Sonoran Desert."

"How do you know this?" Roman asked, leaning into the camera.

"I'm from Arizona, Roman! It's one of the first facts you learn about your home state. If you see a movie with a saguaro cactus, you know it was filmed in the Sonoran Desert. Charlotte said it's scorching where they are, and the Sonoran Desert is the hottest one in both Mexico and the United States."

"You're saying that The Miss is hiding somewhere in Arizona?"

"Not just somewhere, Roman. The Sonoran Desert is less than two hours from the Mexican border."

"You don't think she crossed the border and is in Mexico?"

Marlise shook her head almost immediately. "Not with the girls. She'd have to have passports if she tried to enter legally or a safe route to travel by foot across the border, and those don't exist. If she had gone by herself, I would say it's possible, but not if she has that many girls. She stayed on this side of the border to run drugs. Not a question in my mind. Mina, would you pull up an image of a saguaro cactus and run it down to Charlotte? Ask her if that's the one she intended in the drawing. We'll wait."

Mina nodded and took off, leaving Roman to stare into the camera. "I'm impressed, Marlise." His tone said he was genuine. "That was some great deducting skills. All we saw in those drawings was too much ground to cover."

"This is still a lot of ground to cover. The Sonoran Desert extends into California and down into Baja, but I know The Miss. She never took a girl any further west than Phoenix. She's in Arizona."

"How big is the desert in Arizona, mileage-wise?" Cal asked. "Do you know?"

"It extends above Phoenix to the north, the border on the west and about Tucson to the east," she said without hesitation. "It's still a lot of ground to cover, but I would concentrate on the area near the southern border. If she's running drugs and they're coming from someone in Mexico, she would want to be close. Hell, she might even cross the border legally with a passport and bring the drugs back herself."

Roman raised a brow. "I have some friends south of the border. I'll get the image to them and see what they know. It's risky on her part to use a passport, but we still have to check on the off chance she did."

Mina came back into the room and plopped down in the chair. She must have sprinted to get to the med bay and back that quickly. "Charlotte said yes. Those are the cacti she saw around their camp."

"I cannot believe that a woman with no law enforcement training managed to home in on a woman hell-bent on being a ghost with nothing more than a picture of a cactus. Mary, I'm in awe," Cal said, wearing a grin. He wasn't kidding around. She'd impressed him, and her heart soared.

With her head held high and her shoulders back, she smiled too. She suspected the feeling she had inside her chest was pride. "I want this to end so you can all be free again. Until we find her, we can't even rid ourselves of The Madame."

"What is the news on the trial?" Cal asked Roman, who was still on the screen.

"The trial is on hold. The defense is working hard to convince the judge they need to move forward, but so far, they've failed. The judge put everything on hold for two weeks. She has sequestered the jury but allows family visits in the hotel while supervised. At the end of the two weeks, I suspect the trial will go on, with or without Marlise."

"We have ten days left of those two weeks?" Cal asked, and Mina nodded. "Then we'd better get a plan in place and execute it before we run out of time. We've been here too long and need to get out of this town before bad characters stop by and hurt innocent people. I'm giving Mary point on this one. Are you guys in agreement?"

"Me?" Marlise asked in shock. "Why are you giving me point?"

"Isn't it obvious? Thus far, you've been the one to find all the little crumbs The Miss didn't know she dropped. You know her and her habits. I'm putting my bets on you being the one to locate her and bring her down."

"I am too," Mina said with a wink.

Chapter Fourteen

The plane was in descent, and Cal was on high alert. They'd made it out of Kansas on a commercial flight to Phoenix, but that didn't mean they'd make it out of the Phoenix airport without picking up a tail. If The Miss was in Arizona, as Mary suspected, they would have to watch their backs until they secured her location.

"Are you sure this is safe?" she asked from the seat next to him. "I'm worried about Mina and Roman."

"They'll be fine," he assured her, holding her hand on his lap. "The Miss hasn't tried attacking Secure One since she sent her team in to scout it."

"That part is weird," she agreed with a head nod. "Why wouldn't she strike if she knew I was there?"

"Because she doesn't know you're there," he said immediately. "She doesn't know that we went back there after the failed attack at the courthouse. Since her women couldn't confirm you were at Secure One, attacking would be wasted resources without confirmation you're there. We also have to consider that she doesn't have a team big enough to attack a compound far from her camp."

"I wondered about that too," she whispered. "I figured

she'd have a team watching Secure One at the very least. That's why I'm worried about Roman and Mina."

"That was a chance we had to take. We're running out of time, and driving to Phoenix was time we didn't have to give. We'll meet up with them at the hotel and make a plan in person. We need the backup they afford us, and we all work well together."

Her nervousness was making his belly skitter. Risking his brother's life wasn't high on his list of favorite things to do, but if Roman and Mina weren't with them, they didn't stand a chance against The Miss. His brother was smart, and his wife was brilliant, so Cal was confident they'd make it to Phoenix safely and without extra company. Then again, if Roman brought company with him unexpectedly, it could work to their advantage. They needed to find the woman, and following the fox back to her hole was an easy way to hunt. He wasn't going to tell Marlise that. She didn't need to worry more than she already was.

"I hate to even say this, but would it be such a bad thing if The Miss was watching Secure One? We will have to make contact with her somehow. If she followed us here, that would make it easier."

How does she always know what I'm thinking?

"Let's worry about getting out of the airport to start with, okay?" he whispered as the wheels touched the tarmac. "Remember, head down, follow my lead and don't let go of me at any time."

He stood and gathered their backpacks from the overhead compartment, then helped her up to stand in line. He'd have to stop and pick up his checked luggage, which contained nothing but his firearms and electronics, but he couldn't risk leaving them behind. He might need both sooner rather than later if The Miss was waiting for them.

The trip through the airport was quick, and when he tossed the backpacks into their rental and climbed in, he refused to breathe a sigh of relief. They weren't out of the woods by any means. Anything could happen once they got on the road.

"Buckle up," he said, securing his own seat belt and ensuring hers was set up for her height. "The hotel is only ten minutes away, but anything can happen in ten minutes." He handed her his firearm. "You're on guard duty. Shoot first and ask questions later."

She glanced down at the gun and then to his face. "I've got your back, Cal."

He nodded once and started the car, but he couldn't keep the smile off his lips when he backed out of the lot and hit the highway. They had a date with destiny, and in his opinion, the sooner, the better, before he did something with this woman he couldn't take back.

MARLISE PACED THE hotel room floor, wishing it was bigger than a cardboard box. That wasn't fair; the room was decent sized, but Cal's presence made it feel smaller than it was. She was also trying to keep her focus off the one bed in the middle of the room. Once again, he'd gotten a room with a giant king-size bed covered in pillows and a plush comforter. It would be a great place if they were in the room for pleasure rather than business. Then again, Marlise wasn't sure Cal even knew what pleasure was anymore. He'd shut himself off from the world for so long that his life revolved around business and nothing else. Maybe she could change that one day, but today was not that day.

They'd gotten word that Roman and Mina had arrived in Phoenix and were on their way to the hotel. Cal was setting up a communications center with Secure One while they waited, but Marlise couldn't sit still. Phoenix was her hometown, and it brought back memories of Mary's life. The faces, names and pain the people in her past caused. The faceless people who had taken advantage of her, first as a child and then as a desperate young adult.

Hands grasped her shoulders, and she jumped at the intrusion to her memories. "Stop for a minute. Remember, there is no one left here who can hurt you. Once Roman and Mina get here, you have three layers of protection from anyone outside of these walls who want to hurt you."

She rested her head back against his strong shoulder and sighed. "How did you know that's what I was thinking?"

"Human nature. Phoenix is your hometown, and the memories will rise to the surface. Don't get sucked under by them. You're above all of that now. You fought against those old biases and now you're here to finish the job. You're here to win the gold against the people in your past who hurt you."

"That doesn't make me any better than them then," Marlise said with a shake of her head.

He turned her to face him and held her close. "That's where you're wrong. You will finish the job by standing on the moral high ground they couldn't find if it were right before them."

"Good prevailing over evil?" she asked, and his head tipped in slight agreement.

"If you want to put it that way, sure. You're in the right, they're in the wrong, and that's all there is to it. We're one step closer to bringing this woman in and handing her over to stand trial with her old boss. I look forward to your day in court because you will annihilate their defense and show the world who they are."

"You sure have a lot of faith in me, Cal," she said with a shake of her head. "I hope I can live up to it."

"I have faith in what I know, and I know you. I've known you were the one who would put an end to this since the day you ran onto my plane with a broken arm, broken nose and fierce determination in your eyes when there should have been nothing but pain. We will follow your lead because you know her world. That will be the advantage she didn't account for when it came to this game of cat and mouse."

"I sure hope so," Marlise said, swallowing around the nervousness caught in her throat. She wanted to be the woman he saw in her, even though it scared her to death to be that woman. Facing The Miss again in any arena was terrifying, but doing it when she wasn't in shackles was downright deadly.

"I know so," he said, kissing her nose as he gazed down at her. "Deep breath in, and remember, your friends have your back."

"Are you a friend, Cal?" she asked, their foreheads still connected. "Sometimes, I don't know if you're a friend or someone who puts up with me."

Before she blinked, his lips took hers on a ride of passion and desire that involved more tongue than the last time. She was breathing heavy and was desperate for air but didn't want the kiss to end. His lips still on hers, he answered the question. "If I were putting up with you, would I kiss you like that?"

"No?" she asked against his lips, and he nipped at hers, making her squeak. She knew what he wanted, and she gave it to him. "No, you wouldn't."

"Damn right," Cal hissed before he attacked her lips again and showed her just how passionate he would be if he let himself go.

Chapter Fifteen

The knock on the door dragged a groan from Cal's lips as he ended the kiss. His breath sounded heavy as he stood in front of her, still gazing into her eyes. What she saw there was lust, fear and an emotion she couldn't name.

"That will be Roman," he said as he grabbed his gun and stood to the side of the door to check the peephole.

"Secure two, Romeo."

Marlise heard Roman's muffled voice just as Cal lowered the gun and opened the door. The moment Mina was inside the room, she had Marlise in her arms in a fierce hug.

"I'm so happy to see you again. I've been worried sick."

"No need," she promised her friend. "Cal always takes excellent care of me."

Mina smiled and turned to face the brothers, who had walked into the room after securing the door. "He does, but we both know The Miss is ruthless and will stop at nothing to shut you up. I'll be worried until the day she's behind bars."

"Or dead," Marlise said with a shrug of her shoulder. "Prison is good but dead is better. Is that a terrible thing to say?"

"From your position, absolutely not," Roman said. "If I needed more proof of how evil she truly is, Charlotte is example C. That poor girl. The Miss put a tracker meant for a car inside her with no regard for the damage or infection it could cause."

"Not to mention she's forcing them to be assassins and run drugs," Cal added.

"Then let's shut her down," Mina said. "Charlotte wanted to come, but Mack wouldn't allow it."

"Mack wouldn't allow it?" Cal asked on an eyebrow lift. "Why?"

Roman lifted his right back at him. "On the defense that she wasn't strong enough to run if need be. Selina agreed. She has an infection in her leg from the tracker. Selina is running IV antibiotics, and said it will clear, but she has to stay off it."

"Mack is keeping everything on track at Secure One, then? Do I need to reach out?"

Roman let out a bark of laughter, then crossed his arms over his chest while he grinned at his brother. "He's multitasking. It'll do him some good to concentrate on more than work for once."

"All of that said, or not said," Mina grunted on an eye roll, "Charlotte is ready to help with whatever she can from Secure One. She sketched the positions of the spotters on The Miss's compound with some realism worthy of a gallery show."

"Charlotte was an artist living on the streets before joining the Red Rye house," Marlise said. "She would tag buildings whenever she wanted three squares and a bed. When The Madame came calling, she told me that she signed on the dotted line to get her record wiped. Supposedly, they'd hired her to do graphic design for their new start-up company. She had no inkling that they were starting up an escort service."

"I'm sure none of the women The Madame trafficked thought that would be the case. You certainly didn't," Cal said, his voice softer than usual when he addressed her.

She worried that Mina and Roman picked up on it, but there was nothing she could do if they had. Cal was right. None of the girls knew they were selling their souls down the road for a chance at stability. The only one who knew that was The Miss, and it turned out she had ulterior motives.

"Marlise, where did The Madame troll for women when you lived here?" Roman asked, picking up a tablet off the bed. "Were there specific places she'd send scouts to hunt for women?"

A chill ran through Marlise at the memory of that time. Cal put his hands on her upper arms and kept them there. It was a reminder that he was there to take care of her, and he wouldn't let her get hurt again.

"The train station, bus station and YMCA. They also rotated through the public parks with restrooms and shaded areas. Girls hung out at the parks where they had access to water and toilets. They're too smart to pick up girls from shelters, but they do troll the campgrounds. That's where they found me." A shiver went through her when she remembered that first interaction with a scout. If only she hadn't gone with her that day.

"That's still a lot of ground to cover," Cal said, squeezing her shoulders to offer comfort.

That was when she remembered if she hadn't gone with the scout that day, she wouldn't have these people in her life. Wishing for a redo in the past always changed the future. Even after suffering so much pain and trauma, she wanted this future with these people in it. She could only hope that was the case after The Miss was caught.

"I need to talk to Charlotte," Marlise said, grabbing Mina's hand. "Can we call her?"

"Tell us why first," Mina said calmly while her gaze flicked to Cal's.

"Tell us what you're thinking, Mary. We'll listen," Cal promised.

Marlise glanced between them all for a moment. "Well, it's important we know if she's sourcing girls from the bigger cities. If she is, that tells us her camp is somewhere closer to the center of the state than the border," Marlise pointed out. "But my gut tells me she's further south of Phoenix."

"How far is it from Phoenix to south of the border?" Roman asked, pecking around on his tablet, but Marlise could answer him faster than Google.

"It's two and a half hours, which doesn't sound like that long, but if you get a nervous girl in the car, two and a half hours is a long time for her to change her mind. The Madame always kept the commute down to an hour. She also had the scouts talk up all the pampering the girls would get when they arrived."

"How does that apply to calling Charlotte?" Cal asked, and Marlise turned to him, grasping the front of his shirt.

"She lived with those girls for at least a year, Cal. Chances are, she knows where they're from, at least the new girls The Miss brought in."

"She has a point," Roman said, but she waited for Cal to agree.

When he gave the nod, she did an internal fist pump. While Roman got Charlotte on the phone, she forced herself to stay calm. If her theory was correct, they were in the wrong place and had to move farther south if they had a hope of finding this woman before the trial resumed. It might be a shot in the dark, but you missed all the shots you didn't take, and honestly, they had no other shots.

"Marlise has a question for you, Charlotte," Roman said, snapping Marlise back to the conversation.

"I'm happy to answer it if I can," Charlotte said, and Roman motioned for Marlise to ask her question.

"Charlotte, did you get to talk to the new women that The Miss brought to camp?"

"Sure, just like in Red Rye, we lived together, and the new girls were scared and wanted to talk."

"Did any of them tell you where they were picked up?"

The other end of the line was silent, and Marlise was about to ask Roman if the call had dropped when Charlotte spoke. "I should have thought of that before Roman and Mina left," she said. They all heard the disappointment in her voice that she hadn't.

"Don't feel bad," Marlise said immediately to calm her. "You haven't felt the best since you got to Secure One, and I just thought of it myself. I'm hoping to plot a few of them on a map to give us a better idea of where to start the search."

"Give me five minutes? I need to think when I'm not on the spot."

"That's fine," Roman said. "Have Mack call us back or text us the information."

They ended the call and stared at each other with frustration until Cal spoke. "What if The Miss didn't get the women from Arizona?"

Marlise started to pace, but she shook her head while she did it. "I'm sure she did, at least in the beginning. She was setting up shop and didn't have the time or the scouts to extend her tentacles too far. I wouldn't be surprised if the first few girls she got were snatch-and-run homeless girls off the street."

"You're saying The Miss had to build her army fast?" Cal asked.

"Exactly," Mina agreed. "If she were running drugs through Red Rye, she wouldn't want those clients to defect to a different supplier. We know she was prepared to leave, which means her home base was likely ready, but she still needed women to get it running."

"When Charlotte gets back to us, I want to plot the cities on a map. We'll find the center of all of them and start looking for The Miss's girls there."

"Needle in a haystack though," Cal said with frustration. "When the sun comes up tomorrow, we only have nine days until the trial resumes without us."

"If you'd rather, we can—" Marlise's sentence was cut off when the phone rang.

"I remembered six girls," Charlotte said, "but I don't know if these towns are in Arizona, California or Mexico."

"I think we can rule out Mexico," Marlise said immediately. "You didn't need passports to move around the country, right?"

"No," Charlotte agreed. "That's a good point. Then if we're talking about that desert you mentioned, these towns have to be in Arizona or California."

"I'm ready," Cal said, holding a sheet of paper to write them down.

Charlotte listed off three names, and Marlise stopped her. "Wait, Three Points and Sahuarita are near the San Xavier Indian Reservation. Were any of them Indigenous women?"

"That was the vibe I got," Charlotte said. "Do you know where these towns are?"

"The first three are south or west of Tucson. What are the other three?"

Charlotte listed them off, and Marlise bit her lip as she leaned over Cal's shoulder. "Those towns are all within driving distance of Tucson." If The Miss was taking girls from just one town or specific area, that meant she didn't have time to be picky about who she was taking.

"Thanks, Charlotte," Marlise said before Roman hung up with her.

"The Miss must be desperate if she's taking women all from one area," Mina said, mirroring Marlise's thoughts. "That could put her on police radar."

"Unlikely," Marlise said, sitting on the end of the bed. "She's still only going to source homeless girls. They're already lost girls, so no one will miss them unless they have a close friend on the street."

"True," Mina agreed, glancing at the two men. "It looks like we need to get to Tucson."

"That's less than two hours by car," Marlise said before anyone could ask.

"Once we're down there, do you know where to start looking?" Roman asked, his gaze holding Cal's.

The breath that Marlise blew out was long and frustrated. "That's the problem. There is so much area to consider there. You've got Catalina State Park, Santa Catalina Natural Area, the Catalina Foothills, Saguaro National Park and Tucson Mountain Park. Those are just the ones around Tucson. There are many other wilderness areas along that route going west."

"You're saying we have found the haystack, but it's big, and the needle is still small," Cal deduced.

"We only have nine days," Roman said. "We don't have time to search all those places on the off chance The Miss has sent a scout out."

Her three friends continued to toss around ideas on finding the needle, while Marlise considered something even more important—finding the eye of the needle. They had nine days, and that wasn't much time when the scouts spend at least a week grooming a girl before they take her back to meet The Miss. Maybe when she first arrived, The Miss wasn't grooming the girls out of time constraints, but by now, she'd surely be back to her usual tactics. She wasn't dumb, and she knew that taking too many girls from one area was bad for business. That made a person too memorable to the other girls on the street. The last thing The Miss wanted was for her scouts to be followed back to the base.

"I doubt she's even taking girls from Tucson anymore," Marlise said as a hush fell over the room. "She may not even be recruiting right now."

Mina pointed at her. "She's right. She could be sitting fine with women, other than losing Charlotte. With what happened at the trial, she could be laying low and waiting for that to pass."

"We're going to have to draw her out, and there's only one way to do that," Marlise said, sitting up straighter. "We let her know I'm in town."

"Absolutely not!" Cal bellowed before the words were barely out of her mouth. "You aren't trained for that, and we don't have the backup!"

Mina grasped his arm to quiet him. "She's right, Cal. If we don't draw The Miss out, we'll still be trying to find her when the trial resumes."

"We'll drive around the whole damn desert looking for her pods before we risk Marlise's life again!"

"We don't have time, Cal!" Marlise exclaimed with frustration as she leapt to her feet. "Some of the roads west of Tucson are nothing but dirt and lead deep into the desert! We don't have time to find the needle. We have to find the eye, and then we have to thread it. If we don't, she will always haunt us. I'm tired of this cat and mouse game, and every minute we stand here safely, another girl could be dying. I have enough on my conscience. I don't need more deaths weighing heavy there."

"It's too dangerous," Cal ground out, his insistence loud and clear, but Marlise noticed an underlying layer of fear.

She walked to him and braced her hands on his chest, but he stepped back, putting that wall back up between them. "You can tag me. You'll know where I am at all times."

"Tagging you doesn't help if The Miss dispatches you on sight."

"She won't," Mina said. "She won't do that in public. She'd have to deal with a body if she did it anywhere other than home base, and Marlise is too well-known because of the trial. The authorities would know immediately that The Miss did it and she was in the area."

"She'd still be dead, Mina," he hissed. "I'm not taking that chance with her life."

"I'll go with her and be her backup."

"Forget it!" Roman exclaimed from the end of the bed, where he was sorting out information coming in from Secure One. "The FBI is already going to have a cow that I took their star witnesses out of town to find a madwoman. Imagine if they get kidnapped! No, this is a bad idea for both of you."

Mina's eye roll at her husband was powerful, and Marlise had to bite back a smile. "The FBI isn't going to say a thing if we catch The Miss for them, which is something they've been unable to do. Besides, they don't own us anymore."

"Even if I wanted to, which I don't," Cal emphasized, "there's no way to tag you without The Miss finding it when you get to her. The first thing she'll do is search you."

"I'll already be there, and you'll have the location," Marlise said logically. "After that, it doesn't matter."

"It matters if she kills you when she finds it."

"You could tag me instead," Mina said, tapping her prosthesis. "She can't take this."

Roman took Mina's face in his hands. "This is not your war to fight, Mina."

"But it is, Roman," she whispered, not backing down. "The Miss took two years of my life and my leg from me. This is as much my fight as it is Marlise's."

"It's a moot point. The Miss isn't dumb. There's no way

she would grab either of you. She'd know it was a trick," Cal said to shut the conversation down.

Marlise's excitement drained away, and she plopped onto the bed. Cal was right. They'd spent the last two years evading The Miss. There was no way she'd believe it wasn't a trap. There was no way she'd believe they'd just throw themselves out there and wait to get snatched. If they were going to get to The Miss, they would have to be subtle. They needed to be found without being obvious about it.

"I know what we have to do." Marlise stood and pointed at Mina. "We need to head to Tucson today, but I'll need you to make a stop. If I give you a list, can you obtain what's needed?"

"Of course," Mina replied. "What's your plan?"

"We know we can't go in dressed as ourselves, so we hit the streets as girls looking for a better life. We visit some parks, knock on some doors and make it known we want out of the street life. Disguised, no one will know who we are, which buys us time."

"No," Cal said, but Marlise spun on him and stuck her finger in his chest.

"Do not tell me no. You gave me point on this in Kansas, and you can't have it both ways, Cal Newfellow! You can't say you want to find The Miss but tie our hands at every turn!" Roman was biting his lip when she turned to face them. "Right?"

Roman shrugged. "I have to side with her on this one, little brother. You did give her point, and you said you trusted her instincts. We're running out of time, and her idea is valid and credible if we put safeguards in place before they go out."

"I'm going with you," Mina said, grabbing Marlise's hand. "We were a team in Red Rye, and we're an even better team now. We have each other's back, right?"

"Right, but Mina, you don't have to," Marlise said, her gaze flicking to Roman, but he didn't look as upset as Cal did. "I'd understand if you'd rather be part of the team monitoring my movements."

"I do have to," she said emphatically. "I want a piece of this woman as much as you do, and I will not let you go out there alone. You've been alone all your life, but not anymore. Secure One has you now, and you've proven yourself to all of us. Even Cal, despite his growling and teeth gnashing."

"Mina," he warned, his jaw pulsing. "Do not push me."

Mina strode up to him and looked him up and down. "Or what? Are you going to fire me? Fine, fire me. I'm still going out tomorrow on the streets of Tucson with Marlise to find this woman. You can get on board or stand in the corner and pout while we make a plan, but we're running out of time. We have no other option."

They stared each other down for long seconds before Cal's shoulders sank, and he shook his head. "I know you're right, but I don't like it. I don't like it at all."

"Neither do I," Marlise said, stepping close to him so he could feel her heat and know she was there for him. "But I trust you, Roman, Mack and the team at Secure One. I trust that Mina will have my back and keep me safe. For someone who doesn't trust easily, that's saying a lot. You've all proven to me with actions rather than words that you're not letting anything happen to me. You only need to prove it one more time. The most important time."

Cal's brown eyes were wide and held the truth that he

hadn't said. He was scared. He was scared for her but also of losing her. His nod relaxed her shoulders, and she gave him one back. The action was of respect for her and her choices, which filled her with pride.

"I will agree to this, but we don't leave for Tucson until morning. We need the rest of today to make a plan and get everyone at Secure One on it."

"Agreed," Mina and Roman said together.

"I can accept that," Marlise said. "It's only ninety minutes to Tucson, so we can still be on the streets by ten."

"If we agree, then let's get to work. I want to find this woman and bring her in so we can get on with our lives without her hanging over our heads."

As Cal, Roman and Mina set up a battle station in their hotel suite, Marlise couldn't help but wonder if the life he planned to get on with would include her, or if he wanted to find The Miss as a way to end his commitment to her. The determination she saw in his eyes told her he was committed to keeping her safe, but the fear she saw in them told her he was just as scared as she was about her role at Secure One once this was over. She suspected they were scared for different reasons, and Marlise hoped that if she came out of this mission in one piece, so did her heart.

Chapter Sixteen

The sun had gone down on them as they'd plotted and planned this mission to the last "what if," but Cal still wasn't comfortable sending Marlise into the field. She knew the streets, but they were always fluid, and she'd been gone for too many years. Roman wasn't any happier about sending Mina with her, but it was better than sending Marlise alone. They could watch each other's backs, and there were better tagging options for Mina than Marlise. They'd tag her prosthesis with a tracker in hopes if they did find The Miss, they wouldn't know she was an amputee. As long as she kept the prosthesis hidden, they could track them.

Roman wasn't going to get any sleep tonight either, and Cal took a bit of comfort in knowing he wasn't alone in his distaste for this mission. Neither of them dealt well with not being part of it. They'd rather be out there clearing the field than sitting on their hands in a car waiting for something to happen. They didn't have a choice this time. Their presence would be noticeable and only hamper the women as they worked the streets. He had to trust Mina and her skills as an FBI agent. He also had to trust Marlise and her skills as someone who'd once lived on the streets. The only part he liked about the plan was disguising them beyond recognition. If they didn't know it was her, the scouts would be more likely to take her to home base as a willing participant rather than a hostage. The women just had to get them onto the property, and Secure One would do the rest.

Mina had gone out and bought the supplies, and in six hours, they'd don their disguises and leave for Tucson. A vast pit opened in Cal's gut, and he grunted, wishing this hell were over and they were back at Secure One. Did he regret bringing Mina and Marlise to Secure One? No, not for one second. This case had cost him time, money and sleep, but he'd gained so much more than he'd lost. He had his brother working with him now, a sister who was also an excellent hacker, and a woman who could be more than an employee and friend if this were a different time and place.

She already is.

He grunted at that voice again. Thinking that way was going to get one of them killed. That voice hadn't listened to him since Marlise stepped foot on his plane two years ago. He fought against it, but it never relented, and it was always loud in his head when the room was quiet. Marlise had gone to bed an hour ago and left him to brood in the corner. He'd sleep there in the club chair, his feet up on the luggage rack, instead of climbing into that giant bed with her. Holding her as she slept would be a terrible idea just hours before he'd have to let her out of his protective grasp. They needed to close this case so he could get Marlise out of his mind and his lodge.

"Tell me what happened," Marlise whispered.

The room was dark, and Cal sighed, glad she couldn't see his facial expression at the request. "I can't, Mary."

"You mean you won't," she replied with disappointment.

"No, I can't. The mission was classified. I can't tell you what happened."

"You can tell me what happened without specifics, Cal. I only need to know what happened to you and Hannah."

"What happened to the meek woman who never said a word when she first came to Secure One?"

"You taught her to stop letting people walk all over her."

Cal snorted, and while he didn't mean for it to be, it was tinged with amusement. "I have to admit that even when you're in my face about something, I still like my feisty Mary to my meek one."

My? Stop. Get that out of your head right now, pal.

"Then stop putting up a wall between us like you don't care."

Cal stood from where he sat near the window and walked to the bed. He lowered himself to the edge of it. "I do care, Mary, and that's why I put the wall up. Doing anything else could get you killed."

"I'm not Hannah, Cal, and it's time you stop treating me that way."

"I'm treating you the same way I would any other witness I had to protect."

"Good sell, but I'm not buying. Tell me what happened."

Why was he even considering her request? He hadn't told anyone what happened since the debriefing the week after the mission. He'd been in a hospital bed, a bullet wound in his chest, but his heart shattered to smithereens.

"We were young and in love. Hannah was, um—" Cal glanced at the ceiling "—on the same team. I'm not purposely being vague, but I have to be careful what I say."

Marlise took his right hand and started to massage his palm below his missing fingers. He wanted to draw his hand away and force her to stop, but her touch calmed the burning nerves. He knew she lived with the same kind of pain and wondered if she knew he suffered too. He tried to hide his discomfort from his team, and the prosthesis helped by protecting the sensitive digits, but he spent a lot of time pretending he was fine when he wasn't.

"I understand. Keep going," she said, her fingers massaging away the pain.

"She was specially trained as an interpreter as well. It was her job to go in and get the information we needed. It was my job to protect her while she did it. The big boss said to move in, but I wasn't comfortable with the lack of recon. When you're working with the government, you're never in control, and they told me the people we were looking for weren't active in our area. My limited recon said the same. We were both wrong. Hannah paid the price. That's the story."

Marlise sat up in bed and turned his hand over, rubbing her thumbs across the scars that crisscrossed it. "What happened, Cal?"

"I just told you!" he exclaimed, sending his hand into his hair on a deep breath.

"What you did was tell me something I already knew. You didn't do your job, and Hannah died. But what happened?"

"It doesn't matter, Mary!" he exploded, standing and walking to the end of the bed. His harsh tone didn't even make her flinch, and that worried him. If she was digging in, he had a problem.

"It does matter, Cal. Hannah mattered to you. You loved her, but you didn't get her killed."

"Yes, I did! I didn't see the rebel hiding in an abandoned building with a rifle! She was a duck in a carnival pond, and I stood there selling tickets!"

"Did Hannah know the risks when she went on the mission?"

"Of course, she did. She was part of the team and had the same training I did, except she was also a linguist."

"I'm not trying to be coldhearted here, but if she was trained and part of the team, she accepted that she might not walk out alive. You did the same thing. If I had to guess, you took a bullet that day too."

"You're wrong."

"I saw the scar, Cal. I may not be highly educated, but I lived on the streets, and I've seen things there. That scar on your chest? The doctors opened you up to get a bullet out of you. A bullet you more than likely took for her. Don't tell me you failed Hannah when you gave everything you had, including nearly giving your own life."

"Is it an option to get the meek Mary back?" Cal asked as he walked to the bed and sat on its edge again. "I'm not sure I like being challenged by this one."

She smiled, but she didn't back down, and that ratcheted up his heart rate until he felt a trickle of sweat down his back. If she didn't stop, he would do something they'd both regret, like take her as his own in this bed.

"Sorry, that woman is long gone. The Mary in front of you tonight has decided to accept the experiences that shaped her and made her the woman she is. You need to accept that what happened to Hannah all those years ago

shaped who you are personally, professionally and emotionally. Stop locking up your emotions to avoid being vulnerable. We're all vulnerable, Cal. We all have an innate need to
connect with another soul that feeds our own. Yes, you loved
Hannah, but she's been gone for thirteen years. When will
you start finding connections again that feed your soul?"

She slipped her tiny hand under his T-shirt and ran her
finger down his scar. The sensation sent a shiver through
him, and he grasped her hand to stop her caress. "That scar
is why I don't make connections anymore, Mary."

"Is that why you covered the scar with a tattoo? To avoid
being reminded of the one connection that was broken?"

"I covered the scar so I wasn't faced with my failure in
the mirror every day. Is that what you wanted to hear? They
cut me open to take the armor-piercing bullet from the muscle near my heart. A few millimeters were the difference
between life and death for me. They may as well have cut
my heart out the day they cut the bullet out. I haven't used
it since, and I have no intention of letting that organ rule
my head ever again."

Her laughter filled the silent room, and that damn organ
inside his chest reacted to the sound with a thump against
his chest wall.

"You're ridiculous. As though every decision you've
made in the last two years hasn't been led by your heart."

"Don't call me ridiculous," he spat. "And you're wrong.
I make decisions based on what's best for my business and
nothing else."

"You helped Roman find Mina and then sheltered them
at Secure One. You risked your life and the lives of your
men to get me out of St. Paul and then nursed me back to

health while chasing down a madwoman. You flew your chopper to Minneapolis in the dark of night because your brother's soulmate was in danger, and you didn't even hesitate. You brought me back to Secure One and gave me a job when Mina batted her eyelashes at you. If you think that anyone believes you don't have a heart, you're dead wrong, Cal Newfellow. It's time you accept that organ has led you plenty the last few years, and it hasn't steered you wrong."

"The potential is there for it to steer me wrong to the point someone dies, Mary. I can't allow that to happen again."

"You can't stop it from happening again, Cal. Don't you see that?" she asked, her hands holding her temples in frustration. "There are people out there who act in ways beyond your control! You can mitigate the risk as much as possible, but you can't predict what someone else will do. Why can't you accept that?"

"Because if I accept that, I'm going to do something I regret! I'll lose someone I care about to something beyond my control again!" His exclamation came from across the room where he'd darted when confronted with the truth he always knew but refused to acknowledge.

She was standing in front of him now with her hand on his chest. "Let's be clear here," she whispered, her gaze holding all the truth she knew about this world. "That statement is coming from fear and not truth. You're afraid you'll lose someone else you care about to something beyond your control. You don't *know* that you will. That's the difference. Unfortunately, that's how life works, Cal. Tomorrow is never guaranteed. Telling yourself you don't care when you do isn't going to make it any easier when that person is gone. You've got to care about people and love them while they're here, or all you'll be left with is regrets."

His silence was the gulf between them, even as she stood inches away with her beautiful, youthful, innocent heart laid bare. The moonlight slipped through the curtains and rested across her face to illuminate the scarred flesh.

She grabbed his wrist when he slipped his hand up the webbed skin of her cheek. "Stop." He could tell she'd wanted it to be forceful, but all he heard was sadness. "Don't touch me there."

"Because?" His voice *was* forceful. He wanted an answer and demanded she give it.

"It's my Mr. Hyde side," she whispered. "I look like a monster, Cal. That's why I wear my hair over it. That way, no one is confronted with the truth of how The Miss abused me. Most especially you. I've been used and abused over and over again in this life, and I wear this skin as a badge of shame. I don't know why you want to touch me at all."

Cal's heart broke, each word splintering off pieces of it until it lay shattered at his feet. His poor girl had suffered through so much at the hands of these people. The burns may be healed but those scars—the scars that were slashed into her memory—would remain open, weeping wounds until someone loved her enough to heal them.

"Sweet Mary," he whispered, trailing his hand up the left side of her face to her temple, where his thumb rubbed the skin to soothe her eye. "Your burns don't detract from your beauty. They add to it."

Her eye roll was strong in her right eye. "Nice try, Cal. I don't even have a real eyelid on the left. There's nothing beautiful about it."

"I'm sorry you feel that way, love," he said, gentleness in his tone. "Because I think it shows your strength and re-siliency to live through an event meant to take you away from this world. It shows your determination to go on with life when you had every reason to call it a day. Your future after that fire was bleak at best, but you didn't care what the future held as long as you were part of it. You want to be here, and you have no qualms about risking your heart or your life to keep someone you love safe."

"I trust you, Cal," she whispered. "I trust you to take care of me and protect me. That's why I can take risks to help those I love. You're the first man I've ever trusted because my heart said you were safe. My heart is connected to yours. Whether you like it or not. Whether it's convenient or not, I can't decide for you. All I know is, when you're near me, I feel safe, even when bullets are flying. If I didn't trust you to keep me safe when we faced The Miss again, I wouldn't have left Secure One to testify. I wouldn't have followed you back to a place that tried to take my life and walked into it with my head held high. I would have been too scared, but you were with me and kept me safe."

I trust you, Cal.

Those four words were a jolt to his head and heart that he couldn't deny. He couldn't deny that everything this tiny scrap of a woman said made more sense than anything he'd told himself over the last thirteen years. Through her eyes, he could see that he'd built his life around getting a redo on that day in a land far away when he'd failed someone he was tasked to protect. Every time he kept a client safe or a mission went the right way, it was another piece of metal he added to his armor when he should have been removing it.

"You're so much braver than I am, Mary," he whispered, his forehead touching hers now. "Your heart leads you to the truth every time."

"It does, Cal," she whispered, her gaze flicking up to his. "You can be that brave too if you start listening to your heart instead of your head."

"My head protects me, Mary. It protects me from all of…this."

"This? Do you mean connecting with someone who wants you to be happy? This? As in having any emotion other than anger in your life? This? Like having to admit that losing Hannah was horrible and the hardest thing you've ever lived through? It wasn't your fault, and you did live through it, so why aren't you living?"

Cal didn't let her finish. His lips were on hers before the next word left them. She wrapped her arms around his neck and fell into him. His strong arm around her waist lifted her off the ground, and her soft mewling mixed with his tight moan as he carried her to the bed. Cal braced a knee on the mattress and lowered her to rest against the soft comforter as he followed her sweet lips down.

This is a bad idea. You'll love her and lose her just like the last time.

"No," she said against his lips, "this is not a bad idea."

How could she know that was his exact thought at that moment?

"I see you, Cal," she whispered. "You wear your self-doubt like armor, but it's invisible to me. The man you hide away is the only one I can see. The good, the bad and the ugly. Just the same as you with me."

"Be that as it may," he ground out, his need pressing

against her in a way that betrayed his words, "that doesn't make this the right choice."

"That makes this the *only* choice," she whispered right before she trailed her hand down his taut belly to his hardness yearning for her touch.

The moan left his lips before he could stop it. He didn't want to stop it. He didn't want to stop feeling this way. Her tiny, sweet hand had slipped inside his jeans and wrapped itself around him. He throbbed against the heat of her hand and the idea that she offered exoneration from his past. He hadn't allowed himself to believe that was even a possibility since that day when he took a bullet for the woman he loved, and it still wasn't enough.

"It was enough," she whispered, her warmth spreading through him as she held him. "You are enough, Cal. It's time to share our pain until it's diluted and insignificant to who we are together."

His lips attacked hers again and stemmed the flow of truth from them. The truth was, he had already lost the battle of not caring about another woman the moment she ran onto his plane. Tonight, as she stripped him bare of his clothes and his demons, he knew it. He knew it when she gripped him in her tiny hand and let her heat soak into him. He knew it when he kissed his way from her lips to her breasts and then to her center. She was everything he'd tried to forget existed. Sweetness. Honesty. Pureness unsullied by his poison. He wasn't poison though. Not to Mary. To Mary, he was salvation.

"I don't have any protection," he moaned against her belly when his senses returned for a moment.

He gazed into her eyes and saw the truth. She was his

protection. Her tiny presence in his life had been what could shield him from the ugly all along.

"Let me protect you this time, Cal," she murmured.

He sank into her, accepting her as the final puzzle piece to his unhealed heart. His lips were on hers when he spoke. "Mary," he whispered on a moan of pleasure. "You make me whole. You are home."

She tipped her hips up and let him slide deeper to rest against her center. "I'm more than home, Cal. I'm redemption."

Chapter Seventeen

Cal didn't recognize Marlise when Mina had finished with her makeup. Her facial scars had been covered, and she wore a disheveled wig along with clothes that hung on her slight frame. An old, threadbare flannel shirt covered the burn scars on her arm, and fingerless gloves kept the scars hidden on her hand. The weather in Arizona had cooled now that it was fall, so pants and a long-sleeved shirt wouldn't raise suspicion on the street.

Mina had done much of the same to hide her identity. A pair of men's cargo pants made her prosthesis disappear inside the material and would raise no suspicion. She had traded out her everyday leg for her running blade inside a tennis shoe, just in case they needed to abort the mission and run. Mina ran around the compound every morning and was confident she could escape any situation. He was confident she could too. Regardless of how things went down a few years ago, she was still a trained FBI agent, and she kept her skills sharp. Marlise, on the other hand, didn't have the skills or instinct that Mina did. He hoped she would default to Mina if she told her to run.

He groaned and rubbed his chest with his palm. He'd had

heartburn since he woke up yesterday. Marlise's lips on his skin were the only thing that soothed it, but it was back in full force when she stopped. The women had spent the day yesterday pounding the pavement and trying to get noticed, but no one approached them. Once the sun went down, they walked back to a rent-by-the-hour motel. Cal and Roman did the same thing. Cal refused to allow them to sleep on the streets, but he also knew they couldn't all be seen together. He had traded off watching their room with Roman last night. This morning they'd given them a head start and followed in the van. They were down to eight days to find The Miss, and Cal had doubts this would work.

"How'd you sleep?" Roman asked from the seat next to him in the van. They were waiting in a park at the moment. They'd move around throughout the day, so they didn't attract suspicion, but they had to stay close to where the women were.

"Didn't get much sleep. Don't tell me you did knowing you had to send Mina back out to the wolves today."

"Mina has been my partner for years. Yes, she's my wife now, but I still trust her skills as an agent. She's going to take care of Marlise. No offense, but you're jumpier than a cat on a hot tin roof, and that's not the Cal Newfellow I know. What gives?"

"You realize that when someone says 'no offense,' it's obvious that whatever they're going to say is offensive, right?"

Roman's whistle was long and low as he shook his head at his brother. "Wow, your deflection game is strong this morning. What are you trying to hide?"

Cal refused to participate in his nonsense. He'd do his job and focus on keeping Marlise and Mina safe from a madwoman. The last thing he would do was tell his brother he'd slept with their witness. He would remember that night for the rest of his life. The power that little thing held over him was unyielding, and he didn't know what he was going to do about it. How was he going to let her go when this was over? He had to though. She deserved a chance to go out and live her life, but watching her walk out of his was going to gut him.

He kept his gaze trained on the empty grass in front of him, hoping for a glimpse of the woman he'd made love to three times the night before last. No. It wasn't making love. That was dangerous thinking. Seeing it as anything other than a one-night stand was a fast way to lose objectivity when it came to this case. He checked his earpiece, listening to Mina and Marlise talking with other women. They'd been asking questions about where to get a hot meal and a shower, but none of the other women were forthcoming.

"Come on, Mary," Mina said. "We'll go find the YMCA."

Cal and Roman knew that was her cue that they were moving. Within seconds their GPS device popped up with a route to the nearest YMCA. Mack was back at Secure One, blazing a path to save them time. Cal started the vehicle and followed the GPS to an abandoned house near the Y. He parked on the street, knowing the women would eventually walk past the van and they could get a glimpse of them.

"Have you told Marlise about Hannah?" Roman asked as he leaned against the door of the van.

"Why on earth would I tell her about Hannah?" Cal growled the question more than he spoke it. The last thing he wanted to do was engage in a conversation with his brother about his dead girlfriend. Roman had been there that day, and he knew too much.

"Fair is fair." Cal glanced at him with an eyebrow down, not understanding what he meant. His brother shrugged. "If she's going to compete with a ghost, you should at least have the decency to tell her."

"She's not competing against anyone, Roman."

His snicker made Cal want to punch him in the nose. He wasn't a violent man, but Roman never eased up on him about Hannah. It had been this way for years. Every time they saw each other, Roman was bugging him about letting Hannah go and forgiving himself for what had happened. Cal didn't know how. Every job he did, every person he saved, was a way to find redemption from the one time he had failed.

"Marlise is more astute than you give her credit for, Cal," Roman said, shaking his head. "If you think she doesn't have your number, you're dumber than you look."

"Roman?"

"Yeah, Cal?"

"Shut up."

"Not this time," Roman said with a shake of his head. Cal was worried their ongoing pact of telling each other to shut up when they didn't want to talk had ended. "Everyone on this team can see how you've looked at Marlise since we picked her up in St. Paul. When will you be honest with her? The moment before she walks out the doors of Secure One, or never?"

"She knows about Hannah," Cal said between clenched teeth. His gaze was pinned to the rearview mirror as he waited for them to approach. It took several minutes to realize Roman was silent. He had his mouth open when he glanced at him, staring out the windshield. "Don't be so dramatic."

"You have to forgive me for being dumbfounded. I never expected you to tell her."

"I tried to use Hannah as an excuse—"

"And our little Marlise called you on your crap, right?"

Cal's shrug said everything. It brought a grin to Roman's face. "They're approaching."

Roman turned his head to watch the side mirror while Cal kept his attention on the rearview mirror. He wanted to catch a glimpse of Marlise to make sure she was okay.

"It's unbelievable how brave she is to go back into this life," Cal said as the women walked by the van without taking notice. He knew they had, but they didn't let on.

"There's one thing I've learned about women, Cal, and it's simple. As men, we always underestimate them. We underestimate their strength, stamina, grit and how their moral compass guides them. After finding Mina a year after her injury, still trying to solve the case, I was never more aware of how much strength it took her to keep fighting when she had every right to give up. Marlise has all that strength and then some. At least she does now that you've taken care of her, built up her health and acknowledged her contributions to the company. You allowed her to lead, a job she's never had before, and that's why she's out there right now. She wants to contribute to solving this case and freeing herself from her past."

"We're on the same page there," Cal said as he watched them walk toward the doors of the YMCA. "I want her to be free of The Miss."

"But you're afraid that means she will walk away from you."

"From Secure One? Absolutely. She's an asset to our team, Roman."

His brother's snort was loud inside the van. "Sure, you're afraid you'll lose her as a team member of Secure One. I almost buy that, Cal. If you think we can't see something has changed between you two, you underestimate my skills as a special agent of the FBI."

"Leave it alone, Roman. We have one focus, and that's keeping our girls safe."

The goofy smile his brother wore on his face told Cal that he already suspected what had happened between him and Marlise, but he wasn't going to confirm it. His time with Marlise was too special to sully by acting like it meant nothing to him. He hadn't had time to process it all, but he knew it meant something to both of them. Cal regretted his decision not to be honest with her, and he hoped he could be before it was too late.

"Don't ask about showers here," Marlise said to Mina as they approached the doors. Roman glanced at Cal with a questioning look, and he shrugged. "If they say they're available, they'll expect us to use them. A shower is going to blow my cover."

"Good point," Mina agreed. "I should have thought of that."

Cal couldn't help it. He was grinning like the Cheshire cat. "That's my girl."

Roman punched him playfully, but all playfulness disappeared when another woman approached them. Cal flipped the record button on and shifted the audio from their ears to the computer. They both held their breath and hoped they weren't going to blow their cover this early in the game by having to rescue them before they found The Miss.

"Yo," MARLISE SAID to the girl as she approached. "Is the Y open?"

The girl looked her up and down and then did the same with Mina. "Sure ain't."

"Damn," Mina huffed. "I guess there's no point in staying then, Mary. Let's hit it."

Both women turned back the way they came when the other girl spoke. "What ya looking for there?"

Marlise turned back slowly and took a moment to assess the woman in front of them. She wasn't a street girl. Her good hygiene and clean clothing made her stick out like a sore thumb in a place like the YMCA. She was a scout. She was also Latina. Marlise reminded herself she could be a scout for any sex trafficking ring and forced herself to remain calm. She slid her eyes to Mina, who had a brow raised in the air. She was going to leave it to her to feel out.

"We're tired of the street, you know? Looking for a place to get a meal and sleep for the night where we don't need to keep one eye open."

"I could find work again if I could get a shower and some clean clothes," Mina added. "We both could. She cooks, and I clean. We were hoping to find a hotel that was hiring."

"I might know a place," the girl said. Marlise noticed she was trying too hard to be casual. She was excited and nervous, two emotions Marlise knew well.

"You saving it for yourself?" Mina asked. "Respect, if you are. We're all out here scrapping."

"No, but I know the owners, and I don't recommend just anyone to them. I gotta trust them, you know."

Marlise held up her hands in the don't shoot position. "Understood, sister. No harm, no foul. We'll be on our way."

"Wait! I could take you over there, and you could maybe show them your skills?" the girl asked before they could turn away. "They might even give you a room for the night as payment."

"How far is the place?" Mina asked. "We've already walked five miles today."

"It's about forty-five minutes from here, but my car is just up the block. I'm Jen, by the way."

"I'm Mary, and she's Amy," Marlise said, hooking a thumb at Mina as she eyed Jen with suspicion. "What are you doing here if the hotel is forty-five minutes away?" She took a step back and widened her eyes, hoping she looked nervous and agitated. Mina did the same thing, and the girl took a step forward but waved her hands innocently in front of her.

"I was supposed to meet some other girl here who was looking for a job, but she's a no-show. I already told the owners I'd found them some help, and now I hate to go back and tell them otherwise. I saw you two coming and thought you'd be interested. If you're not, that's fine, but I gotta get on my way."

Mina held up her finger and pulled Marlise aside. She put on a show of bending her head to whisper as though they had to weigh their options. Their only option was to find out if this girl was one of The Miss's scouts. "Do we go with her?" Mina whispered near Marlise's ear. "No way to know if she's with The Miss or someone else."

Marlise held her gaze and raised her voice to a stage whisper so the other girl could hear. "We have to take any chance that gets us off the street, Amy. I'll do anything to sleep in a real bed again. Imagine not having to worry about men following us or sleeping in shifts. I know you want it just as much."

With a feigned eye roll, Mina finally nodded once. "I do, but we gotta be careful, you know. And we stick together. No matter what."

"No matter what," Marlise agreed, doing some goofy handshake thing they'd come up with as a way to tell Cal and Roman that they should follow at a distance. The guys could hear them, but Marlise didn't want to take any chances that the mic wasn't working. They needed the backup where they were going. She could feel it in her bones.

Chapter Eighteen

"I don't like them getting into a car," Roman said as he buckled his belt and waited for Cal to put the van into Drive.

"Me either, but we have to trust Mina. All we can do is follow them and be ready for any situation that comes at us. Sex trafficking is so common on the streets that you could walk into a ring on any corner. There's no way to know if this scout is one of The Miss's."

Once the women were out of sight, Cal shifted into gear and idled with his foot on the brake. The computer was up, and they were still recording their conversation as they walked up the road. Thus far, the conversation had remained innocuous about living on the streets and the problem with finding a job when you didn't have a permanent address. Mina and Marlise were spreading it on like peanut butter, and he hoped it wasn't too thick. If this girl was from a different ring, they didn't want their cover blown in town.

"The chances are slim this woman has anything to do with The Miss," Roman said as they waited.

"Maybe not, but we have to take any chance we get. We don't have time to be picky. I hate to sound ominous, but the hair on the back of my neck went up when the girl approached."

Roman's response was simple. "Mine too. I guess we'll know soon enough."

"This is a nice BMW," Mina said.

"Come on, my girl," Roman whispered, his pen against the paper as he waited.

"I've always wanted to ride in a Gran Coupe. The lines are sleek, and the silver paint makes it look like a bullet. I bet it's as fast as one too."

"How do you know so much about my car?" the scout asked suspiciously. Cal glanced at Roman with a grimace, but Roman held up his finger.

"My old man. He got this, like, car magazine, every month. He'd go on about the cars in it during dinner and how he would have one someday. He was a mechanic, so he loved cars, but also booze. The two don't mix, and he wrapped his not-so-fancy Chevy around a tree."

Roman did a fist pump and snickered as he eyed Cal.

"Tragic," the woman said with zero empathy in her voice.

"Not really. Daddy was mean when he drank, and he always drank. The only thing I miss about him was the little bit of support he gave me."

They counted three doors closing, and then the engine purred to life. There was a crinkling of bags, and then the woman spoke. "Here are some snacks. Help yourself while we drive so you aren't hungry when we get to the hotel."

"Thanks!" Marlise said, pouring on the gratitude so thick even Cal smiled. "We haven't eaten in a couple of days."

Cal and Roman listened to the crinkling of wrappers and

their fake moaning as they ate whatever snacks the woman had given them. Roman had to hope none of it was laced.

"What do you do for a living?" Mina asked after five minutes.

Cal glanced at the GPS that showed they were headed west toward the California and Arizona border. "Contact Mack and ask him to check for any issues going west on 86."

"Too easy. This is too easy," Roman said with a shake of his head, but he flipped open the phone to call Mack.

"I'm starting to feel the same way," Cal agreed as he stayed out of the car's line of sight but followed the GPS tracker Mina had in her leg. "Maybe not though. The women were out yesterday. Word could have gotten around that they were looking for a job."

"Or one of The Miss's guards was a scout and recognized Marlise."

Roman said the words Cal was trying not to think. Cal didn't respond. He was already thinking ten steps ahead of where they were. If their ride ended at The Miss's camp, it would be up to the women to get that information to them. Once they knew the location, Mack would let the local authorities know in the closest town while Cal and Roman found a way onto the property to protect Marlise and Mina. His experience with The Miss told him it would never be that easy. She was paranoid and wouldn't risk bringing Marlise into the camp without knowing she wasn't being tailed.

Roman hung up the phone and pointed at the GPS. "He's putting in all the roads that branch off 86 up on the screen. I'll focus on the GPS tracker while you focus on making sure we don't get noticed."

Cal set his lips and eased off the gas pedal. He didn't want to spook this woman before they got where they were going. The element of surprise would be challenging to maintain, but if he didn't, he might never see Marlise alive again.

THEY'D BEEN DRIVING nearly an hour when Jen turned off the highway. "We're kind of far out in the sticks for a hotel," Mina said, making a show of looking out the windows on the side and the back. "Who stays way out here?"

"You'd be surprised how many men are looking to play cowboy in the desert. My friend's hotel is always booked."

A shiver ran through Marlise. She knew what kind of hotel Jen meant and wanted nothing to do with it. Not after spending the night with Cal. Was that only two days ago? It felt like an eternity since he'd held her in his arms. She was determined to do anything to get back to him. She regretted not telling him her true feelings for him before they parted ways. If she didn't make it out of this, he'd never know how much he meant to her.

Her mind went to the way he'd made love to her that night, and she wondered if that was true. Maybe they'd used their bodies instead of their lips, but she'd told him how she felt. He would only have to think about how she loved him that night to know she would love him forever. She shook her head. He'd already lost one woman he'd cared about in this life. Marlise refused to do the same thing to him. She'd worked too hard to show him that life and love were worth taking a chance on again. It was time to put the fear aside and do anything she had to in order to get out of this alive.

"How many rooms are in the hotel?" Mina asked as they bounced over ruts and holes in the dirt road.

"It's a unique property. You'll see once we get there. The

owner is very devoted to giving her guests the best desert experience possible. The hotel is in pods, and there is plenty of privacy for the guests."

Marlise glanced over when Mina tapped her knee against hers. Mina nodded. She believed they were headed to the right place. Mina crossed her fingers together, and Marlise understood. They had to stick together and not get separated. Anything else was a death sentence. Marlise's heart pounded with pent-up anxiety when Jen steered the BMW down a driveway and stopped at a gate. Two women dressed in black fatigues stepped out, and Jen put her window down.

Marlise glanced at Mina, who wore total disregard on her face. She turned away and looked out the window as though she didn't have a care in the world. Marlise realized why. The guards were the same two who'd helped The Miss in Red Rye. They were in the right place. The time had come to face the woman who had tried to do everything in her power to break them. She'd failed, and this time, Marlise would finish the job. She bent down as though she had dropped something on the floor and whispered the two words that would set her future in motion. "Red Rye."

CAL ALMOST MISSED the two words that came across the computer speakers. *Red Rye.* He glanced at Roman from where they sat along the side of the road.

"Did you hear that too?"

"Red Rye," he confirmed, and Cal's heart picked up its pace.

"It's go time, brother," Roman said, strapping on his bulletproof vest and then his tactical pack. They needed as much firepower as they could carry. If things went south before help arrived, they'd have to shoot their way in, and out, to get Marlise and Mina.

After alerting Mack, they slid from the van and took off on foot. The sagebrush offered them surprisingly good coverage as they worked their way past the road Jen had turned down, and they followed the GPS on their small tablet that took them along the west side of the property. They'd find cover and then wait for the trackers on the women to stop moving before they approached. They could still hear what was going on through their earpieces. For now. There was no guarantee that the link would remain once they brought Mina and Marlise onto the compound. The recording devices were hidden in a button on their clothing and undetectable to a wand, but that connection would be broken if they made them change clothes.

Cal slowed his breathing as they ate up the distance between them and the women they loved. The word tripped him up, and he went down to his hands and knees, a soft *oof* enough to turn Roman back to him. While he should be on the alert for an attack, he was worried about being in love. It was an inconvenient fact that he would have to face eventually. Now was not the time. Losing focus before they captured The Miss was a death sentence for all of them.

Roman pulled up inside a hoodoo that offered shade and cover from the sun beating down on their backs. "You okay?" Roman asked when Cal reached him.

"Tripped on some underbrush," Cal answered, taking a drink of water from his bottle. He noticed Roman smirking, but he refused to comment on it. "How far out are we?"

"Hard to tell. Two klicks or less from the western side of where they stopped. I've been listening, but it's been quiet, other than the sound of soft murmuring. I think Jen is talking to the guards about her new arrivals." Roman stopped and held up his finger as Mina's voice broke through their earpieces.

"Wow, that's a cool hotel!" she exclaimed.

Roman raised a brow at Cal. Obviously, they'd cleared security and made it onto the compound.

"It reminds me of a satellite or the sun," Marlise said enthusiastically. "I bet the kitchen is a fun place to work."

"Forget the kitchen," Mina said. "Imagine how cute those little pods are on the inside. I can't wait to start working."

Cal rolled his eyes, but he couldn't stop the smile from taking over his lips. It was no laughing matter, but he couldn't help it. "Spreading it on a little thick, aren't they," he said to Roman.

"Fastest way to The Miss is with a brown nose, and both women know that."

"They better slow down until we figure out a way to save them," Cal grunted while checking his equipment. "There are only two of us and an unknown count surrounding them. We don't stand a chance if we have to go in before the authorities get here."

"We need to move as close to the property as possible in case we have to go in. My wife will not be injured by this woman again."

Cal squeezed his brother's shoulder. "I'm hoping they can buy us some time. If they're going to prove themselves to the boss, they'll have to work for a few hours, right?"

"We can hope," Roman said as their earpieces came to life again.

"This will be your pod while you're here," Jen said after

the car doors slammed shut. "There are clothes on the beds, and you're welcome to shower and clean up. Once you've had a few minutes to rest, I'll take you to meet the owner."

"Already?" Marlise asked with fake nervousness. Then again, Cal wondered if it was fake. "Don't you want us to work a little bit to prove ourselves?"

"That's up to The Miss. She prefers to hand out the assignments each day. If we're short-staffed, it's my job to find new helpers."

A trickle of sweat ran down Cal's spine at the mention of her boss. They had found her. His brother's face had turned white. Cal understood the feeling, which told him more about how he felt about Mary than anything. "This cannot be a repeat of thirteen years ago," he spat. "I'm not going to watch another woman die, Roman."

He took off for the property, but Roman grabbed his pack and pulled him back.

"You can't run in there half-cocked, Cal!" Roman hissed into his ear. "We're surrounded by rocks. She could have snipers at the ready. You already know she was training them to kill. Use your head. We're of no use to Mina and Marlise if we're dead."

Cal took a calming breath and nodded, settling back against the wall as he listened to Marlise and Mina question Jen about The Miss. "Tread lightly, Marlise," he hummed, not wanting them to blow this operation before they had people in place to round up The Miss.

Roman leaned in when the mics went quiet. Marlise and Mina were in the pod now, and he had to hope they assumed it was wired for sound. "Let's head north. We're one klick south from where they stopped moving, according to the GPS."

One klick, Cal thought. A little more than half a mile separated them, but it felt like there was an ocean between them. Rather than speak, he nodded at Roman and headed north with his brother tight on his heels.

Chapter Nineteen

Marlise looked around the pod, surprised that it was clean
and cool. There was a small efficiency kitchen in the middle and a bathroom, but the beds made a shiver run up her
spine. There were two, one on each end of the pod, complete with a door that closed them off from the rest of the
world. The bed behind the door was much bigger than necessary for one person, and the mountain of pillows, not to
mention the mirrors on the ceiling, told the rest of the story.

Mina pulled her into the bathroom, turned on the shower
and leaned into her ear. "I didn't see any obvious cameras,
but that doesn't mean there aren't any. I would guess this
place is bugged for sound." Marlise nodded, fear filling her
now that they had found the woman who had already tried to
kill them too many times. There was no way to know if help
was coming or if Cal and Roman would find them in time.

They'd made sure to put on a show about how cool the
pod was while Jen was with them. The more time they
bought, the higher chance the guys would get to them before
The Miss did. Before she left, Jen had told them to shower
and dress in the new clothes left on the beds. Marlise had
already noticed that the black T-shirt and pants were what

Charlotte had described when explaining The Miss's new business plan. That was your welcome home outfit. Once The Miss decided where you'd be the most useful, you were given new clothes and a new identity. Marlise knew their disguises might fool the woman for a few moments, but their voices had probably already given them away. If not yet, they would once they stood in front of the woman.

"We're in trouble, aren't we?" Marlise asked, her voice wavering from fear.

"Stay calm," Mina ordered, leveling a brow at her. "Once we change, your tracker will be gone, but mine will remain. Roman and Cal will still be able to find us."

"That doesn't help us if we're already dead," she hissed, swallowing down her regret about agreeing to this mission. It was her idea, but now that she knew she was back in The Miss's grasp, the fear had taken over her courage.

"You have to keep your cool," Mina scolded. "Trust in Cal. He's not going to let you die in here. He loves you. You know that, right?"

"No, Mina, it's not like that," she insisted, even though she knew it was exactly like that. At least for her.

Mina put her finger to Marlise's lips. "It's been like that since the day he met you. He will find a way to get us out. Besides, you know Roman isn't going to let The Miss have her way with me again."

That brought a smile to Marlise's lips, and she nodded once. "What's the plan then?"

"We stall as long as we can, and once it's dark, we get the hell out of here and hide."

"This entire property has to be under surveillance, Mina."

"Maybe, but the one thing I noticed on the way in is they

run on generators. There's no power way out here. Chances are, there's minimal lighting once it's dark. All we have to do is avoid the guards and hole up until the authorities arrive."

Marlise finally nodded, but she knew there was no way they were getting out of this pod tonight unless it was by invitation from The Miss.

ROMAN TOOK A knee and pointed ahead through the underbrush. "There are those tree cacti that Charlotte said lined the property."

Cal dropped down behind him and did a three-sixty search of the area around them. "They're big but not big enough to hide us from view. We need cover to reach out to Mack and find out how long until the authorities arrive."

"If they're arriving," Roman said. "We're practically on the border here, and I didn't see too many towns along the highway with a police force big enough to make a dent in this place."

Cal had thought the same thing on the way down, but Tucson wasn't that far away, and all they had to do was hold out long enough for the big guns to arrive. A skittering of rocks raised the hair on the back of his neck. Roman heard it too. He noticed him unsnap his holster, but Cal hoped they didn't have to resort to guns. The sound from a gunshot would travel for miles in a place like this, which would alert The Miss. She could kill Marlise and Mina before they were close enough to save them.

"No guns unless necessary," Cal whispered, and Roman nodded his understanding. "The sound was on our left. Could be wildlife."

Roman's sarcastic snort told him what he thought of that. The sun was setting, and they had to make a decision. They needed cover. Before Cal could move, there was a soft grunt, a thud and two more grunts before silence filled the desert again. Then came a sound that had never filled him with as much relief as it did today.

"Secure two, Mike," a voice said from their left.

Cal and Roman turned and scurried to a rock outcropping several yards to the west. When they reached it, Mack stood guard with a rifle while Eric tied up three women who were out cold.

"Mack, what the hell are you guys doing here?" Cal asked, trying to make sense of what he saw.

"Maybe you could show a little gratitude for us saving your unsuspecting butts from these three. They had you in their sights," Eric said, finishing with the zip ties. He stuffed gags in their mouths and dragged them behind some shrubs.

"I didn't like the idea of you two down here alone. Once you told me the women were going in, we headed down. The rest of the team is covering the clients while Selina keeps an eye on Charlotte. We have news," Mack said, crouching down. "We finally got The Miss's identity off that picture Marlise took."

"How?" Cal asked in surprise.

"Roman's people came through. Her name is Sofia Guerrero. Her father is Alejandro Guerrero."

"*The* Alejandro Guerrero? He's been suspected of running drugs and guns for years."

"One and the same," Mack agreed. "Turns out, he wanted to branch out and encouraged his daughter to continue his legacy across the border. Her mother was American, so she can come and go as she pleases."

"Is Alejandro involved in this compound?" Roman asked, his head motioning at the property east of them.

"That's less clear. No doubt he is, but we'd have to follow the paperwork."

"We'll leave that up to the authorities. Our only objective is to get our girls back safely. They're in a pod and waiting to be taken to The Miss. How far out are the authorities?"

"On their way from Tucson, but they're at least an hour out. They've been keeping an eye on the property, suspecting it was running drugs, but couldn't prove it. It didn't take much convincing to get them down here on a reported kidnapping."

"Do you have any idea how many armed guards are inside?"

"All we know is two at the gate. They're guards from Red Rye, according to Marlise."

"How do you want to handle this?"

"I want the innocents alive. I don't care if The Miss lives or dies, but I'd like there to be evidence left to prove she was behind the fire and the attacks on Marlise and Mina."

"Avoid setting anything on fire," Mack said with a grin. "Got it."

"My wife is in there," Roman said. "We need to get them out before the authorities arrive. I had hoped to get a confession out of The Miss, but confirmation that she's here is enough for me. We get the women out and let the police round up the rest of them."

All men nodded in agreement. "Eric and I will create a diversion at the front gate. What pod are Marlise and Mina in?" Roman showed Mack the tracker that had remained still for the last hour other than walking about the pod. "That's beneficial. They're on the west side of the satellite. We've already taken out those guards," Mack said, motioning at the women in the bushes. "This might be our only window to get them out before the cops arrive and the element of surprise is gone."

"We need ten minutes to get there, get them out and then to relative safety," Roman said, judging the distance to the pod on the map. "If things go bad, shoot your way out of it and get clear of the compound. We'll meet up at the large rock wall three klicks west."

"At which point we will discuss disobeying direct orders," Cal huffed.

Mack rolled his eyes. "Whatever. You're glad we're here. Give us five to get in place, and then we rock and roll."

His men took off, and Cal took a deep breath. He was glad they had come, but he would be happier when he had them out of that pod and The Miss in custody.

"I'm running point," Roman said in a way that told Cal not to argue. "You've got my flank."

"Every time, brother," he whispered, and then they headed for the cactus and two people who meant everything to them.

THE SUN HAD SET, making Marlise nervous as they waited for someone to get them. They'd been there for hours now, but Jen hadn't returned to the pod. Maybe they were going to wait until morning. Let them sweat it out for the night or see if they'd try to escape. They had already tried the door, and it was unlocked. They weren't trusting. They were self-assured. Girls who left a bad situation on the streets were going to be blinded by the comforts the pods had to offer.

"Hey!" a voice yelled, and Mina instantly stood up from the chair by the table. There was more yelling and commotion, but it was a long way from their pod.

"The front gate?" Marlise asked, and Mina shrugged, her widening eyes reminding Marlise not to blow it.

"Who knows," Mina said with ease. Marlise could tell she wasn't at ease though. She was standing by the door of the pod listening to the yelling. "Who cares?"

There was a knock on the door, and Mina cut her gaze to Marlise, who rushed to her side before she opened the door. What she saw nearly brought her to tears.

"Secure two, Romeo," Roman whispered and motioned with his head to follow.

He didn't have to tell them twice. Marlise realized the commotion at the front gate was a diversion, and she prayed it wasn't Cal. She nearly fell to her knees when she saw him in a squat with his gun aimed into the darkness while he waited for them.

"Mack and Eric," Roman whispered as they ran toward Cal. "Authorities on their way."

That was all the information they would get as they were sandwiched between Cal in the front and Roman in the back. Cal hadn't so much as acknowledged her when he turned to motion for them to follow. She had to admit it hurt, but she understood he had a job to do. If he was going to get them out of this alive, he had to focus on nothing but the mission. The last time he split his focus, he lost Hannah. She tripped and nearly fell at the comparison. Roman righted her, but she could hardly breathe. They had to get out of this alive. Cal couldn't take losing another person he cared about in this life.

A shot rang out, and all four of them came to a halt as Cal held up a fist. The darkness was working against them now, and they couldn't see anything.

"Well, well, I've seen two ghosts as I live and breathe," a voice said from behind them. They turned in tandem just as a bright beam of light blinded them. When their eyes adjusted, The Miss stood before them flanked by two guards bearing guns. "Don't worry, my girls have already taken care of your men at the front gate. I'd love to chat, but first, I'll have to insist you lower your weapons and toss them over."

Roman held up his hands before he followed her orders, skittering the small pistol across the sand where the guard picked it up.

"You too," The Miss said to Cal. From the corner of her eye, Marlise watched him toss the gun behind him into the dark. "Did you think you could just waltz in here and take my girls after they'd just arrived? All the work I put into finding our perfect little witness, and it turns out, I should have just been patient."

"You can't kill us all," Mina said. "They'll never stop hunting you if they find us dead."

"Who said they were going to find you?" she asked. "You always were a little too by the book, Agent August, or is it Agent Jacobs now? I heard the happy news. Congratulations."

Marlise had a strong desire to punch this woman, but she bit her tongue to keep from aggravating her.

"We know who you are, Sofia," Cal said from behind her.

"Is Daddy helping you keep the women hooked on heroin, so they'll stay and run drugs for you?"

"I don't need to hook them on drugs to get them to stay, right, girls?" she asked her guards, who nodded robotically.

Marlise knew drugs, and they were definitely on them.

"Is that why you had to put a tracker in them when you sent them out?" Roman asked. "Just in case they forgot their way back?"

"I would be a fool not to know where my assets are at all times."

"Sad that your team was so unsuccessful at Secure One."

"Were they though?" she asked in a voice that skittered fear down Marlise's spine. "From where I'm standing, I've been quite successful in procuring not one witness but two witnesses for the prosecution. Not that I care what happens to The Madame. She was a stepping stone to bigger and better things for me and my daddy. You four are the last thorn in my side, and then I can finally be free of her."

"The police know," Cal said. "They're on their way here."

"Doubtful," she replied with a reptilian smile. "The police around here look the other way since my daddy funds their departments and their habits."

Marlise noticed the yelling at the front gate had ceased, and her heart sank. If what The Miss had said was true, then this was it for them. She would go to her grave without the chance to tell Cal she loved him. Part of her wanted to turn around and tell him, just take a moment before The Miss took her life, but fear froze her in place. Not of The Miss or of dying, but of the look on his face when he realized he would watch her die right before his demise.

"Girls, you know what to do." The Miss waved her hand

at them. "Take out the trash." She turned just as a shot rang out.

"Cal!" she yelled, jumping to the side.

"Get down, Mary!" he screamed, and she dove to the ground, but not before she saw The Miss stumble backward, her body jerking left and then right. Cal threw himself over her as more shots rang out, and then there was silence for a moment before she heard the most welcome sound of her short life.

"Secure one, Charlie."

"Secure two, Romeo."

"Secure three, Whiskey."

"Secure four, Mike! You'll stay down if you're smart!" Mack yelled, probably at one of the guards. What was Mack doing here?

"Mary," Cal whispered, his voice filled with the pain and terror of the last five minutes.

"I'm okay," she promised, sitting up when he gave her a hand, but he kept her face turned away from The Miss. "Are you okay?" She frantically patted him down, checking for bullet holes and blood.

He grabbed her hands and held them. "I'm okay, and I love you. I should have told you that two nights ago, but I convinced myself if I didn't say the words, I could pretend that wasn't the emotion in my chest every time I looked at you. I shouldn't have denied it though. My heart convinced me of that when I thought I was about to lose the woman I loved in the same horrible way as the last time."

"You didn't. I'm here, Cal. I'm here."

He pulled her into him and held her so tightly she couldn't breathe, so she sank into his warmth.

"I love you too, Cal. I have since the first day I was at Secure One, and you ordered everyone away and sat with me, helping me stay calm through the pain and terror no one else understood. That was when I knew you'd always be my only one, even if you sent me away."

"I'm not going anywhere, Mary, and neither are you. I'm always going to be here when you need me."

"Will you be here when I wake up?" she asked, the dots in front of her eyes making it hard to form words.

He held her out by her shoulders. "Wake up? What do you mean, baby?"

She gazed into his terrified eyes and smiled, running a finger down his cheek before it fell to her lap. "I couldn't let them take you from me, Cal."

"Roman!" Cal screamed as he rested her back on his lap and frantically searched for an injury. He found it and pressed his hand to her shoulder, the pain sparking a cry from her lips. "Roman! I need medical!"

Her vision dimmed, but she grabbed him and pulled him to her lips, kissing him until her body went slack and the darkness surrounded her.

Epilogue

"It's over," Marlise said, resting back against the headrest of the SUV. "After all this time, she's finally out of our lives."

"I think she'll always be part of our lives. She brought me you, and I'll always be grateful for that," Cal whispered as he steered the car toward Secure One.

"To The Madame?" Marlise asked with surprise.

"To the universe. To whatever path you took to get here," Cal said with a shrug.

After three long months, the sentencing day for The Madame had finally arrived. They'd made the trip from Secure One to the Minneapolis courthouse to witness it with their own eyes. Cynthia Moore, aka The Madame, had been sentenced to twenty years in prison with no early release. She would be spending her time in Waseca while her husband, former special agent David Moore, spent his twenty years in Leavenworth just outside of Kansas City.

"Conjugal visits don't look promising," Cal said, trying not to laugh.

Marlise snorted at the thought and shook her head. "No, but they both got what they deserved, or they will once they're locked in with the general population."

The mastermind and her flunky would be in their seventies when they got out. If they didn't die behind bars, that is. Chances were good they wouldn't make it long once the other inmates learned who they were. They were initially facing life in prison, which would have been better in Marlise's opinion. Then The Miss died, and her secrets were revealed, so the prosecution offered them a plea deal to avoid another stay on the trial while they sorted through who was responsible for what in the sex trafficking ring. With The Miss dead, they were sure to find evidence, real or fake, proving The Madame had been the one to order girls to be killed for refusing to perform. If they could prove it, Cynthia was looking at life without parole, and she knew it, so pleading to twenty years in prison was an easy decision. It also meant Marlise and Mina didn't have to testify, which was a big relief.

The FBI never found the bodies of Emelia, Bethany or any of the other girls who had disappeared from The Miss's grasp. Where they were, no one knew, but Marlise suspected they were buried in the desert somewhere, or had been sold across the ocean to a land far away. Her heart ached at the thought of either situation. She wanted them found. The FBI assured her they were still looking, but they all knew the truth. The FBI wasn't going to waste resources on lost girls. The thought dampened her joy about the day a tad.

Cal turned the car down the driveway to Secure One as she pondered how it had only been a few hours since they'd left, but her whole life had changed again. Roman and Mina had headed back immediately after the sentencing while she and Cal had done some business in town that was long overdue. She finally had a legal name—Marlise Strong. She thought it was a bit too on the nose, but Cal said it was the perfect fit. She also had a social security card and a legal identification card. After nearly dying at the hands of The Miss twice, she was finally living.

Marlise had followed all the steps she needed to take to have a future. Each new accomplishment was a way to take back what everyone had taken away from her over the years. Her identity. Her passions. Her belief in herself. One man had a hand in giving her back all of those things, and today, he'd held her hand with a giant grin on his face when they'd presented her with a little card that promised a better life.

"I've given it a lot of thought. I'll do the interview for the book, but I'm not interested in the television or the public speaking events. I want people to learn about sex trafficking and the signs to watch for, but I prefer to be behind the scenes," Marlise said when the lights of Secure One came into view. She'd been offered so many opportunities to be an advocate for young women, and she wanted to help, but she didn't want to leave Secure One to do it.

Cal smiled, then shoulder bumped her after he'd parked the SUV below the lodge.

"What are you smiling about?"

"I'm just glad you aren't going to disappear from Secure One and my life to chase the Hollywood dream."

Marlise turned his chin to face her and kissed his lips. "I don't have a Hollywood dream, Cal. My dream is right here in this car," she whispered. "I love you."

"I love you too, Marlise Strong."

He climbed out of the car while she rubbed her right shoulder. It was sore after their long day, but it would be okay after she rested for the night. After surgery to remove the bullet from a guard's gun, she'd spent months doing physical therapy to strengthen it again. She hadn't considered that Cal was wearing a bulletproof vest and she wasn't. When she jumped in front of that bullet, it was a gut reaction to the threat against the man she loved. He'd saved her from The Miss, and it was her turn to do the same at that moment.

When he'd declared his love for her, he wasn't kidding, and he'd proven it every day for the last three months. He'd made sure she got the best care and therapy available and refused to let her do anything but rest and heal.

Cal helped her down from the car and linked his hand to hers. "How do you feel?"

"Free," she whispered.

"I only need that word to understand the emotion. It was the same emotion I felt in the fall when I let the past go and focused on my future."

"I feel like we should celebrate," she said as they walked into the lodge and toward the large dining room. It was where Marlise had found comfort those first few months she was at Secure One. Cal had put her in charge of cooking meals for his staff. That gave her a purpose and something to focus on besides her pain and trauma. There was something gratifying about seeing her friends enjoy something she made for their pleasure. Little by little, it had helped her regain her self-confidence and self-esteem.

"Funny you should say that," Cal said, motioning her into the dining room.

It was dark, so Marlise snapped the lights on, and everyone from Secure One jumped out and yelled, "Happy birthday!"

She turned to Cal with laughter on her lips when she leaned into him. "What's going on?"

"It's your birthday," Mina said from where she stood by Roman, a party hat on her head and a party blower in her mouth.

"Mina, my birthday is in January. You know that."

Cal kissed her cheek and gave her a wink. "We all know that, but when your ID came off the printer with today's date, I decided there was no better day to pick as your new birthday. Today we will celebrate the first birthday of Marlise Strong."

Marlise wiped away a tear as she accepted hugs from her friends and coworkers in the room. It was the final hug from Charlotte that pushed the tears over her lashes. Her friend was living through the same hell she had years ago, and she understood how hard it was to try and assimilate back into society when you were scared of everything. When they'd returned to Secure One after her surgery, Charlotte was still recovering from the infection in her leg, and Cal insisted she stay until she was healed. That would give her time to decide where she wanted to go and what she wanted to do. He'd suggested that she help in the kitchen since Marlise couldn't do a lot with one arm in a sling.

For the last three months, they'd worked together, but lately Marlise was spending more time in the control room learning the business of private security. She hoped that Charlotte would decide to stay and use Secure One as a safe place to heal and find herself.

"Did you make all this food?" Marlise asked after the hug.

"I did! It was fun, and Mack helped."

Marlise resisted the urge to glance at Cal. Mack spent a lot of time helping Charlotte, but no one said a word about it. She supposed Cal felt like it would be the pot and the kettle if he said anything to his friend about his devotion to the tiny, broken girl in the kitchen.

"Thank you. I know how much work it is. I appreciate you, Charlotte. When you're ready, say the word, and I'll help you find a new future."

Charlotte nodded and then motioned at the table. "We should eat before the food gets cold."

No one argued with her. They all took heaping plates of food back to the large tables to eat, chat, laugh and celebrate the end of a long case.

Cal stood up and walked to the middle of the room. "Mary," he said, motioning for her to join him. Abandoning her birthday cake, she walked toward him with a smile. He handed her a small package and motioned for her to open it. "I decided today was the perfect day for this."

Marlise opened the box and found a security badge every team member wore while working. "Secure One, Marlise Strong, client coordinator." She gazed up at him for an explanation. "Cal, what is this?"

"It's your new job. If you want it," he nervously added. "You've more than earned the right to that position. We all know you can do the job. Right, everyone?"

The room erupted in clapping and hooting as she lifted it from the box. "That means I'd have to give up the kitchen manager job."

"I think we've got that covered," Cal said with a wink at Charlotte, who smiled shyly.

"Then I'm ready," she agreed as everyone started clapping for her again. "Why does it say Bravo at the bottom?"

"Secure two, Romeo," Roman yelled.

"Secure three, Mike," Mack yelled.

"Secure one, Charlie," Cal whispered, and the meaning struck her.

"Secure four, Bravo," she called out with tears in her eyes. She hugged the badge to her chest. "Why Bravo? My name starts with *M.*"

"Because I'm Charlie, and I'll follow you anywhere."

She threw her arms around him. "Thank you."

"No," he whispered. "Thank you for being mine. You are mine, right?"

"Always," she promised, accepting his kiss. "You never have to question my love for you or my dedication to the place that saved me."

"Then I have one more question to ask on your birthday, Marlise Strong." He pulled away from her and reached in his pocket, pulling out a ring that made her breath catch in her chest.

"Cal…"

"My sweet Mary," he said as he lowered himself to one knee and held up the ring. "I am so incredibly proud of you, do you know that?" he asked, and she nodded, her chin trembling with emotion. "You have come so far since we first met two years ago, and every day I stand in awe of your strength to make a difference in this world. To do good and spread love, even when you suffered at the hands of evil and hatred. I'm twice your size, but I know you're twice as strong. I know you just got that last name, and I'll respect it if you want to keep it, but today, I hope you're willing to add mine to it as well. Will you marry me, Mary? Will you make your life here with me on this land and continue to make a difference in the fight against evil? Will you love me forever and give me the honor of being your husband?"

Marlise dropped to her knees and nodded, her eyes glistening with tears as he slipped the ring on her finger. "Nothing would make me happier than loving you forever, Cal Newfellow."

He captured her lips as their friends clapped and hooted. Someone turned the radio up, and everyone danced around them as they knelt with their lips and hearts connected. Cal helped her up, and Mina grabbed her in a hug, squeezing the daylights out of her in excitement.

"You deserve this," Mina whispered. "Enjoy every second of it. He loves you so much."

"Thanks, Mina," she said, just as the man in question pulled her back into his arms.

"Dance with me," he said, spinning her out and back into him, where he enveloped her with the length of his body to dance to a slow song on the radio.

"Breaking news alert," a voice said, as an alarm cut off the song. "The body of a young woman was pulled from the Red River today…"

Marlise pulled back and lifted a brow at her new fiancé. In return, Cal lifted one right back.

* * * * *

COLTON'S DANGEROUS COVER

LISA CHILDS

With great appreciation for the talented authors also contributing to this Colton continuity—it's been an honour and a pleasure!

Chapter One

The music was loud, even in the alley. Pulsating. Throbbing. It was alive. Like the rage burning inside the Slasher.

After the third assault a couple of years ago, that was what the media had named the attacker: *The Slasher.*

The Slasher smiled, enjoying the name and the attention. That attention was finally being paid for the right reason. For the power. Not the weakness. *This* was all about taking power back, about taking it away from them.

He would have found the note by now. The invitation for this tryst in the alley. He wouldn't know for certain who'd left it for him, but he would think he was going to get lucky. He had no idea…

A door creaked open, letting some light and louder music seep into the alley. "Hello?" a man's voice called out. "Are you out here?"

Still deep in the shadows, the Slasher called out in a husky whisper, "Over here…"

The guy chuckled, low in his throat, and stumbled away from the door, letting it click closed behind him. Darkness enveloped the area again, but for a thin sliver of moonlight slicing between the tall buildings on either side of the alley.

That thin sliver provided just enough light for the Slasher to see the victim, and for there to be a glint off the sharp blade as the Slasher swung the knife toward the head of the next victim.

FLETCHER COLTON WAS dealing with his last case with Salt Lake City PD before he would head home to Owl Creek, Idaho. It was another slasher case. He hoped this job wouldn't cause him to postpone his start date for the position he'd accepted with Owl Creek PD as lead detective.

This case was getting a little personal for him. This was the second time the Slasher had struck in Salt Lake City. Fletcher hadn't worked the first case; he'd already been working a homicide, which had taken priority over an assault. So far, the Slasher hadn't killed anyone.

But the wounds across the victim's face and chest were so deep that the man was going to have to spend some time in the hospital while they healed to make sure they didn't get infected. These wounds were even deeper than the ones the last victim had received. The violence seemed to be escalating.

So it was just a matter of time before someone died, Fletcher thought. And even if they didn't, the Slasher's victims were going to be scarred for life—physically and mentally as well. The Slasher had to be stopped. These two cases in Salt Lake weren't the only assaults. Over the past few years, there had been random attacks outside nightclubs in LA and Vegas. And now Salt Lake City. The randomness made it impossible to figure out where the Slasher would strike next.

Fletcher wanted to make sure that it was nowhere. He'd

already interviewed the victim at the hospital. Now he was at the scene, watching as the techs collected evidence. Or at least he hoped they were collecting something that could be used as evidence. Lights had been set up in the alley so that nothing would be missed. The light illuminated the spatters and pools of blood from the attack that had been violent and vicious.

And somehow personal...

But the victim had no connection with the last one. At least none this victim, Eric Holt, was aware of. Fletcher couldn't find any association to the victims in the other states.

What the hell was the motive?

Maybe there wasn't one.

Was this just some psycho who randomly picked victims to disfigure?

"Not much here, Detective Colton," one of the techs said. "Not even footprints, and given the amount of blood, I would have expected to find something."

Fletcher pushed a hand through his dark hair, which probably needed a cut, like usual, and sighed. "The victim wasn't able to give us any useful info either. Everything happened so fast. He couldn't even tell if it was a man or a woman who attacked him." The guy had been vague about all the details, but then he was pretty drunk—with a blood alcohol level that was twice the legal limit.

That was the one thing all the victims had had in common. They'd been drinking. A lot. This guy had been at his bachelor party. So had one of the other victims...

But the others had just been at the club as far as Fletcher knew. He had to find something else. Another lead. "I'm going inside to do some interviews," he told the tech. "Let me know if you find any—"

His cell rang, and he pulled it out of his jacket pocket. The contact information read *Uncle Buck*. In the middle of interviews, he would have ignored it…if not for what had happened recently with his sister Ruby, for how close they had come to losing her forever. But that case had been closed and the deranged guy was locked up. She should be safe, especially with Sebastian Cross so determined to make sure she and their unborn child stayed out of harm's way.

Still, Fletcher was concerned enough that he swiped to accept the call. "Uncle Buck, what is it? I'm at a crime—"

"It's your dad, Fletcher. He's had another stroke. It doesn't look good. He's been life-flighted to Boise Medical. You need to get there as soon as you can."

Fletcher cursed. His relationship with his dad was complicated, but Robert Colton was still his dad. Fletcher loved him even though he got frustrated with him, like he was now. "After the last stroke, he was supposed to quit the drinking and smoking…"

And whatever the hell else he'd been doing that he shouldn't have been doing, that he wouldn't have been doing if he'd cared about anyone but himself.

"Fletcher, it's too late for all of that now," Buck said, his voice gruff with emotion.

A twinge of guilt struck Fletcher. He shouldn't have been thinking about that, let alone voicing his thoughts aloud. He shouldn't have been thinking about anything but his dad's health and about his family. Buck's relationship with his brother hadn't always been the easiest either, but they were brothers. If his dad didn't recover from this stroke like his last one, it wasn't going to be easy for anyone to handle, especially not Fletcher's mother.

"I'll be there as soon as I can," Fletcher assured his uncle.

He had already turned in his resignation to leave Salt Lake City PD for Owl Creek. Someone else would have to take over this case. Someone else would have to catch the Slasher before anyone else got hurt.

KIKI SHELTON'S HAND shook as she scrolled through the messages and posts popping up on the screen of her cell phone. *Oh, no...*

Not another one...

She had to call, had to make sure everyone she knew was all right. She glanced toward the closed door off the kitchen that was dark but for the dim glow of the under-cabinet lighting. Soft snores emanated from behind that door. Her grandfather had gone to bed a while ago, but he was a light sleeper, especially when they were fostering a puppy for Crosswinds.

Fancy was a little two-month-old shepherd mix with tan fur everywhere but her muzzle, which was as black as Kiki's hair. Except for her deep auburn tips. The puppy bounced around Kiki's bare legs, excited that someone else was awake at this hour. Kiki wanted the two of them to be the only ones, so she opened the patio door and stepped onto the deck attached to the back of the cottage.

She didn't want her grandfather to overhear her talking on the phone. He already worried about her too much. He didn't need to know that there had been another attack. In addition to the texts and calls sent directly to her, news of the slashing had also popped up on all her social media accounts.

Thank God Jim Shelton still refused to pay attention to any of them. But he would probably catch it on the news. He never failed to watch the network broadcasts every morning and every night, flipping from channel to channel to get different takes on the same story.

There was only one take on this one. There was a maniac brutally attacking people.

Concerned that someone else had been hurt, she made the call she'd been anxious to make.

"Kiki!" the male voice cracked with the exclamation of her name.

"Are you okay?" she asked Troy. He was usually her assistant, but she'd loaned him out to another DJ since she hadn't had a gig this weekend.

He'd been there. In Salt Lake City. At that very club where the attack had happened…

"It's messed up, Kiki," he said. "I stepped outside to smoke and saw the guy lying there…"

"I'm so sorry, Troy," she said, her stomach churning over the thought of what her friend had found, had seen. And that poor man. "That's horrible. Are you okay? Is he?"

"Yeah, I'm okay. It was way worse for him, but I think he'll live. But it was so bad…" His voice cracked again, and she could hear his shudder through the home. "It's just messed up, Kiki…" He slurred a bit; maybe he'd had something to drink or maybe he was just tired.

It was late. But Kiki was used to staying up late; so was Troy. "You need to get some rest," she suggested.

"Every time I close my eyes I see him there, all cut up and bleeding..." She heard the shudder again.

"Take some time off for a while," she said.

"If I'm not working, I'll just keep thinking about it..."

"Then join me early in Owl Creek," she said. She had some gigs set up for them in the area in a few weeks. "It's safe here. Nothing much happens."

She wouldn't tell him about what had happened at Crosswinds—how she could have lost a good friend. But that criminal had been caught, so Owl Creek was safe again.

Like it had always been...

Kiki's safe haven. After she'd lost her parents in a horrific car accident when she was six, she had come to live with her grandfather along the shore of Blackbird Lake. She leaned on the deck railing and stared out at the surface of the lake, which reflected the night sky and the stars twinkling in it along with the big crescent moon.

It was beautiful here and so quiet, just cicadas chirping in the night as fireflies flitted around like sparks, appearing and disappearing. Fancy tore around the yard, chasing after them, her little teeth snapping as she tried to capture them in her mouth. But it was still quiet, despite the antics of the puppy.

So quiet and so beautiful that it always seemed to recharge Kiki, especially after a long winter and spring of playing clubs in LA and San Francisco and Salt Lake City. But the money she was saving and the reputation she was building was worth all the hard work.

She should have been working the club in Salt Lake this weekend, but she'd wanted to stick around Owl Creek to make sure Ruby was okay and that her grandfather could handle the new puppy. Every time she came home, it seemed like he'd aged while she was gone. And she didn't want him being alone so often, even though he insisted he was as spry as he ever was. And the truth was, he probably preferred to be alone. Either working with puppies from Crosswinds, at his tackle shop or his favorite place, out on his boat on the water, fishing.

"You sure, Kiki?"

She had pretty much forgotten Troy was still on the line. "What?"

"You sure it's safe there?"

She thought of what Ruby Colton had just gone through. But that was over now. "Yes, it's safe here, Troy. Come to Owl Creek."

But as she clicked off the cell, a strange shiver chased down her spine. Maybe it was just the night breeze. Maybe it was foreboding. After what had happened with Ruby, was Owl Creek as safe as Kiki had always believed it was?

Or maybe that just proved that something bad could happen anywhere…

Chapter Two

The past week had passed in a blur of hospital vigils and now this: the funeral.

Fletcher's dad hadn't survived this stroke like he had the last one. After days in a coma, Robert Colton's body had given up the fight. He'd slipped silently away from them.

"Are you sure you don't want to say anything?" Fletcher's older brother asked him.

He shook his head, uncertain what he could say about his father. Sure, he'd loved him, but he'd also sometimes wondered how well he'd really known him. Robert Colton had spent more time at work than with his family.

"No, Chase," Fletcher said. His older brother, who'd worked with his dad at Colton Properties, knew their father far better than Fletcher had. Fletcher just wanted to make sure that Mom was all right and made it through this day. To find her, he moved through the crowd of family and friends and Owl Creek residents who'd gathered in the funeral parlor to mourn or at least to support the mourners.

Every one of his siblings had someone standing beside them, offering their condolences and probably memories of his father. He'd heard his share already, during the hospital vigils, and at the visitation the night before. He really just wanted this to be over, for his sake, and for his mom's.

Over the past week Jenny Colton had been strong and loving, as she always was, comforting her *kids* instead of letting them comfort her. Maybe that was because she was a nurse and was just used to taking care of others. Maybe that was just because she was an amazing person.

She'd raised not just her own six kids pretty much on her own while Dad had worked crazy long hours, but she'd also helped Uncle Buck raise his four kids after Aunt Jessie, Mom's twin, had abandoned her husband and family. They were all adults now, but Jenny Colton still always put them first, before herself.

But she always made time to take care of her physical health. Fit and active, the only indication of her age were the streaks of gray in her short, dark blond hair. Fletcher breathed a little sigh of relief that she was all right, that she was healthy.

But how was she doing emotionally?

It had been a long week for him. He couldn't imagine how it had felt for her. He found her with Ruby and Sebastian, which he totally understood after they could have lost Ruby. Instead, they'd lost Dad.

Mom wasn't the only one standing near them. An older man with thick white hair, Jim Shelton, stood beside Sebastian. He'd been running a bait and fishing business on Blackbird Lake for as long as Fletcher could remember. And the woman standing next to him looked nothing like his little orphaned granddaughter who'd come to live with him so long ago.

Kiki Shelton, with beautiful, thick black hair and ample

curves, had certainly grown up over the past twenty years. She seemed to get more beautiful every time Fletcher saw her, but that hadn't been very often recently. He'd been working his way to detective in Salt Lake City, and she'd been working clubs in LA and Vegas and San Francisco. She'd even worked some in Salt Lake City. Ruby had let him know a few times when Kiki was DJing, but going to a club, with the noise and the crowds, wasn't his idea of a good time. At least on the few times he had ventured out, he'd only wound up with a headache, though, not scarred for life like those other guys.

The wounds across Eric Holt's face flashed through his mind along with the blood spattered and pooled in that alley. He wondered how the Slasher case was going back in Salt Lake, who'd taken it over and if they had found any leads.

It was easier to think about that case than about this day, about the funeral, about his dad's senseless death.

If only he'd taken better care of himself...

KIKI HATED FUNERALS because of the flood of memories they brought back. Of her parents' funeral. Of losing them both so suddenly and shockingly as she had in that traffic accident.

Fortunately, she didn't remember much about that, even though she'd been asleep in the backseat. They'd been on their way to Grandpa's for Christmas. A pang struck her heart, as it always did, when she thought of them. She still missed them so much, nearly twenty-one years later.

But Grandpa had taught her that attending funerals was the right thing to do, to pay your respects to the deceased and to offer your sympathy and support to their survivors.

Robert Colton had a lot of survivors. The Colton family was big.

Ruby Colton was the one Kiki knew best because the veterinarian owned Colton Veterinary Hospital and took care of the animals for Sebastian Cross's Crosswinds Training. The two had an even closer relationship now. Sebastian's arm wrapped tightly around the blonde. He was definitely supporting her.

Ruby had three older brothers, two younger sisters and four cousins, too. A pang of envy struck Kiki. She'd always wished she had siblings. She probably had some cousins on her mother's side, but they were back in Mexico and she hadn't heard from any of them. Her grandfather had reached out, sending letters and pictures over the years, but they'd been returned as undeliverable.

Grandpa had always done his best for her. She wrapped her arm around him, knowing that it was getting harder for him to stand for long periods of time with the arthritis he had in his back. The funeral was due to start soon, so they would be able to take a seat then.

Right now, they stood talking to Sebastian and Ruby and Ruby's mother. Jenny Colton was a strong woman. Although she was a little pale, her eyes were dry and clear. But her second oldest son must have been worried about her because he'd clearly been looking for her when he'd walked up.

Fletcher Colton. He wore a dark suit for the solemn occasion, but his hair was a little long, a little unkempt. A little sexy.

His broad shoulders strained the seams of that suit, and his eyes... They were a deep, vivid green. And his gaze was focused on her right now.

Kiki's pulse quickened at the intensity of his stare, but she tried not to take it too seriously. Fletcher Colton just seemed like an intense guy. A detective.

Detectives probably checked out everyone the way he was checking her out.

"You remember Kiki," Ruby said to him, and her lips curved into a slight smile as if she thought he had another reason for staring at her friend.

"Yes, of course," Fletcher said.

"I'm sorry for your loss," Kiki told him, repeating the words she hadn't understood when she'd been six and standing in this very room. She hadn't been able to comprehend why people were apologizing to her like they were responsible for that crash. She hadn't even known what happened for sure, since she'd been sleeping, but Grandpa had said that it was weather. No one's fault.

But now, since losing them, she had a lot more empathy. She understood how it hurt to lose a parent.

Having probably heard those words a hundred times, like she had back then, Fletcher just nodded.

"Your father did a lot for this town," her grandfather said. "He will be missed."

"Thank you, Mr. Shelton," Fletcher said. "It's great to see you."

"Don't know how long you're sticking around Owl Creek but come by if you'd like to do some fishing," Grandpa told him.

"I'm moving home," Fletcher said.

And Kiki's pulse quickened even more.

"He's taken the position of lead detective with Owl Creek

Police Department," Jenny said, beaming with pride in her child.

Fletcher shrugged. "Probably won't be as busy as it was in Salt Lake City, so I'm sure I'll have time for some fishing, Mr. Shelton. Thanks for the invitation."

Since Kiki helped Grandpa with the tackle shop and fishing excursions, she would probably be seeing Fletcher around, too. That thought unsettled her for some reason.

Or maybe this uneasy feeling she had didn't have anything to do with him and it was just because he'd mentioned Salt Lake City, as it reminded her of the Slasher's recent attack outside the nightclub where Troy had been working.

Her assistant was still shaken over finding the victim, over what he'd seen. But he'd come to Owl Creek. Troy had even found a place to stay since Kiki was going to be here for the summer, helping her grandfather while doing gigs in the area. She'd booked a job at a nightclub in Conners for this upcoming weekend.

Conners was just outside Owl Creek and was just as safe. Well, just as safe since the deranged man who'd gone after Ruby had been caught.

Music began to play, signaling the beginning of the service. Mrs. Colton, Ruby and Sebastian started off toward the chairs nearest the casket. Fletcher hesitated for a moment before following them, probably dreading this.

She could totally relate.

But then he glanced at her, and there was some question in his green eyes as if he wanted to ask her something. But then he blinked, and the look was gone. He just nodded at

Kiki and her grandfather, in some kind of acknowledgement, as he headed off after his family.

She and Grandpa found chairs near the back of the service, since they would have to leave right after it to check on Fancy. So Kiki probably wouldn't see Fletcher again for a while unless he actually took her grandfather up on his fishing invitation.

If he did, she'd probably make herself scarce. She had no interest in getting involved with anyone. Her career was really taking off, and when she wasn't busy working, she wanted to help Grandpa as much as she could.

She had no time for romance. No matter how good-looking Fletcher Colton was.

Not that he was interested in her. He probably just wanted to fish.

FLYERS HAD GONE up around town. Hot LA DJ Kiki Shelton was going to be spinning at Conners Club this weekend. This was an event not to be missed.

The poster had a picture of Kiki on it with her black hair, the ends dyed deep red, and her killer body. A lot of men would probably show up to watch her spin and dance.

A lot of men who would drink too much. Who would get careless.

Who might step into a dark alley.

The Slasher smiled in anticipation.

This attack was soon after the last one. The closest together of the attacks yet.

But this urge burned inside the Slasher. This urge to act again.

To lash out.

To get the attention and the revenge they deserved. And to make sure that some man in Conners got exactly what he deserved, too.

Chapter Three

As if the funeral hadn't been bad enough, Fletcher, his mom and siblings had had to meet with the estate lawyer the next day. Fortunately, he'd come out to the house and Fletcher had been able to slip out of the meeting early. Leaving the others upstairs in the great room, Fletcher slipped downstairs to the walkout level where he'd been staying in his old bedroom.

None of what the lawyer had told them had been a surprise. Jenny got the house and whatever money they'd had in their accounts. Each of the kids got an equal share of Colton Properties while Chase was named the new CEO.

It was pretty much what Fletcher would have expected, probably what they'd all expected. If they'd ever thought about their dad dying...

Even after the first stroke, Fletcher hadn't thought about it. Hadn't considered it was possible.

He'd recovered so quickly and completely from that first stroke. And even though the doctor had warned him to change his lifestyle, it hadn't really seemed possible that Robert Colton would die before he even hit sixty years old. It just hadn't seemed like it could happen.

But it did.

He was gone. But he'd been gone a lot while Fletcher and his siblings were growing up. He'd been away so much that the house didn't even feel different without him being here. Fletcher was staying with Mom, just to make sure that she wasn't alone.

Eventually he would look for his own place. But for now, it was comforting to be home, if not for Mom then at least for him. He'd already lost his dad. He didn't want anything to happen to her, too.

Kiki Shelton had lost both her parents suddenly when she'd been just a kid. When she'd said sorry at the funeral, like so many other people had, it had meant a little more because he knew she knew.

She knew even better than he did about loss.

Maybe that was why she'd intrigued him so much, why he hadn't wanted to stop talking to her even as the service started. No. That was because he'd wanted to ask her about the Slasher.

Or at least that was the idea he'd had at the time. But he realized now it was a reach. Sure. She was a DJ who worked at nightclubs. But there were a lot of nightclubs. And even if she had been at any of the ones where an attack had taken place, she would have already been questioned. She probably wouldn't have any new information to give him no matter what he'd asked her.

And that case in Salt Lake City wasn't his anymore since his dad's stroke had compelled him to cut his two-week notice short. He was glad that he'd been here, though. Glad that he'd been here for his mom and his family.

But now that the funeral was done and the will was read, it all felt so anticlimactic. So strange and surreal.

He had to get back to real life. Fortunately, he was starting at Owl Creek PD in the morning, a week earlier than he'd been scheduled to start. But he needed to get back to work. He needed to help people since he hadn't been able to help his father.

Not even the doctors had been able to help his father.

Knuckles rapped against his door and then it creaked open. He turned away from the window that looked out over Blackbird Lake, surprised to see it was Chase who'd sought him out. "Everything okay?" he asked.

"I was just going to ask you that," Chase said. "You slipped out of the meeting so quickly."

"I thought it was done," Fletcher said.

Chase arched a light brown eyebrow over one of his green eyes. While he and Fletcher had the same color eyes, Chase's hair was lighter brown, and he kept it conservatively cut. And even though this meeting had been at their home, Chase wore a suit. He'd probably come right from the office, though.

Fletcher felt a pang of envy that his brother had had something to keep him busy over the past week.

"Are you upset?" Chase asked.

"About what?" Fletcher asked.

"That I was named CEO."

Fletcher chuckled and shook his head. "You were born CEO, Chase. Everybody knew that was going to happen someday."

"It happened too soon," Chase said, his voice gruff.

And Fletcher knew that even though he'd kept busy, Dad's

death had probably affected his oldest brother the most. He'd certainly spent the most time with him. He closed the distance between them and pulled his brother's lean body into a brief hug. "I'm sorry…" he murmured.

And as he said the words, he thought of Kiki Shelton. Of how she'd said them.

Yeah, it was good he started his job tomorrow. Then he could get his mind off not just his dad's death but off Kiki Shelton, too. He had too much going on to even allow himself an attraction to anyone right now.

He was starting a new position with a new police department while helping his family deal with his dad's death. He didn't need any other distractions.

A couple of days had passed since the funeral, but Kiki hadn't been able to get that image of Fletcher Colton out of her mind. The way he'd looked at her…

What had he wanted to ask her?

Not that she really cared. Or had any time for it.

She needed to stop thinking about him and focus on everything else she had going on in her life. She glanced across the console of her SUV to where Fancy sat, her harness secured to the seat. The puppy whined and quivered.

"You have to get used to riding in vehicles," Kiki told her. If she went into service as a scent dog like Sebastian had predicted for her, she was going to have to travel a lot. Like Kiki did.

But a drive up toward the mountains wasn't a sacrifice at all. She loved coming out this way to Crosswinds Training Center, with the enormous sparkling blue of Blackbird Lake on one side of it and the mountains behind it.

Her heart stretched with love for this place where she'd grown up. Owl Creek was beautiful. And there was actually a creek—well, more of a river—by that name, too. It curved around and through town and emptied into the lake.

Kiki had to steer her SUV around those curves on her way up to the training center. Fancy needed a checkup, and Ruby was working out of the medical offices there today.

Kiki had been a bit surprised that she was working at all. She couldn't even remember much of that time immediately after her parents had died. Just the funeral and Grandpa.

He'd gotten a puppy then as if it would make her feel better. And somehow it had worked.

Fancy, with her tan fur and black muzzle, reminded her of that dog. Buster. Even now, years after he'd passed, Kiki remembered Buster. He'd helped her through a rough time. Just like some of the dogs that Sebastian Cross helped train were used as PTSD dogs to help veterans, like him, through a rough time.

Maybe that was why Ruby had chosen to work, to take care of the animals she loved so much. But, remembering how closely Sebastian had stuck by Ruby's side during the funeral, it wasn't just the animals that the veterinarian loved at Crosswinds. Or that loved her.

A wistful sigh slipped out of Kiki's lips. Not that she was jealous or anything. She liked her life exactly as it was. Focused on Grandpa and growing her brand as a DJ and building her nest egg.

Fancy whined again.

"And you…" Kiki murmured. She enjoyed volunteering with these puppies as much as her grandfather did. A veteran himself, he liked helping out with the ones who were trained to assist with PTSD. But Fancy was special.

Sebastian thought so, and so did Kiki. But probably for different reasons.

"Hang in there, sweet thing," she said as she steered her SUV down the last part of the private road and onto the Crosswinds property. In addition to the big brick and wood training center, there were indoor and outdoor kennels and the medical building. "We're here," she said as she pulled up next to the medical building.

Sebastian also had a cabin on the property that he'd renovated some time ago. He had transformed it from the family getaway it had once been into his home now. Crosswinds was an ideal place with the view of the lake below and the mountains behind it, but Kiki preferred to be on the water.

When she had a gig in Owl Creek or nearby, she often went "home" to the houseboat her grandpa had on the lake instead of back to his cottage. That way she didn't risk waking him up. Maybe she would stay there tonight when she came back from the club in Conners.

She parked the SUV, then went around and opened the passenger's door. As she leaned inside to release Fancy from her seat harness, the puppy's furry body quivered with excitement, and the little dog licked Kiki's hands and then her face.

Kiki chuckled and helped the puppy down from the vehicle, holding tightly to her leash so she didn't run off. That wasn't a really big concern, though, since Fancy tended to stick close to her. "Checkup time," she said as she led the little dog toward the medical building.

Maybe Fancy understood what she'd said because she

tugged against the leash, as if trying to head back toward the SUV. Maybe she remembered being here in the kennels and preferred Grandpa's cozy cottage. Kiki had been spoiling her a bit.

She'd also been working with her, though, on commands. "Heel," she said.

The puppy tensed for a moment.

"Walk."

And Fancy trotted along beside her.

"She's coming along," Sebastian said as he opened the door for her.

Kiki smiled. "She's very smart, so it doesn't take much to train her." But she still had a few bad habits, like chewing things she shouldn't. This time it had been one of Grandpa's favorite slippers.

"I really appreciate you and your grandfather helping out, though," Sebastian said. He crouched down and let the puppy sniff his hand, her little black muzzle wrinkling as she smelled the scent of other animals on him. "She's going to be good to go soon."

Kiki felt a little pang. Sure. She knew scent dogs were necessary for a variety of things, for sniffing out drugs or explosives or for tracking missing persons. But she didn't want to think of the dog ever being in harm's way because of her abilities.

Through the open door behind Sebastian, another person stepped out. Della Winslow was a couple of years older than Kiki, with long, light brown hair and brown eyes. She was a K9 search and rescue tracker, and her black lab, Charlie, was close by her side as usual.

Fancy yipped at the lab, either with excitement or fear.

Kiki tugged on her leash as the puppy tried to clamor around the bigger, male dog.

"I'm sorry," Kiki said.

"Charlie is used to it," Della assured her with a smile.

"This is the pup I've been telling you about," Sebastian said. "The one out of Sable's litter."

"I remember the litter," Della said. "But you placed them with foster families so quickly, I didn't get to know any of them very well."

In addition to her job with Search and Rescue, Della also worked as a trainer at Crosswinds. She crouched down to pet the puppy, looking her over, and nodded. "I see the potential." She glanced up at Kiki. "You and your grandfather always do such a great job socializing the pups."

"You'll have to choose one to keep one of these days," Sebastian suggested.

Kiki shrugged. "I'd love to, but I travel so much. I'll mention it to my grandfather, though."

Sebastian chuckled. "He always says that he fosters them for your sake, but I think he enjoys having them, too."

Or he remembered how much Buster had comforted her and thought she still needed comforting for some reason. "He really does do a lot for my sake," Kiki said.

And she could never repay him enough for all the love and support he'd given her. So she wouldn't ask him to keep a dog for her if it really would be too much for him.

"I think it's mutual," Sebastian said. "You would do anything for him. You could still be working out in LA or Vegas, but you always come home to help him in the summer."

She shrugged again. "I enjoy playing some of the smaller venues around here."

"I saw your flyers up around town for the Conners Club tonight," Della said.

Troy had put up all the flyers. It had given him something to do, to get his mind off that attack in Salt Lake City. "Come out if you can," Kiki encouraged them.

Della gave her a noncommittal nod. But then she probably couldn't commit, never knowing what might come up that would require her help as Search and Rescue.

Sebastian grinned. "Ask Ruby—"

"Ask Ruby what?" the veterinarian asked. She stood in that open door behind Della.

Della smiled and said, "I better get going. Thanks for checking Charlie out for me. He's just been a little off lately."

Kiki could relate. She'd felt a little off since seeing Fletcher Colton at the funeral. Why did she keep thinking about him? It was good that she had a gig tonight, something else to think about besides him and how good-looking he was.

She knew there was a bachelor party that would be stopping in because the best man had messaged her some special song requests. Based on a couple of those requests, she might suggest the groom pick another best man.

"I know you were concerned that Charlie has been sleeping so much, but he's fine," Ruby assured Della. "Might just be a little bored."

That was probably Kiki's issue as well. The reason for her giving Fletcher Colton a second thought—just boredom. Once she was playing and the crowd was dancing, she would forget all about Fletcher.

Della smiled. "Well, in our business, being bored isn't a bad thing."

"It is in mine," Kiki said.

The others chuckled, and Fancy jumped up with excitement over the mood. "Down," Kiki said.

And the little dog immediately dropped down to all fours.

"Yes, she is going to be good," Della agreed with a glance at Sebastian.

Kiki wondered for a moment if they were talking about Fancy or about her. But Della rushed off and so did Sebastian, leaving Kiki alone with her friend.

"So, what was Sebastian telling you to ask me?" Ruby asked as she led the way back to an exam room.

Kiki lifted Fancy onto the table and let the nervous pup lick her face again. "About coming to the club in Conners tonight."

Ruby smiled. "I've been a little tired lately."

"After everything you've been through, that's totally understandable," Kiki said. "I'm sorry again about your dad and that whole…"

"Madman trying to kill me because he thought I was preventing him from getting this land away from Sebastian?" Ruby finished for her. "It's all over now. And it worked out." She touched her stomach and smiled again.

Kiki gasped. "Are you pregnant?"

Her smile widened, and her green eyes sparkled with happiness. "Yes."

"You and Sebastian…?"

Ruby nodded. "Yes, I've actually moved in with him."

"I'm happy for you," Kiki said, and she felt that traitorous little jab of envy again. Not that she wanted a baby or even a significant other. But sometimes, even in a crowded club, she felt so alone. That was another reason she loved to come home to Grandpa in Owl Creek. But then she shouldn't have had that feeling here.

"What about you?" Ruby asked.

Kiki patted her stomach and hips. "I'm not pregnant. Just curvy."

Ruby snorted. "You're perfect, and you know it. I meant what about your love life?"

Kiki snorted now. "What love life?"

"Exactly. How can someone like you not have a significant other?"

"I do," Kiki said.

And Ruby's eyes widened.

"My grandpa," Kiki said. "And this little nugget of cuteness here." She pressed a kiss to the top of Fancy's furry head.

Ruby chuckled. "This little nugget isn't going to stay little long. She's growing like crazy. What was your concern about her?"

"She ate part of one of Grandpa's slippers."

Ruby took out a stethoscope and listened to the puppy's belly. "How long ago was this?"

"Had to be sometime during the night. The only time Grandpa takes them off when he's in the house is when he's in bed. He didn't notice until he went to put them on this morning."

"Did she go out this morning?" Ruby asked.

Kiki nodded. "I let her out before I knew about the slipper. But I think she passed it. I just want to make sure that she's all right."

"Everything sounds fine," Ruby said. She pulled a small

puppy snack from her pocket and held it out for Fancy who gobbled it up. "She has an appetite, too."

The little muzzle wrinkled as Fancy's nose sniffed the air and then Ruby's pocket. The vet chuckled and gave her another treat. "That's your reward for sniffing it out. She does have a natural talent."

"Sebastian does, too, because he already figured she'll be a scent dog," Kiki said. "He really knows what he's doing."

Ruby smiled. "Yes, he does."

"Guess I didn't have to tell you that," Kiki said with a chuckle of her own.

"Nope. We're going to be getting married soon," Ruby shared. "After what happened with us and with Dad, it just proves how short life can be and how very precious." She touched her stomach again.

Kiki laid her hand over Ruby's. "I'm so happy that something good came out of everything you've gone through recently."

Ruby blinked and smiled at her. "Of course, you'll have to be at the wedding."

"I'd love to DJ it," Kiki assured her.

"I meant as a bridesmaid," Ruby said. "I didn't expect you to work it. I'm not even sure how big a wedding we'll have. There has been so much going on here."

"Too much for you," Kiki said.

"Too much for Owl Creek," Ruby said.

"Hopefully everything will quiet down now," Kiki said.

Ruby nodded heartily in agreement but then added, "But not so much that you get bored and head back to LA early. Or that Fletcher heads back to Salt Lake City. He's used to being a lot busier than he'll be here, even with Owl Creek PD covering some of the surrounding areas."

Kiki hadn't considered that—that Fletcher might not stick around Owl Creek. She felt another strange twinge. "Do you think he'd leave?"

"Not anytime soon," Ruby said. "He's worried about Mom. We all are. But she's doing really well."

"That's good."

"Good that Mom's doing well or that Fletcher will be staying?"

Heat rushed to Kiki's face. "I don't even know Fletcher." She sighed. "Don't be one of those happy brides-to-be that tries matching up all their friends now."

Ruby held up her hands. "I promise I won't. I'm really busy. It was just the way you two looked at each other at the funeral…"

Fletcher wasn't the only one in his family who'd been intensely studying her then. Ruby must have been, too. But Kiki had only noticed Fletcher. Despite the warmth of the June day, a little shiver raced down her spine.

"Your pregnancy must be causing hallucinations," Kiki teased. "I doubt Fletcher is any more interested in me than I am in him. And now I better get this little fur ball back to Grandpa and start loading up my equipment for my gig tonight. Sure you won't come?"

Ruby yawned. "Maybe another time."

Kiki nodded. "Sure. Take care."

"You, too."

And Kiki felt that little shiver again. She was safe. Wasn't she? It wasn't as if anything would happen at the Conners

Club that had happened at those other clubs. Those had been in bigger cities, more dangerous areas of town.

Conners wasn't much bigger than Owl Creek, so hopefully it was just as safe as Kiki had assured Troy that it was. Nothing bad was going to happen here.

THIS MUSIC WAS so much better than what had played in Salt Lake City. It was more alive, more melodious, and made the Slasher feel as if it had been mixed to choreograph to their movements, to the swing and swish of the blade cutting through the air and then cutting through the next victim.

He screamed and lifted his hands to his bleeding face. And the Slasher cut through those as well.

And when the hands fell away and the victim dropped to the asphalt in the alley, the Slasher slashed some more…

Chapter Four

His first few days on the job had been uneventful. Despite being lead detective, Fletcher hadn't had many investigations to lead. A stolen vehicle. A suspected driving under the influence incident. The most exciting thing had been a possible embezzlement of a school's booster fund by one of the parents.

With as close as the police department was to his sister Frannie's bookstore café, Book Mark It, at least he'd been able to stop in and visit her a few times. Check on her. They'd always been super close growing up. Not that he had liked books the way she had, but they'd both loved a good mystery.

After some of the things he'd seen in Salt Lake City, like the latest victim of the Slasher, Fletcher should have been relieved that, despite what had happened with Ruby and Sebastian, his hometown was relatively safe and quiet. He *was* relieved for the sake of his family.

But for himself…

Fletcher loved working. Maybe he'd gotten that from his dad. But unlike his dad, Fletcher knew that his overwhelming love of his job meant he was better off single than trying to have a wife and family. He didn't want to miss all the things that his father had over the years. But not working wasn't an option for him.

He had to work. Had cases to solve, criminals to catch and put away even in Owl Creek. So he'd focused on the car thief, the drunk driver and the embezzler and had closed those cases. At least Owl Creek PD covered Conners as well, but nothing had come up yet there that they hadn't been able to handle on their own.

Until Fletcher's phone rang in the early morning hours of Saturday. His cell vibrated across the surface of the bedside table and he reached out for it, answering with a groggy, "Colton."

"Fletcher?"

It was the chief, his boss, so Fletcher roused himself. "Yes, sir."

"You've been requested to help out with an assault that just happened in Conners."

"Requested? Me specifically?" he asked. How did anyone in Conners even know he'd accepted the job at Owl Creek PD?

"You're needed at the crime scene there," the chief continued.

"Needed? Requested? I'm confused, Chief," he admitted.

"Conners PD know there've been some cases like this in Salt Lake City when you were there," the chief explained. "So they need you out at the crime scene ASAP."

Fletcher went from groggy with sleep to wide-awake and tense. "Cases like what?"

"Where a guy is found in an alley behind a club and he's been viciously attacked—"

"The Slasher."

Here? In the Owl Creek area?

Not the big clubs in the big cities.

It didn't make sense, but that made it even more interesting. "Is the guy all right?" He asked the most important question.

Had the attacks escalated, like he'd been worrying they were? Had it become more than assault?

"He's alive," the chief said. "I don't know any more about his condition or what happened. Just that they'd like you to advise." And he gave him the address of the crime scene.

"I'll be there." Fletcher rolled out of bed and dressed in a rush, desperate to get to the nightclub in Conners before it was too late, before all the witnesses were gone. But as fast as he'd dressed and drove, he still arrived too late to interview the victim. And most of the guests had left the club.

Fletcher got an almost dizzying sense of déjà vu. The location was so similar to the last crime scene where he turned up in the alley as the techs were processing it. The blood pools and spatters were the same. "Let me guess," he said. "No footprints? No evidence?"

One of the techs looked up at him, her eyes narrowed with suspicion. "We're not giving interviews."

"That's good," Fletcher said. "Because I think the Slasher is getting off on the notoriety."

Why else had the perp stepped up his attacks? If their victims were really random, then the only reason would have been for more attention. For more media coverage.

The reporters had been out front, but Fletcher had slipped through them unnoticed and then flashed his badge at the officer guarding the entrance to the alley. He flashed it now at the tech. "I'm the lead detective with Owl Creek PD."

The young woman nodded. "I heard they were sending somebody over since we're short-staffed. Right now, we're processing everything. Hopefully we find something."

"If you don't, you won't be the only techs who couldn't," he assured her.

"You've worked these cases before?"

"Not like I've wanted to," he admitted. The first one he hadn't been assigned as he'd had other cases to close first. And the second…

His dad had had the stroke, and Fletcher had been called home early to Owl Creek. And he'd thought then that he wouldn't have the chance to work the Slasher case again.

But the Slasher had come here, too. Maybe.

"Are you sure this case matches the profile of the other ones?" he asked the tech. He couldn't imagine that, if the Slasher wanted publicity, they would choose here for their next attack. Wouldn't they go back to LA or Vegas where there was more of a media presence?

"The victim was slashed up bad across his face, hands and chest," a man said as he stepped out through the back door that was open to the interior of the club. He extended his hand toward Fletcher. "You must be Detective Colton. I'm Sergeant Powers." The man had thin gray hair and a lot of lines in his face.

Fletcher shook his hand and nodded. "I appreciate you calling me in on this."

"I appreciate you pitching in. This kind of a case is above my pay grade, especially since I'm semiretired." He yawned. "I have another officer conducting interviews with the last of the people who actually stayed in the club and didn't take off the minute the police were called."

"Sounds like that wasn't many," Fletcher remarked. That had appeared to be the same situation in Salt Lake City, too. Nobody wanted to get involved, or maybe they were worried about public intoxication or some other charge, depending on what they'd been doing in the club.

"Wrapping up now," the sergeant remarked, and he stepped away from the door so that Fletcher could see inside the club. The lights had been turned up, the harsh fluorescent bulbs illuminating the nearly empty space.

And he saw her.

She wore black, like she had when she'd attended his dad's funeral, but it wasn't a dress. She wore tight leather pants and a cropped top. And her voice was even huskier than it had sounded in the funeral parlor as she replied to the officer's question. "There's really nothing I can tell you about what happened in the alley. I was behind the turntables the whole night, usually with my headphones on."

"So you didn't see or hear anything. You can go," the uniformed officer that the sergeant had assigned to take statements told her.

While they'd called in Fletcher to help, they weren't letting him do very damn much. He'd wanted to conduct the interviews. But he wanted more than that.

He had an idea. With Kiki's help, he might have a way that he could work the case. Maybe he would actually be able to solve it and catch the Slasher.

But when he started toward the door, the sergeant stepped in front of him. "I need to pick your brain about these cases," the older man said. "See if you have any idea where we should start."

He had a damn good idea.

With Kiki Shelton.

SHE HADN'T BEEN lying to the officer when she'd answered his questions just moments ago. Kiki hadn't heard or seen anything. She'd had her headphones on, as she always did, while mixing the tracks. Hell, she'd even had her eyes closed, moving to the music. Feeling her own vibe.

And during that time, someone had been getting attacked in the alley.

She shuddered in horror. The same horror Troy must have been feeling, because he'd disappeared sometime during the night, too.

She wasn't even sure when. One minute he'd been there and finally, when she'd noticed the commotion in the club, she'd also noticed he was gone.

Had he found this victim, too?

She'd thought it was one of the bachelor party guys who had discovered the injured man because he'd been waving his arms around, his hands smeared with blood.

And she'd taken off her headphones to hear him screaming for help and to hear other clubgoers yelling when they saw the blood on the man.

Everything had descended into chaos after that, with people running and shouting. And Kiki had pretty much been trapped behind the turntables, unable to get out and even look for Troy. She'd expected he would show up.

But he hadn't.

Even after the police cleared the club of whoever had

actually remained behind to talk to them. While she had stayed as well, she hadn't been any help to the police. And now she had no help herself.

"Troy, where are you?" she whispered into the darkness of the back parking lot. Her SUV was out here, one of the shadows in the night. She would have clicked the fob to turn on the lights, but her hands were wrapped around the handles at the top of the speakers she rolled across the asphalt.

In addition to her turntables and mixers, Kiki always used her own sound system. Sometimes she patched it in with the club's system, but most of the time hers was better. Because she preferred her own setup, she had a lot of things to schlep from club to club.

That was why she needed an assistant. Even though she was strong enough to carry the equipment on her own, if she was working alone, she had to take more trips for set-up and breakdown. And breakdown, at the end of a long night, needed to be faster because by that time all she wanted to do was go home, shower and drop into her bed and sleep.

That probably wouldn't be possible tonight, not when she was worrying about that poor man. There had been all that blood just on his friend.

How much had there been on the victim?

She didn't want to think about it, but her maudlin mind kept circling back there, to the alley where he'd been found. She'd done her best to keep to the other direction, which was thankfully where she'd parked.

Before the attack, the club owner had offered to let her and Troy unload and load up their equipment in that alley, but Troy had shuddered and refused, saying that he never wanted to set foot in another one after the last.

She'd promised him then that nothing like that would happen around Owl Creek. She'd promised him it was safe here. That the Slasher wouldn't attack anyone here.

Had it been the Slasher?

Maybe it had just been some random mugging.

Not that it made anyone any safer.

In fact, it probably made them less safe because then there were, potentially, two dangerous people out there: a mugger and the Slasher.

No. Not here. Not this close to home.

She shivered despite the warmth of the June evening and hastened her pace across the parking lot. But footsteps echoed hers. She glanced over her shoulder, but nothing was visible in the dark but darker shadows.

What had happened to the streetlights out here? Were there any? It had been light when she and Troy had parked out here, his truck next to her SUV.

She turned back to where they'd parked, but it looked like only one vehicle was still out there. Hers.

Troy had left.

So who was behind her?

She heard the footsteps again, the scrape of shoe soles against the asphalt. Her pulse quickening with fear, she released the handle on the speaker and reached inside the bag slung over her shoulder. She wasn't looking for the key fob. She was looking for her pepper spray.

Nobody was getting close enough to slash her.

Chapter Five

Where the hell was she?

He could hear something in the darkness, something like wheels rolling over asphalt. Like someone was moving a suitcase or something...

Curious, he'd followed the noise. But in the darkness, he couldn't see anything. He'd considered turning on his light and calling out. But what if it was the Slasher?

He uttered a short, derisive snort at the thought. The Slasher hadn't avoided getting caught all this time by hanging around the crime scenes. They probably moved on to the next city shortly after an attack.

But why here?

"Don't try anything! I have pepper spray!" a voice called from the darkness.

"Kiki, it's me," Fletcher said as he turned on the flashlight on his phone. The beam illuminated her standing in the middle of the dark parking lot, a small canister clutched in her hand, her finger ready to press the sprayer.

"It's Fletcher," he clarified. Since he was still in the dark, she probably couldn't see him. So he moved the light closer to his face.

"What the hell..." She released a shaky breath. "Why didn't you say anything? You scared me!"

"I'm sorry," he said. "I couldn't see who was out here either."

"What are you even doing here?" she asked. "You weren't in the club tonight."

Maybe it hadn't been that busy then, since she sounded so certain that she hadn't seen him there. Or maybe she just assumed, correctly, that he wasn't the type to go to clubs. They were too loud. Too crowded. Too full of drunk, obnoxious partiers that he dealt with all too often already as a detective.

"After the person was found in the alley, the Conners Police Department called us in to assist."

She released another shaky breath. "Oh, that makes sense."

Apparently, more sense to her than him being at the club having a good time.

But she wasn't wrong. Fletcher couldn't actually remember the last time he'd had a good time. Certainly not since his dad's stroke and...

"Did you think it was the attacker out here?" she asked and shuddered.

"I didn't know what to think," he said and pointed to the canister in her hand. "Evidently neither did you." But he was glad that she'd been prepared to defend herself had it been necessary.

"This is so damn scary," she said. "People getting attacked like that so viciously." She shuddered again.

"You were prepared with the pepper spray," he said. "But you really shouldn't be out here alone in the dark like this. It's too dangerous. And I'm not just talking about the Slasher. Anyone from the club could have followed you out here."

Her lips curved into a faint smile. "You're the only 'anyone' out here besides me. And you sound like my grandfather."

"Jim Shelton is a very wise man," Fletcher said.

"He worries too much. And after this…" She sighed. "He's going to worry even more."

Fletcher had an idea.

A solution to her problem and maybe to his as well. "Maybe we can figure out a way to allay his fears," he said.

"We? What are you talking about?" she asked.

He glanced around that all-enveloping blankness. Anybody could be out there, hiding in the dark. Even the Slasher.

"Let's talk about it somewhere else," he said. "What are you doing out here?"

She thumped her hand against the top of what looked like a speaker on wheels. "Putting my equipment in my vehicle."

"You parked way out here?" he asked.

She sighed. "It didn't seem that way out when it was still daylight."

"And you're moving all this equipment on your own?"

"I have an assistant."

Fletcher swung the beam of his cell flashlight around the area. But he only saw the two of them. "Where is your *assistant*?"

She sighed again, and this one was heavy. "I don't know. I haven't seen him since the lights came up and the police were called."

"He just took off?"

"A lot of people did," she said. "It was chaos."

"Why?" he asked.

"A man was attacked," she said. "People were screaming. There was blood." She shuddered now, more violently than she had before.

"You saw the victim?"

She shook her head. "No. The guy who found him, his friend, had blood on his hands and shirt and he was screaming for help." Her voice cracked with emotion, with empathy.

"So instead of helping him, people took off," Fletcher pointed out. "Including your assistant, leaving you to move all your equipment on your own."

"I'm sure he was just shaken up like everyone else," Kiki said. "They didn't know how to react. They were just scared, especially Troy. I assured him it would be safe here after Salt Lake City."

"What do you mean?" Fletcher asked. "Just because of what happened there with the Slasher? Or were you there?"

"I wasn't," Kiki said. "But Troy was. He found that victim, and it really freaked him out. I promised him that it was safer here, that nothing would happen."

This Troy had been at the scene of two of the attacks.

Fletcher needed to find her assistant. "When did you last see Troy?"

She shrugged. "I don't know. I was so busy with special requests and people coming up. I don't remember when I saw him last."

So he could have slipped into the alley before the attack.

"Did you try calling him?" Fletcher asked. "Texting him?"

"Yeah, of course," she replied. "But I didn't get any

reply or even his voice mail. It's like his phone is dead or off or something."

Fletcher suspected the *or something*. Like the man took his cell apart so that nobody could track him. And Fletcher could think of one reason why.

So no one would find out he was the Slasher.

INSTEAD OF A police escort, Kiki had had just one lawman tailing her home. Why?

She doubted he was concerned about her safety; she didn't fit the profile of the Slasher's usual victims. She wasn't male. And she was pretty sure, from the way he looked at her, that Fletcher Colton was well aware of that. Just as she was well aware of how very male he was.

Her pulse quickened, but that had to be because of what had happened that night.

She hadn't seen the victim, but she'd seen all that blood on his friend. That poor man.

Who would do such a thing to someone? Attack them so viciously?

Kiki turned her SUV into the driveway of her grandfather's cottage. Lights shone in her back window as a vehicle pulled in behind hers. Fletcher's. He got out of his SUV at the same time she stepped out of hers. "You didn't need to follow me home," she told him.

"You have all that stuff to unload," he said, waving his hand at the rear hatch of her SUV.

He'd helped her load up the rest of her equipment at the nightclub.

"I leave it in there," she said. "There really isn't any room for it in the cottage." Her grandfather's house was small, so she had more storage space in the back of her SUV. With the tinted windows, it was hard to see the expensive equipment stored inside so she didn't worry about it getting stolen.

She hadn't thought she needed to worry about those Slasher attacks here in Owl Creek either, though. Maybe she needed to be more careful. "I should grab my laptop, though," she said, clicking open the hatch.

As it rose, the front door of the house opened and the yard light flashed on, illuminating the driveway while leaving the man standing in the doorway in the shadows.

Jim called out, "You okay?"

She sucked in a breath, worried that he might have heard about the attack already. "I'm fine, Grandpa."

Fancy pushed past him in the doorway and ran out to the SUV, bouncing around Kiki's and Fletcher's legs.

"I heard a man's voice," Grandpa said, "and I wanted to make sure you were all right."

"Fletcher Colton is out here with me," she said, though her grandfather could probably see that for himself now.

"I was just making sure she got home safely, sir," Fletcher called back to Grandpa.

"Something happen?" the older man asked.

Kiki smothered the groan trying to slip out of her throat. Before Fletcher could say anything about the attack, which would upset her grandfather and keep him awake, she grabbed his hand, squeezing it to shut him up and also to make her grandfather think that they were together. "No. He was just being a gentleman, Grandpa."

"Few of them left nowadays," Grandpa said. "I'll leave you two alone then." He chuckled. "Well, except for that little furry chaperone."

Fancy still hopped around on the driveway but her interest appeared to be more in the back of the SUV than in them, since her little muzzle wrinkled as she sniffed. She was so focused that she didn't even react when the door closed behind Grandpa.

"What's she smelling?" Fletcher asked, and his long body seemed to tense next to Kiki, reminding her that she was holding his hand.

She jerked hers away, her skin tingling in reaction. "I don't know. Sebastian thinks she'll be a scent dog. I think he's right."

"Drugs?"

She tensed now with righteous indignation. "What are you saying? You think I have drugs in my vehicle?"

Fletcher held up his hands. "I was just asking what he was training the dog to sniff out."

"Nothing yet," Kiki replied. "Fancy has to get socialized first and learn basic commands. Like Sit." And she turned toward the puppy, held her hand out—palm up—at waist level and then raised it toward her shoulder.

Fancy whined and danced around for a moment.

"Sit." She repeated the gesture and finally Fancy planted her little squirmy butt on the ground. The dog was smart. They'd only been working together a couple of weeks, and she was already beginning to master the basic commands. Kiki reached into the back of the SUV and pulled out her laptop bag. In the front pocket was a small packet of puppy treats. She rewarded Fancy with one. "That's what she was sniffing out. Her treats. Not drugs."

"You're a little defensive."

"I hate that people assume, just because I work in nightclubs, that I'm either a user or a dealer." She groaned her disgust at that all too common assumption. "There are a lot of people who go to nightclubs to listen to music and dance and just have a good time."

"That guy tonight—in the alley—he didn't have a good time," Fletcher said. "The other victims of the Slasher, disfigured for life, didn't have a good time."

She flinched. "I know. But that had nothing to do with the music or the nightclub."

"Those attacks have only happened outside nightclubs," Fletcher said. "So they definitely have something to do with nightclubs. So does your assistant."

She sucked in a breath. "You suspect Troy?"

"You don't?"

A laugh bubbled out of her, but it cracked a bit with nerves. "God, no. I can't believe you do. He was devastated when he found that body in Salt Lake City. And tonight."

"Yes, what happened to him tonight?" Fletcher asked. "Where did he go?"

She shrugged. "I don't know. I'm sure he just got freaked out that it happened here after I promised him it was safer in Owl Creek. I told him things like that didn't happen here."

"Things like that can happen anywhere," Fletcher said.

As a detective, he probably could have given her examples, but he didn't need to. She knew what had nearly happened to his sister Ruby here.

She just sighed. "I know. And I shouldn't have made him a promise I couldn't keep. He's probably angry and disillusioned—"

"Or guilty," Fletcher interjected. "I need to talk to him. Tell me where he is."

She shivered at his tone and his intensity. Now she knew why Fletcher had been hired as lead detective. He could probably get a confession out of anyone with that look, that edge to his voice.

Probably even out of an innocent person, which was what she believed Troy was. But Troy was also a bit flighty at times, emotional, reactive.

That had to be why he'd taken off like he had. He was scared. And Fletcher interrogating him would scare him even more.

"I've known Troy for four or five years now," she said. "He's a good guy. He works hard and is very helpful."

"Helpful to whom?" Fletcher asked with a pointed glance into the back of her SUV.

"He would have helped me with this equipment, but that attack, so soon after the last one, must have scared him," she said, her voice heavy with concern for her friend and for the victim. "That's why he took off like he did."

"Without a word to you," Fletcher said. "Without checking to make sure you were okay."

"I'm okay," Kiki said. "I was in the club the whole time. I was never in danger."

Fletcher nodded. "No, you weren't. You're not the Slasher's usual victim." His gaze flicked down her body in her leather pants and cropped top. "You're definitely not male."

And despite the warmth of the June night, Kiki shivered a little with goosebumps, not of cold but of awareness, rising on her skin. "Are you flirting with me, Detective?" she asked.

His lips curved into a slight grin. "Just making an observation."

She smiled and mused, "Strange observation to be making during the course of your investigation." Then, because she'd been wondering, she asked, "Why did you follow me home?"

Fletcher chuckled and his grin widened. "You definitely aren't in any danger," he said. "You're too perceptive to have anyone sneak up on you."

"Are you trying to sneak up on me?" she asked. "Just as I was never in any danger, I wasn't the danger either, in case you consider me a suspect. I was behind the turntables in front of a hell of a lot of witnesses when that attack must have taken place. And I was here when the man in Salt Lake City was attacked."

She'd been in some of the same cities for those other attacks, but she wasn't about to point that out to him. Not when he clearly considered her assistant a suspect.

"Troy was there," he said, confirming his suspicion. "And I need you to help me find him so I can question him. Will you do that?"

She sighed and nodded. "Only because I know that once you question him, he'll be able to provide alibis and prove his innocence to you."

"Let's hope that's the case," he said.

"Liar," she said. "You'd probably like it to be Troy, so that you can close this case."

"You are perceptive," he said. "The Slasher needs to be stopped. What he's doing to these victims is so cruel, and eventually one of them will probably die from their injuries."

She shivered again with revulsion and dread. "You're right. I'll help you find Troy. But what happens when you realize he's not the Slasher? How will you catch this person then?"

He looked at her again, his forehead furrowing beneath the strands of his overly long hair. And that intensity was back in his green eyes.

The intensity that unsettled her for a lot of reasons.

"I have an idea about how I can do that," he said.

"Why do I feel like that idea involves me?" she asked uneasily.

His grin widened even more, and his green eyes glinted in the light from the porch. "Because you are perceptive."

His idea definitely involved her.

Chapter Six

Fletcher was certain that Kiki wasn't in danger from the Slasher, which was the only reason he'd considered the idea he'd had to be able to investigate from the inside of the nightclub scene. But before he shared that plan with her, he wanted to find out if it was even necessary or if the first real suspect in the case was the Slasher.

Her assistant. Troy.

"You really don't know his last name?" he asked with suspicion as he glanced across the console to the passenger's seat of his SUV. Fancy rode in the back, her harness strapped to the seat.

"No, I don't," she said, her voice a little sharp with either irritation or maybe embarrassment.

"You said you've known him for four or five years."

"I have."

"And he's your assistant. Don't you have to have his full name to put on his paycheck?"

"He just takes a share of the tips. He doesn't want a paycheck."

"He doesn't want to pay taxes," Fletcher concluded.

"You have to pay taxes on tips." Kiki said it so matter-of-factly that it was clear she would never consider not declaring them.

He doubted that Troy was as conscientious about that as she was. The man was either avoiding income taxes or child support or maybe both. What else was he running from? Fletcher doubted that it was really the Slasher.

Every one of the victims had been a clubgoer, not someone who worked at the club. But someone like this Troy, who went from club to club... He made a very interesting suspect.

By that line of thinking, so did Kiki. He would have to double-check her story that she had been working the entire evening. That she hadn't taken a break at all.

And he had an idea of how he could check her story.

If it was necessary.

But if this mysterious Troy was really the Slasher, then Fletcher had no reason to spend any more time with Kiki Shelton. A pang of disappointment struck him at the thought.

But that was ridiculous, just as flirting with Kiki had been silly. She was Ruby's friend, and Ruby had already been through too much even before they'd lost their dad. The last thing his sister needed right now was Fletcher creating any awkwardness with her friend, who was also someone who fostered dogs for Ruby's soon-to-be husband Sebastian.

And Fletcher was pretty certain it would end in awkwardness, as most of his relationships had. Either he got ghosted—like his girlfriends believed he was ghosting them when he was simply busy—or he got cheated on because someone else gave them more time and attention than he was able to.

No. He had no business flirting with Kiki Shelton. But he

couldn't stop glancing across the console at her. She was so beautiful, and the way the black leather clung to the curves of her body had his body tensing with desire for her. He had to ignore his attraction to her, though, and focus on the case.

The Slasher could not claim any more victims.

He slowed his SUV and turned into the driveway for the seasonal RV park where Kiki said that her assistant had parked his van. He drove past some high-end travel trailers and motor homes toward the outskirts of the RV park where the woods had begun to claim back the cleared areas. In a section of weeds, someone had parked a vintage VW bus.

"That's it," Kiki said. "He's here!"

The van was dark, like the other vehicles parked around it. "How do you know?" he asked.

"He drove that to the club tonight," she said. "It wouldn't be here unless he'd driven it back."

So he was here. This close.

The Slasher?

Fletcher reached for his weapon as Kiki reached for the door handle. "No," he told her. "You need to stay here. Wait until I make sure he isn't a threat."

"He isn't," Kiki insisted. "Not to me."

"But if he considers you being here a threat, he's going to be one, too. Somebody dangerous is hazardous to anyone who gets in their way," Fletcher said.

In denial or defense of her friend, she shook her head. But she didn't open the door.

Fletcher stepped out into the darkness and listened. Gravel crunched. Twigs snapped and there was a subtle shift in the air, indicating movement around him. It could have been other RV residents or animals. But somehow, he suspected it wasn't.

He drew his weapon and his flashlight and aimed his beam around the area as he approached the van. Tree limbs rustled. Something was definitely out there.

Or someone.

"Police," Fletcher called out, identifying himself even though he really didn't want to, just in case he needed to fall back on his other plan. The one he had yet to bring up to Kiki.

But whoever, or whatever, was out there didn't come out of the trees. More branches rustled but the sounds were farther away now and getting fainter as the person fled. So when Fletcher shined his light into the van, he wasn't surprised to find it empty.

Troy had taken off again.

The passenger's door opened, and Kiki stepped out. "He's gone?"

"Yes."

Fletcher touched the handle of one of the back doors of the van, and it easily opened. Troy had run off in such a hurry that he'd left it unlocked.

Another door opened and then Fancy rushed up next to Fletcher. The van was lower to the ground, so the puppy easily jumped inside, sniffing through the bedding and belongings tossed about the back of the van.

Then she yipped and pulled something from the bedding and brought it toward Fletcher. He shone his light through the clear plastic to the collection of different colored capsules inside it. The puppy's sharp teeth were already tearing through the bag.

And Kiki gasped with concern. Then she pointed toward the ground. "Drop!"

Fancy whined.

"Drop!"

And the little teeth released the bag, dropping it onto the threadbare carpet next to Fletcher. "Some little pharmacy he has here," he mused.

"These could be his," Kiki said, but even she sounded doubtful now. But she scooped Fancy up in her arms and lifted her out of the back of the van.

"Troy has a medical condition?" he asked.

She sighed. "Not that I know of."

He shone his light over the van, watching for it to glint off metal. And it did. Off beer cans. Not a knife blade.

She tensed and turned toward him. "Don't you have to have a warrant or something to search his premises?"

"Nobody has seen him since the attack," he said. "I have probable cause to make sure that he's all right."

"You can't take those pills," she said. "What if they are medically necessary?"

Fletcher snorted in derision at that, but he didn't have a warrant, as she'd pointed out. He really shouldn't have even opened the door to the van.

And he had no right to open the glove box either. So he shut the door. Then he made a note of the license plate number. He'd run that, see if he could find out Troy's last name and if the van was actually registered to him.

Instead of releasing the puppy, Kiki snuggled it against her as if she needed comforting.

"You're not so sure of your assistant's innocence anymore," Fletcher remarked.

"I know he's not the Slasher," she insisted. "But the drugs…" She sighed again. "Sometimes he seems a little out of it. I thought maybe he drank too much."

"There were a lot of beer cans in the van," Fletcher said.

"And that bag of all those drugs."

"So maybe some of those people who approach you for drugs do it not because of your working in a nightclub but because of Troy?" he asked.

A little breath of air hissed through her teeth. "I don't want to think that."

But she clearly was thinking it now.

"So from his disappearing act, it looks like you're going to need a new assistant," he said.

"I'll be able to find someone here in Owl Creek," she replied. "I know a lot of people willing to help me out."

"You don't have to look any further," Fletcher told her.

"What do you mean?"

But instead of answering her, he just opened the back door of his vehicle for her to buckle Fancy back inside. Then he opened her door too before heading around the hood to his side. He glanced around him again, feeling someone out there. Watching them.

Listening to them.

So he wasn't going to ask her here.

KIKI KNEW THAT Fletcher had a plan that somehow involved her. But he didn't share it with her that night. Or that early morning.

He just dropped her and Fancy back at Jim's and drove away, leaving her wondering. Awake. And worried.

He must not have slept either because he returned a few

hours later, pulling his SUV into the driveway behind hers. Fortunately, Jim had already left to take out a fishing charter on the lake. He had a boat docked near where the houseboat was. After last night, waking her grandfather up when Fletcher had followed her home, she probably needed to stay out on the boat, at least on the nights that she DJ'd.

Fancy barked and jumped on the door, trying to get outside to greet Fletcher before he even got out of his vehicle. "Someone's smitten…" Kiki murmured as she got up from the table where steam rose from her mug of coffee. Then, through the screen door, she watched Fletcher walking toward the house. The wind ruffled his overly long dark brown hair and plastered his shirt against his broad shoulders and muscular chest. She didn't have to be a detective to conclude that this detective worked out and that Fancy might not be the only smitten one.

But when he got up to the house and the wind was no longer blowing his clothes against his body, she could tell that they were a little oversize and wrinkly, like Grandpa's favorite TV detective that he watched reruns of nearly every day no matter how many times he'd already "solved" the case.

She pushed open the screen door and let Fancy out to bounce around his legs, pawing at his khaki pants.

He leaned down and scratched behind the puppy's ears, and the shameless mutt dropped and rolled onto her back, giving him her belly to rub. He chuckled as he scratched that fur, too. "She's seriously cute," he said, and he glanced up at Kiki, his green eyes warm with affection for the pet.

He was seriously cute, too.

She'd thought so every time their paths had crossed in the past. But with him working in Salt Lake City and her working in so many other cities, they hadn't seen each other often over the years. Not even when she came home for the summers to help Grandpa.

Because Fletcher hadn't lived in Owl Creek for a while.

"What are you doing back here?" she asked him, the curiosity overwhelming her.

He tensed for a moment. "I have an idea about how I might be able to catch the Slasher."

She shook her head.

"You're not going to hear me out?"

"No, I meant why did you come back to Owl Creek?" she asked. "It had nothing to do with the Slasher because you probably didn't think the Slasher would show up here any more than I did."

"I came home when Ruby was in danger, and I liked how Owl Creek PD handled the case."

And they'd liked him enough to offer him the job of lead detective. "I know that. But why did you really want to come back? You could have stayed in Salt Lake City or gone somewhere else where there would be more crimes to solve."

"There are crimes here to solve," he said.

She sighed. "Not usually. I can't believe that was the Slasher last night."

"You don't want to believe it," Fletcher said. "But the MO and the wound patterns match the other victims. It was definitely the Slasher."

She sighed again, but it was ragged. And her chest ached. "You still didn't answer my question, you know."

He flashed her a grin. "Maybe you should be the detective. You're good at this interrogation thing."

She laughed. "It's one question. I'm not interrogating you. I'm…"

"What?" he asked. "Interested?"

"Curious," she corrected him. Interested implied something more like attraction, like desire…

And she actually felt those, too, but she didn't want him to know that. He and his family had already been through too much lately. And she…

She had too much going on for a serious relationship. And to her, the Coltons were serious people. At least Fletcher seemed to be with that intensity of his in the strained cord in his neck, in the twitch above his square jaw and in that stare he fixed on her.

"So, are you going to satisfy my curiosity?" she asked.

"If you'll satisfy mine sometime," he said, negotiating with her.

She smiled and shrugged. "Sure." She wasn't sure what he would ask her, but she had nothing to hide. "So…"

He shrugged now, those broad shoulders pulling the wrinkles from his oversize cotton button-down shirt. "I was worried about Ruby and noticing how much older my parents were getting. And Hannah is raising Lucy all alone." He shrugged again. "I felt like I needed to come home. I just wish I'd realized that sooner, before my dad had another stroke."

She reached out for him then, grabbing his hand to squeeze in hers. "I'm sorry."

"You offered your condolences at the funeral," he reminded her.

"But it doesn't hurt just that one day."

He turned his hand in hers and squeezed back. "You would know. I'm sorry about your parents."

She shrugged off his sympathy. "That was a long time ago."

"It doesn't hurt just that one day," he said.

She smiled at him repeating her words back to her. "So it's your turn," she said. "You can satisfy your curiosity now."

His gaze slipped then, to her lips, and his thumb rubbed across the back of her knuckles.

Saliva filled her mouth, and she had to swallow hard so she didn't start drooling over the man. He wasn't thinking about kissing her. That wasn't the curiosity he wanted to satisfy. She was sure of that.

But then she remembered how he'd looked at her in her black leather outfit, his gaze sliding up and down her body like a caress. She wasn't wearing leather now. She was wearing very old and ragged jeans with a light cotton T-shirt. But the material was soft enough that it did cling to her curves, and the holes in the jeans revealed her tan thighs and knees.

His gaze dipped down over her again like it had the night before, and his green eyes darkened, the pupils dilating. Maybe he did want to kiss her.

She wouldn't protest. She was curious about his mouth, too. But then she reminded herself how bad an idea it was to get involved with anyone right now, least of all a Colton. He was mourning. She smiled again and stepped back, breaking the contact of their hands.

And she was busy. She had to help Grandpa with the fishing business and Fancy and…

"I need your help," Fletcher said.

"With what?" she asked slowly, reluctantly, because she'd already suspected he'd wanted to ask her to do something, something she probably wasn't going to want to do. Like when he'd asked her to show him where Troy lived.

"Did you find Troy?" she asked. Maybe he wanted her to talk to her assistant and encourage him to answer Fletcher's questions.

He shook his head. "Not yet."

"He couldn't have gotten far," she pointed out, "without his vehicle."

"I know. I have someone watching it. An APB out for him to be picked up for questioning. Hoover. That's his last name. He's Troy Hoover."

She shrugged. "I didn't know. Like I told you, it never came up."

"You didn't know his last name. Or that he's had a previous arrest for drug possession and that he owes back child support? That didn't come up either?" he asked, and he was definitely doing the interrogating now.

She shook her head. "He helped another DJ I knew, and when that DJ retired, Troy just started helping me out. It wasn't like I had him fill out a job application and checked his references."

"Or even got his last name."

"I knew him for a while—through the other DJ, through the clubs." She sighed. "But yes, I should have asked him more about himself." She couldn't deny that now, especially since he apparently had a record. "When were those arrests?"

"The drug possession was a while ago," Fletcher admitted. "And the child support is just outstanding. No arrest warrant for that yet."

"I didn't even know he had a child," she murmured.

"Two."

Two kids that he wasn't helping to support. She cursed. "I shouldn't have let him take his wages from the tips."

Fletcher shook his head. "No. That helped him evade garnishment of his wages and taxes."

She released a ragged sigh. "Well, I still don't believe he's the Slasher. But I won't let him work with me ever again either." Guilt pulled at her that she, however inadvertently, had helped him avoid his responsibilities. "I really thought I knew him better than that."

"Some people are hard to get to know," Fletcher said.

And she suspected he was one of them. Although he had eventually answered her question about his return, he had yet to tell her what his plan was and how it involved her.

"Yes, they are," she agreed with a pointed look.

He chuckled. "I'm an open book."

"So read the chapter heading to me about why you're here then," she urged him.

"You need an assistant," he said.

She narrowed her eyes and studied his face. "I have managed on my own." But it was work.

"You don't need to. I know someone you can use as your assistant," he said.

"Really? Who is that?"

"Me."

She closed her eyes and tried to picture him—in his wrinkly business casual khakis and button-down cotton shirt, standing behind the turntables with her—and a laugh bubbled out of her at the image. "Everybody would know you're a cop."

He shook his head. "No. I just started the job, and I didn't interview anyone in Conners last night. Only a tech and the sergeant saw me. And I haven't been around much since I moved away from Owl Creek, so most people won't recognize me."

"People might not recognize you as Fletcher Colton, but they'll make you for a cop right away."

He glanced down at himself. "How? I'll hide my holster."

"It's not the gun," she said with another laugh.

"What then? How can I not pass as your assistant?"

"Do you dance?" she asked.

He grimaced.

And she laughed again. "Have you ever gone to a nightclub—" she held up a hand when he started to open his mouth "—that hasn't been a crime scene?"

"Not for a while," he admitted.

Her curiosity piqued again. She asked, "Why not?"

"I've been busy," he said. "With work, with my family."

She sighed. "I understand being busy, but in my business that's a good thing." It meant she was in high demand, that people wanted to come where she was spinning. "Not so much in your business."

He shook his head. "No. It's not. That's why I really need to catch the Slasher."

"And you're right, then, that you need my help," she said. He wasn't going to pass as her assistant without it. "Do you have anything in your closet that isn't khaki and or buttondown?"

"I have jeans," he said.

She pointed at hers. "Like these?"

"I throw them out before they look like that," he said. But the way his gaze moved over her skin that the holes exposed, he didn't seem to mind that she hadn't.

She smiled and stepped closer to him and touched the buttons on his chest. "And something that doesn't button down?"

"I will need the button down to hide my gun," he said.

"Hiding your gun is less important than hiding that you're a cop," she said. "Just your presence alone will scare the Slasher away."

Which wasn't a bad thing. She would rather not have another attack happen here. But she didn't want them to happen anywhere else either.

"I have to catch this person," he said. "Whoever it is, they're so dangerous. Their victims will be disfigured for life, and eventually…eventually…" His throat moved as he swallowed. "Someone is going to die."

Fear clutched her with the knowledge that he was right. Eventually someone was going to die. She didn't want that someone to be him, though.

WHERE WAS THE news coverage? The Slasher scrolled through their phone, trying to pull up stories about the latest attack. But the only one that came up was the last one. In Salt Lake City.

Not this one in Conners, near Owl Creek, Idaho. The area was pretty.

With the lake and the river and the mountains in the distance. It was so idyllic that something bad happening here should have been big news.

Should have incited a panic.

And it had at the club. Once the victim had been found, everyone had been screaming and running in fear, afraid that they might be next.

And maybe they would be.

Because the Slasher was going to stick around town and make damn sure that Owl Creek acknowledged how powerful they were. And how very dangerous...

Chapter Seven

Fletcher hadn't wanted to admit it, but Kiki was probably right about his ability to fit in at a nightclub. His cover wasn't going to be effective if *anyone* suspected he was a cop. Because rumors would spread, and nobody would talk to him.

And the Slasher would just move on to another nightclub and find their next victim elsewhere.

So he'd agreed to go shopping with Kiki for some clothes that would help him go undercover as her assistant. But first he'd stopped by the hospital in Conners to check on the Slasher's latest victim. Some of the guy's wounds had gotten infected, so he was receiving IV antibiotics. He also needed more surgeries to try to limit the scarring he was going to have.

The guy had a long road ahead of him to heal. Physically and emotionally. But when Fletcher walked up to his door, he heard laughter behind it. A man's and then a woman's familiar, raspy laugh. He pushed it open to find Kiki standing next to the man's bed, smiling down at him. Today she wore shorts so short that the bottoms of the pockets hung out of them, and a T-shirt that was so short that it showed off her belly button and the piercing in it.

Fletcher's pulse quickened.

Kiki glanced at him, and her smile faded. "I should leave now and let you get your rest."

The guy glanced at Fletcher, too, and emitted a soft sigh. "Don't think that's happening. Another cop with questions, I presume?"

Fletcher swallowed a groan and nodded. Kiki had been right about people pegging him for police. "I'm Detective Colton." He identified himself, flipping his badge out to show it. "I just have a few questions."

"I should go," Kiki said. "I have a date to go shopping with someone." She glanced at her wrist. "In just a little while."

"You have a date," the man said, and he didn't swallow his groan.

"You're engaged," Kiki reminded him.

"Yeah, but you came to visit me, and she hasn't."

"Are you two friends?" Fletcher asked. And if so, why hadn't Kiki mentioned that to him before?

"I wish," the guy replied. "Her helper never lets anyone through to talk to her."

"I just came to check on him," Kiki said, "after finding out what happened at the club."

"That damn Slasher…" the guy murmured, his voice cracking.

"Did you see them?" Fletcher asked.

"I just saw that damn blade coming toward my face and then…" He shuddered. "I didn't see anything."

"What were you doing in the alley?" Fletcher asked. "Why'd you go out there?"

The guy glanced at Kiki who stood near the door, and as if she'd realized he was reluctant to admit it in front of her, she waved and popped out of the room.

The guy groaned again. "It was stupid."

"What was? Why were you out there?"

"I found a note in my pocket. Someone must have shoved it in there on the dance floor. I thought…"

"What did the note say?"

"Meet me in the alley for some fun." The guy lifted one of his bandaged hands to his bandaged face. "Some fun…"

"Do you have the note?" Fletcher asked.

The guy shrugged. "I don't know. They took all my stuff when I got to the hospital."

It wasn't with his things. The techs had all that stuff now—had already processed it for DNA, fingerprints, whatever they could find to help find the Slasher.

"We'll keep looking for it," Fletcher assured him.

"I hope you find it before my fiancée does." His voice cracked again with fear. "Oh, God, maybe she already found it and that's why she hasn't been here."

Fletcher doubted that, but he would check with her, too. "She wasn't at the club?"

"No, it was my bachelor party. We just stopped in because we knew the DJ was hot." He glanced toward that closed door, as if trying to see her through the solid wood.

"You came there for Kiki?" Fletcher asked.

The guy nodded. "A lot of people follow her around the club circuit. She's good."

"And hot," Fletcher added.

The guy chuckled a bit, then flinched, wrinkling the bandages on his face.

"You need your rest," Fletcher told him. "But please, if you think of anything you haven't already shared—"

"I know," the guy replied. "I know. I should have told the police everything."

"That was it?" Fletcher asked, double-checking.

"Just the note," the guy replied. "That was it. I didn't mention it before because I didn't want my fiancée to know."

But since she wasn't the woman who'd visited him right now, Fletcher had a feeling she'd already figured it out even without the note being found with his stuff.

Where was the note?

"Hope you heal quickly," Fletcher told him before turning to reach for the door that had closed behind Kiki such a short while ago.

"I got a question for you, Detective," the guy said.

Fletcher looked back over his shoulder. "What?"

"Why?" the guy asked. "Why me? Why would anyone do this?"

Fletcher shook his head. "I don't know. But I'm going to work hard to get those answers for you and the other victims and to put this person away."

Tears rolled down the guy's face, wetting his bandages.

And Fletcher felt a jab to his heart. The guy hadn't been a great fiancé, but he hadn't deserved this.

Nobody did.

Fletcher opened the door, and he felt that jab to his heart again. But this was for another reason, for the woman leaning against the wall across from him.

She was definitely hot.

And Fletcher couldn't help but think, as he stepped into the hall to join her, that this undercover assignment was going to be far more dangerous than he'd ever considered. And not just because of the Slasher.

KIKI FOUGHT THE smirk that was trying to curl up her lips. "Hey, what's keeping you?" she called from her place outside the door of the men's dressing room.

Since there was only one clerk in the store, and she was planted behind the register, Kiki had been playing sales associate, picking clothes for Fletcher to try on. After meeting up at the hospital in Conners, Fletcher had followed her to the outlet mall there since all the shops in Owl Creek were a bit higher end. The outlet mall was cheaper with a wider variety of stores—so many that this one wasn't at all busy. They were also the only customers in the store, so nobody would mistakenly think she was calling out to them. Fletcher should also have no doubt that he was the one she was talking to, yet he wasn't replying. Or coming out.

"Fletcher!"

"What's keeping me?" the question bounced back at her from the dressing room. "I can barely move in these pants." He pushed open the door and stepped out, wearing the skintight jeans and silk shirt she'd picked for him. The emerald green made his eyes sparkle even more and the silk molded to his chest and arms like the denim molded to his legs.

"It's either go for this look or the tattoos and piercings," she said. "That's what Troy looks like."

"I'm looking *for* Troy. I don't want to look *like* him," Fletcher said.

"You don't want to look like a cop," she reminded him.

He raised his fingers to his lips, trying to shush her like his undercover assignment had already started.

She laughed and pointed at the teenage clerk. "She has earbuds in."

He relaxed a bit, and when he did, the seams of the shirt strained at his broad shoulders and along his arms. To be built like that, he had to work out. A lot. The guys Kiki knew who worked out like that usually wore clothes to show off the result of their efforts, not hide them.

"You need some better fitting clothes," she insisted.

He reached for the top button of the shirt. "Yeah, and these aren't it."

"They fit better than your usual clothes," she pointed out, "which look like they're two sizes too big."

"I have to be able to run in case I have to chase a suspect down, and I need to be able to hide my weapon."

"Not everybody in the club hides their weapons," Kiki said. "If they have a permit to carry, some bouncers let them in with them."

Fletcher groaned. "Alcohol and guns. What could go wrong?"

"The Slasher isn't shooting their victims," Kiki said. "And not everybody that comes into the club drinks. Some just come for the music."

"Not the Slasher."

"You don't even know if that person comes inside the club. Maybe they just wait out in the alley until someone steps out for a smoke break or something."

He shook his head and glanced toward that clerk again. The girl wasn't even looking their way. She was focused on whatever video was playing on her phone. And nobody else had come into the store yet. "The Slasher doesn't wait for their victims to come to them."

Kiki tensed with dread. "But I've never seen anyone getting attacked like that happening inside." Fights. Sure. There were often fights. Sometimes someone even waved around a gun that Fletcher, with good reason, seemed to disapprove of them carrying while they were clubbing.

"Most of the victims have admitted to getting a note slipped into their pocket without them even realizing it." He tried to shove his hand into the pocket of his jeans, but they were too tight for him to fit more than his fingertips inside. "These aren't going to allow for that."

So he wanted the Slasher to slip him a note? To try to lure him into an alley?

She resisted the urge to shiver as a sudden chill chased down her spine. He wasn't just going undercover then. He was setting himself up as bait. She'd agreed to let him act like her assistant as his cover, but she hadn't realized how dangerous it was going to be. And she really didn't want him getting hurt like that man she'd visited in the hospital earlier today.

"And I thought it was cool to wear baggy pants and flannel jackets right now," he persisted.

She smiled at his persistence and his language. "Cool?"

"Hip, fly, whatever the words are that you kids use nowadays," he said, his green eyes twinkling with amusement.

"So are you trying to sound like my grandfather?" she asked, her smile widening. "Because he sounds more hip and fly than you do." And a giggle slipped out. "But then I guess you are older than I am." Probably five years at the most, but she couldn't help but tease him.

He glared at her, but his eyes were still twinkling. "I am not that old. I am just not that..."

"Cool?" she asked. He certainly wasn't now. Not in those clothes. He was *hot*, and she was getting hot as he undid another button and revealed some of the dark hair on his chest. Her heart beat faster and faster. Then she took a step back and whirled around. "I'll get you some hoodies and other things so you can hide your weapon."

But she wasn't necessarily talking about his gun. His weapon was how damn sexy he was.

He chuckled as if he'd realized he'd affected her. But maybe that was only fair. She'd purposely worn a pair of her shortest shorts just to get to him.

When she came back with an armload of hoodies and flannels and some looser jeans and Timberlands, he opened the door to his dressing room. The clerk hadn't even looked up from her phone while Kiki had flitted around the store picking out more clothes for Fletcher to try on. She wasn't paying any attention to them at all.

And Kiki kind of wished she was because she had no excuse not to step inside the dressing room with Fletcher to dump her armload onto the bench behind him. But when she would have ducked out again, he stepped between her and the door.

"What did you bring me now? Jeans I'm going to have to lie down on the floor to get on?" he asked.

She chuckled. "Bed. People usually lie down on the bed to get their jeans on. But for me." She patted her hips. "It's easier to get them on if I bounce up and down while I'm standing." And when she bounced to demonstrate, his gaze slipped down her body again.

A groan slipped through his lips. "Wouldn't you rather go shopping for you?" he asked.

"No. This is fun. And I already have all the clothes I need for the club." She kept a separate wardrobe of things that fit with the brand she'd built as a stylish and trendy female DJ whose music got people moving. "You need something you can wear this weekend, something that will help you fit in with the club scene."

He rolled his eyes.

"You really don't like clubs?" she asked.

"What's to like? They're loud and hot and crowded and really damn dangerous lately."

She couldn't deny that, not after she'd checked in on the Slasher's latest victim at the hospital. "That's why you need to fit in," she said. "If you want to catch the…" She glanced around him to where that clerk stood at the register, watching her phone. The buds were still in her ears. "Slasher."

Fletcher walked toward the pile of clothes she'd dumped on the bench. "What do you want me to try on next? And why do I feel like a life-size Barbie doll right now?"

"Ken," she corrected him. Then shook her head and corrected herself, "G.I. Joe."

"That's my brother Wade," Fletcher said with a sigh of his own. Wade had been hurt, badly, on his last deployment, so it was no wonder that Fletcher was probably worried about him. His whole family had to be.

"How is he doing?" Kiki asked.

"He's healing," Fletcher said, his voice a little gruff with emotion.

He clearly loved his family very much.

"It was sweet of you to check on the Slasher's latest victim," he said, his green gaze fixed on her with that unnerving intensity.

"I feel bad it happened while I was spinning, and I never noticed…" That someone was getting disfigured while she played. There had been so many bandages on the man, so much pain in his face. She shuddered.

"The music is loud. The place is crowded. There's no way you would have noticed," Fletcher said.

She was touched that he was defending her or at least trying to make her feel a little less guilty that someone had been hurt while she'd been playing.

"So how is this cover going to work for you so that you'll notice what's going on?" she asked.

"Do I have to stick by you all the time or just help with setup and takedown of your equipment?"

"Setup and takedown only," she assured him. "Troy only hung out with me for a couple of songs, usually. We had a little dance thing." She smiled as she considered teaching it to Fletcher.

He shook his head and backed up. "No dancing."

"Nobody will guess you're a cop if you do," she assured him.

He shook his head and some of his hair fell across his eyes. "I should get this cut," he grumbled as he shoved it off his face.

"No!" she gasped, and she reached up to put her hands in it as if the scissors were heading toward it as he spoke. His hair was so soft that her skin tingled from contact with it. "This is the one thing that makes you look less like a cop."

"You say that like it's a bad thing to look like a cop," he said.

"If you want this undercover thing to get the results you want, it is a bad thing," she pointed out. "Otherwise..."

"Otherwise what?" he asked.

"I have no problem with the way you look," she admitted, and she knew she should pull her hands from his hair, but it was just so soft. And he was so good looking with his chiseled features and vivid green eyes.

His mouth curved into a slight grin. "Really?"

Standing in that dressing room with him, trapped between the bench and his long, muscular body, she might have felt a little uneasy. But she didn't particularly want to escape right now. She enjoyed flirting with him entirely too much. And touching him.

"Well..." she murmured. "There is one thing that you could use..."

And he arched a dark brow over one eye. "Are you going to suggest a tattoo or a piercing again?"

She shook her head. "No. What you could really use..." And she leaned a little closer to him, her mouth near his ear, her chest almost touching his.

His body tensed, and he audibly sucked in a breath. "What?" he asked, his voice a rasp.

"You could really use—" she said, her voice all breathy "—an iron."

He chuckled. "Is that why you're picking out all tight clothes for me?" he asked. "So there will be no wrinkles?"

She glanced down his body the way he'd glanced down hers. He still wore those tight jeans, molded to his muscular thighs. "Yeah, that's the reason..." she said with a laugh, her particularly naughty-sounding laugh.

"Are you flirting with me, Ms. Shelton?" he asked.

"Don't take it personally," she advised him. "I flirt with everyone. Occupational hazard."

He laughed. "I'll try to remember that."

And she would have to try to remember that he was only helping her out as part of his cover in the club. He didn't really want to spend this time with her. He just wanted to catch the Slasher.

Chapter Eight

Club Ignition was just outside the city limits of Owl Creek in what had once been an abandoned warehouse. It was all metal and brick with a big open ceiling. And it was also loud and hot and crowded with sweaty bodies. All the things Fletcher hated about nightclubs.

But there was also Kiki.

She lit up the place, shining brighter than the strobe lights flashing around the club. One flashed now, nearly blinding him. How the hell was he supposed to spot any potential suspects when he could barely see at all?

The lights kept rhythm with the music, flashing in time to the beat. So not only was she managing the sound, but the light show, too.

And the sound, while loud, was also rich. Thick and heavy like cream and just as smooth. How did she do it all? He'd had no idea how much was involved with being a DJ. In addition to the expense of buying and maintaining all the equipment, there was also the physical labor of moving and unpacking the equipment. But the work didn't end with setup or takedown.

In addition to the lights, she also worked four turntables,

mixing songs and adjusting bass, and as she turned and mixed, she moved. Her body swayed to the slower songs, jumped to the faster ones and Fletcher wasn't the only one who couldn't look away from her.

Everybody in the club was as fascinated as he was. The men tried to get close to her, but she had a short barricade separating her DJ booth from the crowd. Knowing Kiki like he was starting to, she probably used it more to protect her equipment than herself.

But whatever her reasoning was, Fletcher was glad she had it, that she wasn't vulnerable to that crowd that could include the Slasher. Or just some men that might not respect her boundaries.

Even a group of women jumped up and down near that barricade, screaming her name with excitement on their flushed faces. "Kiki! Kiki! Play our song!"

Despite the headphones she wore, she must have heard them. Because when the song "Where My Girls At" started pumping out of the speakers, those women lost their minds, screaming louder and jumping up and down even higher, their arms waving wildly over their heads.

He'd planted himself near the booth, but closer to the floor so he could watch it. Too close to the floor, because one of the women from that group tried pulling him out with them to dance. He shook his head.

"Come on, Fletcher!" Kiki called out to him over her microphone. "Dance with my girls!"

"Then you gotta dance with us, Kiki!" a guy yelled out, pointing to the floor.

"With me!" another guy yelled.

As the men hollered at her, and she ignored them or just

shook her head, the women tugged Fletcher out onto that floor. He knew how to dance; he'd grown up with three younger sisters who'd needed practice partners for prom and other school dances. But those dances had been a while ago, so he didn't know how to do half the stuff these women were doing.

Even then, he might have stayed out on the floor if he'd thought it would give the Slasher an opportunity to slip a note in his pocket. But while the women were rubbing up against him and touching him, he didn't feel anything being put inside his pockets. And given the damage to the victims, he wasn't sure that a woman could have inflicted it.

Some of the victims had been big guys. Wouldn't they have been able to fight off a woman?

No. It was more likely a man who'd done the damage. A left-handed man, according to the medical examiner who'd studied the wounds of all the victims. So he studied the guys who called out to Kiki, wondering if it was one of them.

And he broke away from the women and leaped over the barricade to join Kiki in her booth that was already over-crowded with equipment. If he was going to dance with anyone, it was going to be her. Hell, he'd rather do more than dance with her.

But he was here to find a killer.

Not a good time.

FLETCHER COULD DANCE. First with the women.

She would have been concerned that he was getting a note slipped in one of his pockets, but she knew those women well. They really were her girls. They came out to the clubs because they loved to dance.

"You've been holding out on me," Kiki said when he joined her in the booth. "Making it sound like you didn't even know how to..."

"I never said I couldn't. Just that I don't because I don't want to," he explained. But he was moving with her, against her, grinding up on her.

Instead of being offended, she giggled. And she'd thought he was uptight.

Fletcher Colton was full of surprises. And damn, he looked good. He wore a tight white T-shirt that changed color with every flash of the strobe lights. To hide his holster and his weapon, over the T-shirt he wore a light checked button-down shirt, but she had insisted that he leave it unbuttoned. And he had.

The jeans were loose and baggy but with enough holes to show off the hair on his muscular legs. And to make her heart race a little every time she looked at him. Or felt that brush of hair against her bare legs. She wore leather again, but shorts and a vest. And instead of black, she wore red—nearly the same color of the tips of her hair that swung around her shoulders as she danced.

Music filled her. Lifted her.

It had always been like that, ever since she was a little kid. She moved to it as if it was inside her, guiding her arms and legs. Her heart thumped in perfect tempo with the beat, just as heavy and deep. Except for now.

With Fletcher dancing with her.

Now her heart beat faster and faster with every touch of his body against hers.

She twirled in his arms and leaned close to his ear, whispering, "Aren't you supposed to be investigating?"

"I'm making sure my cover works," Fletcher said, grinning as if he knew how badly he was getting to her.

How much he was making her want him.

Like in the dressing room earlier this week, when she'd touched his hair and had wanted to keep on touching it. She'd touched it earlier when he'd showed up at the club to help her unload the equipment. She'd put some mousse in it, played with it, all on the pretext of making him look the part of her assistant.

Troy had never looked like this. While some women had probably found him attractive and danced with him, the crowd hadn't reacted to him like they had Fletcher.

And, while she had danced with other people before, she hadn't reacted to anyone like she was reacting to dancing with Fletcher. Because she wanted to do more than dance.

Her heart pounded so hard that she struggled to breathe. She needed air and some distance from her sexy assistant. "You can man the turntables while I take a bathroom break, then," she told him.

"What?" His green eyes widened with shock and fear.

She wasn't really leaving him to play anything, she explained. She'd already put a set of songs in order, including the requests from some bachelor party attendees. The music would keep pumping from the speakers while she caught the breath she'd lost, that her lungs ached to find again.

She wasn't out of breath from the dancing or from the spinning but from the closeness of Fletcher Colton. Of how he looked and of how he made her feel...

So damn attracted to him.

She slipped past him and down the couple of steps to the barricade that she vaulted herself over. As she moved through the crowd, guys called out to her and tried to dance with her like Fletcher had been. But she didn't stop moving until she pushed her way into the crowded bathroom.

Women moved aside and applauded while they chattered at and around her.

"Kiki, you're the best!"

"Kiki, what a huge improvement over Troy."

"I liked Troy."

"Yeah, we know why."

"Who is he?" one of her usual crew asked. Claire was a blonde who always wore bright red lipstick.

"He's hot!" Janie said. Her hair was dark like Kiki's but wildly curly, even a little frizzy tonight—probably from the heat.

"He yours?" Amy asked. She was a redhead, but probably about as natural a redhead as the tips of Kiki's hair were natural.

Kiki's pulse quickened even more at the thought of that. Of Fletcher being hers.

But she didn't want anyone. Not really. At least not for keeps. That would make life too complicated. She was committed to traveling from club to club, building her brand so that she could get a record deal like so many other DJs she knew.

She shook her head. "He's just an old friend."

Janie snorted. "Looks like more than that."

"Is he?" Amy asked with a trace of disappointment.

Feeling a pang of jealousy that these women were so interested in Fletcher, she smiled slightly, smugly, as if she was claiming him. "Now, ladies, I need to use the bathroom so I can get back to the turntables."

As she slipped into a stall, voices called out to her, requesting songs. Someday, maybe, the song they requested would be one of hers.

That was the dream, one she'd had since she was a little girl and had felt that music moving inside her. But the music wasn't the only thing inside her tonight.

Tonight, she had that overwhelming attraction to Fletcher. And all these women talking about him, drooling over him, only made him more attractive to her. As if he hadn't already been attractive enough.

But he was only here because of the case. She had to remind herself of that, of the Slasher. Detective Fletcher Colton wasn't here to dance with her or to drive her to distraction over how damn attractive she found him.

He was here to catch someone before that person hurt anyone else. That was what mattered most. Making sure nobody else got hurt, or worse.

A little flicker of fear shortened her breath for a moment as she worried that she might be the one getting hurt if she wasn't careful. Not by the Slasher.

But by Fletcher, if she acted on this attraction she felt for him. She couldn't do that for so many reasons. She had her friendship with his sister Ruby, her busy schedule, her life goals...

Their careers were going to take them in different directions. His was going to take him into dangerous places.

And she'd already lost people she'd loved. She couldn't fall for Fletcher.

THE SLASHER NEEDED another victim. The police wouldn't be able to keep another attack from the media. Wouldn't be able to keep the story from spreading, from going national like the other attacks had.

The Slasher needed another victim because they needed the attention, the fear, the respect.

So they were at their usual hunting ground. A crowded club.

There were so many men to choose from.

Even Kiki had brought someone new tonight.

Someone to help her with the equipment. Or was he her boyfriend? The way they'd danced together, the way they'd looked at each other...

They definitely knew each other well. There was an intimacy between them. If not, the Slasher would have been concerned that this man was something else...

Like a police officer.

Would one go undercover to catch the Slasher?

Were they that important?

How many different police departments and agencies were trying to catch them?

Trying to stop them?

Nothing and nobody would. And if anyone tried to get in their way...

They would wind up being the next victim of the Slasher, and maybe that person would lose more than their looks.

Maybe they would lose their life...

Chapter Nine

Fletcher wanted nothing to do with the turntables or with all the requests being shouted at him while Kiki was gone. Where had she gone? Just the restroom?

Not the alley.

His pulse quickened as he thought of that—of her becoming a victim of the Slasher. The serial attacker hadn't gone after women before, but that didn't mean that the person wouldn't, especially if Kiki stepped into the alley at the wrong moment. As he started across the dance floor toward the bar and the door behind it through which they'd dragged all her equipment, he got distracted by the sound of a familiar, raspy voice.

"Let go of me," Kiki said with indignation and determination.

"You danced with that loser but you won't dance with me?" The man sounded indignant as well. "It's my bachelor party. Come on."

"I know, and I've been playing your favorite songs," Kiki replied. "And to keep doing that, I need to get back to my booth."

"Just one dance. Or a drink. I'll buy you a drink. I can buy you a lot of things, pretty Kiki."

"I am not for sale," she said. "Now let me go!"

"Let her go!" Fletcher growled as he pushed through to where some guy, just a little taller than Kiki, was holding tightly to one of her bare arms.

Kiki tried wrestling free, but the man's grip tightened to the point her skin was turning red.

"Oh, here's your lapdog now," the guy remarked with a disparaging smirk. "Come on, Kiki, give up losers like this for real men. Men with means."

"I don't—"

Fletcher didn't interrupt her. He just grabbed the man and jerked his arm behind his back so that it fell away from hers. With the abrupt release, she stumbled back a step into the crowd that had gathered around them.

The guy wrestled in Fletcher's grasp. "How dare you! Get your hands off me!"

"I will break your arm," he threatened. He raised the man's arm a little higher behind his back until he cried out. "Don't you ever touch her again."

"Let me go!" the guy said again, but it was more of a frightened whine than the condescending demand it had been earlier.

Fletcher twisted the guy's arm just a little harder before he released him. The minute he did, the guy swung his fist toward him. Fletcher ducked and swung back, striking him just enough to knock him into the man's friends who'd gathered behind them. "Now get the hell out."

Finally, the bouncers arrived, dragging the man from the

crowd, as he hurled insults and protestations. "This is my bachelor party! Do you know who I am?"

Nobody cared. The mocking laughter of the crowd followed the guy out along with a few of his friends.

"You're going to be sorry!" was his last pitiful proclamation.

The laughter got louder.

Nobody was.

But the way Kiki looked at Fletcher, glaring as she rushed past him toward her booth, he figured he might be sorry later when she had time to talk to him. What had she wanted him to do? Let the guy hurt her?

The thought wrenched his guts, making him feel sick. While she might have been annoyed with him, nobody else was. They all patted his back and shoulders. "Way to protect Kiki!"

"Let me buy you a drink," someone offered, and he was swept up with the crowd gathered around the bar until he was up against the long peninsula of granite and glass.

"Drink's on me," the bartender said when cards and money were extended toward him.

"Just coffee," Fletcher told him. He couldn't drink on the job, especially this job. He needed to be alert to deal with the Slasher. And if he had alcohol, tired as he was, he wouldn't be able to stay awake. Unless he watched Kiki.

"Everybody, get back on the floor!" Kiki's command echoed from the speakers. "I need you all out here. I need you to…" Her voice trailed off, replaced with the upbeat music and song, "Dance, dance, dance!"

The clubgoers shrieked and headed back out, jumping and yelling along with the lyrics. With Kiki.

She wanted the drama involving her forgotten. She wanted to focus on the music, on other people having a good time. That seemed very important to her.

The bartender leaned over the bar, that was a whole lot less crowded now, and said, "Thanks for getting rid of that entitled ass. Too many rich guys come in here thinking they can have whatever they want."

Fletcher focused on the bartender. With dark blond hair and stubble on his pointy chin, he was probably a little younger than Fletcher—maybe late twenties, like Kiki's age. But there was a jadedness to him already, despite his youth.

"Must get sickening," Fletcher agreed with him. "Having to listen to them spout off about how important they are."

The bartender nodded. "You have no idea. Just because they have money, they think they can treat everybody like dirt." He snorted. "Money doesn't buy class or manners, that's for damn sure."

Fletcher was glad that when he'd met the bartender earlier that evening, when he and Kiki had been bringing in her equipment, he hadn't shared his last name. Thanks to his dad's real estate investments, the Coltons had money. Fortunately, thanks to how their mom had raised them, they also had class and manners.

But this guy seemed to lump all rich people together and equate them with rudeness and entitlement. He'd probably had some bad experiences over the years, but it looked like his bitterness about rich guys ran pretty deep.

Had all the Slasher's victims had money?

Fletcher made a mental note to follow up on that. Wanting to show camaraderie with his new acquaintance, he grinned and picked up the mug of coffee. "Thanks," he said. "And cheers to getting rid of entitled jerks!"

The bartender grinned.

"Cheers," another voice chimed in.

Fletcher glanced down the bar to where an older man sat alone, his glass lifted toward Fletcher. With iron gray hair and several deep lines in his face, this guy had to be in his sixties. He didn't look like the other clubgoers. Maybe he owned the place.

Fletcher leaned across the bar and asked the bartender, "What's his story? Owner?"

The bartender snorted. "No. Just a regular customer. He comes around a lot."

"Really?" Fletcher asked. The guy didn't seem to be into the music, but he kept looking at the dance floor.

"Yeah, I thought he was a cop at first, but he's actually just a dad looking for his missing daughter."

A pang of sympathy for the distraught father struck Fletcher. "Oh…"

"Yeah, sucks. He hasn't seen her for a few years. Don't know why he thinks he's going to just happen to run into her in a club someday." He shrugged. "But whatever…"

"Bart! Bart!" a male customer called from the end of the bar.

"Gotta go," Bart said. "Don't wanna keep these entitled jerks waiting."

When the bartender walked away, Fletcher approached the older guy. "Cheers," he said to him again.

Unlike the bartender, who wore a black uniform that was fading to gray from age and frequent washing, this guy wore a suit that looked tailored and expensive. He also wore an expensive watch on his right hand, which probably made him a lefty. He could have been one of the entitled jerks that Bart and Fletcher had been talking about.

Hell, with the shares of Colton Properties that Fletcher had just inherited, he could probably be one of those entitled jerks. But he hadn't even stuck around for the reading of the will to find out what the value of those shares were. It had been too hard.

Losing someone sucked.

"Cheers," the stranger repeated. "Better enjoy your drink because I think you're in a little bit of trouble."

"How's that?" Fletcher asked. "Think that guy is going to call the police?" It would be funny if he did.

But Fletcher didn't want to blow his cover.

"Kiki doesn't seem too happy with you," the guy said with a slight grin.

Fletcher groaned. "Yeah."

"She can take care of herself."

The way she'd whirled on him with that pepper spray last weekend, she'd proved that she could. But with the Slasher on the loose...

And the way that jerk had been squeezing her arm...

She would probably have bruises, and that infuriated Fletcher. "I actually showed some restraint," Fletcher insisted. He hadn't thrown the first punch, and he hadn't broken the guy's arm like he'd been tempted to for hurting Kiki.

The man chuckled. "I doubt Kiki's going to see it that way, especially since it was the guy's bachelor party."

"So, you know Kiki pretty well," Fletcher remarked. And he also paid a lot of attention to what was going on in the club since he'd known that the guy who'd hit on her was the guest of honor at his bachelor party. Was this stranger so observant just because he was looking for his daughter?

The guy shook his head. "No, I don't know Kiki all that well. I've just been at some clubs while she's playing the music."

He definitely wasn't part of the club scene, despite how often he must frequent them. Fletcher could relate.

"You haven't been with her before," the gentleman observed. "She usually has some skinny, tattooed guy with her. Where's he tonight?"

Fletcher shrugged. "Good question. He took off on her last weekend and hasn't been seen since."

Fletcher saw him flinch and regretted that he'd probably reminded the older man of his missing daughter. Had she run away from home? Was that how he'd lost track of her?

Fletcher wanted to ask these questions, but appearing too interested would risk his cover, too. He narrowed his eyes and studied the guy. "Are you a cop?" he asked.

The man grimaced. "No. I don't have much use for the police."

"Why's that?" Fletcher asked.

The stranger sighed. "They don't give some things, some people, the attention they deserve."

The Slasher was all about getting attention, but Fletcher hadn't been able to figure out why yet. Was this it? Because the man wasn't getting the help he wanted to find his daughter?

"I'm sorry," Fletcher said.

"Why?" the man asked, narrowing his blue eyes. "Are you a cop?"

Ignoring the jab of concern that he had risked his cover, he laughed heartily. "That's funny," he said. "Me? A cop?"

"So then you're more like her other assistant?" the man asked.

And Fletcher wondered now if the man was looking for his daughter or for drugs. "No. I'm nothing like Troy either," he assured him. "Kiki and I are old friends. I just stepped in to help her out."

Until the Slasher was caught.

And Fletcher needed that to happen soon, before anyone else got hurt. Or worse.

KIKI SHOULD HAVE been relieved that Fletcher stayed away from her booth. She was annoyed that he'd felt the need to step into that situation on the dance floor.

Like she'd needed his help.

Like he thought she couldn't take care of herself.

She'd been handling jerks like that for a long time on her own. She knew how to get rid of them. A few sharp words cut up their egos like the Slasher.

No. Nothing compared to what the Slasher did to their victims. Nothing.

She couldn't get over the sight of the victim she'd visited in the hospital. And she hadn't seen him until after he'd been treated. She couldn't imagine what Troy must have seen when he'd found that victim in the alley behind that Salt Lake City club. No wonder he'd taken off when he'd heard about another attack.

Though apparently, he had other reasons to avoid the authorities. She felt a pang of guilt over that, over helping him evade his responsibilities. But she'd had no idea he had children. And just because he was a deadbeat dad, it didn't make him the Slasher like Fletcher clearly suspected he was.

But why?

What would his motive have been?

What was the Slasher's motive for hurting people so horrifically? For disfiguring them like that?

She shivered despite the warmth of the crowded club. And she tried to peer through that mob of people to catch sight of Fletcher.

Where had he gone?

Was he still wrestling with that creep who'd hit on her? Or was he wrestling with someone far more dangerous? Trying to get a better view, she climbed onto one of the speakers in the booth. She danced along with the music she played while searching the crowd.

She caught sight of him, his dark hair mussed despite the mousse she'd put in it for him—or maybe because of it, since she'd kept playing with the soft strands. Or had one of the women who'd danced with Fletcher messed it up? Or maybe it had happened during his tussle with that boor of a bachelor who had acted like his money could get him whatever he wanted from any woman.

She snorted at the thought. She would play song requests, but those were the only requests she fulfilled. And most everyone who came to her shows knew that.

Did Fletcher know that? And if he did, why hadn't he let her handle that creep on her own?

She'd done it plenty of times. She hadn't asked for his help. She didn't need him, but she damn well wanted him. He was so attractive.

From her vantage point on her speaker, she peered around

the club, trying to find him. He was at the bar talking to Mr. Sullivan. She'd met the guy a couple of years ago, and every time she saw him, her heart ached for his sadness and desperation.

He'd shown her a picture of his daughter, asking if Kiki had seen her. If she had, she wouldn't have recognized her as the girl wearing a school uniform, her hair pulled back into a tight ponytail. If Kiki had ever seen her, the girl had probably looked like so many others who hung around the clubs, desperate to have a good time.

Some were a little too desperate.

Desperate to look older, prettier, more desirable. So desperate that they sometimes made bad choices. Kiki didn't know for sure if that was what had happened to Dan Sullivan's daughter any more than she knew for certain if she'd ever seen her before.

She'd disappointed the older man because she couldn't help him. Fletcher could. But was that why he was at the bar talking to the man?

Or did he wonder if he was the Slasher, just like he'd suspected Troy, too?

Fletcher's head turned from the bar toward her. Across that crowded room, she couldn't see his eyes, but she could feel the intensity of his gaze.

That look he'd been giving her every time they came into contact. Lately, they'd connected a little too often for unfortunate reasons.

His father's funeral.

The attack at the club in Conners.

But every time they saw each other, they had this bizarre connection. He found her as attractive as she found him.

But neither of them could afford a distraction right now, not with that dangerous attacker out there, probably prowling clubs for another victim.

Was that Fletcher's real reason for going undercover at the club? Not just to find clues to the Slasher's identity but to get the Slasher to try to attack him?

He'd wanted the loose jeans—loose enough to chase after a suspect, but also loose enough for a note to be slipped into his pocket.

That was why she'd been so desperate to find him in the crowd. To make sure he was still inside the club and not out in the alley.

Because ever since their shopping trip, she'd had the horrible feeling that Fletcher was using himself as bait for this vicious person. That he was setting himself up to be the Slasher's next victim.

Chapter Ten

Fletcher had avoided Kiki since he'd saved her from that drunk because, like the man at the bar, Fletcher doubted that was how she'd seen it. That he'd saved her.

She probably just figured he'd interfered. And he had no doubt that he would hear about it when the night was over, and when he was alone with her. Despite knowing he would probably get told off, he couldn't wait for the night to end. And not just so that he could be alone with her.

He was so damn tired. It wasn't for lack of sleep. He was used to working late, sometimes even around the clock, when he had a case to solve. He was tired because of the noise and the music and the definite attraction he felt for Kiki.

She was amazing.

The way she worked all that complicated equipment left him in awe. The sounds she made…

Especially when she sang along with some of the lyrics. Her voice was amazing. Sexy and vibrant and hauntingly beautiful. Just like her.

When she danced, she moved like the music was inside her, pouring out of her every pore. She was so captivating it was nearly impossible to look away from her. Like everybody else in the club, he watched her now, dancing away behind the turntables.

She'd even been on top of one of the speakers earlier tonight. As if she'd been looking for him—and maybe she had been, because once their gazes had met, she'd jumped down. And he'd felt a little flicker of excitement that she might have been concerned about him.

With the way she kept distracting him, just by being her, how the hell was he going to catch the Slasher?

Sure, he'd been working, subtly interviewing that distraught father and the bartender. He'd gotten Dan Sullivan's name and his daughter's name. Caitlin.

He'd gotten the bartender's full name, too. Bart Taylor. Fletcher had even managed to sneak one of the glasses the man had touched beneath his shirt and then into the duffel bag he had slipped in with Kiki's equipment. He would run it for prints. Check out the man's past.

Find out why he hated rich guys so damn much.

If only the Slasher had ever left prints at the scene— something to match them to. But while several prints had been found at every scene, in every alley, none of them had been the same. The wounds and the weapon that had made them had all matched, though, so the Slasher must be just one solitary person committing every assault.

A left-handed person. A coroner had studied the wounds and determined that from the depth and direction of the cuts, a left-handed person had swung the blade.

The bartender was left-handed.

So was Dan Sullivan.

Fletcher hadn't realized there were so many left-handed

people until he'd started looking for them in the club. The bartender and Sullivan hadn't been the only ones. The way other patrons had waved at the bartender to order drinks or some of the women had waved at Fletcher to draw his attention had shown they were probably left-handed, too.

What about Troy?

Kiki's former assistant was still high on his list of suspects. Where was he? The bartender had mentioned to Fletcher that he'd thought he'd seen him earlier. Someone else had said the same, but Fletcher had searched the crowd and hadn't caught any sight of him. He'd even searched the alley, too. Hell, he'd made a point of going out there at least once an hour to see if the Slasher was lying in wait for someone.

Or if they'd already attacked.

Did Kiki have any idea where her assistant was? She hadn't even known the guy's last name, or about his drug possession charge and back child support. Fletcher doubted she knew anything else about the man that would help locate him. But maybe she would know if he was left-handed or not.

If she would talk to him…

So far all she'd done was glare at him since he'd pulled that drunk off her on the dance floor.

Fletcher had wanted to check on her, to see if her arm had bruised from how tightly the guy had been gripping it. But the one time he'd gotten close, when he'd slipped that glass into his duffel bag, she'd given him such a look, all tight lips and lowered brows.

He was probably in more danger from her than from the

Slasher right now. Nobody had tried to slip him a note. His pockets were empty. And the night was nearly over.

No. The night was over. It was early morning now.

Kiki had shouted "last call" and the songs were winding down in tempo while the lights gradually got brighter.

And the crowd thinned out.

Dan Sullivan had left a while ago.

The bartender had slipped away after fulfilling the last call orders. He was probably in the back, washing dirty glasses. Or maybe looking for one.

No. He wouldn't miss the one that Fletcher had tucked into his duffel bag. He wished he'd managed to get Dan Sullivan's glass, too, but the guy had only had one drink and he'd kept his hands around it the whole night, as if he'd been worried that someone would slip something in it.

Was that what he'd thought happened to his daughter?

While Fletcher had gotten him talking about his daughter, the man had just showed him his picture and said that she'd always liked going to nightclubs, even when she wasn't really old enough to get in.

So maybe he blamed nightclubs for her going missing. And the attacks on clubgoers was his way of getting revenge.

Because the viciousness of those attacks made them feel so personal.

Like someone was after something.

Notoriety or revenge?

Or both?

Fletcher sighed, which turned into a yawn so big that he closed his eyes and leaned against the barricade he'd been standing near, just outside Kiki's booth.

"Hey, old man, try to stay awake," Kiki chastised him, her voice soft and close to his ear.

Realizing that her voice was the only sound he heard but for a buzzing echo, he opened his eyes and blinked against the brightness of the lights. "Is it over?" he asked, letting his eagerness slip out. Maybe it hadn't been the eventful night he'd hoped it would be, but while he hadn't had a note slipped in his pocket, he had found some more potential suspects. Besides Troy.

The bartender had mentioned seeing him in the club, but when Fletcher had looked around, he hadn't seen anyone who'd matched the description he'd had of the man. Had he been there? Maybe he'd intended to help Kiki after all.

And then he'd seen Fletcher. Too bad Fletcher hadn't seen him.

"Yes, it's over," Kiki said, "and I have a lot of equipment you need to help carry out, since you're so helpful and all..."

Fletcher flinched. "I figured I would pay for that."

"For making a scene? For embarrassing me?"

"The scene was already being made," he said. "That guy was a jerk."

"He was drunk and acting like a bigshot in front of his friends," she said. "It was his bachelor party."

"That doesn't give him the right to harass you," Fletcher said, appalled. "I'm glad I decided long ago to never get married."

"You don't want to get married?" she asked.

He shook his head. His parents had not had the ideal marriage. He wasn't sure if it was just because of how much his dad had always worked but knowing how his own relationships hadn't withstood his work schedule, he wasn't going to risk anything more permanent. "Nope. And really, I don't think that guy should either. What a dick."

Those lips, which had been tightly drawn together, twitched up into a smile. "Yeah, he was, but I would have handled him so that I didn't ruin his evening."

"I doubt his evening was ruined. I'm sure he went on to another bar," Fletcher assured her. "Or maybe a strip club."

She sighed. "He did kind of act like that was where he thought he was."

"I'm sure their bouncers would toss him out, too, if he tried anything," Fletcher said, and he was smiling now at the thought.

"You are not a bouncer, though," she said, and she reached over the barricade, poking him in the chest. "You didn't need to rush to my rescue because I am not some damsel in need of saving."

He tried to fight his widening smile so that he wouldn't infuriate her even more than he already had. But she was so damned beautiful when she was feisty like this. Hell, she was always so damned beautiful. He nodded. "I know. But I didn't want you to get hurt."

He looked at her arm now. The bright lights illuminated the mark on her skin that was still red from how tightly the man had gripped her. And Fletcher wished he'd hit the guy a little harder.

She glanced down at where his gaze was focused and shrugged. "I get bigger bruises than that hauling this equipment around," she said. "That's nothing. And if he'd not let me go, he would have gotten an injury that would have had a terrible effect on his wedding night."

Fletcher chuckled. "Okay. Remind me not to piss you off again."

She nodded. "Oh, I will," she promised.

He chuckled again. "Oh, I have no doubt that you will."

"You're kind of pissing me off right now," she said.

"How's that?"

"You're stalling when we have work to do," she pointed out. "Let's get this equipment out to the SUV."

He tensed. "Are you going to come around to the alley again like when we unloaded it?"

"You're too tired to schlep it out to the parking lot?" she asked with a teasing smile.

"No," he said. "We can do that. But first, I do need to check the alley."

Especially since all his suspects had disappeared a while ago.

What if one of them had attacked someone else while he'd been in the club, drooling over Kiki? He would never forgive himself for getting so distracted.

But he would also never forgive himself if something happened to her. "No. I'll check the alley after I walk you out to your SUV."

She narrowed her eyes and glared at him. "If I thought I needed a guard dog, I'd bring Fancy to work with me."

He chuckled. "Fancy is pretty young to be a guard dog."

"She's feisty."

"Like her owner."

"I'm not her owner," Kiki said with a trace of regret. "Just her foster mom."

"You never get attached to these puppies you foster and want to keep one?" he asked.

She shook her head. "No. I travel too much to have a pet or a relationship."

Was she warning him off? She probably couldn't miss how attracted to her that he was. But it was just attraction. Nothing more.

Attraction and concern.

"We'll carry out some of the lighter things to your vehicle," he said. "Then you can drive it back to the alley and we'll get the heavier stuff."

She sighed but nodded. "Okay."

He was going to make her wait until he checked the alley before she pulled her vehicle into it, though. He didn't want her to find another victim, either with him or without him.

KIKI'S IRRITATION WITH Fletcher slipped away the minute they stepped outside the club. The parking lot wasn't very well lit, like the one in Conners.

And the night was eerily quiet. Not even a cicada sang or a cricket chirped.

Apprehension raced over her like a cold breeze, and she shivered.

"Here," Fletcher said. "Take my shirt." While holding one of her turntables, he managed to pull off his shirt and drape it over her shoulders.

She would have refused, but it was warm, and it smelled like him—like soap and man. "Aren't you worried about someone seeing your holster and gun?" she asked.

"If they're out here in the dark, it might be a good thing if they do," he said.

The Slasher hadn't ever attacked an armed man. So it was definitely a good thing, especially since she suspected

Fletcher was going to insist on checking the alley alone once he'd walked her to her vehicle.

Her grandfather would have been charmed by Fletcher's protectiveness and chivalry. Kiki kept trying to tell herself that she was annoyed.

But she might have been just a little bit charmed as well. Not that she was taking it personally. As a lawman, Fletcher had taken that whole oath to protect and serve or serve and protect… Whatever it was.

He was really undercover to protect any more men from being attacked by the Slasher.

Even though she was happy that she wasn't out here alone in this eerie and all-encompassing darkness, she felt compelled to say, "You really don't need to walk me to my vehicle. I'm not in danger from the Slasher."

"We already talked about that," he said. "If he or she feels threatened…"

She snorted. "I'm not carrying the gun, and I have no idea who would do something like that." She certainly hoped she didn't know someone that vicious and evil.

"I'm not just concerned about the Slasher," Fletcher said. "I don't entirely trust that bachelor party groom wouldn't come back after the club closed."

"Then once again, you're probably in more danger than I am," she said. She'd considered that, though, and her pepper spray canister was hooked to one of the belt loops of her red leather shorts. Just in case.

Kiki believed in being better safe than sorry, which was why she wanted to ignore this attraction she felt for Fletcher. But the heat from his shirt, and the scent of him in the fabric, titillated her senses.

"Why'd you park so far out?" Fletcher asked. Clearly, he was more annoyed than titillated.

"I parked out here because I couldn't leave my vehicle in the alley where we unloaded," she reminded him. "And by the time we unloaded it, the lot was already starting to fill up so I had to park out here."

Fletcher groaned.

"We're almost there," she assured him, clicking the key fob so that the lights on her SUV blinked on. "Despite all that coffee I saw you drinking, you're still tired. Not used to staying up so late?"

"It's more these boots you had me buy. As expensive as they were, I expected them to be more comfortable," he grumbled.

"You need to break them in first," she said.

"I thought I was…with the dancing." He did a couple fancy cha-cha steps.

Kiki laughed. She clicked to open the back of her SUV, setting her stuff inside the hatch.

"You've been holding out on me, Colton. You're going to have to salsa with me." She reached out and grasped his hips, trying to move them back as she took a couple of steps toward him. But he didn't move, and suddenly she was flush against his long, hard body. "You're supposed to dance."

"I don't know how to salsa," he said, his voice a little gruff. And even in the dim light from the hatch of her SUV, his eyes glittered as he stared down at her.

The intensity of that stare moved inside her like the music did, making her want him so damn badly. With her heels on, she wasn't that much shorter than he was, so his face wasn't that much above hers. Her gaze moved to his lips, and yearning filled her, making her stretch just a bit until their mouths were so close that there was only a breath between them.

Fletcher groaned.

And Kiki smiled. "Feet still hurting from those new boots?"

"It's not the boots that are bothering me now," he admitted in a husky whisper.

"What's bothering you?" Kiki asked. But as close as she was to him, she could feel his body's reaction to hers.

"You are," he said, and his breath whispered across her mouth.

She parted her lips, breathing him in before releasing a shaky, wistful sigh. "Fletcher…" She couldn't remember the last time she'd been this attracted to someone. And they hadn't even kissed.

She stretched up a bit and brushed her mouth across his. And heat swept through her body.

"This is a bad idea," Fletcher murmured.

"What?" she asked, playing coy.

"I can't afford any distractions right now, not with this investigation, and my cover…" But then he kissed her back, as she'd kissed him, just brushing his mouth across hers before pulling back.

"What's the distraction?" she asked.

"You are," he repeated. "So damn distracting…" And he kissed her again. Deeply. His mouth settling firmly against hers.

She parted her lips and deepened the kiss even more. Their tongues touched, flirted, teased and, again, desire coursed through her like music, making her body want to move with his.

But then that eerie silence broke, something smashing against something, like the sound of glass breaking. They jerked apart, Fletcher reaching for his weapon.

"What? Where..." she murmured.

"Stay here," Fletcher whispered, and he moved back toward the club, disappearing into the darkness.

Had the sound come from the alley? The way it had echoed, it probably had.

Maybe it was just the bartender or someone else who worked at the club dumping something into the trash behind the building. Or...

It was the Slasher attacking another victim, and Fletcher was either going to stop it or put himself in danger as well. Her heart pounded fast and hard with fear.

For him.

Then she heard something closer. And she was scared for herself.

She'd parked so far out that the SUV was near a field. Something moved in the grass, making it rustle softly. It was probably just an animal.

The real threat was in that alley, where Fletcher had rushed off to.

He was the one in danger.

She had no reason to be afraid, except for worrying over him. Maybe she was also afraid over that kiss.

Another sound emanated from the field, something low and forlorn.

Maybe that animal she'd heard was in pain. Hurt.

She took a few tentative steps away from the SUV.

Fletcher hadn't meant for her to stay exactly where he'd left her. He just hadn't wanted her to follow him.

She understood that. She had no gun. And she didn't want to be a distraction to him, like he'd already accused her of being. She didn't want him to get hurt because of her.

And she didn't want any other living creature in harm's way either. Peering into the darkness, she walked closer, until she stood just inside the tall weeds of that field. She tilted her head and listened.

Not just for that sound she'd heard but also to the soft rumble of Fletcher's voice. He'd found something in the alley. But he hadn't fired his weapon.

Maybe everything was fine. It had just been what she'd thought: an employee throwing trash into the dumpster. Fletcher was fine.

But then something reached out of the weeds and darkness and grabbed her, and she knew she was the one in danger. As she fumbled for the pepper spray on her belt loop, she opened her mouth and screamed. But if it was the Slasher who'd grabbed her, help would probably come too late to save her.

Chapter Eleven

One minute Fletcher had been talking to the bartender, Bart Taylor, in the alley where the man had dropped a crate of empty bottles, and the next that scream had rung out.

Kiki's scream.

God, he'd thought she was safe. Safer out there than if she'd followed him into the alley. Fear gripping him, he ran back toward the lot, toward where he'd left her.

But he didn't see her standing near her SUV. The dome lights casting a glow out of the hatch didn't illuminate her. "Kiki?" he called out, his voice cracking a bit with his concern for her.

"Here!" she yelled. "Over here! Call an ambulance!" Her voice was high with fear or adrenaline or both.

"Are you hurt?" he asked, that alarm gripping him still, squeezing his heart.

"Not me. But…there's another victim…"

Fletcher found her standing in a field just beyond her vehicle. She seemed fine, just slightly shaky as she pointed down at the ground.

"I don't want to move him."

Fletcher holstered his weapon and pulled out his cell. The

light from the screen illuminated the area and the body lying in the weeds, blood pooling all around it. He was facedown, the back of his head bloodied with maybe a cracked skull.

Fletcher dropped to his knees next to the man, reaching for his wrist to check for a pulse. "Is he dead?"

"No," Kiki said. "He—he grabbed my ankle…"

And Fletcher could see now that the man's arm was outstretched toward Kiki. And there was blood smeared on her skin.

The man's hands and arms were cut. But there was a pulse, albeit faint and slow. Fletcher called in to dispatch, requesting an ambulance and a police response. He glanced around, making sure the bartender wasn't close enough to hear, then he identified himself, gave his badge number and added, "Make sure no one acknowledges me. I'm undercover so question me like any other witness."

But he wasn't like any other witness because he hadn't seen a damn thing. He'd been distracted, just like he'd told Kiki, with her. While he'd kept checking the alley for the Slasher or for another victim, he hadn't thought to check out the parking lot. Hell, he hadn't even noticed anything when he'd walked Kiki to her SUV, and given the blood, the guy had been lying here for a while.

"Should we do something?" Kiki asked. "Roll him over? Make sure he's breathing?"

"With his head wound…" Fletcher was hesitant about moving him. "I don't want to hurt him any worse than he already is."

"But he could be dying."

Fletcher touched the guy's wrist again, and that thready pulse was gone now. His skin even slightly chilled. He hated to move the guy, but in order to administer CPR, the victim had to be on his back.

Fletcher slowly rolled him over, being so careful of his head, and even he gasped while some strangled sound slipped through the hand Kiki had clasped over her mouth.

"Oh, my God…"

There were deep slashes across the guy's face, but despite the wounds, Fletcher recognized him. He was the groom with whom he'd tussled on the dance floor.

"Oh, my God…" Kiki murmured again.

Fletcher didn't know if she recognized him, too, or if she was just horrified by the injuries, the deep lacerations across the guy's face and chest and arms.

He leaned closer to him, listening for breath, watching his damaged chest to see if it was moving, and he heard a soft rattle from it. He was still breathing, but his lungs were filling, probably with blood. "He doesn't need CPR," Fletcher said.

He needed far more help than Fletcher's first aid training had covered. Sirens whined in the distance, gradually getting louder and louder as the ambulance and police approached. And Fletcher let out a little breath of his own—of relief that help was arriving.

He wasn't sure, though, if they would be able to save the guy either, not with how badly he was wounded. He was by far the most seriously injured of the Slasher's victims.

Just as Fletcher had feared, the level of violence was escalating. And it was only a matter of time before an attack became fatal and claimed a life.

KIKI WAS SHAKEN. Too shaken to sleep. Too shaken to stay at Grandpa's cottage and not accidentally wake him up while she paced. So she just stopped at his house, picked up Fancy and drove around the lake to the marina where the houseboat was docked.

She wouldn't disturb anyone else here. She'd left a note for Grandpa just in case he had heard her drive up. Knowing how light a sleeper he was, he probably had.

That was why she'd rushed around to get out of the house, with Fancy and a bag of clothes and toiletries, before he came out of his bedroom. She hadn't wanted to talk about what had happened that night.

What she'd found.

The latest victim of the Slasher.

What a maniac. A monster, really, because how could one human being do that to another?

She shuddered despite the fact that she still wore Fletcher's shirt. The cotton was pretty thin, though, and it had lost the warmth of his body that it had when he'd first given it to her.

He'd lost his warmth, too, when the ambulance and the police had arrived. He'd been all business, talking to everyone else almost furtively, probably because he hadn't wanted to blow his cover.

And another officer or detective had questioned her. Kiki had been so shocked by what she'd found, by that hand reaching out of the darkness and the weeds to grasp her ankle.

The scream had been instinctive, but her throat burned a little from how loudly she'd uttered it. And she trembled again from the terror she'd felt in that moment.

Fancy whimpered. Either the puppy had picked up on

Kiki's fear, or she was nervous walking down the dock toward the houseboat.

Water lapped against the boats they passed and against the posts of the dock, swirling around them in the faint light of the sliver of the moon overhead.

Where had that moon been earlier?

She could have used that in the parking lot. Then maybe she would have found him sooner.

The way the EMTs had looked—from how furiously they'd been working to the way they'd sped away, lights flashing and siren ringing out loudly...

It hadn't looked good.

She didn't know if he was going to make it. And she felt a pang of guilt for how she'd felt about the man earlier that evening, when he'd grabbed her arm.

It had been him, hadn't it?

Another groom-to-be celebrating his bachelor party like the last victim of the Slasher. What the hell did that person have against men like that?

Sure, this guy, whoever he was, had been a jerk. But the other man...

The victim she'd visited in the hospital hadn't seemed arrogant like that one. He'd even managed, despite his injuries, to laugh with her.

She wondered if tonight's victim would ever be able to laugh again. She wondered if she would, after finding him.

No wonder that Fletcher always seemed so intense. This was his life, the career he'd chosen for himself. To investigate crimes like the one that Kiki had literally stumbled across tonight.

The body.

No. The person. He had to live.

"Oh, Fancy…" Kiki murmured, her heart heavy with dread. With regret.

Maybe if she and Fletcher had done things differently…

Maybe if the man hadn't been evicted from the club…

Maybe he wouldn't have been hurt so badly.

Maybe he would be…

He had to be fine.

She wasn't sure that she would be again, after what she'd seen. She needed a beer and some soft music. Grandpa kept beer in the fridge in the galley on the boat. And she always had music with her. Either on her phone, or just inside her.

Maybe if she sang to herself…

People had said she was singing when she'd been found, in the wreckage of the crash that had killed her parents.

The wreckage she had escaped without a scratch on her. She didn't remember any of that. Maybe wiping the memories from her mind had been her childlike way of dealing with that horrific tragedy.

But she wasn't a child anymore. And she doubted she would be able to forget anything about tonight. About finding that man.

Or about that kiss she'd shared with Fletcher. If not for whatever had happened in the alley, maybe they would have…

No. Not in a parking lot. She wasn't some wild teenager. She never had been. She'd been tempted in that moment to act like a hormonal teen, though, to give in to her desire for Fletcher.

Thinking about that kiss should have been better than thinking about what had happened after it, but her pulse quickened even more. And the adrenaline was rushing through her again.

That kiss had been dangerous to her.

But why?

Fletcher had said he wasn't ever getting married, that he didn't have time for relationships either. And she certainly understood why. His work was definitely more important. Catching the Slasher was absolutely more important.

That was why, after answering the officer's questions, she'd left. The club had been pretty much sealed off, probably as a crime scene, so she trusted that her equipment would be safe there overnight.

She had another gig there this weekend, if the club was allowed to reopen, so it made sense to leave it there anyway. It was just so expensive, though, that she usually preferred to keep it with her.

But after what had happened to that man, she'd realized how inconsequential material things were. People mattered more. Maybe she should have stayed at Grandpa's.

But he was safe. Nothing was going to happen to him.

He was long past the age when he used to come to the clubs to watch her. She didn't have to worry about the Slasher attacking him.

But she still worried about him.

He'd always been there for her. She couldn't imagine a world without him in it.

Fancy whimpered again, reminding Kiki that she'd just stopped on the dock. She was near the houseboat, but her thoughts had been weighing so heavily on her that it seemed hard to step across the side and onto the boat deck. As if she might slip and fall between the boat and the dock.

Fancy probably feared that, too, because the puppy whimpered again.

"It's okay," Kiki assured her, and she bent over to scoop the puppy up in her arms. She held her close for a moment, burying her face in the dog's soft fur. Instead of reassuring the puppy, she was looking for comfort.

Maybe she should have woken up Grandpa. He had always been so good at comforting her. At making her feel better about everything.

But he was getting older, and she didn't want to burden him with things like this, things that would make him worry more about her than he already did.

And he already worried too much.

She understood, though, because she worried about him, too. She didn't want to lose him like they'd already lost her mother and father. She didn't want to lose anyone else she loved. Another reason she needed to make sure this attraction she felt for Fletcher didn't go any deeper, didn't become real feelings.

After tonight, she realized all too well just how dangerous his job was. That could have been him bleeding out in the blood-soaked, overgrown field.

She shuddered. And Fancy bristled in her arms. "Sorry," she murmured to the puppy. She was definitely not making the little dog less nervous.

"Here," she said. And she passed the dog over the side of the boat before stepping onto the deck herself. The boat rocked a bit on the softly lapping water.

Then Fancy headed toward the door to the cabin. The open door.

It should have been locked. Kiki had certainly locked it

the last time she'd been here. What about Grandpa? Had he forgotten?

He certainly believed Owl Creek was safer than anywhere else, which was why he preferred it when she was home. He had no idea how dangerous this place could be.

But after tonight, Kiki knew.

And she wondered if that danger had found her here.

Chapter Twelve

"Where the hell is she?" Fletcher asked.

But the night had no answer for him as he stood outside Jim's cottage. Her SUV wasn't parked in the driveway like it should have been, like he'd hoped it would be.

Sometime after she'd been questioned, she'd slipped away from the club. From the crime scene.

She'd even left her equipment behind, which had alarmed him. Why wouldn't she have waited for his help to load it up? Why would she have taken off without it?

While her equipment had been there, his duffel bag had gone missing. With that glass inside.

The bartender had stayed to answer questions, though, as had a couple of the waitresses, bouncers and dishwashers. They had all made certain to share that the last time they'd seen the victim had been when he'd been fighting with Fletcher over Kiki.

Was that why she'd taken off?

Did she suspect him of being involved like the club employees had?

No. The officer who'd questioned her had assured Fletcher that she'd alibied him. Even if the officer hadn't known that he was a detective, the young woman would have ruled him out as a suspect then.

Not that she was running the investigation. He was.

He told himself that was why he needed to find Kiki. But even he knew he was lying about that. He needed to find Kiki to make sure that she was all right. That she wasn't too upset about finding the latest victim of the Slasher and that the Slasher hadn't followed her from the crime scene.

Could they have been worried that she'd seen something?

Was that why they'd attacked the latest victim so far from the alley? So it would be harder for anyone to see the attack? Or to find the body?

This assault had been far more vicious than the others. And the blow to the head…

That was new. None of the other victims had had a wound like that, none had been hit over the head so hard that it had rendered them unconscious.

The wounded man hadn't regained consciousness after the paramedics had arrived either. Would he? On his way to Kiki's house, Fletcher had called the hospital in Conners where the man had been taken since there was only an express medical clinic in Owl Creek. After identifying himself, Fletcher had asked for an update on the victim's condition.

From the wallet found on him, with all his money and credit cards in it, Fletcher knew the guy's name was Gregory Stehouwer. Stehouwer was in a coma. His head injury had been that severe, and they weren't sure he would wake up. Maybe he'd seen the Slasher. Could that be why he'd been hit so hard in the head? Maybe the Slasher had tried to kill him so that this victim wouldn't be able to identify them.

From the extent of that blow, Fletcher was beginning to lean toward a male assailant or a very strong female. The only thing Fletcher knew for certain about the Slasher was how dangerous they were.

So dangerous that he'd needed to make sure that Kiki had gotten safely home. But she wasn't home. Where the hell was she? And had she gone there on her own or had someone forced her to go where they'd wanted her to?

Or was he just overreacting because he'd been so damn shaken when she'd screamed?

He sighed, uncertain of whether or not he should knock. If he woke up Jim and alarmed him and she was fine, she would be furious. But if something had happened to her and he'd done nothing to find her...

"Who's out there?" a gruff voice called from the darkness within the house.

"Mr. Shelton?" he called back. "It's Fletcher Colton, sir."

A bright light flashed on, momentarily blinding him. He squinted and turned slightly away from the porch light.

"It is you," Jim Shelton said as he pulled open the interior door and peered at Fletcher through the screen. "Has something happened? What are you doing here?"

Fletcher's tongue stuck to the roof of his mouth for a moment as he considered his answer. Then he cleared his throat and said, "I saw Kiki at the club earlier tonight, and I had to follow up about something she saw."

Shelton released a heavy sigh. "Something happen again like that one in Conners and the other in Salt Lake City?"

Those weren't the only places where the Slasher had attacked, but those were the most recent. Fletcher gave a noncommittal shrug. "I don't know for certain, sir." And as he said it, he realized that it was true.

The whole MO of this felt so different than the other attacks and not just because of how severely the victim had been injured, but because he'd been so far from the club. The other victims had been left in the alley, where someone would almost certainly find him when they were cleaning up after the club closed.

This victim had been left out in a field beyond the parking lot, as if nobody had wanted him to be found. Or, at least, maybe not with enough time to save him.

"And you think Kiki will know what happened?" Shelton asked, and he stared intently through that screen.

Fletcher shrugged. "I don't know." Then, because he was being honest, he added, "Probably not."

Instead of being concerned, the older man chuckled. "Thought there was something-something between the two of you even at your daddy's funeral. Sorry about that, son. I really thought that Robert was too tough to die, at least so damn young."

To a man in his late seventies or early eighties, fifty-nine was young. Hell, to Fletcher, fifty-nine was young no matter how hard his dad had lived those years. Working too much, drinking, smoking and eating too much.

"How's your mama doing?" Shelton asked.

While not everybody had been a fan of his dad's, they all loved his mom. "She's doing well, sir," Fletcher replied. "More worried about the rest of us than herself."

"Sounds like your mama," Shelton said with a smile. "My Kiki is a lot like her—always worrying about me when she should be worrying about herself."

Fletcher was worried enough about her right now for the both of them. But he didn't want to concern her grandfather too much. At least not until he knew where and how she was.

"Have any idea where she might be, sir?" he asked.

Shelton chuckled. "Of course. She left a note when she picked up the puppy."

Fletcher should have realized that he hadn't heard the little shepherd yet. And if it had been here, the puppy probably would have been jumping on him. "Where did she go, sir?" he asked.

"The houseboat."

Blackbird Lake was so big that there were a few marinas on it as well as many, many private docks. Obviously, the houseboat wasn't docked at the cottage, or Kiki's vehicle would have been parked in the driveway where Fletcher had been hoping to find it.

"Where is that, sir?"

The older man pushed open the screen door and stepped onto the porch with Fletcher. "I'm not sure I should tell you since she didn't leave you a note."

Fletcher smiled. "I think she figured I was busy, so she didn't bother saying good-bye when she left." At least he hoped that was reason she had.

"And you really want to say good-bye to her?" Shelton pushed. The older man was shrewd. He obviously knew Fletcher was interested in his granddaughter.

But Fletcher didn't want him to know how worried about her he was. "I need to ask her a few questions, too."

Like if she regretted kissing him now. Or if she regretted it having to stop, like he did.

Most of all, he just wanted to make sure that she was safe.

"What the hell happened tonight?" Shelton asked, his voice sharper now as if he was irritated. "You know I'll hear about it."

Fletcher had made certain that there had been no reporters at the club tonight, and the ones who'd shown up in Conners had been denied a story. Nobody had answered any of their questions, and he'd also taken steps to protect the investigation from the Freedom of Information Act for now. Since it was an ongoing investigation, no reports could be shared with the public. He wanted to starve the Slasher of the very thing he or she seemed to crave most: fame.

But maybe that was why the Slasher had struck again so close to the last attack. Maybe he or she was chasing headlines, trying to get into the news again. Trying to get attention.

And if so, maybe Fletcher was to blame for that man's attack tonight. Not directly, like the bartender and other club staff had seemed to imply, but indirectly.

And when he'd thrown the man out of the club, he'd just about delivered him to the Slasher. But the guy hadn't left alone. Some of his entourage had left with him. Had he returned on his own?

For Kiki? Maybe that was why he'd been attacked near her vehicle.

"I really can't say, sir," Fletcher said. "You know how quickly gossip spreads in Owl Creek."

"But would it be gossip?" Shelton asked.

Fletcher sighed. "Not exactly gossip…but not exactly fact either. Until an investigation is complete, it's all pretty much just speculation."

Fletcher had been doing a lot of that because he'd had no

real leads to the Slasher until now. Now he had many leads to follow. The bartender. The distraught father.

And Kiki's missing assistant.

He just hoped none of them had followed Kiki from the club and then to wherever this houseboat was.

"You're about as slippery as that minister from that strange, fairy-tale church."

"Fairy-tale church?"

"You know. The Ever After Church."

Fletcher tensed. That was the church that the guy who'd gone after Ruby had been obsessed with, so much so that he'd been trying to get Crosswinds for them. Supposedly unbeknownst to the pastor, though.

Or was it?

"Markus Acker?" Fletcher asked.

"What?"

"The minister you're talking about," Fletcher prodded him.

"Yeah, that's probably it," the older man said with a shrug. "I've only seen him a couple of times, usually running around the countryside." Then Jim Shelton yawned.

Fletcher had been so tired himself earlier, but once he'd kissed Kiki...

All hell had broken loose in more ways than one. "Sir," he prodded the man. "I really need to talk to your granddaughter."

Shelton sniffed as if he was smelling a load of bullshit. And he kind of was.

Fletcher wasn't being entirely honest with him. And even the old man must have realized that Fletcher wanted to do more than talk to her. What had he called it? The something-something between them?

Fletcher grinned.

And the old man chuckled and shook his head. "You can go see her." He gave him the name of the marina and the slip number. "But don't say I didn't warn you."

"Warn me? About what?"

"Kiki's not settling down anytime soon," Shelton said. "She only comes here as much as she does out of obligation for me."

"Love," Fletcher corrected him.

And Shelton grinned. "Yeah, she's a sweetheart. But she's also as stubborn as…" His grin widened. "As her grandfather. Nobody's going to tie that girl down or tell her what to do."

"I don't want to tie her down," Fletcher assured him. But now…

He shook his head to clear those kinds of *something-something* thoughts from it.

He just wanted to make sure that she was all right.

"I know," Shelton said with another yawn. "You want to *talk* to her."

Fletcher nodded. "Thanks for telling me where she is." And he hoped like hell that the old man was right that she was at the houseboat.

Safe.

But a sudden chill rushed over him, and his fear returned. And he felt like he had when he'd heard her scream.

Like she was in danger.

KIKI MAY HAVE stood there for seconds, frozen on the deck as she stared at the open door. But it wasn't just open. The glass in the door had been broken; shards of it littered the deck, sparkling in the faint glow of that crescent moon.

Grandpa hadn't forgotten to lock the houseboat. Neither had Kiki.

Someone had broken in. Were they still there?

She'd stood there, frozen, wondering what to do. Call the cops? Grab her pepper spray? But Fancy hadn't stayed beside her. Instead she'd walked over that glass and into the cabin area of the houseboat.

Now she barked and then yipped, like she'd been hurt. Thinking of that man, how badly he'd been injured, Kiki charged forward, her pepper spray clasped tightly in her hand. She wasn't even scared. She was furious.

"Don't hurt her!" she yelled. "Don't you dare hurt her!" With her free hand, she fumbled for the switch inside the galley kitchen. Light flickered on over her head and spilled into the living area of the boat and onto the man who lay on the couch, the dog nipping at his worn jeans. "Troy!"

"I'm not hurting her," he said, as he pushed the dog back.

The puppy nipped at his hand.

"Fancy!" she called. The dog turned toward her, and she made the gesture of her hand at her side, palm up, and then bent it toward her opposite shoulder. The shoulder of her hand that still held the pepper spray. "Come."

The dog glanced back at Troy, as if still uncertain of him, before finally obeying Kiki's command. She planted her bristling little puppy body, her hair raised, between Kiki and Troy. Her protectiveness was as instinctual as Sebastian considered her "scent" skills. Maybe Fletcher's need to protect was just as instinctual.

If only he could have protected her from what she'd seen…

Did she need protection now? From Troy?

"What the hell are you doing here?" she asked. "The police are looking for you."

"I know," he said. "That's why I'm here. You showed me this place when I first got to Owl Creek."

On the way to show him the campground where he'd rented a space, she'd stopped off at the marina to check on the boat. He'd been nervous around the water, though, as nervous as he'd been around the club.

She'd thought he'd just been on edge after what he'd seen in Salt Lake City. After finding that victim…

Was Fletcher right? Was that too much of a coincidence?

But then she'd been working the club in Conners and then tonight…

She resisted the urge to shudder over the memory of what she'd found, of how that hand had wrapped around her ankle and she'd thought it was the Slasher that grabbed her, not the Slasher's latest victim.

"I didn't intend for you to use this boat, especially not to hide out from the authorities," she said.

"I'm not… I can't…" he stammered.

"They just want to talk to you about what happened at that club in Conners last weekend," she said. Had he been here all week?

He swung his legs down from the couch and sat up.

She tensed, worried that he was going to jump up, that he was going to come at her since she was between him and the door. The door that he'd broken to get inside.

Could she trust him? She knew now how very little he'd told her about himself.

But instead of getting up, he leaned forward and put his head in his hands. "That's so messed up, Kiki."

"Yes, it is," she agreed.

"I'm sorry I didn't get there in time to help you tonight," he said.

She tensed. "You were at the club tonight?"

"Yeah. I showed up late, though, and you had someone else there," he said, with a hurt tone, almost as if she'd betrayed him. "Who is he?"

The lawman who considered him the prime suspect in his Slasher case.

"An old friend," she said. "I've known him for years." That was true. But she'd left out important details, just like Troy had about himself. Troy had left out that he was a criminal. She'd left out that Fletcher was a cop. "I thought you were a friend, too, Troy, but then I realized how little I know about you."

He looked up at her then. "You know me, Kiki. We've known each other for years."

"Yes," she said. "But how is it possible that I didn't even know your last name?"

"You never asked."

She could kick herself now for not vetting her assistant more thoroughly. That another DJ had been using him for years wasn't an excuse. She realized that now. "And I didn't know about your criminal record either."

"The cops told you about that?" he asked, and he sucked in a breath.

Was he worried about her knowing? Or that the police

knew? Probably the police, since he was hiding from them. What would he do to stay hidden?

She tightened her grasp on her pepper spray. She didn't want to use it, but she would if she felt threatened. "Yes, they were concerned with you taking off after that man was wounded at the club. You need to talk to them."

"I didn't see anything," Troy said, his voice rising with irritation. "I've got nothing to tell them!"

Fancy barked.

"Heel," Kiki told the puppy. She didn't want Troy doing to Fancy whatever he'd done that had made the dog yelp before Kiki had followed her into the houseboat cabin. "They still need to speak to you, Troy. To rule you out—"

"I'm a suspect?" he interjected and jumped up then.

And Fancy jumped too, her body bristling as she growled low in her throat. The puppy obviously didn't trust Troy any more than Fletcher did, and probably any more than Kiki should.

She needed to call the police.

Or Fletcher.

Troy raised his foot, as if to kick Fancy who'd jumped toward him.

"No!" Kiki screamed. "Don't hurt—"

Pounding cut off her protest. The sound of running footsteps against the dock. She whirled around and Troy shoved past her, knocking her back against the kitchen cabinets. Then his footsteps echoed that other pounding. And then a splash.

And the boat rocked, hitting against the dock.

Somebody had gone into the lake.

Troy?

Or whoever had been running down the dock?

To rescue her?

Or…

Chapter Thirteen

Kiki's scream affected Fletcher the way it had at the club. His heart pounded with fear for her, for her safety. For her life.

She'd only let out the first note, and he'd started running down the dock, toward the slip number where her grandfather had said he would find the boat.

She had to be on it. Probably inside, because her scream had been a bit muffled. He'd heard the "Don't hurt—" and panicked. He'd drawn his weapon and started running.

He didn't need to check the slip numbers to find her boat because a man leaped off it, onto the dock, and started running toward the end of it. Toward the water.

In the moonlight, Fletcher could see the guy's long, straggly hair and the tattoos on his arms. Was this Troy?

The same Troy others had seen at the club tonight?

And then he'd come back here?

Had he been hiding? Or had he suspected that Kiki would come out to the boat and he'd been lying in wait for her? She had to be okay. Through the glass window of the cabin, Fletcher could see her standing.

She didn't look to be injured.

And Fletcher couldn't let Troy escape from him again. So he chased after him. And when Troy jumped off the end of the dock into the water, Fletcher holstered his weapon and followed him into the lake.

Despite it being mid-June, the water was surprisingly cold. And it sucked at Fletcher's clothes and boots.

Those already heavy boots got heavier as the leather sopped up the water. And they began to drag him down, like cement blocks tied to his feet. He kicked and chopped at the water with his arms, trying to fight his way back to the surface as the breath he'd held burned in his lungs.

He had to get out of the lake now, or he might not be able to. He couldn't see anything in the water. Troy might have gotten out. Or Fletcher might have gone so deep that he couldn't see even the moonlight on the surface anymore.

He kicked harder, using his strength. Suddenly light shone on him, and he realized he was at the surface again. But the boots kept pulling at him, dragging him down. He reached out for the dock, grabbing one of the wood posts.

The light shining on him was from a cell phone held in Kiki's hand. "Are you all right?" she asked. "Do I need to call 9-1-1?"

He panted for air, dragging in deep gulps of it while hanging on to that post. He had to pull himself up and out before his grasp on that post slipped. "I'll be fine…" he said between pants.

The light dimmed. And then Kiki reached down to grab his arms and try to pull him up. He worked with her until finally he lay on the dock, water dripping from his saturated clothes.

"Are you all right?" she asked again as she knelt beside

him, leaning over him. She was so beautiful and held so much concern in her dark eyes.

And he remembered that kiss in the parking lot before everything had gone to hell.

"Want to give me mouth to mouth?" he asked, unable to resist teasing her.

She chuckled and leaned back. "I guess you are all right then."

He nodded then tensed. "Troy? Where is he?"

"He got out of the water before you did," she said, her breath hitching a little.

"Did he hurt you?" he asked, reaching up to grasp her arms.

She flinched and shook her head.

"But you're hurt."

"That's from that other guy on the dance floor."

He had hurt her, but despite that, he hadn't deserved what had happened to him.

"Did he make it?" she asked, her voice cracking slightly now.

"The last update I got, he was alive, but in a coma," Fletcher shared. And he'd just let one of the suspects in his attack get away. He used his elbows to push himself up so that he was sitting. "Where did Troy go?"

She shrugged. "He got out of the lake farther down the shore." She pointed in the distance. "And ran off into the woods."

Fletcher struggled to roll over onto his knees and then push himself up to his feet. But his legs were weak from all the kicking he'd had to do to keep from getting sucked to the bottom of the lake, and they nearly folded beneath him.

Kiki caught him around the waist. "You're not going to catch him even if you could run."

He could barely take a step; his boots were so heavy with water that it was hard to lift his foot. "These damn boots," he grumbled.

"Yeah, it's the boots," Kiki said. "Grandpa leaves some clothes on the boat. Let's get you something dry."

"But Troy…" He'd been so damn close to catching him. To maybe catching the Slasher. He had to stop that maniac, had to make sure that he didn't hurt anyone else.

"He's gone," she repeated. "And he got a hell of a head start on you. You're not going to find him."

He pulled his cell from his pocket, and water streamed out of the case. He cursed.

"Do you want to call 9-1-1?" she asked. "I have my phone."

Fletcher shook his head and spattered water around the dock and across her face.

"You're like a dog," she remarked.

And he glanced around. "Your grandpa said you had Fancy. Did something happen to her?" He hated to think of the sweet little pup being injured.

"I locked her in the bathroom on the boat," she said. "I didn't want her getting in the water. Or Troy hurting her."

"Troy hurt her?" he asked. A man who could hurt an animal could easily hurt people, too.

Her teeth lightly nipped her bottom lip and she shrugged. "I don't know. She got onto the houseboat before I did, and she made a yipping noise. She seems fine though."

"Want me to call Ruby?" he asked. "Have her check Fancy out?"

"No," she said. "Ruby's pregnant. She needs her rest, especially after what she went through and then losing your dad so soon after that. We can't wake her up."

Fletcher's heart warmed with a flood of appreciation for this woman. "You're a good friend to her." So good that he shouldn't have involved Kiki in his undercover operation. He'd put her in danger.

And Ruby would probably never forgive him if something happened to her friend because of him.

"This was a bad idea," he murmured.

"What?"

He glanced around, wondering who else he and Troy might have awakened when they'd run down the dock. There were quite a few other boats in the marina. And maybe Troy wasn't as far away as Kiki thought he was.

Maybe he had circled around and come back. Maybe he was out there somewhere, listening.

Waiting.

Fletcher couldn't talk to her here. And he had to make sure that his weapon worked after jumping in the lake with it, in case Troy came back.

"Where's that boat?" he asked. And he pulled his T-shirt away from his body.

"I'm sorry," she said. "You must be getting cold." But she was the one that shivered as a breeze blew across the lake, making all the boats rock. "It's this way."

Her arm was still around his waist, as if she thought he needed help walking. While his boots were still so heavy, his strength had returned along with his usual reaction to her nearness: attraction. So he pulled away from her.

She still wore his shirt—the one he'd given her at the club. And it was wet now, her red leather vest showing through it.

"You're probably cold," he remarked. But he sure wasn't, not when just looking at her had heat flashing through him. Along with that damn desire he had no business feeling, not in the middle of a dangerous investigation. Not when his cover was putting her in danger.

"I'm fine," she said as she led the way down the long dock. She stopped outside a houseboat. Whimpering emanated from somewhere inside it.

"Poor Fancy," he said. "Are you sure she's all right?" He jumped over to the boat deck. And glass crunched beneath his wet boots. "He broke in here."

"Yes."

"To do what?" he asked. "Wait for you?"

"I think he was just hiding out," Kiki said. "But he admitted to being at the club earlier."

Fletcher cursed. Had he been that close to the Slasher just to lose him in the water?

FANCY MUST HAVE heard Fletcher's voice because her whimpering became yips again. But not yips of pain. Yips of excitement.

The puppy had fallen hard for Fletcher.

Kiki had to make sure the dog was the only one who fell for him. Not her.

She couldn't stop shaking, but it wasn't with cold. She'd been so scared when he hadn't surfaced from the water. She'd known it was him when she'd heard that splash. Him who'd come clomping so loudly down the dock in the boots that had probably nearly killed him.

But he was strong. He'd fought his way to the surface again. And now he rushed inside the houseboat.

Fancy's yips got louder when he opened the bathroom door. And when Kiki joined them inside, she found him running his hands over the little dog as if checking her for injuries like his sister, the vet, would have.

His genuine concern for the puppy got under Kiki's skin in the best possible way. As if he wasn't hard enough to resist with the way his wet clothes had molded against his muscular body.

With the way his slick hair highlighted all those chiseled features of his handsome face...

"I think she's okay," he said. "She's not flinching or pulling away from me."

That was because the dog was smart. She liked those big hands of his moving over her little furry body. And suddenly Kiki was very jealous of the puppy. She wanted those big hands of his moving over her body. But she wanted to be naked. And she wanted him naked, too.

"I'm glad she's okay," Kiki said.

"That's why you screamed," Fletcher said. "Because you were worried he was going to hurt her?"

She nodded. "But I don't want to talk about Troy right now," she said. She didn't want to talk at all. "You need to get out of those wet clothes."

Maybe he'd picked up on the huskiness in her voice as the desire she felt for him grew, because he tensed and met her gaze. His green eyes darkened as his pupils dilated. "Kiki..." he murmured, and his voice was even raspier than hers.

And Fancy wriggled down from him to go over to the

couch and sniff at it before dropping down on it, her head on her paws as if exhausted.

Maybe she was.

Kiki should have been, too, but adrenaline still coursed through her body, making her tremble. "Is this what you think is a bad idea?" she asked, referring to that comment he'd made on the dock but hadn't expounded on.

He clenched his jaw so tightly that a muscle twitched in his cheek. Then he sighed. "I shouldn't have involved you in this investigation. I shouldn't have put you in danger."

"You didn't," she said.

"But Troy—"

"Is my assistant," she reminded him. "I know you think he's the Slasher, too, but I can't imagine…" She shook her head. "I don't want to talk about Troy. And everything else that happened would have happened whether you were there or not. You didn't put me in danger."

She had.

And she was probably the most at risk right now. But she didn't care. She stepped closer to him and told him, "Take off your clothes."

He sucked in a breath and murmured her name again almost as if he was warning her. He didn't have to say anything else.

"I know," she said. "This is a bad idea. But nobody needs to know about this but us."

"You're already distracting me," he said. "If we—"

She shrugged off the shirt she wore over her vest. His shirt which was wet from where she'd touched him. Then she reached for the zipper at the front of her vest. "Maybe if we do this, we'll be less distracted," she suggested.

He chuckled. "Somehow I don't think it'll work like that." But he leaned down to take off his boots. His holster followed. He took a few minutes to take his weapon apart, probably to let it dry out.

Before he could do anything else, Kiki took his hand in hers and tugged him toward her bedroom. She had her own on the boat just like her grandpa had his, although he rarely stayed there now. After pushing open the pocket door, she stepped into the room, which was so small that there wasn't much floor space around the queen-size bed. So she climbed onto it and reached again for the zipper on her vest, pulling it down so that the red leather fell away from her.

Fletcher groaned as if he was in pain.

"Did you get hurt when you jumped in the lake?" she asked, concerned now that she hadn't called 9-1-1.

He shook his head. "No. You're the one killing me. You're so damn beautiful." He leaned over then and pressed his mouth against hers, kissing her deeply, sliding his tongue between her open lips.

She groaned now. No. She moaned. Then she pulled back. "You need to take off your wet clothes," she reminded him. And she reached for the button on his jeans.

He shoved what looked like the ammo clip from his gun into his pocket. Then he pulled his wet T-shirt over his head as she lowered his zipper.

His breath hissed out as her fingers brushed over his boxers, over his straining erection. As she pushed his jeans down over his lean hips, he slid her open vest from her shoulders, freeing her breasts.

And his breath hissed out again. "You are so beautiful."

He cupped her breasts in his hands, running his thumbs over her skin and then over her nipples.

She moaned again as pleasure coursed through her. Her breasts had always been sensitive, but never more so than now. In this moment.

He lowered his head then and closed his mouth around one breast and stroked his tongue across her tight nipple.

"Fletcher," she whispered. She wanted him so badly.

Then he was undoing the button and lowering her zipper and pulling off her shorts and underwear. "Are you sure?" he asked, his voice gruff with the desire burning in his eyes.

Like it burned inside her.

She eagerly nodded. "Very sure and very impatient." She wanted to go fast and furiously, joining their bodies.

But he took his time. As he turned his attention to her other breast with his mouth, his hands moved over her body. He caressed her skin, traced her curves and then he touched her core.

And she whimpered like Fancy had.

And Fancy yipped with concern.

Fletcher got up and closed the door. Then he was back between her legs. And he made love to her with his mouth and his tongue, driving her out of her mind until pleasure coursed through her with an orgasm that left her quivering.

But it wasn't enough. She wanted more. So she pushed him back onto the bed and pulled off his boxers. Then she lowered her mouth to his shaft. She closed her lips around him, and he tensed. Then he was gently pushing her shoulders back.

"No. I want to be inside you," he said, his voice hoarse.

"I need to be inside you." Then he cursed. "But I don't have any—"

She fumbled inside a small cupboard next to the bed, feeling around until she found a packet. She tore it open with her teeth and rolled the condom over him. He was so big. So hard.

She straddled him, easing him inside her until he filled her. The sensation had her muscles tensing again, pressure building inside her. She leaned down, her breasts rubbing against his chest. The hair tickled her skin, teased her nipples. She moaned and moved.

And he grasped her hips and thrust up, driving deeper. Driving her out of her mind.

It was like they were dancing to the same music, the same beat inside them, their hearts pounding together. They moved in unison.

Then his hands moved from her hips to her breasts, and he stroked her nipples with his thumbs.

She came again, intensely, and a cry of pleasure slipped through her lips. Then he tensed beneath her and began to pulsate inside her as he found his release.

His pleasure.

Her name slipped through his gritted teeth.

She couldn't remember the last time she'd ever been so in sync with a lover. Maybe never.

Fletcher rolled her onto her back and kissed her, brushing his mouth lightly across hers, as he drew out of her body. Then he opened the pocket door and disappeared for a while.

She had just begun to wonder if he'd left when he came back, smelling like soap and midnight rain and sex. And she welcomed him back into her bed, into her arms.

They made love again, slowly, savoring every second. And after another soul-shattering orgasm, she fell asleep. She didn't know how long she'd been out when she felt Fletcher jump next to her.

He must have fallen asleep, too, only to jerk awake. Then she heard it, the noise he must have heard. The sound of Fancy's low growl. Was she warning them of an intruder?

Had someone broken into the houseboat once again?

Chapter Fourteen

Tension gripped Fletcher as he silently cursed himself. How the hell had he fallen asleep?

He knew how, though. He'd been completely satiated and exhausted and comfortable. And he hadn't wanted his time with Kiki to end.

But no matter what she'd said, he'd put her in danger once again. The way Fancy growled outside the bedroom door indicated that there was some kind of threat out there.

Had Troy come back? Was he going to finish whatever he'd intended to do to Kiki?

Because Fletcher wasn't as convinced as she was that the man had just been hiding out on the houseboat. What if he'd been waiting for her to come back here?

What had he intended to do to her?

And if he was the Slasher, and armed with that dangerously sharp weapon that had already wounded so many others, how the hell was Fletcher going to defend her and himself?

He'd left his gun in pieces, drying out on the counter in the main cabin area. The magazine of ammo was in his jeans. Jeans he quickly stepped into and pulled up.

But before he could reach for the door, Kiki grabbed his arm as if trying to hold him back. "What is it?" she whispered, her voice a little shaky. She was as wide awake as he was now.

"I don't know," he whispered back. But he was going to damn well find out.

"Take my pepper spray," she said, pressing a small canister in his hand.

He closed his hand around it. While it wasn't his gun, it was better than nothing. If the Slasher couldn't see, maybe he or she wouldn't be able to slice Fletcher up like they had their other victims.

He drew in a breath and then opened the pocket door. Morning had come, and sunshine poured through the windows in the houseboat cabin. In the middle of the living room area, Fancy did battle, growling and gnawing on one of the Fletcher's new boots.

Fletcher released the breath he'd been holding and chuckled.

Kiki leaned around him and peered out. Then she pushed past him and ran over to the puppy. Fortunately, for Fletcher's sake, she'd pulled on a terry cloth robe. "Drop it," she commanded the dog as she pointed at the floor.

The puppy whined and wagged her tail as she kept the boot tightly clamped in her mouth.

"I understand why she'd want to destroy those things," Fletcher said. "I'm not too fond of them myself."

"Drop it," Kiki repeated, pointing at the floor again.

Fancy whined one more time, as if pleading with Kiki before she finally dropped the mangled heap of damp leather.

"Impressive," Fletcher said. "You really know a lot about dog training."

Kiki shrugged. "I wanted to learn so that we can start getting her familiar with commands right away."

"Show me," he said. He wasn't really interested. He just didn't want to leave her. Not yet. Maybe not ever.

He pushed the thought aside and focused on the commands that she showed him.

"She doesn't know all of them yet," Kiki said. "We introduce them one at a time." She showed him Sit, which was holding out her hand in front of her, with her palm facing up, then raising it toward her shoulder. "Wait and Stay are almost the same." She held her hand out in front of her, her palm facing Fancy. "And probably the most important to keep her out of trouble."

She showed him a couple more. Lie Down and Up.

"She knows quite a few."

"She's a smart dog," Kiki said.

"And you're a good trainer. Maybe you've missed your calling."

"Music is my calling," she insisted. "I love it."

"I can tell that, too," he said.

"Do you love being a detective?" she asked.

He nodded. "It can be frustrating at times." Like now, trying to catch the Slasher.

"And dangerous," she added.

He shrugged. "Life is full of dangers."

And he'd faced one of the most perilous situations last night. Not when he'd jumped in the lake and nearly drowned. But when he'd drowned in her last night, in the emotions overwhelming him.

He wanted to be with her again. But he'd already dropped the ball on this investigation too many times. "I have to go," he said. The clock on the wall alarmed him. "I didn't realize it was so late already."

Her bedroom had been dark and so very comfortable with her soft bed and her softer body curled up in his arms.

"You were up late," she reminded him.

He wasn't sure if she was talking about the club or about what they'd done in the bed. But he nodded. "I need to go, to check on the victim from last night."

She tensed and nodded. "Yes, let me know how he's doing."

They both hesitated, staring at each other. He didn't want to leave her. He found an excuse for that. "You shouldn't stay here by yourself. Just in case Troy comes back."

"After you chased him off the dock, I doubt he's going to come back," she said. "But I should go back to Grandpa's, make sure he knows I'm okay, just in case he heard anything about last night. Did you tell him about it?"

He shook his head. "No. I didn't want to worry him."

"He already worries too much about me," Kiki said.

"He's going to hear about it," Fletcher said. "I'm trying to keep it all out of the press, but people are going to talk to the media eventually or post something somewhere."

"Like they did after the attack in Salt Lake City," she said. "I saw the reports about it right away."

"These last two attacks weren't discovered until after closing," Fletcher said. "That's why they were easier to keep quiet. And club employees don't want to talk about them and risk losing business for their bosses. Too much bad press could cost them their jobs."

She nodded. "That make sense."

"It's about the only thing about this that does."

She smiled. "Are you talking about the case or what we did last night?" she asked.

Thinking about what they did had him taking a step toward her, almost involuntarily.

But she held up her hand, palm facing him, like she'd done with the puppy.

"Wait or stay?" he asked her.

"You have to go," she reminded him. "And last night was to get rid of the distraction of whatever this is between us."

"Something-something," he said.

"What?"

"That's what your grandfather called it," he shared. "That's why he told me where to find you."

Her face flushed. "Oh, Grandpa…" she murmured.

"You're right," Fletcher said. "He is cooler than I am."

"Yes, he is," she agreed with a smile. "And I should go, too, back to the cottage to check on him."

"And I should go," Fletcher repeated. But he really didn't want to leave her and not just because he was worried about her safety.

But if he stayed, he was going to have to worry about *his* safety. He had to leave before he really started falling for her. Because her cool grandfather had already warned Fletcher that she wasn't going to settle down anytime soon.

Not that Fletcher wanted her to. He never wanted to settle down either. All he really wanted was to do his job and catch the Slasher.

He had a feeling that he'd been close to doing that last

night, but the man had escaped. And Fletcher had nearly drowned. "I have to ask you something, Kiki," he said.

She tensed. "If it's about last night, you were probably right. It was a bad idea."

He sucked in a breath, feeling like she'd punched him. "That's not what I was going to ask you about," he said.

Her face flushed. "Then what?"

"Troy. Is he left-handed?"

Her forehead furrowed as if she was trying to remember and then she nodded. "Yes, I think he is. Why?"

"Because the Slasher is, too."

"SHE'S FINE," RUBY said as she lifted Fancy down from her exam table and placed her on the floor of the medical office area of Crosswinds Training Center.

Kiki released a shaky breath of relief. After the puppy's run-in with Troy last night, she'd been worrying about her. She and Grandpa fostered puppies to help them, not hurt them. "That's good."

"How are you?" Ruby's green eyes narrowed slightly as she studied Kiki's face, but not with that same unnerving intensity that Fletcher did.

Fletcher.

Just thinking of him had a rush of heat flashing through her body. He was such an incredible lover. Last night, or this morning—whatever time it had been—had turned out to be more than a distraction. But like she'd told him earlier this morning, it had been a bad idea. Because, after how incredible it had been between them, she was afraid that she was going to want to do it again. And again.

"I'm—I'm fine," Kiki said.

Ruby's eyes narrowed. "I hate to say this because I was sick of hearing it myself, but you look kind of tired."

Kiki was well aware of the dark circles beneath her eyes. "It was a late night at the club," she said, which was the truth. But she knew that Fletcher wanted to keep the attack as quiet as he could, so she wouldn't share that with his sister. She also didn't want to worry Ruby. The pregnant woman had already been through enough.

"Is that all?" Ruby asked.

"Yes."

"Because I heard about those attacks outside some nightclubs," Ruby said. "And I've been worried about you."

"The victims have all been men," Kiki said. "So I'm safe." She wasn't worried about her life. She was worried about her heart.

Not that she was going to give it to Fletcher. She was too busy, and he certainly was as well. Last night was not going to be repeated. A pang of disappointment hit her, but she ignored it.

Instead of looking relieved, Ruby's face tensed with concern. "Mom said Fletcher didn't come home last night."

"I'm sure he wasn't attacked," Kiki said, wanting to reassure her friend, who'd already been through too much, but also not reveal why she was so certain.

"I know," Ruby said. "He's probably fine. He's a really good detective. He's obsessed with work. Maybe too obsessed. The reason he didn't come home was undoubtedly because he was working all night. So there must be something criminal going on again in Owl Creek." She shuddered. "I was just hoping the danger was all behind us now."

"He's a detective," Kiki gently reminded her friend. "He's always going to be working some case or another."

"He wouldn't have stayed out all night unless it was something serious, though," Ruby said.

Kiki shrugged. "Or maybe he's seeing someone." He'd certainly seen a lot of her the night before. Or actually morning.

Ruby laughed and shook her head. "I doubt that. He's only been back a little while. And with the funeral and staying with Mom, he wouldn't have had time to meet anyone. Unless…" She looked at Kiki almost hopefully.

Kiki bit her tongue so that she wouldn't say any more. Fletcher didn't want anyone to know about the Slasher, so he probably wouldn't want his sister to know he'd gone undercover with Kiki to investigate. He'd also gone undercover with Kiki last night, but that had been for an entirely other reason, for pleasure. Heat rushed to her face and her body, just as it had last night.

"It's probably for the best if you two don't get involved," Ruby said.

Kiki fought hard to maintain a neutral expression, to give nothing away about how involved she'd gotten with Ruby's brother.

The veterinarian continued, "Fletcher has never had good luck with relationships."

"Why's that?" Kiki asked as if she was only mildly curious and not wildly so.

Ruby sighed. "He's too much like Dad maybe. Throws himself into his work and doesn't leave time for anything else."

"Seems like I remember another Colton doing the same thing," Kiki teased.

"Ditto, my friend," Ruby said. "You're so busy yourself, always going from city to city, living your dream."

"Chasing it," Kiki murmured. She needed to make a few more connections. Maybe this fall, once fishing season was done and she returned to LA. Maybe there she would find the connection to get a record label interested in her music.

Or maybe she needed to spend some time in Nashville or Detroit.

She could find the connections she needed there, too. Probably anywhere but Owl Creek. But the connections she had here were for her heart. Grandpa. And Ruby.

And Fancy.

"Thanks for checking her out for me," Kiki said.

"What did you think happened to her?" Ruby asked. "She seems fine, if just a little tired like you are." The puppy had passed out in a corner of the exam room.

"She was eating leather again," Kiki said, omitting the fact that Troy might have kicked her. Or done something else that had made her yip in pain like she had.

She definitely hadn't known her assistant very well at all. What if Fletcher's suspicions were right and he was the Slasher? Would she be able to forgive herself for not realizing sooner how dangerous the man was?

Maybe she would have saved some of the victims from disfigurements—or worse if the one she'd found last night hadn't made it.

Maybe that was why she'd wanted Fletcher so badly last night. Because she hadn't wanted to think about any of the horrible things that were going on.

She'd certainly forgotten for a while.

And she'd gone to the houseboat because she'd thought

she wouldn't be able to sleep. But she'd slept in Fletcher's arms. She'd felt safe.

But that was kind of ironic given that she might have the most to fear from him if she did something stupid. Like fall for him.

Because his sister had made it very clear how badly Fletcher sucked at relationships. Not that her track record was any better.

She'd never found anyone who'd been supportive of her dreams and not critical. She'd never found anyone who was willing to work around her crazy schedule. She'd never found anyone who'd loved her besides her grandfather and her friends.

"Are you sure you're all right?" Ruby asked with concern.

Kiki nodded. "Yes, just tired. Like Fancy. Now that I know she's okay I'll be able to get some sleep." But she wondered if she would without Fletcher's arms around her, holding her close.

But that was just because of what had happened. She'd needed the distraction of sex with him and the comfort of his closeness so that she could forget about the Slasher for a little while.

But when she carried Fancy out to her SUV and opened the passenger's door, she noticed a piece of paper lying on the floor that she hadn't noticed before.

She opened it up and noticed, from the direction of the cursive, that a left-handed person had written the note: *I am not the Slasher.*

Troy.

He must have slipped it inside her vehicle last night or this morning. He'd realized he was a suspect. Or he was defensive because he was guilty.

And maybe Fletcher was right. Maybe she was in more danger than she thought from the Slasher. Because if she knew who he was, he might consider her a threat.

Chapter Fifteen

The club closed for a week, under the guise of maintenance, after Kiki had found the latest victim. This had been a good thing for Fletcher because he hadn't had to worry about maintaining his cover. If he hadn't already been compromised...

One of the other officers or techs who'd shown up at the scene might have slipped up and revealed that he was not really a suspect. That he was actually running the investigation into the Slasher. He would know when the club reopened in a couple of days.

But his cover wasn't all he had to worry about losing, though. He'd lost his objectivity and his resolve, too. He needed to be focused on finding the Slasher, not on Kiki. But despite working hard to find out all he could about Troy Hoover, Bart Taylor and Dan Sullivan, he hadn't been able to stop thinking about her.

About what they'd done.

About how damn amazing it had been, and *she* was.

She'd dropped off the note Troy Hoover had left in her vehicle, probably when it had been parked at the marina. Hopefully not while she'd been at Crosswinds.

Hopefully Troy was not following her around, but if he was, at least he knew that she'd gone to the police with his note instead of blindly accepting his word that he wasn't the Slasher.

Fletcher hadn't been at the station when she'd brought the note by. After going home to change clothes, he'd made the drive to the hospital in Conners where Greg Stehouwer, the Slasher's latest victim, was still lying in a coma. Not wanting to blow his cover, Fletcher had avoided the waiting room where the victim's family was and had only spoken with the doctor who hadn't been able to tell Fletcher anything but that the prognosis wasn't good.

The Slasher's attacks might have escalated to murder, just as Fletcher had feared they would. And so, he'd spent the past few days trying to find out as much as he could about all his suspects.

But he couldn't help but think that he was missing something. Or maybe he was just missing *someone*. Kiki. Despite how tired he should have been, he wasn't sleeping well because he wanted to sleep with her.

To get some perspective on his case, and maybe on his life, he'd stopped by Book Mark It, his sister Frannie's bookstore café. The long three-story building on Main Street squeezed narrowly between other buildings. This one was all exposed brick and cement floors. Until the Slasher had struck in Conners, he'd been spending a lot of time there because there hadn't been much else to do.

Frannie bustled around, working the café and the book counter, serving drinks and suggesting book choices to her patrons.

His sister was in her element, like Kiki was in the club.

Frannie didn't quite have the adoring fans that Kiki had, though. Nobody screamed her name and tried to grab her, except for an older lady customer who gave her a hug over the loss of their dad.

After she was released, Frannie blinked furiously, clearing a rush of tears from her hazel eyes. Fletcher flinched over the twinges of concern and guilt that struck him. He should have been checking in more with his family, making sure that they were all doing okay after Dad's death. The first week, he'd stopped by the bookstore often, but he and Frannie hadn't really talked about Dad. Just his boring cases.

He hadn't checked on his other siblings. And even though he lived with his mom, he hadn't been seeing much of her either with the long hours he'd been working. So much for staying there to be a comfort for her.

He hadn't been a comfort to anyone.

As Frannie walked to the door, Fletcher glanced around the shop. He wanted to talk to his sister, but he didn't want anyone else to overhear them. About their recent loss or about his case.

Fletcher had noticed a man sitting in the corner when he'd first walked into the store. While he didn't know the guy's name, Fletcher recognized him from his other visits to Book Mark It. He'd been here before, planted in a corner, reading a book. Even sitting down, it was easy to see that the guy was tall, with his long legs stretched out in front of him. He had a book open, but it was almost as if he was using it to hide behind instead of to read. The guy was still there, and he seemed to be watching Frannie even more intently than Fletcher had been.

Maybe the stranger kept coming around because he was interested in the bookstore owner. Frannie was pretty, with golden highlights in her hair and hazel eyes that sparkled. But there was something about the way the stranger seemed to be watching, but not wanting to be seen, that unsettled Fletcher. And it wasn't just brotherly protectiveness gnawing at him, but police instincts.

He tried to get a better look at the guy's face. But the book blocked most of it. He only lowered it when Frannie walked back from the door, and the guy's dark eyes focused on her again. He had dark hair, too, cut very short, which seemed at odds with the scruff on his face. Some gray was mixed in that scruff, so he was probably older than Frannie's twenty-six. Maybe older than Fletcher, too.

"Looking for a book?" Frannie asked him as she nudged Fletcher's arm. "Or a tall coffee?"

"Looking for my favorite sister," he said.

She smiled and replied, "Ruby isn't here."

"I'm not looking for Ruby."

"Hannah isn't here either," she said, her smile widening as she teased him.

He chuckled. "You know you're my favorite." They'd grown up sharing their love of mysteries. While Frannie had looked for hers in books, though, Fletcher looked for them in real life.

"Shh," Frannie told him. "We're not supposed to have favorites. That's what Mom has told us."

"That's because there are so many of us, especially if you include our cousins." Which their mom always had after her flighty sister had taken off and abandoned her husband and her kids. "And we all know who her favorite is now."

"Lucy," Frannie said, her voice warm with affection for their niece. "Mom loves being a grandma, which is a good thing with Ruby and Sebastian going to have a baby."

"At least something good came of that whole ordeal," Fletcher murmured, thinking of the danger Ruby had been in, similar to the danger that he might be putting Kiki in.

Since she'd found that note from Troy, he had an officer making frequent drive-bys of Jim's cottage and the houseboat. If Troy saw that cop car, maybe he would keep his distance.

If Troy was the Slasher...

"How is Mom doing?" Frannie asked with concern.

Fletcher shrugged. "She seems fine when I see her, but I really don't see that much of her."

"Is that because you're too busy or because she is?"

Fletcher shrugged. "I don't know what she's been doing, honestly."

"So *you've* been busy," she said.

Fletcher nodded. "Still doesn't excuse my not being by more to check on you."

She raised her hands. "On me? Why?"

"We just lost our dad, Frannie."

"Yes, *we*," Frannie said. "We all did. And Mom lost a husband. And I should be checking up on her myself instead of asking you how she is."

"Stop being so hard on yourself," Fletcher said. "Looks like you're busy with your own business here."

Frannie gazed around her shop, and her chin lifted with obvious pride. "Yes. I love it."

"I can tell," he said. Just like Kiki loved what she did as well. But what Kiki did was going to keep leading her away from Owl Creek. If anything ever happened to Jim Shelton, she would probably stop coming back altogether.

"How about you?" Frannie asked. "Do you love your job, Fletcher? Solving mysteries for real?"

He glanced again to that man in the corner. Was he close enough to hear them? He leaned closer to his sister and whispered, "What's that guy's story? He seems a little stalker-ish."

Frannie laughed. "No. He's a regular. He's harmless."

If she really believed that, Frannie hadn't given the guy much of her usual attention. Because there was something *off* about him, and usually she would have picked up on that.

"Stop," she said.

He tensed. "What?"

"Stop being so intense and suspicious of everyone, Fletcher."

"Occupational hazard," he reminded her.

She laughed. "You were always like that. Every date Ruby, Hannah or I brought home got the third degree from our big brothers. But you were the hardest on them."

"I wasn't hard enough on Owen," Fletcher said. Hannah's deadbeat husband had abandoned her and their daughter before Lucy's first birthday.

Frannie nodded and gave a fake shiver. "That's why we're smart, staying single and all."

Fletcher nodded. But staying single didn't sound as smart as it once had to Fletcher, not since that incredible experience he'd had with Kiki, and that hadn't been just what they'd done in her bedroom on the boat. He'd even had fun shopping with her. "I wish I was smarter," Fletcher said.

"Tough case?" Frannie asked. "I can make us some cappuccinos and help you figure it out."

He was tempted. He would love a sounding board about the case. But he was waiting for information back on Bart Taylor and Dan Sullivan, seeing if they had been present at the times and places of the Slasher's other attacks. Troy had been around for at least one other of them. Two, actually, for a total of three times.

He'd been in Salt Lake City and had found the victim. Then Conners. And he'd admitted to Kiki that he'd been at Club Ignition where Greg Stehouwer had been left for dead, not just disfigured.

Had that attack escalated because Troy knew he was a suspect and that the police were closing in on him?

Or was Fletcher's other instinct right and he was missing something? He glanced again to that man sitting in the corner, and he narrowed his eyes to glare at him. "Are you sure he's harmless?"

"Fletcher!" Frannie exclaimed, her face flushing with embarrassment. "Don't scare away my customers."

"Want me to make sure that's all he is?" he asked. "What's his name?"

Frannie shook her head. "No. I'm not giving it to you. Aren't you staying busy enough in Owl Creek? Already bored with a smaller police department?"

Fletcher thought of that other night, in Kiki's bed, in Kiki's arms. "I'm definitely not bored," he said. And that had nothing to do with his case.

KIKI WAS BEING FOLLOWED. She wasn't a fool. She hadn't missed that vehicle driving by her house. Past her grandfather's charter business and the boathouse. Even slowing down in front of the club when she'd checked on her equipment.

And she knew who it was.

Or at least who was responsible for it.

Fletcher had undoubtedly asked an officer to keep an eye on her. Was it for her sake though? Or was he just trying to catch Troy?

He hadn't called or texted her since that morning on the boat, so he was probably just trying to catch Troy. The Slasher.

Were they one and the same?

Kiki shuddered to think that she might have been known someone so long and been working that closely with someone capable of such violence. Uneasy now, she glanced around her as she stood at Fletcher's front door. Had the officer followed her here?

The door opened, and she jumped, startled.

"Kiki," Mrs. Colton said with a smile. "What a lovely surprise."

"I'm sorry," Kiki said. "I should have called first." She hadn't wanted to call Fletcher since he hadn't reached out to her first. But she should have called Jenny before just dropping by.

"You are always welcome," Jenny assured her. "And it's always lovely to see you." She reached out and hugged Kiki.

And Kiki, who could barely remember her mother, felt a pang of jealousy for Fletcher. Then she remembered that he'd lost his father. Jenny had lost her husband.

"I'm stopping by for two reasons," Kiki admitted. "I know you have a ton of family, but if you'd like help with anything that might be hard for them to deal with, I'd be happy to step in."

Jenny's brow furrowed with confusion so Kiki explained, "Like cleaning out closets for instance. Grandpa still had so many of Grandma's clothes in his closet when I first moved in with him that I didn't realize she was dead for the longest time. I thought she was just gone on a trip."

Mrs. Colton smiled. "That's sweet, and I expect that he might have wanted to think that, too. Maybe that's why he kept her things for so long."

Kiki held up her hands, indicating she would back off. The bag from a shoe store dangled from one of her hands, though, the box bumping against her arm. "I'm sorry. If you're not ready, I totally understand. It hasn't been that long."

Jenny shook her head. "No, it's not that. I've already taken care of Robert's things."

Kiki had no idea what that meant. Had she tossed everything out? Or maybe she'd given his things to their sons.

"I'm sorry. I didn't mean to overstep," Kiki said. God, if Jenny told Fletcher about this, he would think she was stalking him.

"Please stop apologizing, Kiki."

Heat flushed her face with embarrassment. She was acting like a fool. Like the mother of the boy she liked had caught them making out or something.

She was being ridiculous. But being here, after being with Fletcher, unnerved her. Her offer to help Jenny had been a sincere one. But she was beginning to wonder about her own motives now. Had she just hoped to run into Fletcher while she was here, at the house where he was staying?

Had she missed him, so she was being pathetic and hoping to catch a glimpse of him?

She had another gig at Club Ignition this weekend, just a couple of days away, so she would see him then. Unless he'd chosen to pursue his investigation a different way than going undercover.

"You're not overstepping, Kiki," Jenny assured her. "I appreciate the offer so very much. Come inside, and we can visit."

Kiki's stomach flipped with nerves at the thought. She would have had a reason to be inside if she'd been helping Jenny with something. But since she'd refused, Kiki needed to gracefully extradite herself before Fletcher came home. Not that he wouldn't realize she'd been here when his mom gave him what Kiki had bought for him.

Why hadn't she thought this out more thoroughly before she'd decided to do this? Why hadn't she considered how it might look to Fletcher and to his mother?

This was a bad idea. But she found herself going inside, because she couldn't come up with an excuse. While Jenny poured them iced teas in the kitchen, she glanced over at the bag Kiki had sat on the counter.

"Is that for me?" she asked.

Kiki was tempted to press the cold glass of tea against her face. "This is actually for Fletcher," she admitted.

Instead of being offended, Jenny let out a breath of relief. "Good. I received so many lovely flowers and cards and casseroles, but I would just like life to get back to normal now."

Maybe that was why she'd already gotten rid of her husband's things. Or dealt with them somehow.

"I'd like everyone to stop worrying about me," Jenny continued, then her face flushed. "I'm sorry. That sounds rude."

Kiki shook her head and assured her, "No. I totally get it. You're used to taking care of other people." As a nurse and as a mom and doting aunt. She was more comfortable in the role of caregiver.

"And nobody needs to take care of me," Jenny said. "I'll be fine."

"You will," Kiki said. "I've always admired how strong you are."

Jenny reached across the counter and squeezed her hand. "You're the strong one, Kiki. You've already been through so much, but you put yourself out there, in those big clubs, pursuing your dream. That takes a lot of guts."

Pride suffused Kiki, but she shrugged off the praise. "That's not difficult for me. It would be harder giving it up than going on." That was true. Music was such a part of her life. She couldn't ever give it up. For anyone.

Jenny glanced at the shoe store bag with curiosity and confusion. "So you brought this for Fletcher?"

It didn't make very much sense to Kiki now either. But Fancy had chewed up his boots. And he'd hated them so much that she'd been determined to replace them.

"I didn't even realize you two knew each other very well," Jenny said.

"We don't," Kiki said. "Not really."

And he obviously hadn't told his mother about his investigation. "We just ran into each other, and the puppy I'm fostering damaged one of his boots. I just wanted to make sure it was replaced."

"I'm sure Fletcher wouldn't expect you to do that," Jenny

said. "He doesn't care much about material things. Just his career." She uttered a soft sigh.

Maybe she'd compared him to his father.

Though she was close friends with Ruby, Kiki wasn't around Owl Creek enough to understand all the personal dynamics of the Colton family.

Jenny's forehead furrowed with concern for her son. "I'm worried about him. He works so hard that even though he lives here, I barely see him." She let out another sigh, this one a bit shakier than the last. "I hate to think that there is that much crime in Owl Creek to keep him as busy as he's been lately."

He'd been successful in keeping the Slasher's latest attacks out of the news. But it was only a matter of time before someone leaked the stories. Then Jenny was going to be even more worried about her detective son.

As worried as Kiki was. Because she'd seen firsthand how vicious the Slasher was.

WHAT THE HELL was wrong with this town? Why was there no mention, anywhere, of the attacks? Social media in the area had commented some about a mugging in Conners and a bar fight in the parking lot of Club Ignition. The gossips in the local gathering spot, Hutch's Diner, had been spreading the same rumors. Of muggings and bar fights.

There had been no mention of the Slasher. Not that the Slasher could take credit for everything that had happened.

But wasn't copycatting the highest form of compliment? Or maybe someone else was wanting to get some attention.

Either way, it hadn't worked.

Was trying to hide the truth some new police strategy?

Had someone profiled the Slasher and figured out how necessary attention had become to them?

And now they were trying to cut it off?

The Slasher would show what they thought of that. And whoever had put the gag order on the media was going to damn well regret what they'd done.

Chapter Sixteen

Greg Stehouwer wasn't coming out of his coma. At least that was what his doctors believed. His head injury was so severe. The doctors had advised his family to pull the plug. The Slasher would be a killer.

Fletcher felt sick that he hadn't managed to stop whoever the hell it was before it had escalated to murder, just like he'd feared it would. When he showed up at the hospital to speak to the medical examiner who had agreed to inspect the wounds on Greg's face and chest, one of the family spotted him.

"It's you!" the man yelled. "You're the one who got in the fight with him. Why aren't you in jail?" The man looked a lot like his brother with fine blond hair, blue eyes and the same athletic build.

Fletcher pulled out his badge. "No. I'm the one in charge of this investigation. And I am so sorry about your brother." Sorrier than this man would ever know.

The guy stammered, "But—but you're the one who fought with him—"

Fletcher shook his head. "I never went out to the parking lot. I didn't leave when your brother left. You did, though."

The man's face flushed with fury and he glanced around, as if making sure nobody had overheard them. An older couple sat together on a couch, hugging each other and crying. Probably his parents who had refused to give up hope despite the doctors' grim prognosis. They'd refused to pull the plug so far, believing he would come out of it.

"He's—he is my brother," the man said. "I wouldn't hurt him."

"Where did you go after you left?" Fletcher asked.

"We started driving back to Conners. We were going to hit the clubs there."

If the groom-to-be had acted like he had at Club Ignition, Greg probably would have gotten tossed out of them, too.

"But then Greg changed his mind. He wanted to go back to teach you a lesson."

"I never saw him again until after he'd been attacked. So you let him go back alone?"

"I have a wife and kids," the man replied. "I wasn't going to get into a fight in the club." He glanced at Fletcher's badge again. "What were you doing there that night?"

"The DJ is a friend of mine," Fletcher said.

The man's blue eyes narrowed. "You're investigating that Slasher thing, aren't you? Is that why you were there?"

Fletcher clenched his jaw. While he felt badly about what had happened to Greg Stehouwer, he didn't want to reveal too much of his investigation to this man or to the press or to the people he wanted to fool tonight in the club.

Tonight. He had to drive back to Owl Creek. Had to get dressed to play the part of Kiki's assistant. His pulse quickened at the thought of seeing her again.

He'd wanted to stop by so badly this past week or at least

run into her around town. But he'd also had to work this case, had to try to follow up and find all the information he could about Troy Hoover and Bart Taylor and Dan Sullivan. His possible suspects. But he couldn't help but think he was missing someone.

The man nodded. "That's why you were there. You're trying to catch that Slasher. That's who did this, isn't it? That damn Slasher!"

"I don't know," Fletcher honestly replied.

A short while later, when he spoke with the medical examiner who had inspected the deep slashes on Greg's face and chest, he was even less certain.

"His wounds don't look the same as the other ones," the doctor said. The guy was older, with iron gray hair and a mustache. "I took photos of his injuries to compare to the injuries the other victims had sustained."

"You had no problem matching the wounds from the victim at the club in Conners to the wounds on the Slasher's other victims. But you have some doubts about this one?" The same uncertainties had been going through Fletcher's mind since Kiki had found Greg so far out in the club parking lot and with such a serious head wound. One that had essentially killed him, if the doctors were right and he was brain-dead.

The medical examiner lowered his voice to a whisper and told Fletcher, "My preliminary assessment is that blade seems to have been duller and maybe a little wider. Plus, the angle doesn't match the others."

"So a different weapon?" Or a different assailant?

The guy shrugged. "I don't know yet. To say conclusively,

I'll need to compare these wounds more closely to the photos taken of the other victims. If you want to wait around..."

Fletcher glanced at his watch. If he didn't hurry, he was going to be late getting to the club. Most of Kiki's equipment was still there, so she wouldn't need his help loading and unloading it until later tonight. But he needed to see her.

Hell, he'd needed to see her all week, but he'd forced himself to stay away, in case Troy Hoover was watching. The officer checking on her hadn't noticed anyone suspicious hanging around, though.

So she'd been safe.

And she had to stay that way. But going back to the club was dangerous. So would telling her not to do the job she loved, though.

Fletcher didn't want to get between her and her music. He just wanted to get between her and the Slasher.

"Call me later with what you find out," he told the medical examiner. "I have somewhere I need to be."

And someone he desperately wanted to see again. She'd bought him boots.

His mother had thought the gesture was sweet on her part, but she didn't know how much he hated those boots. Kiki did. Was it a joke? Or revenge for his not calling or texting her all week?

God, he was a coward. He hadn't known what to say to her or how to act. And knowing she was as averse to relationships as he was, he hadn't wanted to act like they were a couple, even though...

No. He had no time for relationships. A man was essentially dead now. Fletcher had to focus all his energy on finding his killer and making sure that nobody else got hurt.

Hopefully tonight ended without another victim or casualty. But Fletcher had a bad feeling about it, especially when he walked into the club and found Dan Sullivan inside already, arguing with the bartender.

"You have to give this up—" the bartender cut himself off when he noticed Fletcher. "What the hell are you doing here?"

Fletcher pointed toward the DJ booth. "Checking to make sure all of Kiki's stuff is still in the right place, so she'll be all set when she gets here." He'd had to rush to beat her there. Thankfully Mom hadn't been home when he'd run in and changed into Kiki-approved club clothes and those new boots.

"Nobody touched her stuff," Bart said, defensively.

"Are you sure?" Fletcher asked. "The bag I left up there went missing that night." With the glass that had Bart Taylor's prints on it inside. He looked pointedly at Dan Sullivan. "Seems like people can come and go here pretty freely."

"I guess so," Bart said. "Figured you would have been arrested for what happened to that guy in the parking lot."

Fletcher tensed, wondering if the bartender knew just how seriously Stehouwer had been wounded. He shook his head. "Kiki backed me up that I never went out to the parking lot."

The older man snorted. "Of course she would back you up."

"Some security footage did, too," Fletcher said. "Never showed me going out there."

"The camera at the front door doesn't reach that far out into the parking lot, and there aren't any farther out there," Bart said. "You kept going out to the alley that night."

Was that why Stehouwer had been attacked in the parking lot? Because the Slasher had noticed how frequently Fletcher had been checking their usual crime scene?

"You could have walked out through the alley to the parking lot," Bart said.

"Seems like you really want me to be guilty of this," Fletcher said, "and I thought we were going to be friends." He glanced from one to the other of them, wondering what they'd been arguing about. "Just like you two are friends." They hadn't acted like it the other night.

But Bart had known a lot about Sullivan. Maybe they were more than customer and bartender. Bart shook his head. "He's just asking me to help him find someone."

Dan's daughter.

But was she anywhere to be found?

Fletcher had turned up a couple of Jane Does that might have been matches for the girl. Deceased.

He wasn't going to say anything to the desperate father until he could confirm it, though. He really needed the guy's DNA. And Bart's.

If only the Slasher had ever left any behind. But they hadn't left anything that would have proved their guilt.

"There are no cameras in the parking lot," Fletcher repeated back to the man. "But there are some inside here." He pointed toward the ones hidden up among the lights in the tall ceiling that had been painted black like the brick and metal walls.

The bartender shrugged. "I gave all that footage to the police."

Liar.

But if Fletcher called him that, Bart and Dan would realize that the only way Fletcher could know what he'd turned over was because he'd seen what had been turned over to the police. They'd gotten the parking lot footage and some from maybe one camera inside, but there was more than one. So why hadn't the guy turned it over?

What was on it that he'd been trying to hide? And how the hell was Fletcher going to be able to get a look at it?

KIKI HAD NO idea if Fletcher was even going to show up at the club. Maybe he'd decided to go another direction with his investigation. Maybe he was worried that his cover had been blown the other night.

Or maybe…

He just didn't want to see her again after what had happened. Not that she cared. Sure. It had been hot. Pretty incredible.

But that didn't mean they should do it again. Maybe it meant that they shouldn't. That they couldn't risk getting used to that level of passion and pleasure.

Kiki already had a playlist together in her head. Nobody had sent her any special requests this week. Not even her girls, Janie, Claire and Amy. They'd messaged her to make sure the club would be reopened, but that had been it, which was weird.

Usually Claire asked for a few slow ones. And Amy wanted the music without the lyrics. Janie was the one after Kiki's heart and usually requested all the ones about female empowerment. Beyoncé and Joan Jett and Aretha Franklin and even The Chicks. Janie was going to be happy tonight because Kiki had gone really old school and queued up some Nancy Sinatra. *These boots…*

That had been more for Fletcher, though, if he showed up in those boots she'd bought for him. Even though she didn't have much equipment to carry in, she arrived a little early. Just to make sure everything was set up how she liked it and to get her new playlist perfected. Not because of Fletcher.

But when she walked in and found him standing at the bar, her heart did a little flippy thing in her chest, like Fancy when Kiki tried to get the puppy to follow the Spin command. She tried to ignore it and him, like he'd ignored her this past week.

"Ah, Kiki's pissed at you, too," Bart remarked.

"Nobody has any reason to be pissed at me," Fletcher said, but he didn't sound very convincing, like he didn't quite believe it himself. "Kiki, tell them that you weren't lying when you gave me an alibi the other night."

"What?" she asked. "Why would I lie about that?"

"Because you two are a little closer than you and Troy ever were," Bart called back to her.

She shrugged. "Yeah, we're old friends. So there's no way he would have left that guy out there for me to find." She didn't have to fake the shudder that swept over. "And if he had, he wouldn't be here right now. He'd be in the hospital, too. I was mad when he interfered on the dance floor. You think I would condone him doing something like *that*?"

Bart and Dan Sullivan both shook their heads and laughed. "Sorry," Bart said.

And she didn't know if the bartender was apologizing to her or to Fletcher. Then he set up a mug of coffee on the bar in front of the undercover detective and made it clear.

"I didn't mean to give you such a hard time," Bart said. "With all this crazy Slasher business, everybody who works in clubs and all the owners have been on edge. I had to talk the manager into reopening Club Ignition tonight. She wasn't sure she wanted to."

"Is that why Troy hasn't been around?" Dan asked Kiki, walking across the floor toward her. "The Slasher scared him off?"

Or he *was* the Slasher.

That was what Fletcher believed.

She nodded. "Yeah, he was freaked out. He was at that club in Salt Lake City and the one in—"

"Hey, hon," Fletcher interjected as he rushed over to her with that coffee in his hand. Obviously he still needed his caffeine to stay up late. He set the mug on top of one the speakers and asked, "What do you want me to help you with?"

Kiki realized she'd probably been about to say too much. Did Fletcher consider Dan a suspect, too? Or Bart?

Her?

As a detective, he probably automatically thought the worst of everyone he met. Maybe that was why he hadn't called or texted this week.

Maybe he hadn't known if he could trust her.

She narrowed her eyes at him in a bit of a glare. "I got this, *hon.*"

He grinned. "Good thing the equipment is already here. I have another new pair of boots to break in…" He raised his foot, holding up one of the work boots she'd bought him. He'd laced them a little looser, maybe in case he went into a lake again and had to get them off fast.

She hoped he didn't go in the water again. But she felt a bit like she was drowning as she stared at him, desire overwhelming her. With the boots, he wore another pair of distressed jeans. A white tank top type of undershirt underneath a light flannel jacket. And his hair was still a little damp from what must have been a quick shower. He looked sexy as hell, like one of the rock stars whose posters she'd hung on her bedroom walls growing up.

She'd like Fletcher in her bedroom again but not on the wall. Maybe holding her up against it.

His green eyes dilated, as if he was feeling the same overwhelming attraction that she was. She'd really thought that making love with him would remove the distraction. They wouldn't have to wonder anymore how it would be because they would know.

But now that they knew...

She just wanted to do it again.

He jumped over the barricade to join her in the small confines of the overcrowded booth. And her pulse quickened with his nearness, with the heat and hardness of his body so close to hers.

"Thanks for the boots," he said, and he leaned down as if he was going to kiss her.

She pulled back slightly. "I just didn't want you to sue me, you know, over my dog destroying your boots."

"You're claiming Fancy as yours?"

She shrugged. "For the moment. Just fostering her." But she was getting more attached than she'd been to the other puppies she and her grandfather had fostered. Just as she was getting more attached to...

She tensed at the thought she didn't even dare let herself fully formulate. "And don't go reading anything into me dropping off those boots," she continued, lowering her voice to a whisper. "I know that the other night wasn't anything special. Just a one-off, a hookup, a release of all that—"

He closed the distance between them and pressed his mouth against hers, kissing her deeply, passionately. When he finally raised his head, she couldn't think at all.

She could only feel. How very badly she wanted him. But had it been real at all? Or just part of his cover?

"Why did you do that?" she whispered.

"Because I really, really wanted to," he said.

"I thought it was a bad idea," she reminded him of what he'd said last weekend and that had been even before they'd made love.

"It still is," he said, "because now I want you even more, and I know it's going to be even harder for me to stay away from you."

"Why do you want to stay away from me?" she asked. Was he worried about falling for her like she was beginning to worry about falling for him?

"Because I don't want you in danger," he said.

She wanted to argue that she wasn't in any danger. But it had been strange the way that Troy had showed up on the houseboat and then how he'd left that note in her vehicle. He must have shoved it through the window or something because she always locked it.

But even if Troy wasn't the Slasher and she wasn't in any physical danger, she was in danger of another kind. Because when Fletcher had kissed her, she hadn't wanted him to stop.

Chapter Seventeen

The weekend had passed without incident, unless Fletcher considered what had happened after the club, later that night. How he'd gone home with Kiki to that houseboat again.

How they'd made love all night.

That night and the next and the next after that. Mom probably thought he'd moved out. He *had* been looking for a place of his own.

He was staying in Owl Creek, in his new position as lead detective, so he needed a house. He'd pulled up a couple that were listed online and had done the virtual tours. That was about all he had time for.

Around his investigation.

And Kiki.

She wasn't staying. She was working on music that she'd played for him a couple of times when he'd awakened to find her working. She'd written songs to sell and songs to sing and produce on her own. She was going to be big someday soon. Bigger than Owl Creek.

So he had to protect his heart, just like he had to protect his life. Just because nothing had happened last weekend didn't mean that the Slasher had left Owl Creek. In fact, Fletcher was pretty damn certain they were still here.

Troy Hoover. Bart Taylor. Dan Sullivan. Troy had definitely had some means and opportunity to commit those crimes. Bart wasn't always tending bar here in Owl Creek. He worked other clubs, too. And Dan Sullivan had been looking everywhere for his daughter, hitting clubs all over the west coast and neighboring areas. He could have been in those other cities where the attacks had taken place.

Fletcher needed to step up his investigation even though nothing had happened last weekend.

At least nothing at the club. A lot had happened on that houseboat between him and Kiki.

But he was extra uneasy as they unloaded her equipment tonight. He had a feeling that the Slasher was going to act out again. If it was for attention, though, they had it now. Greg Stehouwer's brother, Gerard, had talked to the press, insisting that the Slasher had attacked Greg and that the police were doing nothing to find the psychopath.

Instead of being insulted over Gerard's complaint about the police, Fletcher was relieved that Gerard hadn't blown his cover. And that the man had no idea how Fletcher was working his brother's case. It hadn't become a murder yet. Though Greg was still in a coma, his parents were holding out hope that he would regain consciousness.

Fletcher wasn't as hopeful, even though the doctors had sounded a little less bleak the last time he'd checked with them. Apparently, the guy had started breathing without the ventilator.

While it was a sign of improvement, there was no guarantee that he would wake up. And even if he did, he probably wouldn't be able to help Fletcher identify the Slasher.

According to the medical examiner, the person who had attacked Greg Stehouwer wasn't the same person who had disfigured the other victims. The wounds had been too different. So, was the Slasher one person or two different people working together?

Once again, as he and Kiki carried equipment into the club, he found Bart Taylor and Dan Sullivan together at the bar, their heads bent close as they kept their voices so low nobody could overhear them. Fletcher tried. They seemed to be working on something together. When they noticed him, they jumped apart. They were definitely hiding something.

But what?

Had they figured out who and what he really was?

"Hey, Fletcher," Bart called out. "Want your usual?"

He chuckled because his usual wasn't an alcoholic drink like bartenders usually served but a cup of coffee. Strong. After how little sleep he'd gotten over the past week, he definitely needed it. He stopped at the bar to stick his finger through the handle of the steaming mug while he juggled the other equipment he carried. "Thanks."

"How about you, Kiki?" Bart asked.

"Got my usual tea and honey," Kiki said, raising her thermos.

Fletcher grimaced, remembering when he'd tried her concoction. Like a hot toddy without the whiskey and the heat, it had been lukewarm, overly sweet tea. No wonder she had so much energy all the time.

Fletcher yawned then. He really needed his caffeine.

After rolling a speaker into place, he took a long sip from his mug.

"You still not used to the late nights, old man?" Kiki teased.

He chuckled and whispered, "I'm not the one who fell asleep on me last night."

Her face flushed, and her dark eyes glittered with desire. "I'm wide awake now, though. And you're not."

"Maybe because someone woke me up so early this morning," he said.

"Do you have any complaints about that?" she asked, and she ran her fingers down his chest.

Through his thin T-shirt, he could feel the heat of her touch, and his skin tingled while his heart pounded fast and hard with excitement.

"No complaints at all," he assured her. He didn't remember the last time he'd been so happy or satiated. That thought brought on a rush of guilt that swept away some of the happiness. His dad was dead. Greg Stehouwer was basically brain-dead and other men had been permanently disfigured. He had no right to feel happy, at least not until the Slasher was behind bars. Permanently.

While the last weekend had been quiet, Fletcher didn't believe that the Slasher had left Owl Creek. He or she was here. Or maybe there were two of them, like the medical examiner had speculated after ruling that Greg Stehouwer's wounds were different from the other victims.

Two people.

Like Dan Sullivan and the bartender.

Or two totally unrelated people. Maybe whoever had attacked Greg Stehouwer was hoping that the Slasher would be blamed for it. Greg was as rich and important as he'd claimed that night on the dance floor, and once he got married, he was going to get even richer with a payout of a trust from his deceased grandparents. Money was always a strong motive for murder. And whoever had attacked Greg Stehouwer hadn't been simply trying to disfigure him.

Was that what the Slasher had been doing to the other victims? Trying to ruin their lives for some reason like he or she believed theirs had been ruined?

Like Dan Sullivan.

He'd lost his daughter. Did he blame every guy he saw in a club for taking her away from him? Fletcher had sent out her picture everywhere, and he was waiting for a call back from a few coroners whose Jane Does had matched the description of Dan's missing daughter.

One was in LA. There was another in San Francisco and one in Salt Lake City.

After helping Kiki set up her equipment, Fletcher headed toward the bar where Sullivan was sitting. He set his empty mug on the granite bar for Bart to refill.

"You've been the first customer here the last couple of weekends," Fletcher remarked to Sullivan. And Bart had been letting him in before the club even opened. "Do you have a lead that your daughter is in Owl Creek?"

Dan shook his head. "No. No leads. But I think I'm starting to fall for this town. All the fishing and hiking."

"You been doing a lot of that during the week?" Fletcher asked.

The guy shrugged. "Some. It's a beautiful area. Did you grow up here?"

Fletcher tensed, wondering if his cover had been blown.

Just as he'd been checking out Dan Sullivan and Bart Taylor, they might have been checking him out. Since he had grown up here, Dan and Bart could have run into a lot of people who knew him and knew what he really did for a living. And it wasn't acting as Kiki's assistant but as the lead detective for Owl Creek PD.

"I did grow up here," he admitted. There was no point in lying about that if Sullivan had already figured out the truth.

"Is that how you know Kiki?" A female voice asked the question.

And Fletcher turned, expecting to see a waitress behind him. But it was one of the women he called Kiki's superfans. He didn't know which one was which, but this one was the redhead with the frizzy hair and bright smile.

He smiled back. "Yes, it is."

"She's amazing!" one of the other ones gushed as the blonde and the brunette walked up to the bar, too.

"Doors open, huh?" Fletcher asked.

"The bouncer let us in a little early," the blonde said with a wink.

"He always lets the prettiest women in first," Fletcher said.

They giggled at his compliment. He had a soft spot for them because of their adulation of Kiki. He had become one of her superfans, too.

"Are you going to dance with us tonight?" the brunette said with a bit of a whine. And then Bart handed her a glass of wine across the bar.

"If I'm going to keep up with you ladies, I'm going to need more coffee," he said.

"I already refilled your cup," Bart said, pointing at it. "It's probably getting cold."

"Let's get this party started!" Kiki's voice echoed throughout the nearly empty club. More people were coming through the doors, but they obviously hadn't been lined up around the block like that first weekend Fletcher had gone undercover as her assistant.

Greg's brother going public about the Slasher attacking him here had definitely affected their business. The only reason anyone had probably showed up at all tonight was because of Kiki. She was amazing.

She wore the red leather vest and shorts, probably because she'd left it on the boat that first time they'd made love and she hadn't gone back to the cottage to grab any of her other club wardrobe. This was Fletcher's favorite, though, because it reminded him of that night, though not everything that had happened then had been good.

He could have drowned. And maybe he had in a way.

He'd drowned in the pleasure she gave him. In her.

To get the dancing started, she sang along with the songs she played, mixing them between two of her four turntables. He didn't know how she kept everything straight, especially when she had to be as tired as he was.

He reached for the mug of coffee. It was getting a little lukewarm, so he drank it fast and had Bart fill it again. He had a feeling he was going to have to stay alert tonight. That something was going to happen.

Because that feeling was an uneasy one that had goose bumps lifting on his skin. And he wore a flannel shirt over his undershirt, so he shouldn't have been cold. He should have been too hot in the flannel, especially with the way Kiki looked.

Just the sight of her, her body moving to the music she played, had him a little light-headed, a little dizzy on her beauty and the sound of her husky voice singing along with that music.

He was in danger. And not just from the Slasher. He was in danger of falling for Kiki.

KIKI WAS SO pumped with excitement that she couldn't stop dancing. The music flowed through her like her blood. She'd written some great stuff over the past week. And she'd made some incredible love with an incredible man.

A very sweet man in the way that he played with Fancy and worked with her on her commands and the way that he listened to all Kiki's songs and acted so in awe of her. Sometimes just the way he looked at her with that strangely intense look of his...

He hadn't been looking at her that way tonight, though. It was as if he could barely hold his lids up over his eyes. At the moment, he was a very tired man.

She felt a pang of regret that she'd kept Fletcher up late and then woken him up early. He was obviously tired, so tired that he'd been nearly nodding off in the booth.

So it was probably good that her girls had cajoled him into joining them on the dance floor. But he wasn't moving with his usual rhythm. He seemed sluggish, and he stumbled and nearly fell. It was almost as if...

He was drunk.

But his coffee cup sat atop the speaker, vibrating with the beat. She leaned forward and sniffed it. She didn't smell alcohol in it, though she wouldn't have expected to since she'd never seen him drink anything but coffee. But the way he was acting...

He was more than tired. It was as if he'd been drugged.

Alarm shot through her. Was that what had happened to those other men? Why they hadn't managed to fight back harder against the Slasher? Because they'd been drugged first?

She gazed out into the crowd, looking for him. But now, later in the night, the dance floor was full. She couldn't even find her girls now.

Maybe they'd taken him back to the bar. Or outside for some air.

He definitely needed it. But if he went into the alley tonight as he usually did, to check for victims, he might become the next one.

THE SLASHER HAD figured out who Fletcher really was. A Colton. Rich and spoiled like all those other victims.

After the recent death of his father, he was probably even richer. It had been easy enough to figure out who he was after just following him around for a bit, like to that bookstore his sister owned.

There were a whole lot of Coltons in this town. So if one more died, like his father had, he wouldn't be missed. Would Kiki miss him?

The Slasher felt a pang of regret. But it couldn't be helped. Kiki would realize, in the long run, that the Slasher had done her a favor.

Had saved her from that inevitable speech rich guys like Colton gave to women like her.

It was fun while it lasted, but it wasn't going to work out in the long run. They were too different.

And what they really meant was that they were better.

And they wanted someone better.

The Slasher knew what Fletcher Colton wanted. Not just someone better.

Detective Colton wanted the Slasher and he'd just been using Kiki. So really, this was a favor to Kiki.

Getting rid of Fletcher Colton for good.

Chapter Eighteen

Fletcher's head pounded, and his vision blurred, the strobe lights blinding him with blue, red and purple flashes. He needed more coffee. Or maybe some fresh air.

He'd gotten away from the girls and off the dance floor with the excuse that he needed to use the restroom. And he had…

To splash cold water on his face. But that hadn't woken him up. And when he stepped back out into the club, those lights flashed at him, making his head pound harder than the music. The music.

Kiki. He needed to talk to Kiki. To tell her something…

But he couldn't think any clearer than he could see. He moved back into the bathroom, where the lights didn't flash, just buzzed overhead from the fluorescent bulbs. That light was harsh but shouldn't have made him feel as dizzy and light-headed as he felt.

Maybe he needed air.

His stomach roiled, too, though. And he stepped into a stall to use the toilet bowl as his stomach expelled everything he'd eaten and drank that day. Just coffee.

So why was he so tired? So light-headed?

Maybe his blood sugar was too low. Or…

He reached into his pocket for the handkerchief he'd shoved into it earlier, but paper crinkled in his fingers instead of cloth. A note.

He pulled it out and had to blink a couple of times to focus on it, to read the scrawled writing. *Looking for me? You know where to find me. If you're brave enough…*

The Slasher. He or she hadn't signed the note, but they hadn't had to. He knew who had given it to him even though he hadn't noticed when it had been shoved in his pocket. Who had passed it to him? And when?

On the dance floor?

Or when he'd been standing in the short line for the men's room? A couple of guys had pushed past him. And he'd also walked by Dan and Bart at the bar. When he'd stumbled, Dan had jumped up and helped him steady himself.

"Whoa, there, you must be burning the candle at both ends, Fletcher."

He had been. But the way he felt now was more than tired. He'd probably been drugged.

So he knew he shouldn't go out to that alley. Not now. Not alone and definitely not in this condition. Whatever this was.

But maybe throwing up would help clear his head. And the fresh air…

Not that the air in the alley was fresh. And not that he should go out there alone.

His head had cleared enough from vomiting that he knew to call for help. He reached for his cell and sent a picture of the note to the officer who was always on standby in the area when Fletcher was working undercover at the club.

His back-up would be here within minutes. Would meet him in the alley...

He left the stall, stopped to wash his hands and his face and to gulp mouthfuls of water from the faucet. Now, if he headed to the alley, the officer would certainly be almost there, too.

The alley was behind the kitchen, so that only employees were supposed to use it. Maybe that was why Fletcher hadn't found anyone out there yet when he'd worked undercover at Club Ignition.

Maybe that was why Greg Stehouwer had been attacked in the parking lot instead. But he hadn't received a note. Or if he had, it hadn't been on him when Kiki had found him.

Of course, the detail of the note hadn't been leaked to the press. And if the person who'd attacked Greg had been a copycat, they wouldn't have known that detail.

But this person, the one who'd slipped Fletcher the note, knew it. They had to be the Slasher.

He started down the hall toward the bar area and just as he neared it, he stumbled again. But Dan Sullivan wasn't there to catch him this time. He didn't see Bart either. One of the cocktail waitresses was behind the bar serving drinks.

Where had those two gone? Were they waiting in the alley for him?

And where was Kiki?

Even though music played, it wasn't with the energy and mix that she gave to the beat. He glanced across the dance floor to the booth. It was empty.

Where was she?

Hopefully in the restroom. But he had a horrible feeling

she'd gone into the alley. Maybe looking for him. And she was going to find what was waiting for him.

The Slasher.

He couldn't wait for backup, not if Kiki was in danger. He had to go out there now and hope like hell that he wasn't too late.

KIKI HADN'T FOUND FLETCHER. She had found someone else, though, hidden among the dancers on the floor. Troy. He'd caught her wrist when she'd tried to pass him. And she'd nearly used the pepper spray she had clasped in one hand.

"Kiki."

"Troy! What are you doing here?" Was he the one who'd drugged Fletcher? He'd had to be drugged to be as sluggish as he'd been. Because he'd been tired before but had never moved like that.

"I need your help."

She shook her head and tried to pull her wrist free of his grasp. But, like the groom from the bachelor party a couple of weekends ago, he tightened his grasp instead of releasing her. "Let me go!" she told him.

She didn't want to pepper spray him. Not there in the middle of a crowded dance floor.

Too many other people might get hurt. But she didn't want Fletcher getting hurt. Or was she already too late for that?

"You need to listen to me," Troy implored her. "I'm not the Slasher. But I think I know who is."

"That's why you need to talk to the police, Troy," she urged him. "You need to tell them what you know."

He shook his head. "They're not going to listen to me.

And I don't really have any proof. You need to listen to me, Kiki. I want to tell you."

She shook her head. "I'm not the police, Troy. I can't help you with this."

"I thought you were my friend."

She shook her head again. "No. I don't even really know who you are."

He released her then, so abruptly that she stumbled back into some other dancers.

"Kiki! Kiki, play my song next."

She wasn't going to play any songs. She had to find Fletcher. She had to make sure that he was okay. She shoved her way through the other dancers, ignoring them as they tried to catch her attention, as they tried to stop her. She kept her grip tight on her can of pepper spray.

She had a feeling that she was going to need it. Either because of Troy or because of Fletcher.

He wasn't at the bar. She would have seen him, in his blue and pink flannel shirt, if he had been. He claimed to hate that shirt, just as he claimed to hate the boots that he kept so loosely laced now. But he'd worn that shirt a few times. Just to cover his holster, he claimed.

He had his gun.

The pressure on her chest eased a little with that realization. He was armed.

But if he'd been drugged, like she was worried he'd been, he might not be able to fire that weapon in time to save himself from the Slasher's attack. Because if he had been drugged, it had probably been the Slasher who'd done it.

Where would the Slasher be waiting for Fletcher? The

parking lot where Greg Stehouwer had been attacked? Or the alley?

She chose to check the alley first. Because it was closer and because she could rush through it to the parking lot where she'd found Stehouwer bleeding in the weeds.

One of the waitresses who was tending the bar glanced at her as she ducked under the counter and passed through the doorway into the kitchen. A lot of employees went to the alley to smoke, but Kiki rarely went into the kitchen and definitely not into the alley unless she'd been carrying her equipment in or out through that door.

With the location of the parking lot and the front door, though, she could park by the entrance and bring her stuff in that way. But because those spots were designated for people with disabilities, she had to move it after she unloaded her equipment.

But even though she hadn't used the alley often here, she knew where it was. She rushed through the kitchen, past the enormous dishwashers that leaked steam into the room, to that steel door.

When she pushed it open, she saw Fletcher in the faint glow from the light at the top of the short stairwell that led down to the asphalt where he stood, his gun gripped in his hand. But she saw only him.

A dumpster was just below that stairwell, jammed between this old warehouse and the one next to it that was still abandoned. Nobody had renovated it yet like they had Club Ignition.

She'd thought once or twice about how it would make a great sound studio. It was all brick and metal and thick insulation. The acoustics in it were even better than in the club.

But she didn't have the money for something like that—at least not yet. And right now she didn't have the interest.

All her focus was on a certain detective.

"Fletcher!" she called out to him.

He tensed, then turned slowly toward her, as if he was about to pass out. He had definitely been drugged. And as he turned, something jumped from the shadows on the other side of that big dumpster. It didn't look like a person to Kiki—who couldn't see anything but plastic, like some kind of synthetic suit with a hood and mask—but then a knife blade flashed.

And she knew who it was. The Slasher.

She screamed again. "Fletcher! Behind you!"

But the blade was already swinging toward him as he turned with the gun in his hand.

Kiki rushed down those steps as she raised her can of pepper spray. With the Slasher wearing a mask, it might not affect them at all. But Kiki had to try to protect Fletcher.

She had to make an effort to save him. Because he wasn't aiming or firing his weapon. Instead, when that blade came down across his arm, he dropped it onto the ground. And then he fell onto it, too, his blood sprayed across the asphalt beneath him.

Kiki screamed again as she rushed toward the Slasher. She pressed hard on the canister button, sending that pepper spray out toward the attacker who turned that knife on Kiki now.

Instead of saving Fletcher, Kiki might have become just another victim of the Slasher.

Chapter Nineteen

Fletcher felt no pain from his wound being stitched, just the tug and pull of the needle moving through his skin. The cut across his forearm wasn't all that deep, but it had bled like hell, the torn sleeve of his flannel shirt saturated with blood. It continued to ooze through the stitches pulling the wound together.

At least they'd numbed the area on his arm.

His head still hurt from whatever drug had been in his coffee. A doctor at the hospital in Conners had taken a sample of his blood to test it. To see what had been slipped to him.

"This is going to take a lot of stitches," the ER doctor warned him as he continued pushing the needle through his skin like he was hemming some curtains.

Fletcher knew he was lucky that it was just his arm. And not his face like the Slasher's other victims. Or his chest.

Or his heart.

Because he didn't think the Slasher had just intended to disfigure Fletcher. They had probably intended to kill him. If not for Kiki, they would have probably succeeded.

"Kiki Shelton. Is she here, too?" he asked, and his voice

was raspy—probably from that drug. He knew he'd asked already, but his mind was still a little foggy from whatever he'd been slipped.

"Yes," the doctor replied. "She's fine."

"So she's in the waiting room?" he asked. That was the only way she would be fine. If she'd been in the ambulance with him, which was how he vaguely recalled things, then she wouldn't be fine.

He couldn't remember what all had happened in that alley. Between the drugs and then the blood loss.

And the pain.

He'd felt that then. Not just in his arm or his head. Even his eyes stung. They burned still, so much so that he lifted his free hand toward his face.

"Don't," the doctor warned him. "I'm not sure we got all the pepper spray off you. You might have some on your hand that you'll get in your eyes."

"Pepper spray?"

"Yeah, it probably saved your life," the doctor replied. "The woman who rode in with you—"

"Kiki Shelton." She had been with him. He could vaguely remember her hand on him, touching him, as if she'd wanted to make sure that he was still alive.

"She probably saved your life. She used it on the attacker, but with that alley being so narrow and the air conditioner condenser being right there, the pepper spray went all over the place."

"How is Kiki?" he asked with concern. "I'm a detective, Doctor, with Owl Creek PD. I was working undercover at that club as Kiki's assistant." And if she'd gotten hurt because of him…

"She got it the worst," the doctor admitted. "We had to flush out her eyes and then put bandages over them so that she doesn't strain them."

So she was essentially blind. Was that why she'd held onto him in the ambulance? Or had she been worried about him? She must have been, or why else would she have come out into the alley like she had?

"And the Slasher?" Fletcher asked, his voice raspy. Now he knew it was probably from the pepper spray.

"Slasher?" The doctor's hand stilled midstitch. "Is that who—of course. That's who."

"Who what? Did they come in, too?"

The doctor shook his head. "No. They got away."

Fletcher cursed.

And the doctor nodded now in agreement. "That psycho needs to be caught. I saw what they did to those last two victims."

"How is Greg Stehouwer?" Fletcher asked.

"A frickin' miracle," the doctor replied. "The neurologist said there's brain activity now. He'll probably wake up soon. But he'll still have a long road to recovery after he does."

At least he was alive. That was something.

"I see why you put yourself at risk like that to catch this sociopath," the doctor said. "You're lucky Ms. Shelton was there."

He was lucky. She wasn't. "You think she'll be all right?" he asked, his heart beating fast with fear for her. And with something else.

Something he couldn't let himself acknowledge.

The doctor nodded. "Pepper spray doesn't cause permanent blindness. Usually that lasts for up to forty-five minutes at the most. Ms. Shelton's case is a little different because I think she rubbed it in. She made it worse. But I'm sure she'll be fine."

"And she didn't get cut?" Fletcher's stomach lurched with the horror of her being harmed like those men had been.

Already the numbness in his arm was beginning to wear off and he could feel the nip of the needle, the strain of his skin, as the doctor finished closing his wound.

He didn't care about his pain, though. He just didn't want Kiki to be in pain.

"She didn't get cut," the doctor assured him.

"Where is she?" Fletcher asked. He had to see for himself that she was okay.

"We put her in an individual room in the ER area," the doctor said. "She needs to rest for a while, and then hopefully her vision will be fine and we can remove those bandages."

Hopefully.

But what if it wasn't?

If Kiki lost her vision because of him, because of his involving her in this investigation, he would never forgive himself. And he doubted she would either.

SOME RESCUER KIKI WAS. She would stick to playing music from now on instead of playing detective. Rather than helping Fletcher, she'd probably distracted him. And he'd gotten wounded because of her instead of catching the Slasher like he'd been trying to do.

In addition to the laceration on his arm, the pepper spray had also affected him, making him cough and gag like she'd been doing.

And the burning.

It hurt so much. Even now, with the cold bandage wrapped over her eyes, her skin burned. And her throat ached from all that coughing. She needed her honey lemon tea right now more than she needed the sleep the doctor had advised her to get.

Like she could sleep at all with that image in her head. Of that person, bundled up in a hazmat suit, lunging at Fletcher with that huge knife.

It had been like a machete. So sharp.

It could have killed Fletcher easily. Or taken off his arm.

The wound had been bleeding so much. She needed to check on him more than she needed to rest her eyes. She couldn't rest without knowing how he was.

Hinges creaked as the door opened. And even through the bandage, Kiki could see a faint lightness. But then the hinges creaked again, as the door closed, shutting out the light.

"Hello?" she called out.

Had a doctor or nurse come back to check on her?

"Can you take these bandages off now?" she asked. "I'm fine. Really."

She waited a beat, but nobody responded. Had someone just opened the door and then closed it again?

But then she heard the squeak of a shoe sole against the linoleum flooring. And another sound…

Of someone breathing.

She was not alone.

"Hello?" she called out again. "Who's there?"

But only that eerie silence greeted her again. Who was

it? And why wouldn't they identify themselves? Was it because they didn't want anyone to identify them?

Was it the Slasher?

THE SLASHER'S EYES burned with nearly the same intensity as their rage. Why had Kiki Shelton messed everything up? She was supposed to stay up in her damn booth, playing her music like she always did.

Except for those rare instances when she came out into the crowd. But even then, she never made it farther than the dance floor.

She shouldn't have come out to that alley. Shouldn't have interfered like that.

Fletcher Colton should have been dead. Or at least hurt a hell of a lot worse than he'd been.

He had to be the one who'd stifled the story about the attack in Conners. He'd been working that case, too. The Slasher had found that out, too.

That the lead detective of Owl Creek Police Department had been helping out in Conners. Like he'd claimed to just be helping an old friend when he'd posed as Kiki's assistant.

But maybe they were old friends. Maybe that was why it seemed like there was something between them. Something that could have cost Kiki her life.

Something that still would if she was stupid enough to get in the Slasher's way again.

Chapter Twenty

The hospital rushed his blood work results. His coffee had definitely been tainted with rohypnol. As out of it as Fletcher had been, he wouldn't have survived that skirmish with the Slasher in the alley if it hadn't been for Kiki and her pepper spray. She had saved his life.

The backup officer hadn't gotten Fletcher's text right away. Since Fletcher had had no issue with the cell reception when he'd called to report finding Greg Stehouwer, there must have been a cell signal jammer inside the club. Or maybe the Slasher had brought one.

It seemed as if they'd thought of everything, like the hazmat-type suit they'd worn. No wonder they never left any DNA or fingerprints at the scene.

Eventually the text had gone through, though, and the officer had arrived and then called the ambulance that had brought him and Kiki to the hospital in Conners.

So Kiki had been his backup instead of an officer. She'd saved his life. And he had to make sure she was really all right. So even though he knew she was supposed to be resting, he wanted to check on her and had wheedled her location out of the ER doctor.

But Kiki wasn't resting. As he approached her room, he heard her voice rise, demanding to know, "Who's there? Who are you?"

He could hear the fear in her voice, too. So he pushed open the door to the darkness of the room. Only the light from the hall spilled into the space, revealing a bed and a shadow looming over it.

That shadow lunged toward Fletcher, or maybe toward the door, but he blocked them and shoved the person to the floor. Then he fumbled against the wall and turned on the light.

It illuminated the man lying on the floor. He was thin with long, stringy hair that looked like it hadn't been washed in a while. And his eyes were wild and bloodshot, like an animal that was starving for food or...

The guy tried to scramble up from the floor, but Fletcher held him down with one of those heavy boots Kiki had bought him. "Sit back, Troy. You're not getting away from me this time." And he used his cell to call for the backup that had followed him and Kiki to the hospital.

Kiki.

She sat up in the bed now, pushing at the bandage that had been wrapped around her head. The compress dropped onto the sheet that covered her. Her eyes and skin were red, but she blinked and focused on the two men.

"Why didn't you say something, Troy?" she asked, her voice sharp with anger. "Why'd you just stand there in the dark?"

Troy lay back on the floor as if resigned, but he didn't answer her.

Then she focused on Fletcher and said, "What are you doing! You shouldn't be out of bed! You're hurt."

Fletcher would rather have her angry than afraid, even if she was angry with him. "I'm fine," he said. Thanks to her. "How are you?"

"Pissed off," she said. She pointed toward his arm. "You're still bleeding."

The bandage covering his wound was turning red with fresh blood. He must have reopened the stitches when he shoved Troy to the floor. "No reason to be mad about my cut. It's been stitched up."

"I'm mad that you went into that alley alone."

"I couldn't find you," Fletcher said.

"I couldn't find *you*," Kiki said. "And I could tell from the way you were acting that somebody must have slipped you something."

"They did," Fletcher confirmed. He looked down at Troy. "What the hell are you doing here in her room? How did you even know she was here?" Unless he was the Slasher.

"He was at the club," Kiki answered for him.

Fletcher nodded. "Of course he was. You've been everywhere the Slasher has attacked someone, Troy. Why is that?"

"It's not me," Troy said, his voice quavering with fear, and his body started shaking so badly it seemed like he was more than afraid. He could be having a seizure, or maybe going through withdrawal. Fletcher had seen people acting similarly in his years as a police officer.

Fletcher struggled to imagine this guy as the Slasher. How would someone like him have eluded the authorities for so long in so many different places?

The organizational skills it had taken to plan and execute the attacks didn't seem like something Troy was capable of doing. The Slasher had been so careful and had made certain to leave behind no clues.

No DNA. No fingerprints.

The note. Fletcher had the note. Maybe there would be something on it since the Slasher hadn't managed to take it back like they had from the other victims.

Was that why Troy was here? But then he would have been in Fletcher's room and not Kiki's.

"What the hell are you doing here?" Fletcher asked again.

"I had to talk to Kiki," Troy said. "She has to know the truth."

"You said that you know who the Slasher is," Kiki said. "You told me that on the dance floor. Who is it, Troy?"

The guy's skinny body shook harder, as if he was convulsing.

"What's wrong?" Kiki asked.

"I think he's going through withdrawal." Fletcher stepped away to call out, "We need help!"

But then Troy was up from the floor, trying to shove past Fletcher. Fletcher caught him again and dragged him down to the floor, holding him against the linoleum. Pain throbbed in his arm and in his head. He was in no condition to subdue a suspect. And no matter what Troy claimed, he was still a suspect.

Maybe he was even faking the shakes. He was doing it again, clicking his teeth together and trembling.

"What's wrong with you?" Fletcher asked.

A nurse appeared in the doorway and gasped. "What's going on?"

"Get security."

The officer Fletcher had called stepped around the nurse. "Detective Colton, I'm sorry—"

Fletcher shook his head, forestalling another apology. The guy had been apologizing since he'd found Fletcher and Kiki in the alley. "You're here now. We need to arrest this guy."

"Is this the Slasher?" Officer Blaine asked.

Fletcher shrugged. "I don't know." And he really wasn't certain. "But he has an outstanding warrant for drug possession and another for failure to pay child support."

"We need to assess his medical condition," the nurse said. "Before you take him out of here. He appears to be having a seizure." She stepped into the hall and shouted for a doctor.

Troy's shaking body pushed against Fletcher's wounded arm, loosening his grasp. Maybe he was faking, just trying to escape. But with the officer standing inside the room now, there was no escape.

"Wait," Kiki said. She swung her legs over the side of the bed, and she joined him and Troy on the floor. She wore a thin gown instead of her club clothes. "You wanted to talk to me, Troy," she reminded the guy. "You wanted to tell me who the Slasher is."

But the guy's eyes rolled back into his head, and he convulsed even harder. And Fletcher had a feeling that he wasn't faking now.

The doctor, the one who'd stitched up Fletcher, rushed into the room then with the nurse. Fletcher and Kiki and the officer stepped back into the hall to get out of the way. But then they had to flatten themselves against the wall as the doctor and nurse rolled out a gurney with Troy on it, his body still convulsing.

"Do you really think he knows who the Slasher is?" Officer Blaine asked Kiki the question.

She shrugged. "I don't know."

"Stay here," Fletcher told the officer. "Make sure he doesn't get away. We need to arrest him for those outstanding warrants and hold him for questioning."

The officer nodded and rushed off to catch up to that gurney, leaving Fletcher and Kiki alone. Even with the red and swollen eyes and skin, she was so beautiful. He wanted to close his arms around her and hold on and never let her go. But being close to him had already put her in danger.

"I'm sorry," he said. "I never should have gotten you involved in this investigation." Unable to stop himself, he reached out and touched her face, skimming his fingers along her cheek. "I'm so sorry you got hurt."

She shivered a bit, probably cold in her thin gown. "I'm fine," she said. "But you're not. You're bleeding more now. The wound must have reopened." She pointed at his arm where the bandage had gotten saturated, and blood trickled down over his hand to drop onto the floor.

"It could have been much worse," he said. The Slasher had lured him out to the alley to do more than maim him. "You saved my life."

But it killed him that she'd been so close to the Slasher that the Slasher could have done to her what they'd done to so many other people. And he had to make sure that she was never put in that kind of danger again.

At least not because of him.

KIKI WASN'T USUALLY SQUEAMISH, but all that blood on Fletcher's arm made her light-headed. Or maybe that was still the aftereffects of the pepper spray that had gone all over her and probably all over him, too, since his eyes were scarlet and swollen like hers.

She couldn't stand and watch as the doctor unbandaged and stitched his arm, so she slipped back into the room where she'd left her bandage lying on the bed, the bandage that had covered her eyes and made her feel so helpless. She hated that feeling, hated how it brought her back to the edge of a memory she never wanted to let into her mind again.

Of her parents' accident, of being in that car with them and not able to help them. And so, she'd shut it all out with music, singing to herself until help had arrived.

But it had been too late for her parents. Just as it had almost been too late for Fletcher and for her. The siren in the distance had probably scared off the Slasher more than her pepper spray had.

The pepper spray had covered her clothes, too, so the red leather outfit was sealed into a plastic bag. She had nothing to wear home but her gown. And she wanted to go home.

She couldn't call Grandpa, though. She didn't want him to see her with her eyes and the skin around them so red and puffy. She didn't want to worry him like she was worried. The Slasher was still out there.

She didn't think it was Troy, and she didn't think Fletcher did anymore either. But he still had Officer Blaine sticking close to him, making sure he didn't escape again.

She needed to escape. She could have called Ruby to bring her some clothes and give her a ride back to Owl Creek, but she didn't want to wake up the pregnant woman at this hour. And she didn't want to worry her either.

A knock sounded at the door, and it creaked open to

Fletcher. He walked inside, a bag dangling from his hand. "I had Frannie bring you some clothes," he said.

"Frannie's here?" she asked. While she knew Ruby best, from Crosswinds, she liked all of Fletcher's sisters.

"I just had her drop some stuff at the desk that you could wear home. And I had your vehicle towed here, too. The doctor said you'll be able to go home. So you can get dressed and leave."

"Trying to get rid of me?" she asked.

"Trying to get you out of danger," he said. "You never should have been in that situation tonight. It's my fault."

"It's the Slasher's fault," she reminded him.

"But still, until the Slasher is caught, you should stay away from the clubs," he said.

"Now you're really pissing me off," she said. "You have no right to tell me how to live my life."

He stared at her with that strangely intense gaze of his. "I have no right?" he asked, and a muscle twitched along his tightly clenched jaw.

Was he mad at her?

Or just mad about what had happened?

Kiki got that; she was angry, too.

She was mad at the Slasher. At Fletcher for putting himself in danger. And mostly she was mad at herself for caring so damn much about him. This was his job—catching criminals. Of course, the work could put him in danger because of the treacherous people he was determined to catch.

But after losing her mom and dad, Kiki didn't want to lose anyone else she loved. Not that she loved Fletcher.

But she could fall for him. If she wasn't careful...

She was on the verge, feeling kind of like she was balanced on the edge of a cliff, and it wouldn't take much of a push for her to fall over it. To fall in love.

The past few weeks had been amazing. In the bedroom and out of it. Fletcher was fun and funny and sweet. And sometimes the way he looked at her…

She felt like she might not be the only one on the edge of that cliff. But he was looking at her differently right now. He seemed to want to push her away from the cliff and away from him.

"You have no right to tell me I can't do my job," she said. "Any more than I have a right to tell you that you can't do yours."

That muscle twitched along his jaw again.

"You were the one who was really in danger tonight," she pointed out. "You're the one the Slasher drugged and lured to the alley. Not me."

"But you put yourself in harm's way," he said. "Because of me. If I hadn't been there…"

"I might have gotten nervous about some other guy getting hurt and followed him into the alley," she said. "So don't take it so personally, Colton."

His lips twitched now along with that muscle, as if he was tempted to grin no matter how mad he was at her. "I will take it personally if you get hurt," he said. And then almost reluctantly he added, "I don't want you getting hurt because of me, Kiki. Because of this investigation."

"The club will close down for at least another week," she said. If not permanently since another attack had taken place. She hoped that didn't happen. She really enjoyed spinning at a venue in her hometown. "So you don't have to worry about anything happening to me there."

"I will worry until the Slasher is caught," he said.

"Maybe Troy really does know who the Slasher is," she suggested.

If so, she had no doubt that Fletcher would find out. He would get the truth out of him. And then maybe all of this would be over. But to her, right now, it felt like it was already over between the two of them.

And she wasn't sure if that was because Fletcher wanted to keep her safe or if he wanted to keep himself safe from falling for her.

She could relate to that. She didn't want to love anyone else and lose them like she had her folks. Maybe it was best if it ended now before anyone got hurt any worse.

Chapter Twenty-One

Troy Hoover had recovered remarkably fast, getting released from the hospital within just a couple of days. Maybe it was the methadone he was given, or maybe he'd just been faking all along. Fletcher didn't know. And he didn't care because now that the man had been released from the hospital, he was in police custody in Owl Creek. At the moment, he was in the interrogation room with Fletcher seated across from him.

"The Slasher wants to kill me," Troy insisted.

Fletcher furrowed his brow. "Why? The other victims were all rich and were usually at the clubs for bachelor parties." Troy was neither rich nor a bachelor.

He owed child support, but he'd never officially divorced his children's mother.

"I don't know," Troy said. "Maybe he thinks I saw him or something. That I know who he is."

"If you do know who he is, then he's right about you," Fletcher pointed out. "Who is it, Troy?"

"That old guy that hangs around the bar," Troy said, his voice cracking with fear. "He even paid Bart to try to get me to come into the club. That's why I kept going in because Bart kept calling me and telling me to show up."

That explained those quiet conversations that Fletcher had interrupted between Bart and Dan Sullivan. "Why?"

Troy shrugged. "I don't know why. The only thing I can think of is he's the Slasher."

"But you have no proof of that?"

"He's real rich and real smart. I'm sure he's covered his tracks."

"Then why would he think you're a threat?" Fletcher asked. "If there's no evidence to link him to those attacks?" Sullivan wouldn't worry about the testimony of a known drug user implicating him when there was no evidence that could back up Troy's wild claim.

"I don't know." Troy yawned. It was getting late. After his release from the hospital, he'd had to be driven to Owl Creek, processed and arraigned. "I don't know."

Because Troy was a drug user and, from his doctor's report, had done some significant damage to his body, it wasn't likely that he'd been able to execute those crimes like the Slasher had. But Dan Sullivan...

He was a distinct possibility. And even Bart.

Troy had only the bartender's word that Sullivan was the one trying to lure him into the club. What if Bart was acting on his own? Why would either of them want Troy at the club? As Fletcher had pointed out, he wasn't the Slasher's usual victim. But maybe this had nothing to do with the Slasher.

Maybe there was another reason they'd wanted Troy at the club. Who knew? Maybe he owed Bart the bartender some money. Fletcher wasn't as concerned about Troy as he'd once been, so he stood up and stepped out of the inter-rogation room. "He can go back to his cell," Fletcher told an officer. He was still wanted on those other warrants and had to make whatever bail the judge had set for him.

Having shut off his phone while he was in the interroga-tion, Fletcher turned it back to the buzz of notifications of voice mails. His pulse quickened with hope that one was from Kiki. He hadn't seen her since that night at the hospi-tal. But that had been for her sake as much as his.

He didn't want his investigation to put her in danger again. But the only way to make sure she was really safe was to close the case. To find the Slasher.

He checked his voice mail and found two messages. One from the hospital in Conners and another from the medi-cal examiner in San Francisco. He played the one from the hospital first. The doctor thought that Greg would be re-gaining consciousness soon.

And if that happened, Fletcher wanted to take his state-ment. If he could talk, that was. If he remembered anything after that blow he'd taken to his head and if he'd avoided the potential brain damage it may have caused.

But if he could talk, Fletcher wanted to know if the man had seen his assailant. Though, given what he'd discovered about Greg's trust, Fletcher wasn't all that certain that the Slasher had attacked Greg or someone else had.

He rushed off to Conners, but it was late when he ar-rived. This late at night, the ICU was relatively dark and, except for the beep of the machines monitoring the patients, mostly quiet. Visiting hours had ended long ago. Only doc-tors and nurses walked around the floor, and patients were monitored through the glass walls separating their rooms from the nurses' station. It must have been a shift change or something because nobody sat at the station now.

And when Fletcher glanced through the glass wall to Greg Stehouwer's room, he noticed a shadow looming over the bed, reminding him of how, just a couple of nights ago, he had found Troy looming over Kiki's bed.

But Troy had just been standing there.

This person clutched a pillow in their hands, and they pressed that pillow over the face of the patient lying in the bed. Over Greg Stehouwer.

Fletcher rushed into the room, locked his arms around the person and pulled them back. The person thrashed in his grasp, trying to break free. But Fletcher dragged the attacker to the floor, like he had with Troy that night. This time, at least, his arm was healing and the stitches didn't reopen like last time.

Troy was skinny and not very strong. But this guy fought back, throwing elbows, trying desperately to break free and escape.

"I'm Detective Colton. You're under arrest," Fletcher told the guy. "Stop resisting!"

An elbow landed in his ribs, knocking the breath from his lungs, and the guy surged to his feet. But Fletcher drew his weapon then. "I will shoot you!"

The guy froze, and light suddenly flooded the room, illuminating Greg's attacker. His brother. Gerard stood over Fletcher, his face flushed, his hair disheveled. He glanced at the nurse who'd entered the room. Her face was flushed, too. And the glance they exchanged...

"I'm Detective Colton," Fletcher said again. "Call security." He didn't trust her to do that, though, because it looked like she might be part of this. Had Gerard paid her to make sure that the nurses' station was empty when he'd attempted to end his brother's life? "No," he said when she started moving toward the doorway. "Stay here with your coconspirator." And he called Conners' police department for backup instead.

FOR THE PAST couple of days, the houseboat had felt so empty without Fletcher that it was difficult for Kiki to stay there. And even harder to sleep.

But she didn't want to put her grandpa in danger, just in case Fletcher was right to be so worried about her safety. Although, if he was worried, why hadn't he checked on her? Why hadn't he called?

Or better yet, why hadn't he come home?

No. Not home. This wasn't his home. It wasn't hers either. She was just staying there while she was in Owl Creek and that was just for the rest of the summer.

Fletcher had sent that patrol car past the place several times. She'd seen it earlier that evening when she and Fancy had started out for their walk. Maybe a long walk in the night air would clear her head and hopefully her heart, too, because it was too full of feelings right now. Feelings she didn't want to have.

Kiki had taken such a long walk that both she and Fancy were worn out. All she wanted to do was go back to the boat and crawl into bed. But then she remembered that the sheets and pillows would smell like Fletcher. And she knew she would just lie there, yearning for him.

To be with him. To have his arms wrapped around her,

holding her close like he had every night for the last several nights.

Her footsteps slowed on the dock as she neared the slip where the houseboat was anchored. She didn't want to be there without Fletcher.

Was it already too late? Had she already fallen for him?

It didn't matter how she felt if he didn't return her feelings. And even if he did, how in the world could a relationship between them last?

His life was here in Owl Creek. His job. His family.

She only had her grandfather here and some friends. But her life, her career, was taking her other places and probably always would.

"Ah, Fancy…" she murmured with a weary sigh.

The puppy whined and pulled at her leash, tugging Kiki toward the boat. Then Kiki looked up and saw what the puppy must have spotted. A light was on inside the cabin. A light that Kiki hadn't left on since it hadn't been dark out yet when she and Fancy had left earlier.

Since she hadn't left that light on, who had?

Fletcher?

Had he come back to the boat after all? Maybe she'd read him all wrong at the hospital the other night. Maybe he hadn't been trying to create distance between them the past couple of days; maybe he'd just been busy.

Eager to see him, she helped Fancy onto the boat deck and then jumped onto it herself. Fancy, her leash trailing behind her, rushed through the open door of the cabin. But instead of yipping with excitement, as she did every time she saw Fletcher, she growled instead.

And Kiki knew that it wasn't Fletcher who'd turned on

that light but someone else. Someone Fancy instinctively didn't like or trust. And the little dog had very good instincts about people.

If Fancy didn't like or trust the person, Kiki shouldn't either. She should turn and run for help.

But she couldn't leave the little puppy alone on the boat with whoever was in the cabin making her growl like she was. Kiki couldn't let anything happen to the dog she was supposed to be fostering and protecting.

She just had to figure out, with her pepper spray gone, how she was going to protect them both.

Chapter Twenty-Two

Fletcher was lead detective for a reason. He was good at breaking a suspect. And it had taken only a few minutes in the interrogation room for him to get the nurse to talk. She'd openly shared how Gerard had spent the past couple of weeks trying to charm her into doing what he wanted. Into killing his brother.

She'd refused to unplug his machine when he'd needed it to breathe. Or so she claimed.

But Fletcher intended to find out exactly how the doctors had realized Greg was able to breathe on his own. Maybe she *had* unplugged it. She was demanding immunity, though, to spill all on Gerard. So Fletcher encouraged her to talk some more.

And she'd admitted to making sure that he had a clear shot at his brother. That he'd intended to suffocate him and just make it look like he'd stopped breathing again.

Greg was still alive, though.

And Fletcher made sure his brother knew it when he walked into the interrogation room where he'd left him. He glanced around. "No lawyer? I thought you called your parents. Your wife…"

Nobody had retained a lawyer for him, probably not once they'd realized that he was going to be charged with the attempted murder of his own brother.

Gerard didn't say a word, just gritted his teeth as if it was a struggle to hold back what he really wanted to say. Maybe it wouldn't take Fletcher much longer to break him than it had the nurse.

"Your little friend had no problem talking to me," Fletcher shared. "She gave her statement about how you tried to hire her to kill your brother. You wanted her to finish the job you weren't able to do on your own."

The guy glared at him.

"So you're not what I expected the Slasher to be," he said. And he still wasn't. "But it's going to be good to charge you for all those crimes, too, in all those other states. Close all those cases. And you can pick what prison you'd like to spend the majority of your life in."

"I'm not the Slasher."

He wasn't. He had alibis for the other attacks. Fletcher had already checked that. "Those other precincts can't wait to close those cases—put the Slasher away for good."

"I'm not the Slasher," Gerard repeated.

"No, but you borrowed the Slasher's MO when you tried to kill your brother in the parking lot of Club Ignition. And I know you're the one who did that, Gerard. The warehouse next to the club, the one nearest the parking lot, is in the process of being renovated, too. In order to protect the materials being delivered, they installed a security system."

Gerard shook his head. "That's not true."

No. It wasn't, but Fletcher needed his suspect to think it was.

"You would have said something sooner if you saw..." Gerard trailed off and swallowed deeply, nervously.

"If I saw you trying to kill your brother on camera," Fletcher finished for him. "We didn't know about that security footage until the other night, when there was another attack outside the club." He gestured at his bandaged arm. "It's all over now, Gerard."

Tears rolled down Gerard's face. "He doesn't deserve it. He doesn't deserve it," he murmured.

"No. He didn't deserve to be attacked like that," Fletcher agreed.

"No. Greg doesn't deserve the trust. He's only marrying Melanie so he can get his hands on our grandparents' money. He never visited them. He was never nice to them. Not like I was. He doesn't deserve it."

So, as Fletcher had suspected, it was all about money. "And if Greg is gone, the rest of that trust will go to you?"

Gerard nodded. "I deserve it. He doesn't. He doesn't deserve it."

Fletcher sighed and stood up, leaving the man to cry alone in the interrogation room. He'd closed that case, but the Slasher's identity was still up in the air.

And that was the person Fletcher wanted to catch the most, especially since his arm was throbbing again. That dull ache kept reminding him of why he was staying away from Kiki—that it was to keep her safe.

But he missed her so damn much.

After stepping out of the interrogation room, he checked his phone again like he had earlier. But there were no new voice mails. Kiki hadn't called him.

He hadn't returned the medical examiner's call yet. But

since it was earlier in San Francisco than it was in Owl Creek, he hit the button to call the ME back.

"Detective Colton returning your call," he said.

"Detective Colton," the doctor greeted him. "I'm glad you called back. I have some interesting information about Caitlin Sullivan."

"You found her?"

"I did, and her father knows it. He identified her body but refused to take it."

"What?"

"She had overdosed on drugs," the doctor said. "And he was furious about it. Said she got what she deserved and her dealer would be next."

Was that why the Slasher attacked those men? Did he think the men he'd targeted had been drug dealers? Was that the motivation for all those attacks?

KIKI RUSHED INTO the cabin after Fancy, trying to catch her leash, trying to pull her away from the man kicking out at her as the puppy tugged on the already frayed legs of Troy's tattered jeans. "Come!" she commanded the dog. She just managed to catch her leash as she moved to make the hand gesture. She didn't want Fancy anywhere near Troy.

She didn't want Troy anywhere near her. Wasn't he supposed to be in the hospital? Or jail? Fletcher had been determined to arrest him.

"What are you doing here?" she asked as she held tightly to the leash. Fancy struggled to get to Troy who sat on the couch where she'd found him the last time he'd broken in.

There was no broken glass this time. Not since she'd

fixed the door. But she must have left it unlocked. Maybe she'd done that in the hopes that Fletcher would show up.

She wished he was here now.

"I wanted to talk to you, Kiki," he said. "To say I'm sorry…"

She was, too. So sorry that she hadn't checked him out more thoroughly before she'd asked him to help her. "No. I mean… Why are you here? And not in the hospital or…"

"Jail?" he asked. "Your old friend arrested and interrogated me."

"And let you go?" Fletcher wouldn't have done that if he still suspected Troy was the Slasher.

His usually pale face flushed in the glow of the lamp that he'd turned on next to the couch. "He didn't let me go. But I got bail."

"And you had the money for that?" But not to pay his child support?

"I—I thought you paid it," he said.

She stared at him in disbelief. "Really? Why?"

"I—I thought we were friends, Kiki," he said. "We've known each other so long."

"I don't know if I ever really knew you," she said. And she didn't want to get to know him. "I had no idea about the drugs, Troy."

"I'm going to get clean," he said. "I'm going to go to rehab."

"And your kids?" she asked. "How could you just abandon them? Stop supporting them?"

"I-it's more complicated than that, Kiki," he said. "There's more to the story. I'm no good for them. Not now. But maybe after rehab…"

"I hope you go," she said.

"I already signed up at the hospital," Troy said. "A doctor got me a room at a place. I can go now that I got out of jail. That's why I thought you paid the bail. I thought…"

She shook her head. "It wasn't me, Troy. I want you to go to rehab. But I really just want you to leave. And please, don't come back again."

She didn't think he would have been given bail if he'd actually been charged with the attacks the Slasher had committed. But it didn't matter to her. She didn't want to deal with Troy anymore.

"Kiki, I'm really sorry," he said.

"I'm sorry, too," a deep voice said from behind Kiki. And she whirled around as Fancy snapped and snarled at the man who'd snuck up on them both.

"Mr. Sullivan?" she asked, staring at him in shock. "What—what are you doing here?" And why had he apologized to her?

Troy's face paled again until he looked like death, and he stared at Mr. Sullivan in shock. "It was you," he murmured. "It was you."

"What was him?" Kiki asked. The Slasher? Was Mr. Sullivan the Slasher? He stood between her and the door, and she didn't know how she would get away from him, especially if he had that knife she'd seen in the alley. That long, sharp machete that had cut through the air and slashed Fletcher's arm.

She should have checked on him and made sure that he was okay. That his wound had healed.

Regret weighed heavily on her for so many things.

Fletcher. And not replacing her empty canister of pepper spray. She had a feeling that she was going to need it now.

"I bailed Troy out," Mr. Sullivan said.

"Why—why would you do that?" Kiki asked. "I didn't even know you knew each other."

"We don't," Troy said. "I've just seen him around the clubs when he's been looking for his daughter."

Mr. Sullivan shook his head. "I know where she is. Thanks to you, Troy. You're the one I've been looking for. I didn't know it was you until Bart told me, but now I know you're the one who got my little girl hooked on drugs."

Troy shook his head. "No, no. Not me."

"You don't deal drugs out of the clubs?" Dan Sullivan snorted. "Don't lie to me."

Troy's pale face flushed again. "I—I might have from time to time when I needed money. And people needed something to feel good."

Dan's face flushed now. "Caitlin didn't need to feel good. She needed to grow up. To deal with life like an adult instead of running away and hiding from her problems like a child. Like you've been running away and hiding, Troy. It's time to face the consequences of your bad choices now, just like Caitlin faced her consequences."

Kiki tensed. He'd always acted like such a distraught father. "You knew where she's been all this time?" she asked with surprise. "You knew she was dead."

"Caitlin paid for her mistakes," Dan said. "Now it's time for Troy to pay for his."

"What about me?" Kiki asked. "I didn't know what he was doing."

Dan snorted. "Really? You worked with him for how long and had no idea what he was doing?"

She shook her head. "I really, really didn't know." But she doubted that was going to matter to Dan Sullivan. Because she saw now what he'd been holding behind his back...

It wasn't a knife like the one the Slasher had used in the alley. This was a gun, which was even more dangerous. He wouldn't even have to get close to them to kill them. And she had no doubt that was what he intended to do, or he wouldn't have brought the weapon with him.

"Then I really, really am sorry," Dan said.

Troy shook his head. "C'mon, man, she's not part of this," he said. "Let her go."

"What? So she can get help for you? Like that rehab you think you're getting into?" Dan shook his head. "I can't have that. I can't have you getting better, getting your life back when you took mine."

"I didn't have anything to do with this," Kiki said. "So if you kill me, that's going to make you as bad as you think Troy is. Actually, worse. He didn't know that your daughter was going to die." And Dan had every intention of killing her.

And Kiki had every intention of making sure that didn't happen. She wasn't going to die like this. But she wasn't sure how to stop Dan from shooting her and Troy.

Chapter Twenty-Three

Fletcher had intended to talk to Troy again about Dan Sullivan. But when he went to see him in the cells, he found that he'd been bailed out. And when he found out who had bailed him out...

"Dan Sullivan," Fletcher murmured. "Why in the hell would he have bailed out a drug user like Troy?" But then he knew why.

For revenge.

Troy could be more than a drug user. He could be a dealer as well. He'd mentioned something about rehab during their interview earlier. But a call to his doctor confirmed he hadn't checked in yet. So where would he have gone?

Security footage from the jail showed him walking out on his own. Nobody had picked him up. He'd just walked off. The marina wasn't far from the police department. Every other time he'd come around town, Troy had sought out Kiki. Fletcher figured the man was in love with her. He understood all too well how easy it would be to fall for her, especially after watching her DJ, after hearing her sing and seeing her dance and how the music flowed through her like joy.

And how that joy flowed over onto everyone around her.

Troy might not have been the only one who fell for Kiki. Fletcher didn't think Dan Sullivan had, though, so he probably wouldn't care if Kiki wound up as collateral damage in his quest for revenge.

Fletcher jumped in his Owl Creek PD vehicle, but he didn't engage the lights and sirens. He didn't want to alert anyone that he was coming. Except Kiki.

He hoped she knew if she was in danger that he would rush to her rescue like she'd rushed to his. But he had to make sure that he could actually rescue her and that he wasn't already too late.

Once he parked his SUV, he hurried along the dock, but this time he was careful to keep his footsteps as quiet as he could. He didn't want anyone to hear him coming and he kept to the shadows the boats cast on the dock despite the brightness of the full moon. But as he neared the boat, he knew someone had noticed him.

Kiki and Troy stood on the rear deck, near the railing, with Dan in front of them, his back toward the dock, toward Fletcher. Fancy stood next to Kiki, quivering and snarling with fear and anger.

She knew the man was a threat even if she didn't understand that he was holding a gun. The barrel pointed directly at Kiki's big heart. Fancy was the one who saw him, and she started yipping until he held up a hand the way that Kiki had taught him. The hold command.

Stay.

Don't Move.

Don't React.

He silently told her all those things, and somehow the

puppy must have understood his commands because she stayed next to Kiki and she stayed quiet, barely betraying any interest in him. So he was able to creep closer.

But if he jumped on the boat, it might shift beneath his weight and reveal his presence. He hadn't ever seen anyone on the boat docked next to hers when he'd stayed with Kiki. He could probably get on it without bothering whoever the owner was. But if he stepped onto it, would it shift enough in the water to move her boat, too?

From where he was, he couldn't get a clear shot at Sullivan. The cabin blocked most of his body, leaving just his hand and that gun most visible to Fletcher. Fletcher was a good shot, but hitting a hand wasn't easy.

And if the man pulled the trigger convulsively, he was going to put a bullet right into Kiki's heart. And that was like putting a bullet in Fletcher's, too. He couldn't lose her. Not like this...

FLETCHER WAS THERE. Kiki knew it from the way that Fancy's tail had wagged and the way that she'd whined. Kiki couldn't see him, but it was enough that Fancy had, enough that she'd minded the command he'd given her.

Wait.

Stay.

Kiki had to tell herself to do the same thing. She had to stall for more time, like she had earlier, when she'd convinced Dan not to shoot them within the cabin but to come up to the deck.

To make them jump into the water with the anchor tied around their feet.

"People will hear the gunshot," she'd told him. "I'm not

the only one living on their boat. Other people will see you, will stop you. You won't get away."

She wasn't sure that he'd wanted to, though. Maybe, because his daughter was dead, he intended to kill himself once he'd killed her dealer.

And Kiki.

But clearly, he wasn't done yet. "I have to kill Bart, too," he told them as he pushed them closer to the railing behind them. "I know he's part of this." He pointed the gun at Troy. "He works with you, with the drugs."

Troy let out a shaky breath. "He didn't have anything to do with your daughter, sir. I don't think I did either. I didn't recognize her picture when you showed me. I don't think I knew her."

"You sold to her," Dan insisted, waving his gun in a hand that shook with his fury.

As upset as he was, he might accidentally pull that trigger. She tried to ease between him and Troy. He might be less likely to pull the trigger and kill her since he knew for certain that she had nothing to do with his daughter's death.

"There are a lot of dealers in the clubs," Troy insisted. "Customers. Bouncers."

"Bartenders and you," Dan said. "I know you and Bart work together. That's why I paid him to get you into the club. I was going to kill you by cutting you up like that maniac cuts up his victims in the alley." He focused on Kiki again. "But you brought that cop into the place."

So much for Fletcher's cover.

She didn't want to lie to Sullivan and set him off any more than he already was. Because she'd felt that faint motion as the boat moved in the water. Either someone had stepped onto it or onto the boat next to it, causing a ripple along the surface of the water. "He is a cop," she admitted. "He was going undercover to catch the Slasher. How did you know that?"

Dan pointed his gun at Troy again. "He told Bart. He saw you both outside his van that first night, saw that he drove a police vehicle."

And so, Troy had given him up, maybe warning Bart to lie low with the drug dealing while Fletcher was there.

"Not all clubgoers are that bad," Kiki said in defense of her job. "Some people are just there to dance, to enjoy the music, to meet other people."

Dan snorted. "You're naive, Kiki."

"No, I see the good in people. I don't think the worst of everyone I meet."

"That's why you're here," he said. "With an anchor tied around your ankles."

She'd done the tying. It was about as tight as Fletcher laced his boots now. She would be able to get it off, and so would Troy if he didn't panic. He was panicking now, his body shaking, his breath coming in pants that were getting higher and shallower, like he was about to hyperventilate.

If he went into the water like that, he was going to drown before they ever got the rope and anchor off. She had to keep stalling to give Fletcher time to rescue them. But would he rescue them or put himself in more danger, like he had the night he'd gone into that alley looking for her?

"It's time now," Sullivan said. "Enough stalling. Time for the two of you to jump over the railing. Time to end this."

Troy started crying now. Soft, gasping sobs. And tears rolled down his face.

Instead of being moved, Dan Sullivan laughed. "You're not making me feel sorry for you. Not at all." He looked at Kiki and his mouth slid into a frown. "You, I feel sorry for—having to die with a scumbag like him. It would be better for you to die alone."

Even if Dan and Troy weren't there, she wouldn't have died alone. Fletcher was there. She could see him now inside the cabin of her boat, moving toward them. Fancy saw him, too, and whined deep in her throat, as if anxious to rush toward him, to leap and lick all over him like she usually did.

Kiki wanted to do the same, but she was too scared. For her and Troy and for Fletcher, too.

Dan had to think he was in charge. He seemed like a man who was always in control. Could that be why his daughter had rebelled with the clubbing and the drugs? Maybe he'd been too controlling.

Instead of crying, Kiki shook her head as if she pitied him. "This is sad."

"What do you mean?" he asked.

"That you're not strong enough to deal with your grief and your regrets about your daughter," she said.

He bristled and tightened his grasp on the gun. "You don't know what you're talking about!"

"I lost my parents," she said. "In a traffic accident. I didn't blame the other driver even though he left the scene. I didn't have to chase him down and avenge my parents."

"You must have been a kid when that happened," Dan guessed. Correctly. "And you would have felt better if you had."

"I felt better letting them go with grace and with honoring their memories by being the best person I could be," she said. "I didn't become bitter and crazy. I didn't lose control so badly that I turned into a monster."

"Shut up!" Dan yelled at her. "You don't know what you're talking about! Shut up!" And he swung that barrel back from Troy to her, focusing it on her heart. And his finger moved toward the trigger.

Troy stopped crying to gasp and he even pointed at Fletcher, tipping Dan off to him sneaking onto the boat. Kiki reached out, trying to lower his arm, trying to get him to stop. And Troy toppled back, falling over the railing. The rope wound through the anchor and lashed around both of their ankles. If Troy was heavy enough, he might pull that anchor over with him, and then Kiki would go into the water, too.

But she cared less about that than about Fletcher as Dan spun around toward the cabin, his gun raised and his finger moving toward the trigger, squeezing and firing off a bullet in Fletcher's direction.

Fletcher's gun was out, too, but he might not fire back, might worry about hitting her and Troy with the way they were behind Dan. But then they weren't there as Troy fell into the water, taking a piece of the deck railing with him as the anchor struck it, breaking it.

And that rope tightened around Kiki's ankles, pulling her off the boat and into the water, too. And then down into the depths of the lake.

She was worried about herself and Troy, but she was the most worried about Fletcher. She had a chance to loosen that rope again, to free herself and Troy from the anchor.

But if Fletcher had been shot…

Chapter Twenty-Four

The first bullet missed Fletcher. The second was never fired because Fletcher didn't miss. He dropped Dan Sullivan to the deck. And then he went over the railing after Kiki and Troy. She broke through the water, coming up as he sank down into the lake.

She tossed her head, sending water spraying, and then she started slipping under again. And Fletcher could see Troy pulling her down as he flailed and panicked.

Fletcher swam to him, trying to break his grasp on Kiki. But he kept pulling at her, pinching her skin, pulling her under the water. So Fletcher swung his fist, knocking the guy out. And then he carried him up as Kiki shot back to the surface.

Sirens whined in the distance. Fletcher had sent out a text to dispatch. They'd been on their way with the order to come in stealthily. Maybe a report of shots fired had had them turning on the sirens and lights.

Backup arrived too late to save Dan Sullivan. But it had probably been too late to save him long before Fletcher shot him. He didn't know if the same was true about Troy, but instead of going to the hospital, he'd wanted to go to that rehab program. So after giving his statement for the police report, he was given a ride to the facility. Officer Blaine was to make sure that he really checked in, because Fletcher still had his doubts about the man.

Fletcher still had a lot of doubts about a lot of parts of this case. And even about Kiki.

Fletcher had wanted Kiki to go to the hospital, too, but she'd insisted she was fine. He wasn't so sure that she was because she kept trembling even though the water hadn't been cold. And thanks to how loosely she'd tied the anchor rope to her and to Troy, neither of them had been under water for very long.

Fletcher wasn't fine. Physically there wasn't anything wrong with him. He hadn't reopened the stitches on his arm. But emotionally...

He was as on edge as he'd been when he'd seen Sullivan pointing that gun barrel at Kiki's heart. Even after they finished giving their statements to police and everyone had left, he was still jumpy. Maybe more so because it was just the two of them. And Fancy, who'd curled up at his feet as he sat on the deck, watching the sun come up.

Kiki had gone inside to change out of her wet shorts and shirt. And clearly when she walked back out, drying her hair on a towel, she hadn't expected to see him still there. Her dark eyes widened in surprise. And he couldn't tell if she was happy or upset that he hadn't left.

Then those eyes suddenly welled with tears that sparkled in the light. And Fletcher jumped up and rushed to her, closing his arms around her.

Kiki, being Kiki, didn't cry. She didn't give in to tears,

but she closed her arms around him and clutched him close. And they just held each other.

HE WAS ALIVE. When she'd gone over the side, she hadn't known what she would find when she resurfaced. Fletcher dead? The thought had horrified her, making her move even faster to ease out of the rope and fight her way out of the water. She'd helped Troy, too, but in his panic, he might have drowned them both. If not for Fletcher jumping in after them...

Kiki and Troy were probably alive because of Fletcher. So maybe it was just gratitude that had her clinging to him like she was.

Or relief that they were all alive.

Well, not all of them.

Dan Sullivan hadn't made it. But she suspected he'd been gone a long time ago—lost to his hatred and bitterness and madness.

She was just glad she hadn't lost Fletcher. Yet.

She knew he was slipping away from her though. That their time together was coming to an end. They had no future. His life, his career, his family, were all here in Owl Creek.

He released a shaky breath that stirred her hair and made her shiver. "I'm so glad you're all right." But then he pulled back and cupped her face in his hands, and he stared into her eyes with that intense stare that unnerved and excited her so damn much. "Are you really all right?"

She nodded and released a shaky breath of her own. For the moment, with him here, holding her, she was all right.

"I'm not," he said.

She could feel his body shaking against hers now. "Fletcher..."

"I was so scared when I saw him pointing that gun at you, so worried that it might accidentally go off and hurt you or..." He shuddered again.

And she closed her arms around him, then tugged him inside with her, through the open door to the cabin and then through the cabin to her bedroom.

Fancy was on their heels. But Kiki shut the little puppy out. Instead of whining, the exhausted dog just leaned against the door. She wanted to know that they were close.

That was what Kiki wanted, too. Just to have Fletcher close even if it was only for a little while longer.

"Kiki..." he murmured, and then he lowered his head to hers. At first his lips just brushed across hers in a gentle, almost reverent kiss.

Then she reached up and tangled her fingers in his damp hair, and she held his head against hers as she deepened the kiss. She teased him with her tongue.

His breath caught and then he kissed her back just as passionately, just as desperately as she was kissing him. "Kiki..."

"We need to get you out of these wet clothes," she said, as she tugged his damp T-shirt over his head.

He shucked off his jeans and boxers and stood before her, gloriously naked. He was so perfect. His chest and thighs so muscular. His stomach so lean.

She lifted the T-shirt dress she'd pulled on to replace her wet clothes. And his breath shuddered out in a ragged groan.

"You are so beautiful," he said. His fingers, shaking

slightly, traced her every curve with the reverence that had been in his first kiss. Then his lips replaced his fingers.

He kissed her everywhere, and passion overwhelmed her, making her legs shake. She tumbled back onto the bed, pulling him with her. She loved the weight of him, the heat of him, on top of her. His heart beat in time with hers, fast and furiously.

"Fletcher, I need you," she admitted. She felt a flicker of unease as she said it, concerned that she wasn't talking about just now, but forever.

But she'd never needed anyone like that.

Instead of joining their bodies like she needed him to do, he moved down hers. He kissed her breasts, flicking his tongue across each nipple, and then he moved lower, making love to her with his mouth.

She clutched the sheets as the pressure built inside her and then released in an orgasm that left her shuddering and gasping for breath. She closed her eyes, riding the peak of pleasure. And she heard a cupboard open, a packet tear and then he eased inside her, stretching her, filling her completing her.

He began to move, building that tension again. She clutched at him, locking her legs around him, grabbing his shoulders. She met his thrusts, arching up, holding him close, pulling him deeper.

He groaned. And his mouth covered hers, kissing her, imitating with his tongue what he was doing with his body. And that pressure inside her burst again, filling her with pleasure.

Then his body tensed. A deep groan slipped between his lips as he found his release. He flopped onto his back, carrying her with him so that she was on top and their bodies were still joined. And he stared up into her face with such an expression...

Of awe and wonder.

It probably mirrored the expression on her face.

"You are amazing," he whispered. Then he arched up and kissed her, and it was that soft tender kiss that had her heart swelling and warming.

And...

No. She could not fall for Fletcher, but she had a feeling that it was already too late.

They made love again. More slowly, more reverently, before finally settling onto the bed to rest sometime later. But Kiki couldn't sleep. And his body was tense beside hers despite all the orgasms they'd had.

"Why did you come here?" she asked. She hoped it was because he'd missed her like she'd missed him.

"I found out that Dan Sullivan's daughter was dead and that he refused to claim her body. It also sounded like he was going after her drug dealer."

"Troy."

"And when he bailed him out, I figured he was going to go after him, wherever he was."

So he hadn't come to see her. He hadn't missed her the past couple of days like she'd missed him.

"And I figured, knowing how he kept turning up wherever you were, that Troy might be here, putting you in danger and..." His gruff voice trailed off and he shuddered and pulled her closer. "I was so worried that I would be too late."

"You were right on time," she said with a slight smile.

Then she asked, "Is it over?" And she wasn't really asking about the case. She wondered about the two of them...

"I don't think Dan Sullivan or Gerard Stehouwer are the Slasher," he said.

"Gerard Stehouwer?"

"Greg's brother is the one who tried to kill him. Twice, actually. Once in the parking lot and once in the ICU."

She had a feeling that Fletcher had stopped that from happening, just as he'd stopped Dan Sullivan from killing Troy. "Then who is the Slasher?" she asked. "Do you still suspect Troy?"

"I don't know. I have the note the Slasher slipped me. There is some DNA on it. We'll see if it matches Troy's or Gerard's or Dan's."

"And if it doesn't?"

"Then the Slasher is still out there." He tightened his arms around her. "But I will catch whoever it is, Kiki."

At what cost, she wondered. His life? Her heart? She had a feeling they were both in danger.

ACCORDING TO THE latest media reports, the stupid people of Owl Creek believed that the Slasher was either dead or in jail. That the grief-stricken old man or the rich frat boy was the Slasher. The Slasher hated this, hated how other people hadn't just copycatted but tried to pretend to be the Slasher.

That wasn't admiration. That was disrespect.

And the Slasher had already been disrespected enough. It was time to end this once and for all.

Chapter Twenty-Five

Fletcher knew it was a risk coming back to Club Ignition with Kiki. It was a risk to him because the more time he spent with her, the more he was falling for her. And she wasn't going to stay. As she played and sang and danced, he could see the star that she was, burning much too bright for Owl Creek.

He didn't want to hold her back. But he was so damn tempted to try. But that would have been selfish. And he cared about her too much to be that way with her.

"You know your cover is blown," Bart told him as he poured a cup of coffee for Fletcher and pushed it across the bar.

Fletcher had brought his own thermos, like Kiki brought her tea. He wasn't taking any chances anymore. At least not with his life.

With his heart.

He took a chance every time he was around Kiki.

Fletcher chuckled. "I really am an old friend of Kiki's," he said. "And I really am her assistant." But he wanted to be so much more.

Bart snorted and shook his head. "Okay, sure, but you're still a cop, too."

"Lead detective," Fletcher said with pride in the title. Now if only he could live up to it...

His new boss was happy with him for closing a couple of big cases. Greg Stehouwer's attack. And Dan Sullivan's attempted crimes.

His boss thought Fletcher had closed the Slasher case, too. But Fletcher didn't think so.

The Slasher was still out there. Maybe even here tonight now that Club Ignition had reopened.

"Did you get promoted after closing the Slasher case?" Bart asked.

"It's not closed," Fletcher said. At least not as far as he was concerned.

"So that's why you're back here."

"I'm just helping out Kiki until she can find a new assistant."

"I thought Troy was getting clean," Bart said. "That he went into rehab."

"That doesn't mean Kiki will work with him again." Fletcher studied Bart's face. "Sullivan said you worked with Troy selling drugs. He was coming for you next."

"I guess I owe you a thank you then," Bart said. "You made sure that bitter old man won't hurt anyone else. And he was wrong about me. I'm not selling anything but drinks."

Fletcher pushed the coffee mug across the bar toward Bart. "I was drugged that night that Kiki and I were attacked in the alley."

"Then I guess you should have kept a better eye on your cup," Bart said. "Because I didn't put anything in it."

"The other victims had been drugged, too," Fletcher said.

"It wasn't me," Bart said. "I'm not a drug user. And I am damn well not that violent Slasher. Anybody can get close enough to drop something in someone else's glass."

And a note in their pocket?

Fletcher might have believed that Bart had drugged the drinks, but he wouldn't have been able to slip him a note, not when he rarely left his place behind the bar.

"You're the detective," Bart said. "So you must have thought about how a lot of these were at bachelor parties. They usually do shots, line them up at the bar, but a lot of people buy the groom drinks, too. A lot of women."

"Women…" The DNA on that note had recently come back as not a match to Dan Sullivan or Gerard Stehouwer because it had belonged to a woman. An unidentified woman.

Fletcher's boss hadn't considered it that much of a lead. And Fletcher had agreed because the Slasher had never left any DNA behind at any other scene, so he would have made certain not to leave any on the note either. They'd assumed that the woman must have just touched the paper at some point.

Bart's head bobbed in a nod. "Yeah, it's not just guys buying girls drinks anymore. You know, women's lib. A lot of women buy drinks for men, too."

The Slasher was a woman. It made total sense. It was how she was able to get so close to shove a note in the guy's pocket. And how, even though that knife was sharp, the wound on Fletcher's arm hadn't been deeper.

The Slasher was a woman, but which woman? Was she here tonight?

THE CLUB WAS PACKED. Probably because the news had all made it sound like the Slasher had either been arrested or killed. But Kiki knew that wasn't the case. The DNA results on that note shoved in Fletcher's pocket hadn't matched Dan Sullivan or Gerard Stehouwer's. It had belonged to a woman.

Fletcher hadn't been as quick to accept that, though, pointing out how the Slasher had never left any DNA behind before and probably would have made certain to leave none on the note.

Sure, no DNA had been left at the scene of the crimes because the Slasher wore that hazmat-type suit. Ones that had been all too available during the pandemic. But the Slasher wouldn't have been able to wear that suit inside the club without being noticed, especially when slipping a note into the pocket of their chosen victim.

The Slasher had chosen Fletcher once. Had slipped Fletcher that note.

It had to be a woman. And Kiki remembered who'd been dancing so closely to him when he'd started acting so out of it.

Her girls. Amy, Claire and Janie.

She hadn't seen any of them when she'd gone looking for him. Of course, she hadn't looked for him in the ladies' room, so they'd probably been in there.

Or…

Maybe one of them had been in the alley, waiting for him to come out that door. Waiting to attack him.

She shuddered as she remembered that night, how close she'd come to losing him. And the turntable skipped a beat. She steadied her hand and kept spinning while her thoughts spun as well.

She and Fletcher had both been scared about coming back to the club, but they'd each been frightened for the other. She'd promised she would stay inside her booth, and he'd promised he wouldn't drink anything but the coffee that was in the thermos next to hers. And he wouldn't go out into the alley without backup.

An officer from Conners was here tonight, blending in with the crowd. There was another bachelor party here; maybe they thought it was safe, though.

That the Slasher was gone.

But Kiki saw her girls jumping up and down in the crowd. They weren't all dancing together; they'd joined that group from the bachelor party. Some of the guys were grinding up on them. Some of the women were returning the favor.

And then she noticed the slip of paper in Janie's hand, how the strobe light flashed against the white material and bounced back at her.

How had Kiki never noticed that before?

Because she hadn't been looking for it.

Then the paper disappeared. And then Janie did as well, disappearing into the crowd. Had she slipped that paper into a man's pocket?

And which man?

Kiki called out, "Where's my assistant at?" Then making her voice sound like Lucille Ball's, she said, "Fletcher, I need you."

The crowd laughed at her impression. But she didn't see Fletcher among them. Where had he gone? Was he already in the alley? If he was, he was in danger.

Because Kiki was pretty sure the Slasher was heading out there now.

THE MACHETE WAS sharper than it had ever been, the blade honed so that it would slice through skin and maybe even bone now. If Janie could swing it hard enough…

And she was damn sure that she would.

She wasn't just going to maim this idiot. She was going to kill him.

Maybe that was what it was going to take for her to finally get the respect she deserved. The respect her ex-fiancé hadn't given her.

He'd called her stupid and ugly and so far beneath him that he'd been a fool to ever propose to her. He hadn't been a fool when Janie had paid his way through med school.

No. She had been his everything then. He'd showered her with compliments and gratitude even as he'd kept putting off their wedding day.

And even though he hadn't been home much, she'd believed it was just because of his long hours. Especially during his residency.

Residents didn't make any real money, he told her, so they would get married after he became an attending physician. Then he would be making so much money that they could have the wedding of their dreams. The wedding she deserved to have for everything she'd done for him.

But once he'd gotten his job offer and his six-figure salary, he'd asked for his ring back. He'd never intended to marry someone like her. As a rich doctor, he could do so much better than her.

Once Janie had taken care of his face, his new fiancée had thought she could do better, too, and she'd dumped him just like he had dumped Janie.

But that hadn't been enough for her. Because when she'd

gone out to the club, she'd seen all those other grooms-to-be flirting with women, eager to cheat on their fiancées. Janie had decided that they didn't deserve their brides. They didn't deserve their happiness, and she'd taken it away from them.

She wanted to take away more than someone's happiness tonight. She intended to take away his life. And Kiki wasn't going to stop her this time.

Chapter Twenty-Six

Fletcher had the note. *Meet me in the alley and I will show you a good time...*

It wasn't his. He'd taken it off the man who'd stumbled through the kitchen, intent on going out to the alley to meet the woman who had slipped him the note on the dance floor.

The Slasher wasn't going to get the hapless groom-to-be that she'd tried to lure outside. She was going to get Fletcher. He drew his weapon from his holster and pushed open the door to the alley. The metal hinges creaked, announcing his arrival. But nothing moved in the shadows.

Was the Slasher out there?

Or had this been a distraction? An attempt to get Fletcher's attention somewhere else while she attacked...

Kiki?

No. Kiki was safe. Someone had actually helped him out with that, jamming the door to the DJ booth so that Kiki hadn't been able to get it open. She could have jumped over, like he regularly did. But he'd planted an officer in plainclothes next to it to keep Kiki safe.

What about him?

Was he safe?

He started down the wooden steps that led from the door to the asphalt of the alley. And he made sure to clomp his boots and shuffle, so he sounded like he was drunk.

Or drugged.

Fletcher would have him tested to determine what exactly was wrong with the man besides poor judgement. Fletcher's judgement might have been a little poor to walk out here on his own, especially after he made that promise to Kiki that he wouldn't.

But he wasn't alone. As he hit the bottom step and made certain to bang his shoulder, loudly, against the dumpster, the Slasher jumped out from the other side, brandishing that sharp weapon.

But he had his gun trained on her, and then lights flooded the alley and other officers jumped from their hiding place inside the abandoned warehouse on the other side of the alley.

The Slasher held tight to the hilt of the knife, though, as if tempted to swing it. To try to kill him.

"Drop it, Janie," he said. The groom-to-be had told him that the redhead must have given him the note, that she'd been dancing closest to him. "Or I will kill you."

Finally, the knife dropped, clattering against the asphalt. And Janie dragged off the hood and mask and gasped for breath. "I hate you! I hate you! You can't stop me. You can't stop me now."

"It's over, Janie," he said. "You're under arrest."

"But it's not my fault," she said. "They don't have to cheat. They want to. And I want to make sure nobody ever wants them again."

He could imagine what her motivation was. "Jilted bride?" he asked.

"I hate you!" she screamed, and she bent down to grab the knife. But the other officers were there, grabbing her arms, pulling them behind her back to cuff her. "I hate you!"

He didn't doubt it. She was obviously full of hate right now. Just like Dan Sullivan had been.

And he thought of what Kiki had said to the man, about how she'd chosen forgiveness. How she hadn't wanted the bitterness and hatred to consume her. She'd chosen to live with happiness instead.

Just thinking of her, how incredible she was, made him smile.

"I hate you!" Janie raged as the officer struggled to lead her from the alley to where a patrol car waited to bring her to jail. She wouldn't get bail. Maybe a psychiatric evaluation, but not bail.

"I'll meet you at the station," he called out to his officers. He had to collect that groom-to-be and make sure his blood got tested and his official statement taken. But when he opened the door to step back into the kitchen, it wasn't him he found.

Kiki stood near the dishwasher with the officer at her side, and she was shaking. "You promised!" she yelled at him. "You said you wouldn't go out there!"

"I wasn't alone," he said. "I had officers hiding out in the other building. We got her."

"Janie?" she asked.

He shouldn't have been surprised that she'd figured it out. She was as smart as she was beautiful. He nodded. "We got her. It's all over now."

She nodded now. "Yes, it is." Then she turned and walked away.

And he couldn't help but think she was talking about more than his case. About more than the Slasher, that she was talking about them as well.

And he was more scared than he'd been when he'd walked into that alley, uncertain of when and where the Slasher would come at him. At the moment, Kiki scared him more than he'd ever been scared because he didn't want them to be over. Now or ever.

FLETCHER HAD SCARED her again, like that night he'd gone into the alley in place of the Slasher's chosen victim. The thought of losing him like she'd lost her parents had devastated her. She'd come so close so many times.

Thank goodness the Slasher had finally been caught. Janie.

There would be other dangerous cases for him. Other chances for her to lose him. And she'd thought that would be unbearable—more than she could survive because she'd also realized, during all those moments when she could have lost him, how much she wanted and loved him. Too much.

He'd stayed away from her the past week. Maybe he'd been busy wrapping up all the cases he'd closed. Or maybe he'd taken what she'd said in the heat of the moment at face value and believed she didn't want anything to do with him anymore, as her undercover assistant or as her lover.

But because he'd stayed away from her, Kiki had felt like she lost him already. During that week she'd slept very little, missing him too much, but she'd written and, in her songs, she'd found clarity. That there were no guarantees, but that love was worth the risk of loss. And that if it was meant to be, if they were meant to be, that they would figure out a way to be together and to be happy.

But she knew she wouldn't be happy, truly happy, if they weren't together. "Okay, Fancy," she told the puppy, who'd been moping as much as she'd been with missing Fletcher. "We're going to go get him back." This time she had a shirt in a gift bag. A pink and blue flannel one to replace the one that he'd claimed to hate. The Slasher had ruined it that first time she'd gone after Fletcher.

Janie.

Kiki still struggled to understand why, even though she'd talked to Claire and Amy and found out more about Janie. They hadn't been as close to her as she'd made it seem, but they'd known about her broken engagement. They swore they hadn't known that she was the Slasher. She believed them.

Jenny Colton was probably going to believe she was a stalker when Kiki showed up with another gift for her son. But before she could leave the boat, it shifted beneath the weight of someone jumping onto it.

She turned toward the door and saw Fletcher coming across the front deck toward her.

Fancy jumped up and yipped her happiness. While Kiki was excited, too, she contained herself. He'd stayed away for a week. Maybe he'd figured they were over, too. Whatever they were.

She wasn't even sure. They'd never put a label on what they had. What had her grandpa called it? Something-something…

It burned between them now as he stared at her. She wore

a dress today—just a simple sleeveless, button-down denim one. He wore jeans and a T-shirt, like he was dressed to go undercover with her again.

But of course, it was Saturday, so he probably wasn't working today. He also carried a bag in his hand. One from a pet store.

"Hi," he said.

"Hi."

He pointed toward the bag that dangled from her fingers. "Were you going somewhere?" he asked.

She nodded. "Your house."

"My mom's?"

She nodded again.

"I don't live there anymore."

"You don't?" she asked, and nerves gripped her. "Are you leaving Owl Creek?"

He shook his head. "No. I bought a house of my own. Close to the police department and Frannie's bookstore. It has a nice, fenced yard that would be perfect for Fancy."

"You bought a house for Fancy?"

"I'm going to see if Sebastian and Ruby will let me adopt her," he said. "They can still train her and use her as a scent dog. But when she's not working, she can stay with me."

She narrowed her eyes and studied his face. That look was in his vivid green eyes, that intense look that always unsettled her. But this time it had the opposite effect. Her nerves settled and she smiled. "So that gift bag you brought is for her?"

He nodded and pulled out a chew toy. "Figured she might leave my boots and shoes alone if she had this instead." The puppy took the toy from him and dropped onto the floor to gnaw away at it.

"What about you?" he asked. "What's in your bag?"

She pulled out the flannel shirt. "I felt like I needed to replace this. I know how much you love it."

"I really do love it," he said. But he was staring at her, not the shirt. Then he stepped closer to her, until his body just about brushed up against hers.

"You must be relieved this case is over," she said. "You can go to bed early, sleep late... No more loud music or crowds."

"I actually miss it," he said.

"Liar."

"I miss you. And you know you can come to my house and visit Fancy anytime you're in town," he said.

She smiled. "That's generous of you. To let me visit the dog I've been fostering..."

"In addition to that fenced yard, it also has this special sound room in the basement. Former owner was a musician. You might like that."

"I might," she said.

"You can use that whenever you want," he said. "And you can stay however long you want, between gigs, you know... like...forever..."

Kiki's smile widened as joy filled her heart. "Sounds good to me."

"What part? The sound room? The fenced yard?" he asked.

"The forever." And she pulled his head down to hers, kissing him with all the love she felt for him. And all the passion.

The passion swept her up as Fletcher lifted and carried her into her bedroom. He kept his mouth on hers, kissing her deeply as he lowered her onto the bed. Then his fingers were on the buttons on her dress, undoing them all until the material fell away from her body, revealing her lacy bra and underwear. He unclasped the bra and hooked a finger in her underwear, pulling it down until she was completely bare.

And that look was in his eyes still. That intensity that burned for her. And she felt like she was burning up with the desire coursing through her. "Fletcher..."

She reached for him, but he gently pushed her back on the bed. Then he covered her in kisses, from her lips, over her throat and collarbone. He kissed both breasts and flicked his tongue across the nipples.

And she writhed against the bed as the pressure built inside her. She pulled at his clothes, dragging off his T-shirt, undoing his button and lowering his zipper.

He eased back then, pulled off the last of his clothes and pulled out a condom packet. She took it from him, tore it open with her teeth, then eased the latex over his shaft, running her hand up and down the length of it.

He groaned. "Kiki..."

She pushed him onto his bed and straddled him, easing him inside her. She wanted him so badly. Needed him so badly.

They moved together like they were dancing, in perfect sync, and they even came together, screaming each other's names. She collapsed onto his chest, panting for breath, her heart hammering against his.

He held her close, his arms wrapped tightly around her like he never intended to let her go.

She lifted her face to stare into his, which was tense and serious despite the pleasure they'd just given each other. "What's wrong?" she asked him.

"Nothing," he told her. "I just hope you didn't misunderstand me."

She tensed now and eased away from him. "What do you mean?" Had she read the situation wrong?

"I don't want you to give up your career, Kiki," he said. "You're too talented and you bring people so much happiness and joy. I can't be selfish. I know I have to share you with the world—that you're going to be a star."

Only Grandpa had ever believed and supported her that much. Tears stung her eyes and she blinked furiously.

He touched her face. "Kiki, what's wrong?"

She shook her head. "Nothing. I just love you so much."

"I love you," he said.

She had no doubt. Not about his love or about their future. They would figure out how to make forever work.

* * * * *

COMING SOON!

We really hope you enjoyed reading this book.
If you're looking for more romance
be sure to head to the shops when
new books are available on

Thursday 14th March

To see which titles are coming soon, please visit

millsandboon.co.uk/nextmonth

MILLS & BOON

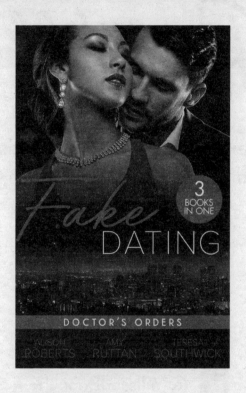

LET'S TALK
Romance

For exclusive extracts, competitions and special offers, find us online:

- **MillsandBoon**
- **@MillsandBoon**
- **@MillsandBoonUK**
- **@MillsandBoonUK**

Get in touch on 01413 063 232